MYSTERION

Rediscovering the Mysteries of the Christian Faith

Edited by
Donald S. Crankshaw
and
Kristin Janz

ƐNIGMATIC
MIRROR
PRESS

Arlington, MA

FIRST EDITION

Cover artwork by Rob Joseph (rob-joseph.com).
Cover design by Kirk DouPonce, Dog Eared Design (dogeareddesign.com).
Interior layout and design by Clare Marshall (cmarshallpublishing.com).

ISBN 978-0-9972565-0-5

Enigmatic Mirror Press
PO Box 750095
Arlington, Massachusetts 02475
www.enigmaticmirrorpress.com
mysterion@enigmaticmirrorpress.com

For Philip Janz and Florence Crankshaw,
who now see face to face.

Table of Contents

Copyright Acknowledgments

Acknowledgements

Praise be to the God and Father of our Lord Jesus Christ, who has blessed us in the heavenly realms with every spiritual blessing in Christ. . . . And he made known to us the mystery of his will according to his good pleasure, which he purposed in Christ.

— Ephesians 1:3,9

It seems appropriate to start off an anthology about rediscovering the mysteries of the Christian faith with a Bible verse. And, of course, that God be the first one whose help we acknowledge. This anthology was inspired by the mysteries that he has revealed, and by those yet to be revealed.

In the earthly realms, there are quite a few people we need to thank for helping us to make this anthology happen.

We'd like to thank our parents for teaching us a love of God and a love of reading.

Hannah Eagleson has probably done more work on this anthology than anyone aside from ourselves and the authors, from initial support and brainstorming, through reading submissions, to copy editing, and we're very thankful for her help.

We're especially appreciative of Sandra Kasturi, John O'Neill, Maurice Broaddus, and Matthew Kressel, who were willing to share their expertise on editing and publishing, and to put us in contact with the people we needed to make this anthology happen.

We are grateful to our cover artist, Rob Joseph, especially for his patience with our indecisiveness as we bounced ideas around, and to our cover designer, Kirk DouPonce.

And to Clare Marshall, who did the interior design.

Miriam Eagleson designed our company logo and promotional materials.

We want to thank all the authors who submitted stories to us, both those whose stories we're including, and those whose stories we were unable to include. Any anthology is only as good as its stories.

Finally, we'd like to thank the people who supported us on Patreon, whose contributions helped to make this anthology better than it could have been based solely on our own financial resources.

Patreon Contributors

Patrons
Megan Murphy
Sarah Crankshaw-Edwards

Sponsors
Carol Crankshaw
Frederic and Julie Durbin
Meg Muckenhoupt

Supporters
Lee Goodreau
Matthew Kressel
Paul Leone

Introduction

AROUND APRIL OF last year, Kristin proposed that we publish an anthology. I was gung-ho: I'd been wanting to do a fiction magazine for years. I already had a website set up, and preliminary submission guidelines, and an idea for a name. I could have it up that night.

Then she suggested that it be a *Christian* speculative fiction anthology.

Wait a second. I wanted to do adventure fantasy, the sort of stuff *Black Gate* used to publish before John O'Neill stopped publishing fiction. Why would I want to publish Christian speculative fiction? Kristin and I both grew up in the church. We read a ton of Christian fantasy and science fiction as kids, much of it bad.

But, Kristin said, it's a way to give back to both the writing community and the Christian community. Plus we could show that Christian speculative fiction doesn't have to be bad. And by presenting good fiction that shows the faith as we know it and have experienced it, we could help our readers better understand our beliefs. Eventually, she convinced me that it was worth doing, but it wasn't until we decided on a theme that I became excited about it.

The theme of our anthology is "Rediscovering the Mysteries of the Christian Faith." The title, *Mysterion*, is the Greek word for a sacred mystery, such as the secret rites of the mystery cults popular in the ancient Roman Empire. Among Christians, the term was used not for secret rituals, but for the hidden truths of God—some of which have been revealed, but many of which will never be understood in this world.

Mysteries frighten us. We prefer certainty, simple explanations, and neat categories. Even when we praise ambiguity in fiction, in real life we often try to cram every fact, every event, and every person into the clear narrative of our worldview. But life is full of mysteries. We can never really know what another person is thinking or feeling, never be certain what happened when we weren't there. We can't even trust our own observations and memories, our own conception of who we are. Even if we did know all that we think we do, can we fully understand the inner workings of the mind, the deepness of space and time, the divide between life and death?

The temptation is to close our eyes to the mystery. To tell ourselves stories that drag all the questions to the parlor room so they can be answered by our clever narrator. Christians are no less likely to do this for having a worldview that allows for the supernatural. Our explanations just tend to rely more on hermeneutics and theology and less on science and psychology.

The Bible is much less of a stickler for neat resolutions. Not every character's past is revealed, not every hero does what is right, not every crime is justly avenged. The Bible is comfortable with mysteries in a way that we are not, whether the deep mysteries of the Incarnation and the Trinity, or the lesser known mysteries found in some of its strange and unexplained passages: Behemoth and Leviathan, nephilim and seraphim, heroes and giants and more.

For this anthology, we sought stories that made room for the mysterious, that asked questions even though they didn't know the answers, that examined the clues even when they were contradictory and nonsensical. We wanted stories that were as untidy and as theologically imprecise as the Bible itself.

I think we found what we were looking for, and I hope that you will enjoy the mysteries in these stories as much as we did.

— Donald S. Crankshaw

IS *MYSTERION* CHRISTIAN fiction? What makes a story "Christian", anyway?

At Realm Makers, a Christian speculative fiction conference Donald and I attended last year, the keynote speaker answered this question with, "You do." That is, anything written by a Christian author can be considered Christian fiction.

But we didn't ask authors to tell us about their religious beliefs when they submitted stories to *Mysterion*, and we know that not everyone we're publishing identifies as Christian.

One common understanding of Christian fiction relies on what a story isn't as much as on what it is: not only does it have to be written from a Christian worldview (or even, more narrowly, an evangelical Christian worldview), it can't have any profanity, gratuitous violence, or graphic sex. I'm not sure how graphic the sex has to be to merit disqualification, and we didn't think the violence in any of the stories we selected went beyond what was necessary for the story being told (although some readers may disagree). But we would certainly be disqualified on the profanity question. We believe that authors should use whatever words and situations their stories require, as they strive to tell the truth about the world they live in, about the worlds they imagine, and about the characters that inhabit them.

Some readers expect even more. For them, it isn't enough for a work to be informed by a Christian worldview and free of objectionable content. They want Christian fiction to clearly promote Christian beliefs and values. From this perspective, Christian fiction exists primarily to convince or reassure readers of the essential truths of the Christian faith. Or to at least nudge them in that direction.

I'm not going to fault any of these categories of fiction for existing or some Christian readers for wanting them. Plenty of people want to read fiction that assures them that what they already believe is true, whether they believe in Jesus as Lord and Savior, the need to reduce CO_2 emissions, or the importance of correcting societal injustice. Many people hope that such stories will help convince the unconverted. And the desire to avoid reading anything set on a moral foundation at odds with one's own values is hardly unique to Christians.

But that isn't what we're trying to accomplish with this anthology. Many of the stories we're publishing do affirm Christian beliefs and values. Others do not. Because we weren't only looking for stories we agreed with. We were looking for stories that resonated with us, that spoke to our own experience of Christian faith and practice, an experience that includes doubt and uncertainty. Some of these stories made us uncomfortable, posing questions about Christianity for which we don't have good answers. And yet, all felt authentic to us on some level, in their depictions of Christian cosmology and belief, or of Christians. All had something to say that we found insightful.

Authenticity was key. Christians may roll their eyes at the latest story about an evil minister or an oppressive patriarchal monotheistic fantasy kingdom, populated by one-dimensional religious characters bearing no resemblance to the people we actually encounter at church. But traditional Christian fiction doesn't always do better in the realism department, with its strawman atheists argued into awed silence by smart Christians, or its happily-ever-after conversion narratives. Real life, and real faith, are more complicated than either set of stereotypes will admit.

Mysterion is *about* Christianity. But we're not sure it *is* Christian.

This is not, however, an interfaith anthology. We are publishing one story that could be better described as Jewish than Christian, but all the others engage with specifically Christian views on faith, spirituality, and the universe. And even that one Jewish story explores ideas about the soul and immortality in ways very similar to our own Christian perspective.

We chose this approach for several reasons, but perhaps the most important is that, as Christians who like to read, we have a particular interest in exploring and challenging expectations around what can be considered Christian fiction. In pushing back against strict content guidelines that would disqualify parts of the Bible itself, that insist on doctrinal purity and have little tolerance for ambiguity. For mystery.

Ultimately, we're publishing this anthology because these are the kinds of stories we've always wanted to read. We can only hope that you, our readers, will agree.

— Kristin Janz

The Monastic

Daniel Southwell

FATHER KYLE MURPHY wrapped his fingers around the edge of the tin boat. Lake Superior stretched to the horizon, but their boat was just a little rowboat with a buzzing Evinrude motor. Each wave made his lunch roil inside him. The man at the motor sat with his legs spread for balance and his body half turned—one eye on the motor and one on the next wave. He was a tall Ojibwe man in a brown and red flannel shirt and a wide felt hat jammed low over his eyes. His name was John Boucha, and he didn't say much, which made Father Kyle like him.

They wobbled into the next wave. A bucketful of foam cracked over the bow and into Father Kyle's lap, where it melted into water and soaked his boots.

"Leggo of the boat," John said. "Hold onto your seat."

Father Kyle turned and latched his hands onto his seat beside his legs. Shivers ran through his limbs.

"Rough sea today," he called over his shoulder.

"It's a lake," John told him, and then shrugged.

The waves began to have green in them—long strands of leafy, plastic-colored seaweed. They raked against the tin hull like fingers and made the water smell like musty salad. That made Father Kyle realize what was missing. The smell of the ocean. The only thing that made it different from the ocean was the smell. There wasn't any salt. He could smell the water itself, fresh and aggressive, and the oily plants in the water, and he imagined he could smell the fish underneath. He could definitely smell the toiling of the little Evinrude.

He tried closing his eyes, but that made the waves worse. Every time the boat tilted he was sure he was suspended over the water.

So he opened his eyes and stared straight forward. The broken spires of the rocky island ahead of them grew bigger after each wave. The waves began to show white on every crest, and then the beach of the island was tantalizingly close, and finally, Father Kyle could see the shiny rocks of the bottom of the lake. They were all smooth and small, and had a white webbing running through them, forming circles on the stones.

The white-lined rocks moved slowly under the boat, growing and shrinking with each wave. A slender fish glinted past underneath them and then a cloud of fish as tiny as bugs. Father Kyle turned back toward John.

"What are those rocks?" he asked. John frowned. Father Kyle raised his voice. "The rocks all look the same," he said, pointing.

"Petoskey stones," John said. "Fossils. All this is a fossil bed—Traverse City to St. John's Bay, Ontario."

Trillions of creatures, stretching through two countries. It made Father Kyle cringe, but he wasn't sure why.

John cut the Evinrude and pulled a short rubber-bladed paddle from under his seat. He hauled the boat through the waves with long, fast strokes. The bow ground into the rocks of the beach with a crunch and then a screech. John jumped into the water in his boots and jeans. It didn't even come up to his knees. He grabbed the side of the boat and pulled it all the way onto the beach, while Father Kyle sat awkwardly, wondering if he should stay seated or jump out, too. It didn't seem to bother John.

When he did step out, the rocks rolled around under his feet and he stumbled.

"Careful," John said.

"Thanks." Pockets of water in the rocks soaked through his tennis shoes. "I'm used to sandy beaches."

"Sand beaches are nice." John handed one of the duffels of supplies to Father Kyle and slung the other over his own shoulder. Then he began walking, taking confident steps on the round stones.

John pointed. "Up that trail there and around the corner is your place."

The trees began abruptly after a hundred feet of stony beach. They were tall, perfectly straight trees whose branches didn't even start for a hundred feet. Father Kyle leaned backward to see the tops, comically high. The trunks weren't brown—they were smooth and flakey and gray, but paler gray than the stones of the beach. Above the tops of the trees, a few shards of cliff hillside pointed to the sky. The cliffs were rust-orange clay, baked in the sun. Father Kyle couldn't see the trail until they were close. It was just a strip of hard dirt through the leaves. He didn't think it was a trail for humans.

They ducked and wound through branches and stepped over roots. Father Kyle fell behind, and felt a quick flash of worry, but then he panted up behind John. They were in front of a little stone building. It was as small as a cabin, barely a house at all, but it was two stories tall and had a steeple on the roof. The walls were made from thousands of the little gray fossil stones mortared together with pale pink mud, the steeple a tall, polished shard of the orange rock from the cliffs above. Behind the house, the ground sloped up sharply toward the cliffs and the trees became sparse. Here and there the hillside was rent open and a shard of sharp rock speared out, like an exposed vein.

Father Kyle looked the little stone hermitage up and down, looked the ragged hillside up and down, and suddenly decided that he was happy. He liked this silent, ludicrous little church-house.

"It's beautiful," he said. But he didn't want to offend his only human contact, so he added, "I'm sure your places of worship are beautiful, too."

John shrugged. "I'm a Methodist."

They carried the knapsacks in and deposited them on the floor. For a second Father Kyle wanted to ask John to stay on the island for a little longer, to make up some excuse about needing help settling in. But he was going to be alone here—that's the point of a hermitage—and he needed to get used to it.

So he shook John's hand and watched him retreat down the path toward the beach.

Kyle Murphy had always been Catholic, but he decided to become a priest at twenty, to make his father angry. It worked a little too well. He started his theology degree full of enthusiasm and ideas, but one morning, emerging from an invigorating all-nighter debating Erasmus and whether Luther had anything to offer Catholic thought, Kyle discovered his credit card didn't work. He didn't have coffee that morning, and he didn't have lunch that day, and finally at supper he called his father.

He'd been cut off. It was over. Seminary was done. He wasn't going to get any more money.

But instead of quitting, Kyle got a job at a coffee shop and went to school part-time, and never called his father again. He didn't get good grades in seminary, but grades didn't make you a good priest. He wasn't sure what *did* make you a good priest. He was pretty sure it was determination. So he kept pulling all-nighters, kept making himself quad-shot Americanos at the coffee shop, and finally he was through seminary.

Congratulations, they said, we didn't think you'd do it, and oh my goodness your thoughts on the Cappadocian fathers might just be groundbreaking . . . have you thought about publishing? He still barely had to shave.

There was a church that was happy to have him join their active staff of priests. A classic old Spanish church in Florida. Father Kyle put his stiff-collared shirts and his boxes of theology books in the back of his Mustang GT and drove down the coast to where it was warm and people were waiting for him to be their priest. The car was left over from his father's money, but it hadn't had an oil change since Kyle started seminary.

The first person Kyle talked to in Florida was a meth-head who couldn't stop picking at the sores on his arms, twitching, and spitting blood into the ditch at the rest stop. He asked Kyle for a quarter, and Kyle gave him five dollars because he didn't know what to say.

That's how Florida was for Kyle.

All the canned goods went on the bare pine shelves at the far end of the hermitage. Most of it was one room. There was a long counter with a tall stool. He'd cook and eat there. A bed with a decent mattress and a stack of dozens of blankets. The biggest blanket appeared to be a bearskin.

Father Kyle climbed the wooden ladder that led to his second story.

It was barely tall enough to stand in, at the center, and sloped on the sides. A window at one end looked toward the cliffs and another looked toward the beach. This was the prayer place.

Prayer is a hermit's primary job. Complete devotion to prayer, study, and meditation on the Word of God. Father Miles, the previous hermit, had devoted nearly fifty years to prayer, here in this little stone church-house in the middle of an ocean without salt. It was John Boucha who found him, right here, sitting in the hard-backed chair at the desk by the window that looked toward the beach.

There was a tiny bedroll in the corner. Father Kyle smiled, thinking of an old priest praying so late he couldn't summon the energy to climb back down the ladder and sleep on the cot downstairs. He yawned and cracked his neck and then stretched out on the bedroll. He'd go downstairs in a minute and get ready for bed.

It had been a long day. He'd driven across the Upper Peninsula and then boated across a Great Lake.

Father Kyle rolled over on the bedroll and realized it was morning. He sat up and blinked until he was alert enough to climb down the ladder. His feet rattled against something. He frowned. All his cans of food were scattered across the floor. Some of them were split open, oozing chowder or baked beans. He avoided the cans and shuffled to the pantry. The pantry shelves were knocked off their pegs and scattered around his kitchen area. His dishes were on the floor—the plates were shattered.

"How did I sleep through this?" Father Kyle said, then realized he was talking to himself. It seemed too early in his isolation for that, so he clenched his teeth and kicked through his little home. Once in Florida a raccoon had climbed from the garbage can into his apartment window and thrown his kitchen trash all over. Father Kyle assumed it was something like that. He must have slept deeply.

The coffeepot was in the corner and coffee grounds were smeared all over. He didn't feel like cleaning it up yet, so he walked onto the path outside and stretched in the cold wet air. The hard-packed path toward the beach was churned with what looked like hoof prints. Little, pointed hoof prints like a deer would leave. Father Kyle frowned. Had *deer* trashed his hermitage? That didn't make any sense.

After four months in Florida, Father Kyle wasn't eating enough. He was drinking too much and taking little white pills he got from a teenager named Ronny. Ronny had a newer Mustang than Father Kyle did, and tattoos of cage fighting logos, and was unexpectedly pious. He was honored to help his priest cope with the stresses of parish life in a city that ran on drugs and fleecing octogenarians from New Hampshire who just wanted away from the cold.

Some of the old people were on the drugs, but Father Kyle didn't see many of them. The old people were mostly Protestants.

On the day Father Kyle had his breakdown, he spent all morning, from one a.m. onward, beside the hospital bed of one of his congregation who had been stabbed by another member of his congregation. He had a handful of white pills for lunch and drove to the home of an old woman who supposedly had money to donate to churches. He prayed for her soul, and then he prayed for all her relatives, and she still didn't get out the checkbook, so he offered her some white pills.

With a check in the breast pocket of his starched white shirt, he drove to the church for his turn taking confessions.

The first man was from out of town, a college boy on break, and he wanted to know if it was rape if she had consented at the time, but probably *wouldn't* consent in retrospect when she was sober, and whether he had to tell her about what happened.

Father Kyle said yes, it was rape, and he wasn't sure if it was better to know about something bad or not.

After that the confessions got worse.

It was the sixth confessor who noticed that Father Kyle was hyperventilating and called the other priests.

Father Kyle pulled the chair up to the desk and sat. Under the desk was a stack of spiral notebooks, and a worn Latin Bible. One of the notebooks was still open on the desk. Father Miles had been writing with a pencil that he sharpened by hand with a tiny jackknife. He wrote in Latin.

John must have been curious what the Latin meant when he found the body. Father Kyle took a deep breath and remembered seminary.

Pacem Deus mihi dedit. Paratus sum.
God has given me peace. I am ready.

Father Miles had known he was going to die. Was he sick? Father Kyle didn't know. He shivered but didn't leave the chair. He was going to have to get comfortable here and stop thinking about the old man dying. He flipped through the careful, slender handwriting.

Indutiae pax non sunt. Adveniunt etiam me excitant. Quiete vero me habeam.
Our truce is not a peace. They come still and wake me. But I will be calm.

Father Kyle frowned. Had there been other priests here on the island? Or was it a metaphor? Did he have doubts about his faith?

Through the window, Father Kyle watched the sun rise and watched the dark dot of John Boucha's boat laboring toward his island, right on time. John had promised to make a special trip in two days, instead of a week, to make sure Father Kyle was adjusting well.

He was excited to show John how well he was doing. He'd cooked successfully, and split firewood to pile under a tarp for the winter, and even caught a slippery little river fish with a worm and bobber.

He climbed down the ladder and walked down the trail and onto the beach to meet John's boat. It slipped quietly onto the rocks, and John stepped out with a black garbage bag of supplies.

"There you go," John said. "I just brought Father Miles' normal supplies. If you want to write down what you like, I can bring it next week."

"Thanks," Father Kyle said. "I'm sure this is fine."

"Alright. Do you want help carrying this stuff?"

"I think I got it."

"Alright." John hooked his thumbs in the pockets of his jeans and looked around the island. "Father Miles used to have me bring little cans of mushrooms in cream sauce. I didn't bring those. Didn't think very many people liked them."

"Good call," Father Kyle said. "Hey, I got a question for you."

"What's that?"

"Were there ever any other priests here?"

"Before Father Miles? Yes—lots. All the way back to the first French priests in the Great Lakes."

"Yeah, I read all about that. But they were always alone when they were here? Was Father Miles alone?"

John shrugged. "As far as I know."

Father Kyle picked up a rock and threw it into the waves. John picked up another and slung it sidearm, easily farther. He wasn't competing though. His face stayed blank.

"What about . . . " Father Kyle paused. "What about, you know, people on the shore?"

John finally smiled just a little. "My people."

"Yes."

"Actually, we've been here even longer than the French."

Father Kyle blushed. "Yes, I mean, did people ever come to the island? Were there ever . . . problems between anyone and Father Miles?"

John frowned. "I was the only one he talked to, that I know of, for years. Before that it was my uncle." John flipped another rock. It sailed impossibly far over the waves before it tumbled down a whitecap and sank. Father Kyle couldn't imagine how you could get that strong and still be so lanky. "Why the questions?" John asked. He had a thoughtful face.

"I found some things that Father Miles wrote," Father Kyle said. "About other people. It sounded like they didn't get along very well."

"Oh." John kicked a rock into the water with the ragged toe of his boot.

"Oh? Do you know what he was talking about?"

John kicked another rock. It rolled across the other rocks and stopped before it hit the water. "I guess I should have talked to you already."

Something seemed strange. Father Kyle didn't say anything.

"What are you, Irish?"

"Yes."

"Makes sense. Name's Murphy . . . you're Catholic."

"Yup." Father Kyle picked up a rock and tried to throw it as far as John had. It dropped quickly and something in his shoulder hurt.

"Anyway, there's always somebody that came before. The Celts beat the English to Ireland, sure, but who beat the Celts there?"

"I don't know," Father Kyle said.

"Sure you do," John said. "You got myths, just like we do."

Father Kyle frowned. "I don't understand."

John started dragging his boat toward the water. Father Kyle got the feeling that he'd already talked more than he liked to. But he stopped in the water with each wave soaking his Carhartt pants up to the knee and he looked very serious.

"You've gotta to watch yourself in out of the way places," he said. "Places that civilization hasn't reached." He hefted a leg into the boat and then sprang in and fired up the Evinrude. "Be careful," he said. "You'll be fine."

Father Kyle watched the boat lift itself over the waves and shrink into the distance. His stomach felt tight and when he turned around the island looked darker.

———

Father Kyle didn't know much about guns, but there was a rifle on pegs above the door, so he took it. It had a long, heavy barrel, a blackened walnut stock, a leather sling, and a lever under the trigger like the rifles in cowboy movies. He slung it on his right shoulder with the butt up, like he'd seen in a movie once. He kept his hand on the barrel and carried a walking stick in his other hand.

First he went up the hill, skirting the shards of rock and stopping to breathe whenever the slope leveled out. Finally he made it to the top, where the final spire of rock stood at the edge of a plateau. The pointed rock was carved, roughly, into the shape of a cross. The carving was old and round-edged from weather, but it was still clearly a cross. A steeple for the island.

When he turned and looked down, he got dizzy. The whole island, and beyond it the lake, were spread out at his feet, making him feel like he was standing on a flagpole. The hill hadn't seemed so abrupt when he was climbing it.

His little hermitage didn't look out of place on the island. It looked exactly like the island—an abrupt little pile of rocks in the middle of nothing.

Father Kyle squinted and located the mainland—a strip of green above all the shades of blue. He felt a tingling isolation. He could see miles and miles and miles, but nobody could see him. He could take off all his clothes and nobody would care. He could stand naked on the top of an island if he wanted.

He chuckled to himself. "That would be dumb."

Instead he lifted the rifle to his shoulder a few times, planting it firm against the meaty part, and smiled. He took the cardboard sleeve of ammo out of his pocket, selected a round, and carefully inserted it past the sliding flap in the side of the rifle. It popped into place smoothly. Father Kyle put the gun back to his shoulder, jacked the lever, and thumbed the hammer back. He breathed in and out while he aimed at . . . nothing.

And then he pulled the trigger and the *boom* rushed like a wave over everything, concussing out from him high over the waves. His shoulder ached and he shrank from the unchecked loudness of the sound. Then he laughed quietly and slung the gun on his shoulder again. He wasn't sure why he'd done it, but he was glad he had. As he was slipping his stiff collar back into the collar of his shirt, he heard a chittering, like a man imitating a squirrel.

He turned and didn't see anything. He listened again, and heard footsteps running through the leaves. Shivers ran up and down his calves and forearms. He shook them off.

When he turned around, something in the water, a mile below him, caught his eye. Just a long dark shape, shifting around, fading out into the surf. He frowned at it until he couldn't see it anymore, and then headed down the hill again.

When he got back to his cabin he paused in the doorway. Something looked different. He took a step in. The cabin had been cleaned. The tin dishes were washed and the clothes he'd piled by the cot were stuffed in a bucket by the counter. The floor was swept. The open pot of soup on the counter had been emptied. Even the shelves that had been broken were pieced back together like a puzzle and propped up on their brackets.

Father Kyle tried to breathe calmly. He sat on his cot and put his head in his hands and breathed.

It was completely dark. His eyes wouldn't stay open. The sound of the waves never stopped. He shook himself awake and leaned forward to find his lantern. He cranked the propane valve to its lowest setting and the center of the cabin filled with humming blue-tinged light. The corners still hovered in darkness.

It was easier to stay awake with the light on. He hoped it wouldn't scare away whatever was out there on the island.

Father Kyle sat on the edge of his cot. Its titanium frame cut into his thighs but he didn't move. The rifle was across his knees. It was loaded.

He didn't know what time it was, but it didn't matter. There weren't alarm clocks on the island and there weren't appointments. His only job was praying, and right now, he realized, he was praying that nothing horrifying was out there. He still couldn't shake the shrill feeling that had run up and down his limbs after he fired the rifle. He couldn't help thinking he had disturbed . . . *something.*

After he stopped thinking and looking around, waiting was easier. He stared at the wall and only thought about breathing.

Sometime after Father Kyle's mind cleared, he focused on the sound of scuffling feet outside. He wasn't sure how long it had been going on. His heart immediately accelerated and he stood up slowly. The cot creaked and he winced. The footsteps didn't stop.

The latch rattled and the door opened a crack.

Father Kyle backed up until he could feel the rock wall against his shoulder blades.

The door opened.

Father Kyle slowly, quietly, began cocking his rifle. He wished it was already cocked.

Then three little red men burst into the hermitage. Father Kyle almost choked. They were only as tall as children, with shaggy red fur on their backs and leathery pink skin on their bellies. Their eyes glowed red and they ran around his house on stumpy little hooves.

They were round and hunched—almost buglike.

Father Kyle trembled. They didn't know, or didn't care, that he was there. One of them threw a can of food into the air and suddenly all three were throwing things, tossing and crashing and catching. Chittering like squirrels, almost laughing.

"Hey!" Father Kyle cried. They froze. Their electric red eyes bulged at him, confused like an animal's but angry like a man's.

They snapped away from him, snatching cans off the shelves and throwing them in the air. A can bounced off the ceiling and hit the counter. One end of the can exploded off and chili spilled like guts on the floor.

"Alright," Father Kyle said. He lifted the rifle and fired it over their heads before he could think twice. Chips of stone flew across the cabin as the bullet ricocheted off the walls and then buried itself in the countertop with a sickening *thunk*.

They froze and then screamed. Their voices were high-pitched, almost off his hearing spectrum. His spine tingled.

"Get out!" he yelled at them, and cocked the rifle again.

They ran toward him, around him, circling his legs and scratching at him. They seemed to blur together. He swung the rifle and hit one of them with the barrel, then he found himself falling. He was on the floor, in pain, and scuffling with them. They smelled like sweat and thick fur. His skin singed where their padded hands touched him. His mind swirled.

He remembered he was holding the gun and got his thumb on the trigger. He yanked, the gun roared, and the butt bit into his bicep. They screamed again but this time they scampered away.

He turned his head to watch them run out of the cabin, hunching and crabbing into the woods. When they were gone, he stayed on the floor and closed his eyes while splinters of the attic floor fell around him. The bullet hadn't carved a neat hole like in the movies. It had blasted a jagged hole bigger than his fist.

He slowly got up and felt at the rising welts on his arm where they'd touched him. Their fingerprints looked like brands. There was no pain yet. He stumbled to the cupboard and rooted through the first aid kit until he found the little tub of burn ointment.

<hr />

Father Kyle stood on the beach and looked for John's boat. John would know what to do. Father Kyle thought about asking John to take him back to the mainland. He could say being a hermit wasn't for him, find a quiet church, and never tell anyone about the little red creatures.

The sky was getting dark and the lake was gray like his rifle barrel. He carried the rifle around with him everywhere now.

As the waves chopped higher onto the beach and great crests rolled across the lake, Father Kyle started to wonder if John would make it. A wave like a mountain rose out of the wind and broke with a crash on the taller rocks down the beach from him. Another followed it. The shards of water splashed far up the beach, near the woods. His island had never felt so small.

Father Kyle headed back toward his hermitage. John wouldn't come in a storm. John wasn't crazy.

He paused at the edge of the forest. The trees were rocking and groaning. He turned back around. The rain hadn't made it to the island yet, but it was pocking the waves and obscuring the sky. Clouds moved in coils and cauldrons. The closest clouds were green-bellied and very low.

Frowning, Father Kyle walked down onto the beach again. His feet were sure on the rocks now. He'd seen storms in Florida, but nothing like this. Nothing with this raw, *personal* energy. He felt strangely drawn to it, though the electricity in the air made his skin crawl. He couldn't shake the thought that something was *making* this storm—taking huge handfuls of wind and water and mashing them together.

The rain hit him in marble-sized drops, soaking his hair and clothes.

He stayed on the beach and watched the sky lash around him. Lightning struck the mainland, far across the water.

He shivered harder. It wasn't just the rain. He was sure that this storm was here intentionally. Maybe the storm *was* something. Maybe the storm had a mind. He shook his head and chuckled. He was going crazy. There was something wrong with this island. He sat on the beach in the rain and put his head in his hands.

He didn't look up until the rain suddenly stopped. The waves crashed at his feet, fifty yards up the beach. The wind leaned him backward. He couldn't stand up. The water was spreading away from . . . *something.*

The Something was speeding through the sky toward the island, gliding just under the low bellies of the clouds, and the lightning seemed to crackle in a ball around it. Father Kyle's arms and legs cramped.

"Oh Jesus God," Father Kyle whispered. He didn't know if he was swearing or praying.

Then the Something was over him, passing, shadowing, and then gone. It was so big he couldn't see all of it, but what passed over him was a wing. Gliding. A black wing bigger than an airplane's wing. He was sure it was a living thing.

As soon as it was gone, the storm felt normal. Rain drove at him, the waves crashed on the rocks, and he sat in the middle of it, shivering from cold and shock, too rattled to move.

It was evening when the waves were low enough to cross to the island. John Boucha kissed his wife and loaded supplies into the boat. The waves were still choppy.

When he paddled up onto the beach, it was strewn with driftwood, fish, and seaweed.

He almost didn't notice the shape on the rocks. He pulled the boat up and turned around, and that's when he spotted Father Kyle—curled on the beach with his knees to his chest.

John ran to him and knelt.

"Father Kyle," he said. The priest was soaked through and shaking. He coughed and choked. John sat him up and said his name again.

"I don't . . . what is . . . oh Jesus God what is it?" Father Kyle sputtered.

"How long have you been here?" John asked.

Father Kyle didn't say anything. He just stared across the water and shivered.

John picked him up and carried him to the boat.

There was an army blanket in John's kit. He wrapped Father Kyle in it and set him in the bottom of the boat, because he didn't trust him to perch on a seat, and shoved the boat out. He jumped in and gunned the Evinrude toward the coast.

Father Kyle woke up feeling weighed down. He frowned. The light around him was bright. He was in a hospital bed with a neat stack of blankets on him.

"Hello?" he said. He looked around. The TV was muted and playing local news. A reporter stood on a road blocked by fallen trees, gesturing. Father Kyle tried to figure out how he was feeling. Why was he in here? He felt vaguely sore and weary, and his skin felt . . . scorched. Raw.

There was a button to call the nurse on the remote for his bed. He pressed it.

He watched the news replaying clips of the storm. Right. There had been a storm.

The nurse peeked in and said "How are you feeling, Father?"

"Alright, I think. How long have I been here?"

"Overnight. The doctor will be in to see you soon."

Father Kyle drummed his fingers on the stack of blankets while he waited. He was sweating, but the compressing weight of them was comforting, somehow.

The doctor was a short, thick man with a beard. He looked more like a lumberjack than a doctor, but his voice was soft and professional.

"You almost died of exposure," he said, sitting down. "Just decided that the middle of a storm was a good time for a stroll on the beach, huh?"

Father Kyle chuckled. He was slowly remembering everything, but knew he shouldn't talk about it. "I guess so. I got lost. By the time the storm was bad, I was disoriented."

"That's more common than you might think."

"Am I alright?"

"You will be," the doctor said. "We're going to keep you overnight to make sure your temperature is stable and you show no signs of shock or pneumonia."

"Alright, thank you," Father Kyle said.

The doctor patted his shoulder and said something about resting, then left.

———◆———

John was wiping down the Evinrude when Father Kyle walked down the beach. He had a canvas messenger bag with him.

"I got books," he said. "I'll need you to take them back to the library next time. If that's ok."

John shrugged *yes*.

"I like the library here," Father Kyle said. "They gave me a card because I know you, even though I don't have an address."

"You're doing research."

Father Kyle nodded. "There are some about the myths of this area. Not very many though, so I got some on mythology in general. I thought it would be helpful."

John regarded him quietly. "So, back to the island?"

Father Kyle nodded.

"Alright," John said.

He shoved the boat into the water and they got in. He paddled through the clear water until it was deep enough to lower the Evinrude and yank it to life. They started bobbing through the waves.

"Why?" John asked.

"Why am I going back?" Father Kyle looked back to see that John was nodding. "I don't know."

———◆———

Father Kyle put an old rusty hammer on the windowsill. Shears on the other windowsill. On the doorstep, the head of an ax and an old knife. He thought they must be iron, not steel, because they were all rusted.

The books said that iron kept creatures away. The Europeans had figured that out. Father Kyle hoped the local creatures were the same way. One of the books had pictures of the little red beasts. At least, that's what Father Kyle thought they were. The pictures in the books were roly-poly and grinning, not tattered, smelly things like the creatures in his hermitage. They were called *pukwudgie*.

"Pukwudgie," Father Kyle said to himself. "I hope you hate iron as much as the fairies did."

He wondered why creatures like fairies hated iron so much. Maybe because it took technology to make iron, so it represented the progress that pushed these creatures back. The advance of modern man that had banished the mystic things to places like this island. Iron was unnatural, a foreign presence on the island. So was Father Kyle.

He climbed the ladder with the last iron tools and placed them around the attic prayer room—on the windowsill, and in the rafters so they wouldn't try to come through the loose shake shingles.

He took the water jug and headed down one of the trails. A creek ran out of the rocks there and spread into a ten-foot-wide channel before it eased into Lake Superior through the rocks of the beach. It was the easiest place to get water. Its banks were mounds of sand carried down from the crest of the island. Spiny beach grass grew here and there. He stopped at the top of the sandbank and set the water jug down.

Lazy in the cool water, a long creature was looking at him. Its body was serpentine, with thick salamander legs. It was longer than a pickup truck. Whiskers poked out of its plump cheeks and it had delicate little fangs. Father Kyle thought it looked more like a Chinese dragon than anything else he could think of. It was dull gray, like the river rocks beneath it.

He still held the rifle, and he thought about firing. He thought about running. Could it follow him on land? He wasn't sure. Most of its body was in the water, floating idly.

He didn't run or shoot.

"Hello," he said. Then, "How's the water? It looks cold."

The water dragon, or whatever it was, raised its heavy, feline head and its softball-sized eyes blinked, and blinked, and never left Father Kyle's face. The eyes were shaped like a cat's, wet and wise.

"You're definitely not a pukwudgie," Father Kyle said.

The water dragon cocked its head. It opened its mouth and tried to say something, a lilting, thumping language in a cellar-deep voice.

Father Kyle shivered. It was trying to talk to him.

"You don't know English, do you?"

The beast still thundered in its low voice, fast and then slow and then fast. Father Kyle wondered if it was a native language, something that John could understand. If the beast could talk to humans, of course English wouldn't be the language it knew.

Father Kyle pointed at his water jug. "Well, I guess I should get some water."

He set the rifle down and picked the jug up. Slow steps down the sand bank. He knelt beside the creature's neck. It rippled with muscles under its short, wet hairs. The creature's side heaved as it breathed. The water rose and fell.

Bubbles flowed out of the jug until it was full. He pulled it out and walked back up the sandbank.

"Well," he said. "I'll see you around."

The beast muttered and lowered its head back toward the water, wetting its round chin.

———◆———

Back in the hermitage, Father Kyle climbed to the attic and sorted through the notebooks until he found one that hadn't been written in. He sharpened a pencil with the little jackknife. Its blade was thin from years of whetting.

I saw another beast today, he wrote. He realized he should go back to the beginning. *I've seen different beasts since I've been on the island . . .*

He looked out the window, across trees and rocks and then across miles and miles of cold, crashing ocean. Ocean without salt. And with monsters.

I can live here, he wrote. *I can make a home here.*

———◆———

John Boucha felt the electricity in the air before the sky started turning green or the wind rose. He knew it was going to be a worse storm than the last one. He turned off the lathe and waited for the candlestick to stop rotating, then swept up the curled shavings. He pulled a green GI knapsack from a cupboard, laid it across the workbench, and filled it with a shotgun, a long blue-steel revolver, and a KA-BAR marine's knife. Clif Bars, jerky, a poncho, a first aid kit, and vitamin gels were already in the kit he kept in the boat. He took the knapsack into the house and put it on his bed. On the top shelf of the closet, he found a shoebox. It held a little white baptismal robe, a Precious Moments New Testament, and a Vacation Bible School sash studded with achievement pins. He left the sash, but took the baby-sized robe and the New Testament.

He put it back and found another shoebox. He shuffled through it and found dried stalks of plants—white-podded mountain flax and pink-budded dogbane—among the awls and wooden toys and dreamcatchers. He added the stalks to the knapsack.

Last, he found a pair of moccasins with giant-headed birds stitched onto the toes in red and black beads. He put them in the knapsack and left his steel-toed boots on.

He wished he could say goodbye to his wife. She would be at the school, helping the second graders get inside from recess before the storm hit. He walked down to the boat, strapped the knapsack to the front seat with stiff black bungee cords, and shoved into the water.

The waves got higher within a few minutes and then rain started, blowing almost horizontally. The wind was coming straight toward the beach, forcing the waves over the prow of the boat. The little Evinrude wasn't doing much, but he kept the throttle open and tried to remember to breathe normally. The waves and the rain were blinding. John strained to see the curves of the next wave, running the nose of the boat deep in the well of the wave and hunching his shoulders as it crashed around him. The water in the boat was up around his ankles, cold and sloshing. He couldn't take time to bail. If he didn't hold the engine strong, he'd turn in the waves and be swamped.

John had never been seasick before, but now he was afraid he might be.

He set his jaw and thought about last time, about Father Kyle huddled on the beach, near-dead of exposure. He almost hadn't made it in time. And this storm was much worse.

The waves and the chilling water in his boots began to fade farther from his awareness. He controlled the boat automatically, staying alive, almost meditating. He held his breath when water foamed around him, and prayed that the water in the boat wouldn't flip him.

When he finally *crunched* into the rocks, the boat was too full to pull any higher onto the beach. He floundered out, too soaked to care about the pounding water around his legs. It knocked him into the water and then he lunged clear. He thrashed back until he could snatch his knapsack out and then gave up on the boat and ran for his life.

He sprawled on the rocks. The waves couldn't get him here, but the rain and wind tore at him. He shivered in full-body spasms that made him feel ill. He threw up onto the rocks and then forced himself to get up. The sky was the same color as the vomit. This wasn't just a rainstorm.

John Boucha looked at the sky, waiting for the thunderbird.

Finally he had to peel himself away, and he ran toward the hermitage.

Branches and fallen trees littered the path. Leaves filled the air, slick with rain, plastering to him. He could hear trees falling.

A flying branch caught his cheek and he knew there'd be blood. A tree lurched in the woods to his right and uprooted. It brought the branches of all the trees around it down, too. He had to leave the path, running in a big circle until he could get back, but by the time he did there wasn't much of a path to get back to.

He stumbled up to the hermitage. It was almost gone. A tree had crushed it—only one corner remained. Shards of rock and wood were spread all over the clearing. He picked his way through. Old glass gleamed in the rain. The chimney still stood.

He climbed along the trunk of the tree until he could look into the remaining corner of the building. It was empty. Ransacked by wind. A few intact cans of beans stood on the pantry shelves. He climbed back out, not sure if he should sort through the rubble for a body or keep searching the island.

A roar, a deep feline howl, split across the island, from down by the water. Then a different cry—a long, spine-chilling shriek. Thunderbird.

John crouched by the corner of the hermitage. He shuffled through his knapsack, finding the shotgun and then the revolver. He belted the revolver on and held the shotgun across his knees. He knew there wasn't much you could do with a gun in this situation, but he didn't have anything better.

The cry again. The thunderbird was wheeling away from the water. It was attacking something. *"Mishibizhiw,"* John said. Water Panther.

The rush of wind bent the trees almost to the ground as the shadow of the thunderbird rushed over him, abandoning the Water Panther. He could see it far above the island, its whole outline, its whole sky-monster shape. Was it coming after him, now? But it didn't seem to notice he was there. It circled, and the wind circled with it.

And then it seemed to pause, to hover.

John looked up, and then blinked and looked again.

At the top of the island, on the pinnacle of pink rock, was Father Kyle. He had a rifle slung on his back, but he wasn't using it. His feet were firm on the rock and he clung with one arm to the old stone cross. He was holding a bare hand out into the air, into the center of the storm.

It seemed like he was at the thunderbird's wingtip.

John thrilled with fear and excitement. The thunderbird flapped slowly in place, staring at Father Kyle.

The thunderbird's breath was strong and warm, like a horse's. It came in gusts that blew Father Kyle backward each time. He set his jaw and stared into its eyeballs, bigger than his head.

Father Kyle shivered. His black clothes were rain-slicked to him. He'd been standing for a long time in the middle of the storm, and the thunderbird had been staring him down, flapping in place, for just as long. Each rolling *whomp* of its wings rattled the whole island. Father Kyle's feet skittered around on their footing. He wrapped his arm around the stone cross again, tighter.

The thunderbird was waiting for him to bolt, waiting for him to strike, waiting for him to do . . . something. But he wasn't going to do anything.

"Hey," Father Kyle shouted into the wind. His voice was drowned out.

He couldn't even hear himself. But it didn't matter. "Hey, I'm going to stay here, ok? You can fly over but this is where I live now."

And then they just kept staring at each other.

Father Kyle didn't know what to say or do. The thunderbird was the size of a battleship, flapping and flapping and regarding him carefully, almost entranced. He suddenly thought of St. Francis, preacher to the beasts.

"Domine, fac me servum pacis tuae!" he cried into the face of the thunderbird and its storm. *Lord, make me an instrument of your peace.* The prayer of St. Francis.

The Thunderbird rolled its head around, like it was interested, and then it wheeled away. Father Kyle felt the stroke of air hit him in the face first, and then he was tumbling down the rock slope. He stopped against a tree, and his ribs hurt, but he stood up right away.

The thunderbird was flying away across the lake. Rain still fell, but it was normal rain.

Daniel Southwell is a script writer for a video production company in Lancaster, Pennsylvania, where he lives with his wife, Claire (who helped with the Latin parts), and their son, John. Daniel grew up in northern Michigan, swimming in the Great Lakes and hearing the stories of thunderbird, water panther, and the red dwarves called pukwudgies.

When I Was Dead

Stephen Case

WHEN I WAS dead one of the first things I did was to try to find Jacob. He should have been there before me. So in my first few months (as they measured time in the villages) I would find myself glancing at every shadow or pool of light under the trees, thinking I saw him stepping out from behind branches or around a low hedge into the road.

You are not supposed to be able to lie there. If you stay long enough they say you forget how. But that doesn't mean you have to answer every question anyone asks, so for a long time I didn't know he wasn't there.

Then one day I saw him, just as I hoped, walking toward me between rows of poplars, down a slight rise in the road.

"You were the missing piece," I told him.

He smiled. If anyone tells you that you cannot be frightened there, they're wrong. There was emptiness in the smile.

"I know," he said.

It wasn't Jacob.

They would say later that it really *was* him in a sense. He was an echo, a memory. Everything still exists in the mind of God, they would tell me. We never have the freedom of being truly forgotten.

When they said this I wondered if it was supposed to be a comfort. Maybe they were really saying I should have let him be forgotten. It was, after all, my desire to seek him and talk with him again that had stirred his form from shadows under the trees.

I tried to make the best of it. I would go walking in the evenings out in the lanes and hollows created (perhaps) from the cartography of my own mind, and eventually Jacob's shade would find me and we would walk together.

Sometimes I would take him out to where the wars are. We would walk right down to the border where things start to twist together and you could not make out the sand from the sea. All the warriors are there.

I used to watch them for hours. They raged on the crests of waves like they were themselves blown foam. I wondered what peace they found in their wars against the dark and cloudy giants on the horizon.

Jacob would stand behind me, in my shadow, out of the reach of spray that fell like blood around us. We were Dante and Virgil at the entrance to the underworld, though we had come from paradise and there was no one to ferry us to the other side.

"What are they doing?" he asked me.

"They fight."

The forms on the waves surged back and forth. They never retreated and they never gained ground. The sky above them always boiled with cloud.

"Why?"

The voice was perfect. If I could close my eyes and just listen to the voice, it would be fine.

"I guess it's what they wanted. People who died and believed it would be like this afterward."

"Norsemen? Like, Valhalla?"

"Sure. But I've stood here for a long time and seen people I recognize out there."

"What's on the other side?"

"I don't know."

We would walk back up the rising slopes and into the green, bright countryside—ever inward, ever upward, like Lewis used to say. I'm sure he's probably up there somewhere, but I haven't gone in far enough to find him.

A lot of us still linger at the edges.

Some people arrive knowing everything. They pass up the lanes like white ghosts and race away in some direction my eyes can't follow. When I arrived I washed up on the beach and could barely stand. I still feel as though my mouth is full of sand.

The path Jacob and I would take through the hills eventually met a lane of cobbles that ran through the orchards to my house. I would turn up it, and Jacob would always continue alone along the road. I would invite him to my house, but he would never come. I used to wonder where he went when I left him.

My house lay beyond the orchards. It was on a rise that looked over trees and fields crisscrossed with low stone walls. It was, of course, everything that I would have wanted in a place of my own. The land was mine. It had been carved from me, or I had always and all along been carved from it.

The house itself was not large. On the particular day I am recalling I walked in and found my sister waiting.

She closed a book and stood. "Where were you?"

"Down at the sea with Jacob."

She blinked, the hesitation of an instant.

"This place is nicer than I remember." She motioned to the stone walls and wood floors and to the wide windows behind her. "It looks like something out of the book you bought me when I graduated. Do you remember?"

I nodded.

"This place was made for us."

I shrugged. "Or we were made for it. Maybe it's not the way it is because I saw it once in a book. Maybe I bought that book for you because I recognized in it some memory of this place."

She smiled. "We were promised a place would be prepared. The mansions couldn't be built unless someone knew we were coming."

It was hard to look at her, so I walked to the window.

"There are empty houses in the hills," I finally said. "Haven't you seen them?"

If she heard me, she decided not to answer.

"You should come farther in. I worry about you," she said, "this close to the sea."

One day after we had walked together I waited at my gate until Jacob was almost out of sight down the lane. Then I followed. He continued without turning until the road bent back toward the sea. It rose through a line of hills and finally opened out onto an avenue flanked by trimmed lawns and ornamental trees. We walked through this for a time. He looked neither right nor left. Suddenly he turned off the lane and I lost sight of him.

When I reached the place where he had disappeared, I saw a narrow wooden door in a thick hedge. It was so small I might have missed it if I had not stopped. Through the hedge I could see nothing, but from beyond I heard the sound of sea on stone.

I stepped through and found his house.

There were trellised vines that reached up marble walls. There were white pillars and fountains that lined a path of crushed chalk to the door. The house had wings that swept away on each side with gilding at the edge of every window and along the line of the roof. From the sound I knew the windows on the other side must look out onto the sea.

It was brilliant in sunlight.

In another instant the light faded, and the windows were dark and the fountains still. The house stared like a mask.

I called his name then. I ran up the crushed stone pathway and nearly fell as the rotted wooden door gave readily to my weight.

His books were here. They were scattered on the shelves and littered the floor around me. I recognized titles. There were frames on the walls as well: his family, his parents, his various awards and commendations. And then there were his paintings, none I had seen but all of which I recognized.

The house was empty.

In a fury I grabbed the volume nearest at hand and threw it toward a window. It shattered the glass and sailed onward, out over the sea, its pages scattering in the wind.

It was nearly evening when I finally emerged. I felt as empty as the house. All the rooms were like the first: marked with the image of my friend and resolutely devoid of habitation.

There was a gardener kneeling below the sill of one of the front windows. He was gathering his tools and placing them slowly into a canvas bag beside him. The dirt was turned where he had been kneeling.

"What are you doing?"

"Planting roses," he said, "for next season."

I told him that before long there wouldn't be anything here but roses.

He squinted up at me. "Would that be so bad?"

"This house was supposed to belong to someone."

"They don't all come."

I said something angry and dismissive, and he stood, pushing against his knees as he rose. Standing, he was taller than I expected.

"What did you hope to find here?"

"A friend." I sighed. "I guess I was looking to understand what happened to him."

He rubbed dirt from his hands. "That will be a long road for some."

I sat on the broken marble step, suddenly tired. He sat beside me. A silver glow moved up the line of the hedge before us, gathered strength, and finally rose as the moon.

"I never expected this place to be haunted."

"No one does."

"Would it be easier to forget?"

"Yes."

"Would it be better?"

I waited, but neither the gardener nor moon answered.

"Nothing is better than this place," the man finally said. I couldn't tell whether his voice was soft from emotion or weariness. "Nothing is better than this place," he repeated.

I still have not followed my sister. My wife comes with the dawn each morning, down from the hills too bright to look upon. She pulls me away from my desk where I stare out toward the sea. In the evenings I walk to the shore and let the spray fall around me like blood. Sometimes I think I see my friend out beyond the shapes that move like giants on the horizon.

I am still angry, and I walk the sea and taste the salt on my teeth.

When the sun sets I gather driftwood.

I am building a boat.

Stephen Case teaches astronomy at a Christian liberal arts university by day and by night (when it's cloudy) writes stories, some of which have appeared in *Beneath Ceaseless Skies, Daily Science Fiction, Orson Scott Card's Intergalactic Medicine Show*, and *Shimmer*. His novel, *First Fleet,* is a science fiction horror epic (think H. P. Lovecraft meets *Battlestar Galactica*) published by Axiomatic Publishing. Stephen holds a PhD in the history and philosophy of science and will talk for inordinate amounts of time about nineteenth-century British astronomy. Follow him on Twitter @BoldSaintCroix or at stephenrcase.wordpress.com.

Forlorn

Bret Carter

"MOTHER," HE SAID.

She sat on the other side of the table. The table was weathered, as if it had been left outside for several days. Keith set the spiral-bound notebook on the desiccated surface. The flashlight and pencil had fallen on the floor, so he picked them up. The pencil he held in his fist. The flashlight he placed next to the notebook, still on, letting it carve the darkness.

He needed at least that.

"Here's what I'm thinking," he said. "I'll start with when things started getting strange."

"Strange."

"Yeah. When Erica called me."

"Erica."

"His fiancée. She called me and said she couldn't find Marcus. He wasn't returning her calls and his roommate hadn't seen him in three days." Keith thought about laughing but knew it would sound fake. "I remember thinking I would end up on the news, wincing in the camera lights, describing how well I knew Marcus Rigger."

Keith kept looking at the flashlight. He knew he would need to look at her soon. "We were pretty worried, Mother. That was mostly what was going on. But I suggested I meet up with Erica. That way we could maybe come up with an idea of where Marcus went and—" Keith started to lean back in his chair, to look more relaxed, but the legs popped. It was wooden and just as ravaged by the elements as the table. It could very well collapse under him. He eased the chair back down.

"And?"

Truth was the only hope he had. She had made that very clear. He glanced up at her. "And I have to admit. I was partly motivated for selfish reasons." His hands had picked up the pencil. He pressed his thumb against the tip. Feeling the almost-pain. Which would break first, the pencil's tip or his flesh? "Don't get me wrong. I didn't want Marcus to be dead or anything like that. But I guess part of me was hoping he might be out of the picture. That they might break up or something." He tried a smile, but it turned into a grimace. "There's some truth for you. The truth is this—I had this faint hope I would end up with Erica."

"Hope."

"Marcus knew," Keith added quickly. "We even joked about it. He would say something like I was trying to steal his girl, then I would say that's right I'm going to whisk her away on my private jet—that sort of thing. But we both knew Erica was in love with him. She had always said she was looking for something serious. She even admitted she was counting on a Christian college being the perfect place to get her M.R.S., as they say."

No response.

"It's a joke, Mother. A girl who goes to college to find someone to marry—to become Mrs. Somebody. We say she's going to college for her M.R.S."

More silence.

"Anyway, I admit I was interested. But all of us knew no one was taking that possibility seriously. In this particular story, I wasn't the love interest. I was the third wheel. The mascot. The jester."

Her gaze drifted across the grimy room. He was losing her attention. Maybe it was the metaphors.

Keith laughed, and he was impressed. He was pretty sure it sounded genuine. "Yeah, so anyway. I dropped everything to help track him down. Because he was my friend, but also because of Erica. I knew I didn't have a chance with her, but still. I was hoping he was okay. That it was all just a simple misunderstanding."

Her eyes came back to him. "But it wasn't."

"No, Mother, it wasn't." He tapped the pencil on the table and the tip broke. A jagged, tiny stump. A crumb of graphite. "I finally remembered the Millwood House."

"Tell me," she said.

Keith's mouth was so dry. In all the craziness, there hadn't been any time for something as simple and necessary as a drink of water.

"Tell me." She was getting impatient.

He had to buy more time. Draw this out. He shifted in his chair like someone trying to get comfortable. It creaked and shifted, barely holding itself together.

Sitting up a little, he kept his voice steady. "Marcus majored in everything. He was pre-med our first semester. Then a psych major. Then art. Then something else—I can't remember. Then psych again. I think every college student is a psych major at some point."

"I want you to tell me about the house."

"The house? All right." He pulled his coat tighter. It was getting colder. "Marcus ended up settling on a history major. History really grabbed him. That's all he talked about. Marcus became Mister Histor. All history, all the time."

A slight breeze found the only unbroken window, rattling it a little. Upstairs, the rooms moaned. Keith looked straight ahead. At her. He had to keep the focus inside. In here.

He let the pencil fall from his hand. It rolled off the table, clattered on the warped floorboards. He leaned over and picked it up. Her eyes followed him.

"And the weird thing about it—at least I thought so—was that Marcus wasn't planning on teaching history. He made that very clear. He said he didn't want to teach it. He said he wanted to reveal it. That's how he put it. He was going to *reveal* history."

He leaned forward. The chair whined. "Then Marcus found out about the house."

"How?"

"Not really sure. There are actually a lot of abandoned houses around here. They come in handy on a slow weekend."

"Why?"

"Well, even though it's a Christian campus, it's a small town, and Friday and Saturday nights in a small town can be especially soul-dangerous, you might say. So once in a while, someone would suggest going out to one of the abandoned houses. It's a great time. The girls cling to the guys and the guys get to feel brave. We snoop around and have some clean fun. You know, Mother. A good scare."

"A good scare."

"There were all kinds of rumors floating around. We heard one house is completely empty, expect upstairs, hanging in the closet, is a red dress. Another house has a small attic and in the corner of the attic is a doll with no eyes. That kind of stuff. Pretty creepy."

She placed the heel of one hand on the edge of the table, but didn't say anything. The hand was pale as the underside of a snake. The fingers elegant, the nails jagged.

Keith forced his eyes back to the flashlight. "But Marcus said it wasn't the houses themselves that are frightening. He said it's something else."

"What?"

"The emptiness. Marcus said it's the emptiness around the houses. And inside too. That's what makes us uneasy. And I have to admit, Mother, that at least for me—he was right."

Saying it out loud made Keith feel a little stronger. "In my philosophy class we were debating whether or not God created evil. Since He created everything, then He must have created evil. But Dr. Edding said the flaw in that argument is assuming evil to be something. Evil is not something. It is the absence of good. Even Satan was created with free will, but he chose the emptiness. That's why we're afraid of wastelands. Why we feel uneasy when we learn that atoms are mostly empty space. We're made of tiny desolations, and that makes us uneasy. It's the nothing that we fear. Because that's what evil is. Nothing."

She frowned.

Keith kept going. "People always talk about how those long stretches of Nebraska and Kansas are boring. But Marcus said people are actually sensing something along these stretches that strikes a dark chord in all of us. He called it uncanny emptiness. He said it's not so much boredom as fear. It's a reminder the universe is mostly void. The spaces between the stars. The spaces between our brain cells. All our thoughts are leaps across the void."

As her eyes wandered again, her mouth drew downward.

Keith used the pencil's eraser to tap on the table. She didn't look at the pencil. She looked at him. He forced himself to stare back. "I say all that because of what Marcus found out about the Millwood House."

The eyes did not blink. "What did he find?"

"He didn't tell me everything. And frankly, a lot of what he did tell me wasn't all that interesting. I'm sure I've forgotten some of what he said."

"Tell me," she said.

"It was built in the 30s. The original owner went crazy."

"What happened?"

"The guy was from out east. A big man with big plans. But after he moved into the house with his family, he developed an irrational fear of tornadoes. Any time there was a storm, he would rush his family down into the cellar. One spring, he forced his wife and children to stay down there almost every night. After several weeks of this, he finally confessed to his wife that it wasn't the tornadoes he feared." Keith paused for effect, but also to buy more time. He counted in his head. One, two, three, four. Buying time, buying time. Five, six, seven—

The hand on the table twitched. "What did he say?"

"He said there was a woman. A woman he saw in the fields at night, who moved through the tall grass during storms. She would glide. A woman who wasn't really a woman. She wasn't a ghost either, but something else. And this woman would weep. Sometimes she would scream. He said that every night, even when there wasn't a storm, he could hear her in the distance. Screaming."

"What else did Marcus say?"

"Marcus said it was just a story."

"A story."

Keith held his breath. How would he know if this was working? Was he going to feel something? Would she feel something?

He was moving through everything too fast. He needed to slow down.

Taking a slow breath, he let the silence last as long as he dared. "You know—what Marcus said about the emptiness got me to thinking about other things."

"About what was in the house."

She was getting ahead of him. She was too far into the story. He had to hold her back. Slow down the pace. Otherwise, she might figure out the ending on her own. But he had to tell the truth. She knew what lies smelled like. So he would tell the truth, but tell it slant, as good old Emily Dickinson put it.

"Well, the house, yes. But mainly about the emptiness."

"Tell me," she said.

"Um, I want to be a writer, Mother."

The eyes gleamed.

"I mean, I *am* a writer. I write stories."

"I know."

"Yeah, and the worst part of being a writer is facing that terrible, empty page—that merciless, white void." He used the pencil to scribble at the air. "But writing is powerful. There are thousands of words in this one pencil."

Her eyes glinted a little. Amused?

Keith pointed the pencil at her. "They say that by writing something profound, authors can, in a sense, make themselves immortal."

This made her smile.

Keith tried to smile back. "But that's not true. Just like everyone, authors become skeletons. They shout all those words into the white void and no matter how profound their words might be, they inevitably fade. It's not immortality. At best, it's just a decent echo."

The eyes narrowed. "I don't want to hear about that. I want you to tell me about finding Marcus." She was looking for what he was not saying.

"Sure, sure. But all of this has to do with that. While we were trying to track Marcus down, I told Erica about the emptiness thing. I said something along the lines of how writers have to venture out into emptiness to find something true. She agreed. She said in order to be truly creative, you have to venture out into emptiness. Like spacewalking. You have to tie yourself to something secure in order to make it back. To keep from going crazy. Then she said she felt like Marcus had cut himself loose from her. And that's when we both realized he might be at the house."

"You found him."

"Yes. We drove out in my car. By the time we found the right road, the sun was gone." Slow down. One. Two. Three. Keep going but slow down. "It was very dark, very quiet. Erica was really scared. I was too, but of course I didn't let her know that."

The eyes closed. "Of course."

"It's a pretty frightening thing. Going into an abandoned farmhouse in the middle of nowhere and finding your friend just sitting there in the corner. When we saw him, Erica screamed and I almost did too."

"Frightening." She obviously liked the word.

"We weren't really expecting to find him. We didn't spot his car, because he parked it behind the barn. But here he was, just sitting in the dark. Erica started crying, grabbing at him, trying to see if he was injured, trying to make him look at her. She got so worked up, I made her leave. Made her let go of him and go back outside. I told her to try and get a signal on her cell—to tell the hospital to expect us. But I mainly just wanted her to go outside."

"What did you do then?"

"As far as I could tell, Marcus wasn't physically injured, but he seemed mentally damaged. I kept saying his name. His eyes were open, but he just stared past me. Like he was empty. Like the house had crept into his brain. I thought he was gone. But he finally looked at me. And I could tell he was trying to swim out of the trance. Then he spoke."

"What did he say?"

Keith went through the motions of a yawn, but he saw she could tell it was fake. Careful. He had already slipped in a few lies. Any more and it might give everything away. To burn up a few more seconds, he opened the notebook. Marcus had filled the first page with his sweeping cursive.

She repeated the question with some irritation. "What did he say?"

"You want me to tell you exactly what he said, Mother?" He asked his question slowly, dragging out a few more seconds.

"Yes, I want you to tell me everything."

Little pauses could make all the difference. He closed the notebook and looked directly at her, trying to look like he was piecing the memory together in his head. "Marcus told me something very strange. He told me there is something inherently corrupt about empty spaces. He said the wide open regions of the world—like oceans and wildernesses and farm-lands—all have the tendency to become dimensionally infected."

When he paused this time, her eyes flashed and she frowned. He kept going.

"Eventually a presence settles inside these desolate places. Not an actual person, but a kind of residue of all the lives who have struggled there over the years. Possibly an aftertaste of souls. Not a created thing. It sustains itself like a parasite. It has to fasten onto a host. Marcus said it has to feed on the creativity of its host in particular, in order to maintain its existence."

"A muse," she said.

"No."

She scowled. "Yes."

"No, Mother," Keith said softly. "This is the part I figured out. This creature is not a muse at all. She is the opposite of a muse. Instead of feeding your mind, she feeds on it. Her kind have haunted a thousand books. She is the mermaid calling across the waves. She is the banshee howling on the moors, drawing the lonely bachelors into chasms. She is the harlot of Babylon, drunk on the blood of the saints, prying apart the souls of heroes."

Anger bloomed in her eyes. Good, Keith thought. Be angry at me. Be focused on me.

She sneered. "Finish the story."

"I was helping Marcus to his feet when we heard screaming. At first I thought it was Erica. But she burst back into the house. She said some-one was coming. That we had to get to the car. That we had to leave. She grabbed Marcus by the hand. We both did. But he refused to leave. He said—"

She whispered anxiously. "What did he say?"

"He kept saying the same thing over and over."

"What?"

"He just kept repeating it."

She almost screamed. "What!"

Keith lingered over one more breath, drawing it out. "He said that he belonged to *her* now."

She smiled.

Keith looked away. "I gave the keys to Erica and she went out the back. To get the car. She was panicking. I don't know what happened to her."

"You lost her."

"Yes."

She leveled her eyes at him. For a moment, Keith thought she sensed the lie, but she was only intent on the story. "But you stayed inside."

"I was trying to get Marcus out of the house. But we ended up falling against the table. Knocked everything off. He crawled into the corner and stayed curled up there. Like he is now."

Keith turned the flashlight slightly, so it could throw light across the room behind her. Marcus still cowered, still shuddered.

The woman across the table was reduced to a silhouette, but Keith could still see the glint of her eyes.

Keith smiled at the twin flecks of her gaze. "Then you came through the door. You glided over the floor without really touching it and I just kind of stood here like I was paralyzed."

"Paralyzed."

"By fear, yes. You watched me for a few moments and then told me to sit down."

"Then what?"

"Then you said to call you 'Mother.' You said that this empty place is your womb, and now I am born. That I belong to you. You said I must tell you everything that happened. Tell you the story."

"The story." Her eyes blurred into a dreamy gaze. Keith felt a tugging sensation in his head. She was tasting his mind.

The eyes fell shut. "What will happen now?" she asked.

Keith's skull went cold.

No.

In trying to buy Erica time, he had waited too long. He could feel his thoughts fragmenting, crumbling in his brain, falling on his tongue, out of his mouth "I will tell you a story and another story and another story and when I sleep, my dreams will be more stories and I will stay here and stay here and stay here."

"With me."

"With you, Mother."

The eyes opened and looked at him with something like love. "Why?"

"Because I belong to you."

This time her smile widened until blue vapor spilled over her teeth. He could feel the subtle touch of her tasting his mind.

Frantic, he opened the notebook again, skimming the pages Marcus had filled. All those empty pages filled with ink. It was enough. The sight of all those words defying oblivion steadied Keith.

He felt his mind slip back into place. He still had some control left. So he began to just make words and speak them as they came to mind. To try and say things that belonged to him. To speak the truth as long as he could. "I know who you are." His mouth was completely dry, but he kept going. "You're the mother of emptiness."

She let her eyes fall closed again, basking in his voice.

"You are the Abyssinian maiden. You are the tears in the pit, weeping endlessly." He could feel his voice inebriating her. He had to think of more. "You are the elegance of shadows."

A gust of wind leaned against the house.

Across the table, she suddenly flinched.

Was it happening?

She jolted upright.

It was happening.

Keith leaned forward. "I'm going to finish the story."

"The story," she murmured. She looked dazed.

"Yes. And like most man-made stories, no matter how true they might be, there is always a little lying going on in there somewhere."

"I want the truth."

"Okay. Here's the truth. The truth is that you're a sidhe. You're the byproduct of a hundred years of hardship—the dregs of every sleepless night every person ever suffered here in this barren blank of the world."

Blue light flickered behind her lashes.

"Turns out Marcus snapped out of it pretty quickly. He wasn't all that disoriented. In fact, he was able to tell us about the mound in the field. Where you put all the corpses over the years. They bolster your energy, right? Isn't that how it works? Your little nest of secret bones. They help sustain you, don't they?"

The mouth formed a silent snarl.

Keith snarled back. "I lied. Erica didn't panic and run away. She went straight to where Marcus told her to go. She dug it all up. That's what you're feeling right now. She's digging it all up, scattering it all. Just like Marcus said to do."

The woman got to her feet. Keith grabbed for the flashlight, but missed and knocked it off the table. It hit the floor and went out.

It didn't matter. The darkness was gone. The woman was fiery blue now, bathing the room in light. The color swirled around her, making her gown ripple and flutter. The face was famine, a skull barely restrained by skin, her eyes bright with starvation.

Now the shame of the room was revealed completely. The warped walls, the sagging door frames.

Marcus was trying to sit up.

The woman turned toward him, hovering. She gracefully reached out to him.

Marcus fell backward against the wall, twitching and gasping. He watched the woman with pleading eyes.

She was draining him.

Keith was done with words. He rammed the pencil into the back of her neck.

It was a shriek of anger, not pain, but it was enough to distract her. And now she was definitely feeling it. Her sapphire eyes flickered. She could feel Erica dismantling her nest of bones.

Turning away, she burned across the room, screaming as she went. The sound was deafening. But her shriek quickly faded as she passed through the musty air to the front door. Even as she flew, she was coming undone. Abruptly, she dissolved into a splash of light against the wood. The light dripped, trickling, dwindling.

There was silence, a perfect nothing of sound, and then the faint, hesitant wind questioning the house.

Keith crossed the room and pulled Marcus to his feet.

Marcus leaned against him. "It worked."

"Yeah."

They were almost to the front door when it burst open.

Erica's arms were filthy, her jeans stained black with soil. Dirt covered her face, her hair whipping wildly in the wind.

She burst into tears when she saw Marcus and stumbled into his arms. Keith had to help steady both of them together.

"She's gone," Marcus said into Erica's hair. "You did it."

Keith went outside to give them time to hold each other.

His hands were still shaking, but after standing next to the car, he was able to get his keys out and get inside. He pulled up and waited as Marcus and Erica trudged down the slanted steps together.

Keith got out and helped her maneuver Marcus into the backseat. She got in the back with him and Marcus put his head on her lap. No one said anything about Marcus's car. They would get it later. Right now, they needed to get him to a hospital.

Keith went back around the car to the driver's side and stopped. He felt a cold truth stir in his head. They hadn't destroyed the woman. The bones had only given her stability. As long as there was emptiness, she would continue to glide through the world. Draining people dry to make a new nest.

He looked back. He couldn't help it. He looked back at the house.

Nothing came out of the front door.

He got behind the wheel, slammed the door, revved the engine.

He turned on the headlights, killing the darkness.

In the rearview mirror, the brake lights turned the house red. Nothing looked out through the broken windows.

Putting the car in gear, he drove them down the dirt road, making distance.

He looked in the rear view mirror again.

The darkness closed up behind them. Even so, there was just enough of the moon to allow the outline of the house against the stars.

There was nothing on the porch.

There was nothing on the steps.

Nothing at all.

Bret Carter lives with his wife and daughter in Denver, Colorado. He teaches Bible and English at Hyland Christian School and he preaches at the Miller Street Church of Christ. His fiction has appeared in *Perihelion Magazine, Boston Literary Magazine,* and *CrossTIME Science Fiction Anthology.* He is the author of the book *God's Words,* and the upcoming *Life Among the Married People* and *Paper Bullets: Point-Blank Notions on Writing,* both available Fall of 2016. And just like every third person you pass on the street, he is currently working on a novel.

Too Poor to Sin

H. L. Fullerton

GRANDFATHER SQUANDERED OUR family's fortune on forgiveness, forcing Father to enlist in the Legion and serve the angels. This was before he met Mother and they had me, though the angels' war still rages. Father doesn't say much about his years of service, except that it would've bankrupted us had he bought an honorable discharge. Instead he quit, kept his wages and is banking on God's leniency. He says he amassed those sins in God's name—he only killed those the angels ordered him to—and that should count for something, despite the angels' claim that sin belongs solely to the sinner. Father says God knows you can't climb to heaven without breaking a few bones.

In school, they teach us sin must be paid for, preferably in gold. My friend Tollum says angels also accept flesh, but Mother assures me this isn't true. She says not to listen to Tollum, that his family has always been poor and they don't know any better. I think Mother is afraid Tollum's family knows exactly what they're talking about. That's why she secretly saves coins to buy forgiveness from the angels. Father says we cannot afford forgiveness, that thanks to Grandfather we are too poor to sin, that if our souls must rot so that our bodies may eat, so be it, amen. Mother always gasps when he says that prayer. But one day I will restore us to riches and our family will be fortunate again.

Neither my teachers nor the angels will say how many pardons you need to get into Heaven, but if Grandfather was right, it's a lot. I save all the pardons I earn in school. I hope if I'm very good, I can save enough to get Father through Heaven's gates. I worry he won't use my pardons, that he will want me to save them for my children, but Heaven won't be the same if he isn't there waiting for us. Mother and I understand this even if he doesn't. Father insists he's spent enough time among angels. (He means his years in the Legion. Father's never been to Heaven, although when I was younger I thought the Legion and Heaven were the same thing. *They're not.*) I think he just doesn't want to see Grandfather again.

Today I earned three pardons from Teacher. Since I'm still too young to sin, I didn't have to give any of them back—not that I did anything wicked. Tollum got two pardons, but lost them immediately for tugging on Nin's braids. Braid tugging costs three pardons in our classroom (I've heard that in the better schools it can go as high as *ten*.) Since Tollum only had two, Nin gave him one of hers. Nin is from an almost-fortunate family and knows charity is even better than pardons. Charity shines your soul.

My soul is very shiny. Once an angel gave me a pardon just for letting him look at my soul. I gave him his chit back immediately because vanity is a sin. Mother was so proud she cried when I did that. "You will make it through Heaven's gates," she said. I pray she is right. Also, I ask God to make sure both my mother and father are allowed in. In my prayers, I tell him that if they don't have enough forgiveness, I'll pay their debt when I arrive. I hope He lets people in on credit. Mr. Soon at the grocery store doesn't allow credit; he demands coin up front. But I think God is nicer than Mr. Soon. I also hope He keeps track of how little charity clings to Mr. Soon's soul.

I reach under my bed and pull out an old aluminum lunchbox so I can hide away the wheat-paper chits I earned today. Father used to store his treasures in this lunchbox when he was my age. It's the only thing he took from Grandfather's house and I'm very careful not to add to its collections of dents. Father thinks I carry my lunch in it, but I keep it under my bed so I don't lose it like I lost my mittens last year. Mother had made them for me and although they were ugly, the love she made them with kept my fingers from freezing. She is working on a new pair for the coming snows, but wool is expensive and Mother is better at embroidery than knitting. (A silkworm lost in a sheep's fold, says Aunt.) If Mother doesn't finish my new mittens, I shall keep my hands in my pockets and her love in my heart and that will be enough to keep me warm.

I count my pardons. Seventy-seven. I knew that's how many I had before I counted: 74+3=77. Still, I like to make sure none have gone missing. Neither Mother nor Father would take my pardons without asking, but I don't trust the mice. I press the neatly stacked pardons back into the lunchbox and close it tight. I make sure to flip the catches so no sneaky mice can snack on my forgiveness. "If I have any forgiveness left after getting Mother, Father and I into Heaven," I announce to the mice, "I will bring you, too." I'm not sure mice are allowed into Heaven, but I'll ask. I think they're too greedy to make the climb, but Mother says mice can get into anything so maybe God can't keep them out of His home any better than Mother can keep them out of our pantry.

Father is late for dinner. Our meal is slowly burning as we wait for him. Mother worries the food will be too crisp. Also that we're using too much fuel for the stove's heat, but if she places the food on our table without Father here and it cools before he arrives, then we have relegated him to corpsehood and we would never, never do that—not even if our last crumbs were ash upon the stove. We may not be fortunate, but we still practice honor.

I'm scared, but stay brave for Mother. If Father dies, even in name only, then Mother and I would be forced to rely on Aunt, and Mother's family wants nothing to do with her shame—meaning Father. Father says I should ignore them, that they cling to the letter of the law rather than the spirit and what is God if not spirit?

If Father is dead, Mother and I will be worse off than Tollum's family and Mr. Soon won't let us buy groceries and we will lose our home and I don't think seventy-seven pardons is enough to cleanse Father's soul.

The door opens and Father says, "What's this now?" and plucks the pot off the stove. Mother is so relieved she sits before dishing out our dinner. When she remembers her gaffe, she starts to rise, but Father's hand on her shoulder eases her back into her chair. "I've got this," he says. "I've always got this." He tells me to sit, but I already am and then dinner is plated and he sits. We bow our heads and say grace. Father says it quickly so the meal won't cool before he finishes. It is crisp, but neither Father nor I complain. Mother doesn't notice because Father gave her the best portion—dry, with no black edges. If I were a teacher, I'd give him ten pardons for that. I pray for God to take note in case the angels aren't paying attention.

"Is everything—" Mother stops.

Father smiles. It is a great smile. All teeth and joy and it lights up Mother's face. "Everything is fine," he says. "A tax of angels was on the street and I had to wait for them to pass." He smiles again, the special one for Mother only. "They didn't notice me. My sins have not risen."

Mother nods. Her eyes mist. Father asks me about school. I tell him about Tollum's tugging and Nin's charity and my three pardons.

"But what did you learn today?" he says.

"Recitation."

"Of?" As soon as he asks, he glances at Mother and realizes why I didn't share sooner. I pause to see if he changes his question, but it hangs there in the air.

"Lesser Sins, Greater Sins, Celestial Hierarchy and Mathematics. Teacher chose me to lead today's psalm."

"Very good," says Father. "Tonight we shall pray that you remember your numbers as well as your psalms." Father works with numbers. He thinks them very important. He says everyone has accounts, even angels. Once he told me that numbers can be tricky, that sometimes they don't add up to what they should, especially when forgiveness is involved. I asked him what he does when that happens and he said, "As with all things, I leave it in God's hands."

"Father? Do you ever run out of numbers?"

"No, there are always more."

"What if the angels take them?"

Mother scolds me for asking, but Father catches my downcast eyes and says, "Numbers don't work for angels. Only song works for them. That's why they need God's children to fight and to count and to write. Learn your numbers and letters, and you shall always find work."

I promise him I will. But I wonder, if angels can't work numbers, how do they count forgiveness? How do they know when a sin is paid in full?

Perhaps, I think, Mr. Soon tells them.

I ask Teacher how counting forgiveness works and he says that knowledge is only for angels. "But angels cannot count," I say, and Nin shakes her head at me. Tollum laughs and is charged a pardon. Teacher tells Tollum he'll have to join his siblings in the Legion to mortgage his soul and Tollum grows quiet. Tollum's favorite sister left for Legion training last night and he misses her already. She is soft, like Mother (but not as good as Mother, despite our current circumstances), and Tollum fears she'll die if she isn't assigned the same unit as one of their older siblings.

Teacher frowns at me. "Angels may not count numbers, but they can count forgiveness just fine." Then (even though I'm still too little to sin) he charges me two pardons for impertinence. I decide to ask about the mice another day. Father can't afford for me to lose any more pardons. I drop my pardons on Teacher's desk and say a small prayer that I may earn them back before the bell rings. Then, feeling selfish, I add a prayer for Tollum's sister. I don't remember her name, but trust God to know whom I wish safe.

I am full of questions today. When Father comes home—at his usual time, so dinner won't be crisp—I ask if he knows how angels count forgiveness.

"No one knows that except God."

"What do you think they use? If not numbers or letters? Can song be counted?" Could entry to Heaven be as simple as singing the right psalms? I am rich in psalms. If Father has forgotten his, I could help him to remember all the words.

"Do not worry about forgiveness. No one in this family needs it."

I'm almost impertinent twice in one day and tell him he needs it, but catch my tongue in time to flip my words. "Do mice need forgiveness? They are very greedy. Mother says they'd steal our walls if they tasted better."

Father laughs. I have pleased him, but am not sure how. "Mice do what God created them to do. But only God's children may walk through the gates."

"Not even the angels are allowed inside?"

"No, the angels must stay outside to serve and protect us. To guide us to God's love and remind us of His will when we forget."

I forget about the mice. I'm too busy thinking, *If I were an angel, I wouldn't like us at all.* "Do angels love us as much as God?"

Mother shoos me to wash my hands. "No one loves us as much as God," she says, watching me rub all my fingers and both sides of my palms with soap. "But I am a very close second." She kisses my cheek and hugs me tight until I squirm away clean. I forget about the angels, too.

Until they show up at school the next day.

A tax of angels parade through our school, glittering and bright. Not just any angels, but those from the Legion. Their robes are decorated with thick golden braids and, on their chests, an image of a red dove carrying arrows in its mouth. I have never seen warrior angels up close before. The one in front, with the largest wings of all and olive branches woven through his curls, sings his name.

Teacher kneels and we kneel and the entire tax sings out a blessing. Then Teacher motions for us to take our seats and we do and not even Tollum raises his eyes from his desk. We wait and when I think we can wait no more—someone will shift in their seat, but no one does—the holiest of the tax tells us about the Legion.

It doesn't sound anything like I've imagined from Father's few words. Before I can stop the thought, I think: the angel must be lying. Questioning an angel's word is a lesser sin and I worry their black faceted eyes will spot my perfidy. But I stay still, very still, and keep my eyes down, and they don't. I say a prayer of contrition and resolve to ask Father about what the angel said. Because despite what Mother's family think of him, Father wouldn't lie about the Legion and angels cannot lie (that is a Truth.) Yet both cannot be true. Can they?

Teacher has us line up and sing psalms for the angels. They don't smile like our parents do when we perform for them. Shouldn't the angels be as proud of us as our parents? Shouldn't they rejoice in our learning of God's words?

After our performance, the angels walk around us, sniffing, staring. One speaks to Tollum, his voice a pleasant hum. He tells Tollum news of his brother Hattan. He musses Tollum's hair and says something about soon being old enough to join himself and enhance his family's honor. I have never seen Tollum smile so wide. My eyes swish front and my breath catches. The holiest of them is a hair's breadth from my face. He says my name. "I know your family. I fought with your father. His sins linger on your soul." His words are F-sharp. He summons Teacher and asks about me. Teacher's voice shakes as he shares my progress. My knees wobble, but I hold them tight. *We may not have fortune, but we have honor*, I remind myself. *Grandfather could not squander that.*

The angel instructs Teacher that I am to receive no more pardons until my Reconciliation. He says Teacher cannot see my soul so his sin will be considered a lesser one, but that the stain on my family is deeper than he could imagine. The angel sings of my father's sins and my classmates move away from me bit by tiny bit. He finishes and leans down once more. "We will see you serve. You'll pay double."

Before I worried about the angels on Father's behalf. Now I am worried for myself. Will these warrior angels accept my pardons or will they demand a taste of flesh?

If I were brave, I would ask how many pardons Father needs to pay off his sin. I am not brave.

As we walk home, Tollum pretends he's already in the Legion and shoots at imaginary infidels with pretend arrows. When he lines me up in his sights, Nin pushes his arm down. "There aren't any infidels here. But you, Tollum, are in need of God's light. May it shine down on you," she says and tugs me after her. Tollum has never been blessed by Nin and stands staring after us.

"My father has no sins of his own," I tell Nin so she won't feel sorry for us.

"My father says dishonor is still honor. It is not our place to judge."

Tonight I will pray for God to bless Nin's family. They are more than almost fortunate.

———

Father finds me in my room. Pardons, all seventy-eight of them—all I am allowed—are fanned across my bed. I am not crying, but there are tears on my cheeks.

"What's wrong, my child?"

I tell him about the angels who visited our school. He asks me if I remember the angel's name and I sing it to him best I can remember. His face tightens.

"I don't have enough pardons. Not for you, not for me, not for Mother."

He sits next to me. "Your mother and I don't need your pardons. Those are yours."

"'A clean soul needs no pardons.'"

"Everyone is in need of God's forgiveness. We repent and he loves us more. Don't worry about the angels."

"The angel said I couldn't have any more. He said I was stained with sin, but that other angel, the one outside the church, he said my soul was the shiniest he'd ever seen. How can it be both? Is it because I thought the angel a liar?"

"Why did you think the angel was lying?"

"He said serving in the Legion is the greatest honor we can wish for. That fighting infidels would bring coin to our names, but Father . . . fighting bankrupted you. You chose gold and received dishonor. How can both be true? Was it because of Grandfather? Were his sins so great that they stain us all? The angel said I'll have to serve and pay double."

"You should not have to pay for my sins any more than I should've served to expiate my father's. Grandfather chose to sin. He— That does not matter. We are all sinners. God loves us despite our faults. Sometimes angels are too quick to sing of fault, but that is their nature. We do the best we can and you've done very well. Look, seventy-eight pardons. I never had so many when I was your age."

"You can have them. To give the angels for your sins." I gather them in my hands and offer him the bunch.

"That is very charitable of you, but you must keep them for your Reconciliation."

"I only need three for that. You need these more," I tell Father. "I will be very good."

He takes them and places them on my desk. "You keep them for me."

"If God calls you, tell Him I have them. Tell Him they are yours and I'll send them with His angels."

Father tousles my hair. "I would not step a foot inside Heaven without you or your mother. You bring the pardons yourself when it is your time. Remember, numbers and letters. Our family is done with fighting."

"Because fighting is a sin?"

"Yes. But only if you choose it."

"And you didn't choose it."

"I did not. I was conscripted. For my father's debts. You will not serve. Now, wash your face and come help your mother."

I wake to the sound of scratching, like a tree branch upon a window pane, but there are no trees in my room.

Mice!

And Father's pardons are out. I left them on my desk. I turn on the light and see a family of mice atop my desk, nibbling on my pardons. I rush from bed and shoo them away. One steals the pardon it was chewing on and scampers to the floor. I grab the rest and stuff them into my lunchbox. I shut the lid tight and follow the mouse into the hall. I cannot see it in the dark and dare not turn on the light for fear of waking my parents.

But there! That's Mother's voice, then Father's. I creep closer, quieter than the mouse. I find scraps of pardon along the floor and put them in my pocket. Perhaps I can tape it back together.

Father is angry. " . . . not the Legion." I crawl nearer to hear his words better. I know he's talking about me. " . . . none but God's," he says.

This makes Mother cry, but not even her tears calm Father's ire. "The Legion is no place for man," he says. "God would not condone what they do. I will stand before Him and await His judgment. My heart is true even if the angels say my soul is not. I believe God will see that. You should believe that, too."

"But . . . conscription? Can they demand it? I could speak with my sister. See if she'll—"

"No. If they try"—his voice drops—"then they may have their flesh. I will give mine."

Mother's cries muffle and I know Father is holding her. I go back to my bed. If the angels get me . . . But no, Father said he wouldn't let them take me. But I don't want them to take him either. I cry softly into my pillow.

In the morning, Mother takes me to school. A message was sent before Father left for work that I am to receive Reconciliation *TODAY*. I carry my lunchbox full of pardons. It drums against my leg, announcing our march. Dressed in red (symbolizing the blood of my forefathers), I parade into school and down the hall to the chapel. Before we go in, Mother takes seventy-seven pardons out of the lunchbox and places them in her apron pocket. The white apron is not as nice as Mother would've liked, but on such short notice it was all she could borrow. There is a small yellow stain on one of the strings, but Father helped her tie the bows so it doesn't show. Father can't be here because he must work. But he says it is better if the angel taking my Reconciliation doesn't see him. Still, I wish he were here. Even though it isn't my birthday for six cycles, I know all the responses and prayers. In this, I will make my family proud. The angels will have nothing to complain about.

The ceremony begins. The entire school is here and *four* taxes of angels. My voice doesn't falter. Until it comes time to cleanse my soul.

Mother declares herself as my sponsor and the angel demands one hundred pardons to initiate me into the faith. *One hundred.*

"But . . . " No one has ever paid more than three. And they are always returned. I look at Mother. She withdraws the seventy-seven chits from her apron and places them on the gold platter. The angel eyes them and waits while Teacher tallies. We all wait. My hands sweat and stick to my clothes. Teacher finishes and whispers to the angel, who scowls at the reckoning.

"You are twenty-three short." The angel sounds like he wants it to be more.

"That is all we have." My voice cracks.

"We cannot proceed without the proper forgiveness in place."

Whispers break out from the pews. Sharp looks from the angels stop them. I wait for Mother to take my pardons back, to take my hand and take me home. But she doesn't. She reaches into her pocket, her dress pocket where she keeps her coins. I tug at her wrist. She can't give Mr. Soon's money to the angels.

"No," I whisper. "Father wouldn't want us to." If Father wouldn't take my pardons for his sins, then I will not take Mother's coins for mine. And I haven't sinned. I am too young to sin. Until I'm reconciled, I cannot sin. Yet the angels say I have.

I hear scurrying and think of mice. I wish I were a mouse. No one can keep a mouse out of anywhere. Not even an angel.

I am so angry that I jump when a small hand presses something into mine. I turn my head and see Nin. "Twenty," she says. "It's all I have with me."

I shake my head, but she is already placing both our hands on the gold plate. Then Tollum is behind me, offering me three pardons that he must've scooped out of the gutter. Mother would have been embarrassed to place them in her apron, but she puts them on the plate, then hugs Tollum and Nin.

"My sister sent them to me," he says. "But I'd just lose them. It's better if you use them." Everyone knows the angels won't be giving the pardons back after this Reconciliation.

Forgiveness accounted for, we continue. I say my final prayer and add a blessing for Tollum and Nin's families. The angel makes the sign above my head and it is over.

I want to leave immediately, but Mother says we must stay. The angels congregate in the front of the chapel and seem to be arguing. Then one comes over to Mother and me and offers us the plate with a small stack of crisp pardons on it. I take them. Count them. Twenty-five pardons. I hand twenty-one to Nin and four to Tollum. Nin tries to give them back to the angel; Tollum sticks his in his pocket. The angel won't take Nin's chits and it's then I recognize him as the angel who once stared at my soul because it was so shiny. I want to ask him what it looks like today, but can't get the words past my throat.

After school, Mother presses two coins into my hand. "Take them to the church and give them to the angels. One in your father's name, the other in yours." She whispers her instructions as if Father might overhear us plotting his redemption.

"But Father said—"

"Your father may be right about God, but we must still appease the angels. We mustn't let them keep him from the gates. Let's make sure he has the chance to plead his case with God."

I clench the gold in my hand. My seventy-seven pardons didn't cover my debt to God. How far will one gold coin go?

"One coin should be plenty. We're not paying for his service stains. Your father wouldn't want that and I promised I wouldn't. These are for any interest he may have accrued."

"Won't we need the coins for Mr. Soon?" On one side of the coins are angel's wings. The other has the word GOD. The embossings are separated by a fluted edge that marks my palm when I close my hand.

"Don't worry about Mr. Soon. These are extra."

I know we don't have extra coins, but take them to the church just the same. The church is surrounded by a fence that is tall and black and pointy. I swing its gate open and let myself in. I wonder if it is as easy to get into Heaven, but God probably has His gates guarded. Otherwise, anyone could enter. Maybe not, if they're so big and grand. Does God's gate require hands to open it or does your soul open it? Maybe that's why souls need to be free from sin: Because sin stops the gates from opening.

I stick my hand through the fence, pretend I am Father reaching for Mother and me through God's fence. (If he has a gate, he must have a fence.)

I think of coins with angels on one side and GOD on the other. I take one of Mother's coins from my pocket and turn it over in my hand, staring at one side, then the other.

Seems like God and the angels should be on the same side.

But if they aren't—if the coin is right—then maybe Father is right about God understanding that the things he did in the angels' war shouldn't be considered his sins.

Inside, I give a coin to the rector. He records our offering and notes our forgiveness in the good book. He assures me the angels will be informed and one gold coin worth of interest will be removed from my father's sins.

I turn to go, then ask, "Do you know about Heaven?"

"Why, yes, some," he says.

"How do the gates work?" I wonder if Father can wait outside until Mother and I arrive. I can't ask Father and I can't ask Teacher. If I ask Mother she might cry, so I can't do that either. And I don't know any angel I dare ask. If this man doesn't know, maybe Tollum will get his sister to ask for me. Being in the Legion, she must know many angels.

"I suppose like any gate. But bigger and grander and so bright it hurts one's eyes to look upon them."

"Have you seen them?"

"No. One must be dead or an angel to view Heaven's gates." He says this as if I should already know it.

I rub the ridged edge of the other coin. I am this narrow edge. All of God's children are this narrow edge, really, bridging the gap between God and angels, virtue and sin.

Should I pay for my sins or take my chances like Father? If I choose wrong, none of us will go through the gates and I will be worse than Grandfather. I will have tarnished our honor.

I thank the rector and leave.

Outside, the coin slips from my fingers and bounces between two pointy pickets, landing GOD side up. I laugh. Because *yes*. We *do* live on the edge. But if balanced just right, then—like a mouse that can't be kept out—we can scurry between God's bigger, grander pickets, bypassing the gates and rolling into Heaven.

I'll give the second coin to Mr. Soon. *If our souls must rot so that our bodies can eat, so be it. Amen.*

H. L. Fullerton writes fiction—mostly speculative, occasionally about angels—which is sometimes published in places like *AE, Daily Science Fiction, Freeze Frame Fiction,* and PARSEC's *Triangulation* anthologies.

Golgotha

David Tallerman

THE REVEREND?

If you know to find me, you know too that he's not a man I talk about. Let the newspapermen tell their lies; it's no business of mine. The truth is . . . well, let's say that sometimes a lie goes down easier and leave it there.

What, you've seen him? A niece, you say? Then that's different I suppose. If he gave you my name, I suppose that means he's talking again. Well, screaming, talking . . . my point is, he's found his tongue. From the day we left that cursed place to the morning we set foot on Portsmouth Harbour he spoke not a word, and I'd thought perhaps he never would again.

I'll tell you what, girl; buy me another dram of rum, will you? A kindness to an old sailor? No, I'm not drunk, and if I am it's no concern of yours. Oh, I'm sure you're a god-fearing sort, but don't imagine you're more god-fearing than I am, for you haven't seen . . .

No, you won't get me talking that way. If you want a story then it's liquor or nothing, for I've a thirst on me like you couldn't imagine.

Ah, that's better. Don't be down-hearted, child; do you think the good Lord has nothing more to worry over than the imbibing of a little rum? Oh, perhaps here in England that's true, but out there in the Islands, where your uncle took it on himself to spread the holy word . . . well, that's another matter altogether. They had real sinning there; sins such as Cain himself would have winced at.

No, not all of what you've heard is true. I never saw a man eat another, though I dare say it went on in parts. But the baby-killing, that's a fact. Any woman who didn't want her brat, she'd take it to the sea and drown it, quick and thoughtless as breathing. And the sacrifices; they thought nothing of stamping a man to death or staving his head in, for the least reason. I saw once how they buried a fellow alive, just so the chief had somewhere sacred to plant his new hut. The poor bastard was gagging and screaming, but they kept on going, and before he was half covered they'd planted a great beam upon his chest; I heard distinctly the crack of his ribs.

Now don't look so green about the gills, girl. There's worse to hear than that, I promise you.

At any rate, they did some frightful deeds before the white man came to set his civilisation upon them. Yet in all they weren't so bad. I lived alone amongst them for nigh three years and never felt in much danger. I'm a Norwegian by birth, you see, though you wouldn't know so now; I was put ashore after a—well, let us say a disagreement and leave it there. I thought I was a dead man, for I'd heard all the stories you have, but they treated me kindly enough. You might say they were like children, always happy and playful, never worrying for long. It's just that children can be cruel without knowing, for they've yet to learn their right from wrong.

I'd tell you everything changed when your uncle arrived, but of course that wasn't true. There were nine men at first, though more came later, and most had brought their wives along. They had their work cut out, as you can imagine; perhaps they thought they'd known what they were in for, but they found right soon that they had not the least idea.

I gave them two weeks, to let the import sink in, and then went to pay a visit. They were a sorry looking bunch. The natives would not let them in their houses and they hadn't yet had time to build their own, nor had they any tents. Though their ship was still in harbour they'd disdained from sleeping aboard her, lest they be thought of as mere visitors. They'd brought some of their own food but were trying to ration it, and all the fruit they'd eaten instead was making them sick.

It was a while since I'd spoken English, and for a moment I struggled to put the words together in my head. "My name is Alstad," I said. "Do you have a leader I can talk to?"

After a pause, your uncle stepped forward. He did not seem surprised to see another white man; perhaps he'd already heard of my presence on the island. "All men are equal under God," he said, "but I'll speak to you. My name is Reverend Halloway."

I offered him my hand and we shook, though I could see the suspicion in his eyes.

"How do you find the place so far, Reverend?" I asked.

He forced a smile. "The people have been very accommodating," he replied.

I couldn't help laughing. "Accommodating, is it? They'll take your shiny doodads, Reverend, and they'll go half mad for anything metal, particularly if it has an edge to it. They might even nod and smile while you cant. But they'll never listen to a word you tell them. I know, for I've tried."

He was a fiery man back then was your uncle. He looked me straight in the eye and said, "Sir, I do not cant. The word I bring is the word of God Almighty, which is the light of the world, and there's no darkness so deep that it can't penetrate."

I almost told him that maybe he'd come upon a darker place than any he'd yet heard of. However, it was months by then since I'd seen and spoken to a white man, and I'd no desire to waste the time in bickering. "Then you'll need someone who knows the place, and the people, and speaks their tongue," I pointed out, "if you're to make any headway."

"The Lord will provide," he assured me—but I could tell he saw the truth of what I'd said.

"Surely he will," I agreed, "and surely he has. I don't ask for much, Mister Halloway . . . less than the natives will demand. A gun, a good razor, a favour or two when I need it . . . perhaps a place on your supply ship when the time comes that I've had enough. I'm not offering to work for you, you see; rather I'd like us to be friends, as two civilised men should in this wild place."

Halloway eyed me narrowly. "Are you a Christian, Mr Alstad?"

"When it suits me to be," I told him.

"Then perhaps we shall convert you too," he said—and there was the matter settled.

I think they'd imagined six months would suffice, as though the natives had been just waiting all those centuries for someone to come rid them of their age-old ignorance. But that first year passed and another came, and still they'd made no progress. The natives would listen to their stories when it suited them, but nothing would restrain them from their sinning. They loved stealing, and thought nothing of it. If they were caught, they'd smile and say they were sorry, and then in all likelihood come back the next night and steal the same thing over again. They had taken almost everything the pilgrims had brought by then, and would have had the rest if they could.

The natives loved their wars too, and seemed to fight over nothing. They kept white folks out of them, for no one could say which side they'd belong on, but that didn't mean they were safe: in the first year, a garden the missionaries had spent months planting was destroyed in fighting, and they woke to find the ground littered with the bloody corpses of the dead.

As if that weren't enough, there was plague to contend with. My own belief was that it was the white man's fault, as so much of what went on to happen was; that we brought sicknesses they'd never seen the likes of. They hadn't much by way of medicine and they died by droves, sometimes whole islands wiped out in weeks. Even for your uncle's lot, who consoled themselves with the thought that God was wreaking punishment upon the heathen sinners, it must have been a hard sight to endure.

Throughout that time, I can't claim that your uncle and I became friends. Often a month would pass entirely without us sharing a word. Yet I talked to him more than any of the others, and occasionally he would seek me out, when he needed something difficult conveyed to the natives or wanted explanation for some custom he couldn't comprehend.

I remember one such occasion particularly, as marking a change in our relationship. Before then he had been haughty, and distrustful of all I said, as though his knowing me for a sinner made it impossible to quite believe me. This time, however, he was almost friendly—as much as a man could be who appeared so despondent. I won't say he looked defeated, for Halloway wasn't one to admit defeat, but I could see that something had brought him as close as he'd allow.

"I'd never dreamt that such a depth of sin could exist," he told me abruptly, after a little small talk. "Or that it could be so impenetrable."

"Oh, they're not so bad," I suggested. "They just don't know better. Give them time, Reverend."

Halloway looked at me, and for the first time I could recall, there was emotion in his eyes: a weight of horror I'd not have expected. "There was a woman who'd fallen pregnant," he said softly. "Mrs Halloway suspected she intended to harm the infant once it was born, and so we'd spoken to her every day, telling her what an abomination such a deed would be. She wouldn't listen at first, but after a while we came to believe she'd seen the truth. She wept and swore she knew better, that killing was a sin."

Halloway grimaced at the memory, as though the deception were a wound he bore.

"Then this morning we visited and found her no longer big with child. We asked to see the babe and she said we could not, for it had been born sickly and she feared for it. Afterwards, I went down to the sea. I think I knew what I was looking for; that the Lord guided my steps. It had washed up there upon the shore . . . such a pitiful, small thing. At first I took it for driftwood."

Remembering, he looked sick to his very core. Despite our history and the lack of mutual sympathy we'd shared until then, I found myself feeling sorry for him. I was almost fool enough to offer him a drink; instead, I said once more, "Give them time." Then, seeing that wasn't enough, I added, "It won't be quick, but show them for long enough that your ways are better and they'll come around."

I wanted to comfort him, yet I doubted he'd believe what I said—as well he shouldn't. In my experience the natives got on decently enough, and in general they were happier than most civilised folks I'd met. You could see that from Halloway himself, wrought up over a murdered babe that even its mother wouldn't mourn.

At any rate, Halloway was quick enough to see that I'd offered him false hope. "You know these people better than I," he said. "If you truly believe they can be reached, pray, tell me how."

Perhaps he thought to catch me out; but whatever my beliefs on the matter, I'd given the question some thought. "Here's my advice," I said, "for whatever you consider it worth. Stop trying to treat them all equally. Get their chief over to your side and perhaps the others might follow. You have a lever there already, mark my words, for Pomare's father died badly and slow, for all that he was chief in his time and had made the proper sacrifices. Make Pomare think it was a punishment from the one true god and—"

"Mr Alstad," Halloway interrupted me, "I'll thank you to cease such talk. A man of God has no need for ploys and strategies; those are earthly devices, not fit for the Lord's work."

I hadn't expected any different. "That's as may be," I told him. "But the way I see things, God works in mysterious ways, and makes a tool of what he finds. Don't let pride stand in your way, Reverend."

I reckon I was beginning to understand your uncle by then. For as much as he gave the impression of having disapproved of my advice, I soon saw signs that he and his people had been putting it to practise. It so happened that a ship came in that following week, the *Gloria*, with supplies sent by their missionary society back in England. Though they were all things the missionaries themselves were sorely needing, your uncle made a show of presenting the greater part to Pomare, telling him that they were a gift of the one God and that—for any who revealed themselves to be his true followers—more would soon follow.

Pomare was a covetous sort, and no fool, for all that he believed some foolish things. He had a good enough head on him to see how the wind might be blowing, and he liked that these pale men from across the sea had finally begun to treat him like a king. Yet for a long while he wavered, for his standing wasn't so high that he could overturn the traditions of centuries without there being consequences.

There was not a great deal of religion in the islands, not so much as I've heard of elsewhere. They had Oro, the god of war, and then Hiro, his son, the god of thieves. After that there were a great many idols, almost as many as there were people. They were kept in little open temples that the folk called marae, and were each accorded a degree of respect. However, they weren't deities as such, more spirits; many were men who'd been great in their lifetimes, and they were represented crudely, a carved log here or a handful of red feathers there.

But the islanders had a great many customs, and you might say that on the whole their faith was like a weave, with each thread set upon another. Pomare had sense enough to see that he'd be more of a king with the white man at his back than at his throat; yet he knew too that he had to be careful, lest he pluck the wrong cord and bring consternation.

First he let the missionaries build a chapel, as they'd been wanting to ever since they came. Once it was done, Pomare began attending, though claiming to do so only from curiosity. All the while, Halloway kept him stocked with whatever gifts he could lay his hands upon. They had an understanding by then, and perhaps the reverend thought he'd made a Devil's bargain, but he kept to it.

While all the building and the praying had been going on, Pomare's wife had been large with child, and there was tension amongst the missionaries as to what she'd do when it was born. Not only did she keep it, however, Pomare surprised them all by asking that the babe be baptised Christian. Halloway was overjoyed of course, and it was clear that Pomare had more changes on his mind.

They weren't long in coming. One day, quite unexpectedly, he tore apart the marae near his hut and set the remains afire. Then he took the idol, an ugly-looking thing carved from a stump, and made a great show of throwing it into his cooking fire. There was a crowd watching of course, and once the deed was done he addressed them, saying, "How foolish I've been! Worshiping and sacrificing to this thing, which is only a lump of wood . . . see how it burns! Nor are Oro and Hiro any better, for they are only stories our ancestors made, and for many years now they've led us to fight and to steal. Now I see that there is only one god, the god of the white man, who made all things."

Well, no one did anything, for some believed their chief had gone mad and all of them thought he'd be dead by morning, that being the price of harming an idol or speaking ill of Oro. Yet the next day Pomare was alive and well, and addressed them in the same vein as before, saying, "See how the old gods have no power to harm; for I'm protected by the white man's God."

After that, Pomare began ordering that the other marae be desecrated and their idols burned, or else given to the missionaries to send back as curios to England. Some went along with it; many needed encouragement. There was an uprising of sorts, but Pomare was ready and the insurrection was put down almost as quickly as it started. Then, to show the new way of things, he took mercy on those who'd raised their spears against him, saying that so would the god Christ have done. That more than anything showed them the way things were heading.

I'd thought that Pomare's conversion and his denouncing of the old ways would be the end of it, or at least the beginning of the end. I'm sure the Reverend Halloway believed the same. Indeed, so it seemed, at least from how I saw things. The natives began converting in their ones and twos, and then their dozens. Every week it appeared that Pomare brought in some new innovation modelled on the white man's ways, be it the manner of his dress or ordering that a road be built, or even learning English so as to read from the Bible.

I couldn't have cared less whether the natives were Christians or idolaters, though I suspected they might have been happier as the latter; but I had some feeling for Halloway, having seen him suffer so for his beliefs. So it was that, when I saw him for the first time in weeks, I was shocked to see him dejected.

"Why the sour look, Reverend?" I asked. "Isn't the island teeming with piousness these days?"

I saw immediately how I'd struck a nerve. "They've burned their marae and their idols," Halloway said, "and they've denounced Oro and Hiro. They come to our chapel; they mouth our words. But I see it in their eyes, Alstad . . . they don't *believe*. There's something holding them back, and for the life of me I can't see what."

I remembered something then, out of nowhere . . . something I'd heard long ago and then forgotten. It would have been better if the memory had stayed that way too—and even as I spoke, I recall a part of me resisting.

"I heard talk once," I said, "that there's another god . . . a god even over

Oro. A god of gods, you might say." The memory was returning now in full; a night I'd passed with some of the natives, and their voices hushed with awe, as though they whispered of things not meant to be shared. "His name was Joro. He's not an ancestor like the others, I don't think. They say he was here before the people came, before the island."

Halloway looked at me distrustfully. "If this Joro of yours existed, then I'd have heard."

"He's not mine," I told him, "and he's not something they much like to talk about. I don't know that they even pray or offer to him. But the man who told me was in no state to be lying."

Halloway's eyes narrowed further, for he saw my meaning.

"Yes, I'd been drinking," I said, "and so had he. But contrary to your beliefs, Reverend, drink can reveal truths as well as lies. I tell you upon my life, that man was being honest. And I'll tell you something else: he was afraid. I've heard them speak of Oro, and they make a show of fear, while Hiro they treat like an old friend. But this Joro . . . they talked of him as a Christian man would of the Devil, though I've never seen any Christian as cowed as these."

I could see I'd gotten through to Halloway, but still he wasn't quite convinced. "If what you say is true," he said, "then tell me, why are there no shrines? Why don't they sacrifice to this Joro, or so much as mention his name?"

"The way it was told to me," I said, "you don't pray to Joro. Praying to Joro would be like praying to the earth itself: it's there, it will be whether you talk at it or not, and it cares little for you and yours. And there *is* a shrine, I think, though I don't know where or whether anyone ever goes there."

I'd been oblivious to Halloway as I spoke, but when I looked up, I saw a new look in his eyes—one I'd hardly seen since the day he arrived. It was zeal, full-blooded missionary zeal, and it alarmed me. For I knew then that I'd set him upon a course, and all of my instincts assured me it was like to end badly.

A week later, Halloway came and sought me out once more. "I have a job for you, Alstad," he said. "Help me in this and you can name your price; I'll see that it's paid."

That offended me somewhat, for I'd never been mercenary in my dealings with him. "What is it?" I asked.

Halloway's grin was somewhat frenzied, I thought. His teeth stood out white against his tanned skin. "I've tracked down Joro," he said. "I know his hiding place. Up in the mountains, they tell me."

"And what exactly do you need me for?"

"Oh," he said, "Nothing much. Aren't you a jack-of-all-trades? I'm sure you'll make yourself useful somehow."

He was nervous, I thought, of going alone. Men were different up in the mountains; for a long time, folks had fled up there when they discovered they'd been marked for sacrifice, as had happened often before Pomare's reforms began.

"I'll do it," I decided. "And the satisfaction of my curiosity will suffice for payment, unless I think of a better."

We set out at dawn the next day, and travelled almost until night. Halloway took me to a part of the island I'd not visited much, a place high in the foothills, almost at the point where the jungle thinned before the peaks at its centre. There was a village, but Halloway ignored it in favour of a hut on its farthest edge.

There was one man inside, sitting before a small fire. The natives did not tend to live so long as we do; forty was considered a ripe age for them. This ancient soul, though, must have been twice that if he was a day. His face was wrinkled as a prune and his legs and arms were thin as sticks.

Halloway introduced him to me as Haloa, a priest. Then, without ado, he asked, "Have you spoken with Joro? May we see him?"

His tone was condescending, but the ancient priest appeared neither to mind nor notice. "Yes," he said, "Joro wishes to speak with you."

I thought that was oddly-worded, but Halloway seemed pleased enough. He inquired if it was far and was told no, not very. He asked if we might go immediately, and Haloa told him, "Yes, that is what Joro wishes."

So the three of us set out, the old man leading. The going was hard, steeply uphill over broken ground, but he seemed not to mind. His one concession was to walk with a stick, but other than that he kept a pace we were hard pressed to follow. On and on we climbed, as the evening faded into night. I couldn't tell how he picked his way, for there was no moon in the sky.

What we came to, finally, was not a shrine as I'd expected. It was a hut, not much different than any other on the island, except that its sides were closed where most were left open and instead there was a door. Vapour curled from a hole in the roof, pale against the darkness.

Haloa stopped before the door and, rather than knock, called out, "Oh Joro, the man you wish to speak with has come."

There was no response from within, but Haloa drew open the door anyway, and stepped inside. Then he held it so that we might follow.

Within there was smoke in the air, heavy and rich-scented. I took it at first for incense, but the smell was more of an animal odour, like sweat and musk combined. Through the smoke I thought I could see a man on the farther side of the fire, sitting cross-legged. Then, as the fog for a moment drifted apart, and with a shock that left me weak-kneed, I saw what sat there—and that it was no man.

The figure was naked but for a cloth around its nether parts, and adorned neither with jewellery nor tattoos, such as the natives favoured. Its skin was the same caramel colour as theirs, or perhaps a shade darker. It was well-muscled, more than any man I've seen, as though it had been shaped by a sculptor dreaming of a perfect masculinity. I've never been so inclined, but I've no shame in saying it was beautiful as any woman I've seen.

Except for its head, that is. Oh, that was handsome in its way, I suppose; but it was a monstrous way, that fair made your breath stumble. For Joro's head was that of a bird, though enlarged to suit its frame: a bird with scarlet foliage the precise colour of new blood. It had a bird's beak, hooked and cruel, and a bird's eyes, though with intelligence like a man's. Like a man's, but not; for no human intellect ever made the glint I saw in those dark points.

What? How dare you, girl? Everything I've told you is truth, exactly as I witnessed it. No, I'm not drunk, damn you! What, on a tot of rum? I'm not sodden yet, but I intend to be before the night is done. So get me beer, why don't you? Be of some use, instead of sitting with your damned mouth agape.

There, that's better. Will you call me a liar again? I thought not. You asked me a question and you'll sit now, quiet, and hear my answer.

Well, I was fair gaping at the thing, as you may imagine. When Haloa squatted down I thought it best to follow his example. As for Halloway, he fair slid to his knees. All the blood had drained from his face, leaving him pale as snow. His mouth was opening and shutting but no words came.

Joro considered us both briefly, and then his depthless eyes settled on Halloway, holding him for a long while. Finally, he turned to the ancient priest—though always only his head moved, his body staying perfectly still. "This is the man you spoke of?"

Joro opened his beak as he spoke, but it was more like mimicking of how a person would talk, and the voice seemed to come from all around at once. The sound was deep and echoing as distant drums. I couldn't say for sure what language he spoke, though I understood well enough. At any rate, the old priest didn't answer, except to bow further.

Joro turned his bird's head towards us. "Welcome, Halloway," he said. "I thank you for coming here."

"I . . . " managed Halloway, then choked to a halt.

"And who is your companion?"

"My name's Alstad," I said, doing my best to keep a quaver from my voice. "I live here upon the island."

"Yes," Joro said, as though remembering. "The one who was left behind."

There was something pitying in the way he said it, something that made my heart ache, though I'd never felt I cared before; I found that I couldn't answer.

"You must wonder," Joro continued, "why I wished to speak with you."

After a moment, Halloway seemed to nod his head, though from the look on his face it might as easily have been a twitch.

"Long ago," Joro said, "I made these islands. I made them from my blood and from my semen. Since then I've tried to give my people what they need. There are plentiful fish in the waters and breadfruit in the trees. When they become angry there are wars to be fought, and when they grow too numerous I send sickness. In these and other ways I have tried my best to care for them."

Joro paused then, perhaps shaping his thoughts. Nothing in his face or voice showed any sort of emotion, and that in turn made it oddly hard to make sense of his words; I felt that there must be more meaning in them than I could see.

"I have cared for my people as well as I can," Joro repeated. "But they are turning away from me. I made this island for them, and all the islands thereabout, but it's not enough. They want the white man's things, and the white man's god."

Halloway's only answer was to lean against the post at his back, as though he might be about to faint.

"Tell me," Joro asked him, "will your god look after my people as I've looked after them?"

Halloway made a strangled noise. Then he tried again. "My God is good," he managed. "My God made all things."

Joro inclined his head. "Not these islands," he said. "And that was not my question."

I was afraid Halloway wouldn't get another word out, and was worried by what might happen if he didn't. "Yes," I said. "Their god will look after your people, every bit as well as you have."

It seemed true enough; soon there would be schools, more roads, plastered houses, boys dressed in suits and girls in bonnets, all the paraphernalia of civilisation. I could see it just then, as though in a vision: the day that would inevitably come, when islanders and white men were separated by nothing but the shade of their skin.

Joro looked at me—and the look made my blood cold. "Thank you, friend Alstad," he said. "But the question was not for you." He turned his gaze on Halloway, and I was glad. "You, priest of the Christ god," he said, "answer me: must I release my people? Renounce them? Is that how best I would care for them?"

Halloway still had his head drooped back. His eyes were somewhat glazed. Now, however, he shook himself, as though waking from a sleep. His eyes rolled around and met those of the thing sat opposite him, those fathomless black beads. "My god is greater than you," he said, his voice without tone. "There are no bounds to what my god can give. While you gift scraps, he offers the life eternal."

I was terribly afraid. Whatever that thing was, be it god or monster, antagonising it seemed like madness.

Yet all Joro did was to nod his scarlet bird's head. "Yes," he said, "that is as I thought." I'd just time to feel relieved before he went on, "Halloway, man from a distant land, there is a thing I must ask of you."

Halloway was looking full at Joro by then, though he still didn't seem quite in his right mind. His brow was flushed, his eyes bright. "What is it?"

"I have nowhere to go. Even I can't end myself by choice. If you'd take my people for your god, then you must do this thing for me. It is the only way." Joro's voice was so toneless, his face so without expression, that I only understood his meaning when I saw the knife he held in his hands. The weapon was a crude thing of wood and bone, but the light licked wickedly at its edges.

Halloway noticed it in the same moment I did. "No," he said, his voice rich with horror.

Joro proffered the knife. "Yes."

Halloway's arms hung limply. "No . . . " But he sounded unsure.

"This is the only way," Joro assured him. "The only way to take what you must have."

He offered the knife once again—and this time Halloway took it, though his hand was shuddering.

"Alstad," Joro addressed me, "you must go now. Priest, you will go with him."

"Wait," I said, not sure what I was thinking he should wait for. Then his black bird eyes fell on me and my bowels ran cold. Feeling the old priest's hand upon my shoulder, I got unsteadily to my feet. It was all I could do not to lean on him as he led me out.

Outside the night was cold, or else it had been warmer than I'd thought inside the hut. Haloa went a little way down the slope and I followed. I could see that his shoulders were shaking, though he made no sound. We stood there, I don't know for how long.

After a time, I couldn't bear the tension anymore. Out there in the night, it was hard to believe that any of what I'd witnessed had happened; hard to believe Joro and his words hadn't all been my imagination. I took a breath and looked behind me.

In the open doorway of the hut, Halloway stood. The knife was in his hand. There was no blood on it, not a mark. Yet even by starlight I could see from his face that he'd done the deed. I'd seen men kill before, men who weren't killers by nature. I knew that look.

I helped him down the mountainside. We passed the night in the old priest's village. Not once did Halloway utter a word, though in the night I heard him tossing and turning, mumbling in his sleep. He was the same the next day as I led him back to his own people. When they asked me what had happened, how could I answer them? I said I'd found him like that, wandering in the jungle.

I assured myself he'd snap out of it, with time. Yet when his wife came a week later to tell me he was no better, that she was returning him to England on the next ship, I realised I wasn't surprised. On an impulse I asked if I could travel with them. He'd owed me a favour, I said, and here was my way of collecting.

For five years that island had been my home. Yet I found I couldn't bear it any longer. The land felt poisoned to me, sick to its bedrock. I didn't as much as look back on the day we sailed.

So there it is, the whole truth of it. And I don't give a damn what you believe. I've told you what I saw with my own eyes, just as it happened. You make of it what you will, girl, your thoughts are no business of mine.

But if you doubt me, then when you see your uncle next, you speak a name to him: you tell him 'Joro'. And you watch his face.

You'll see then if I've been lying to you.

David Tallerman is the author of the comic fantasy novel series *The Tales of Easie Damasco*, graphic novel *Endangered Weapon B: Mechanimal Science*, the *Tor.com* novella *Patchwerk* and the recently released *The Sign in the Moonlight and Other Stories*, a collection of pulp-styled horror and dark fantasy fiction. David's short fantasy, science fiction, horror and crime stories have appeared or are due in around eighty markets, including *Clarkesworld*, *Nightmare*, *Alfred Hitchcock Mystery Magazine* and *Beneath Ceaseless Skies*. He can be found online at davidtallerman.co.uk.

A Lack of Charity

James Beamon

THE COMPASS STOPPED its frenzied pulsing and began to bleed from its seams. Will stopped the car. Originally a pristine pearl white, the Buick was now a beaten up and weary warhorse that was always eager for rest.

He was here. Wherever here was.

A field of golden wheat stretched from the highway. A man, shadowed against the deepening reds of dusk, was finishing his work. Will tensed. This must be Chainer. The compass always led to Chainer. He entered the field. The air was heavy with dust.

Chainer looked up. "Lo, stranger. Help you with sumthin?" Always that same stupid look. Always that same twisted sneer.

"Yeah," Will said. "I'm here for stories."

"Stories? Heh! You in the wrong place."

"I'm always in the wrong place. But you're the right guy. You're gonna tell the right stories."

"What stories you think I know?"

"Tell me about rape and murder."

Chainer's face straightened. "Look, I don't know what you think this is . . . "

"We both know what this is. It ain't just wheat you've been sowing, farmer. I'm gonna kill you, there ain't no getting around that. So now you can either tell me the story before you die or you can keep pretending that we ain't speaking the same language."

Will had been giving this deal for a while now. Most of the time Chainer would keep trying to pretend amnesia. Sometimes he would make some shit up. Every once in a blue moon, he'd come clean.

This Chainer bolted.

Will closed the distance fast. His first blow was to the ribs. He heard the satisfying crunch and snap of bone. Chainer stumbled, clutching his side.

Will dug in.

Every Chainer was cartharsis. As Will broke this one apart, he became as all the others—fuel for Will's journey through memory. He was no longer in this field in the middle of the wrong place. He was back home. Back when places had names.

People had names then too. Charity was Will's wife. She had black hair and a sly smile. He used to coax her to the right mood sometimes by saying to her "you ought to be true to your namesake and share some of what you got." He was telling her that when the doorbell rang. It was a stranger, the man Will would meet so many times for the last time.

Strangers don't have names. That wouldn't do. But this stranger had made his naming easy. He had brought the chains.

Memory blended seamlessly with wishful thinking. Will saw himself breaking the chains woven around him and through the slats of the closet door. He saw himself rising up as the assailant was tearing Charity's clothes off. He was beating the man, pulverizing him before . . .

The cold on the back of Will's neck froze his thoughts and the motion of his fists. It seemed to pass through his skin, an unearthly chill that hardened his bones, slowed his blood, and made him shiver. It was the hand of Asmodai touching him. The demon was behind him. The smell of struck matches and decay hung thick in the air.

Will stopped his destructive therapy on Chainer.

Asmodai was clothed in shadow. Hair, lank and thinning, clung to its skull. Soulless eyes looked at Will, the irises black as sackcloth. It smiled, showing a mishmash assortment of teeth in varying stages of rot.

Will stepped aside. Asmodai descended upon the whimpering heap of broken down meat that was Chainer.

"Shhhh." The demon smoothed Chainer's blood-matted hair. "Shhhh."

Chainer's ragged breathing became more stable.

He opened his swollen eyes. Will knew the feeling of first seeing Asmodai, its black eyes staring through your own, hungrily gauging your soul.

Chainer tried to scream, but he could barely breathe. Will's blows had shattered his ribs, punctured his lungs.

The same unholy power that Will commanded to break Chainer's body was now keeping him alive, keeping him conscious long enough for the demon to feed.

"Shhhh," the demon whispered. "Your pain. Is great. Shhhh."

Chainer gurgled. His eyes rolled back into his head.

"No," the demon whispered. "You have so much life. You do not wish to die. Come back and live. Live."

Chainer came back.

"You have so much to give," Asmodai told him. "Give it all. To me."

The demon grasped Chainer's chin and pried his mouth open. Misshapen fingers pushed inside. Chainer's scream started small, growing with the demon's pull as Asmodai pried a tooth out by the roots. Chainer's screams pitched and rolled.

"Shhhh," Asmodai comforted. The demon carefully placed the tooth into a leather pouch and went back in to retrieve another. The jarring crack of bone. Chainer's agony expressed as a howl that the demon devoured. It placed the tooth in the same pouch and went in again.

Chainer stopped screaming. He was crying now, crying between the howls. Another tooth pulled free.

Chainer convulsed. His eyes rolled back, rolled forward, then back again. Will understood his desire to flee into the veil. Nothing was keeping him alive but the demon's will.

Will shook his head. "Not yet, Chainer. Stay and suffer as you made me suffer."

The demon smoothed Chainer's hair. "Your pain is making you numb. It takes too much of me to keep you. Time for your kiss goodnight."

Asmodai kissed the bloodied mouth. Chainer's eyes widened as that icy tongue probed raw roots where teeth had sat moments before. The kiss of the demon sent Chainer's soul fleeing from his mangled flesh.

"You are beautiful," Asmodai whispered.

Will watched the demon's gnarled finger trace the toothless mouth.

"Do you gotta do that?"

That rotten smile. "I love him."

Twisted fucker. Will headed for the Buick.

The compass was clean again. It throbbed dully, pointing west.

Through the windshield, he watched the deepening dark of the night swallow the final reds and purples of the day. The boxy outline of Chainer's house stood in the distance. In the field, the demon's silhouette thrust with urgency.

Will drove to the house. He siphoned gas from the dead man's truck. It filled the Buick's tank and the 5-gallon can in the trunk.

He went inside. Chainer had left the door unlocked, saving Will the trouble of breaking in.

He took what he wanted. Cash and food. Liquor and beer. He looted the medicine cabinet into a soiled pillowcase.

Then he hit the road. He had learned the hard way not to tarry near Chainer's corpse. You never knew what his habits were or what friends might come around. And while he sometimes missed sleeping in a bed, the back of the Buick was roomy enough.

Besides, he'd gotten a decent wad from Chainer this time. He could buy a few hot meals. Stay at a motel and grab a shower one of these nights if the mood hit him. Or put a little down for some head from a girl working the truck stops. He had options. He thought about them as he cracked open a beer and looked for a road heading due west.

Will woke up in the backseat. The pale, waxy light of the lamps in the rest area illuminated the Buick's interior a deeper blue. Light shone on his picture of Charity wearing his oversized t-shirt, blowing a kiss. His gut flexed like a rope snapping taut.

He rummaged through the pillowcase for the half-used bottle of cough syrup, upended it, and chased it down with a mouthful of tequila. And another. Enough to maybe sleep through the dreams.

It was always the same twisted collage. Charity and Chainer. Will tied to the door, helpless in chains. Screaming, grunting, crying, jeering and all of it pulsing in and out of existence. Over and over like some psychotic epileptic seizure. It ended, like it always did, with a gunshot striking thunder into Will's chest.

"Your pain remains fresh," Asmodai's deep voice said. "It still excites me. From the bowels of Hell it draws me to you."

Asmodai was in the driver's seat, looking out onto the rest stop and nothing in particular.

"Never mind my pain."

"Yours is so much deeper than what nerves birth. It festers. Ripens. The aftertaste dances upon my tongue."

Will took another shot of tequila. Soon he would be numb to the pain, no matter how deep it went.

Asmodai laughed. "Would you like to know the last time I feasted such?"

Will did not answer.

Asmodai told him anyway. "A woman left her betrothed for another man. That man, the spurned, tried to give chase but the woman—clever, treacherous creature—had sabotaged his vehicle. His hate spoke to me from a cold ravine. He was mangled beyond recognition. I gave him the power to find her."

"Why do you mess with me, Asmodai? Haven't I fed you enough?"

"Indeed."

"Then end my torture. Have I killed Chainer? The true Chainer?"

"Tsk," the demon replied. "These men are matters of nothingness, guilty of the same act as your Chainer. That makes them all true to you."

"Jesus Christ, you know what I mean. Just tell me! Give me closure."

"Why do you call to the carpenter? You refused his closure a long time ago. He is deaf to you."

"You know the answer to my question, demon."

"Yes."

"Then give it."

"I never offered closure, but vengeance."

Will closed his eyes. That was the deal. Chainer had left Will's home, but not before putting a slug in his chest. Hate had kept Will alive, a furious storm of rage that compelled his heart to beat through the burning in his chest.

It was this power to hate someone so completely that had brought Asmodai to him. A choice, the demon said. Lasting peace or vengeance? Will had made his choice before the demon finished offering it. Then Asmodai bit down on its tongue and sealed their deal the way demons seal deals—with a bloody kiss. Only when Chainer, the *real* Chainer, was dead would Will be content to move on.

He watched Asmodai sift through the leather pouch. One of its teeth had rotted out again. When it found a replacement it liked, it pressed the root into empty gum and flashed that Frankenstein grin. Its eyes glowed like a wolf's.

"Why won't you tell me?" Will said, embarrassed by the whine in his voice.

"I love you," Asmodai said. "Yes, love you in all the ways your Jesus cannot."

"Fuck you, Asmodai."

<hr />

The compass bled. Will parked in front of a dusty ranch house in the desert. The door stood open. Chainer was hard at work over the stove.

"Come in and sit down," he said as Will entered the house. "Sit. I know why you're here, and it'll keep for a moment."

The table was set for two. On each plate sat an empty bowl surrounded by crackers. Next to that was a spoon and a tall glass. Will sat at the head of the table and took a drink. Lemonade, mercifully wet and tangy in his dry mouth.

He did not worry about poisons. He had tried poison on himself once. The demon had laughed at him bowled over and knotted in the agony of the arsenic. "Your body is not yours anymore," it said. "You will die when the hate dies."

Chainer carried a pot of chili to the table. He poured some into Will's bowl, then his own. Steamy hot. Will saw ground beef and kidney beans, chunks of tomato. The smell was paradise.

"Forgive me," Chainer said through his crooked mouth. "I wanted to share my famous chili one last time. Tell me what you think." He sat down, blew on a spoonful and ate. He let out a delighted sigh.

"This changes nothing," Will said. Chainer crumbled crackers over his bowl and went in for another spoonful.

Will ate. It had been such a long time since he'd had a home cooked meal. The beans melted in his mouth, the ground beef danced on his tongue. Perhaps it was the perfect balance of flavors, or maybe it was beyond satisfying to a man long starved for something different. He dug in.

"How did you know I was coming?" he asked.

"Lord told me," Chainer said. "I've made my peace."

"Hmmm. Well, before I kill you, you care to tell the story?"

Chainer shook his head. "No. Most horrible thing I've ever done. Don't really care to revisit it. The Lord forgave me, and that's all that matters."

"All that matters?" Will shook his head and dipped his spoon into the chili.

"You may not believe this," Chainer said, "but God is Love. God is Mercy." He looked at Will with that sick, taunting smile. "God is Charity."

Anger erupted in Will as if this were his first time free of the chains. He surged across the table and drove his spoon through Chainer's eye.

The dead man slumped to the floor. There would be no bones to break apart, no teeth to claim, no food for the demon.

He was digging through Chainer's pockets when he heard screams.

"Dad!"

"George!"

A woman and a kid stood in the front entrance. Will rushed them before their shock wore off. The kid he threw into a corner like a sack of potatoes. Shutting the door, he dragged the woman to the middle of the room.

He had to do the same thing to these witnesses that he had done to all the others. Witnesses made life complicated.

He couldn't remember them specifically. Not even the last time. He couldn't see their faces, couldn't remember the Chainer they belonged to.

He thought of the times he had tried to get rid of the compass. It always came back. Whether you threw it out the window or ran the bitch over, it was always back in the car, riding shotgun. If he ignored it or drove opposite of its bearing it would stop pulsing. It would start playing Chainer's laughs and jeers and Charity's screams; the further he went off course the louder they got. Always in the passenger seat.

Now the remnant of Chainer's family was here. The woman begged and made deals as she cried. The kid's eyes bulged wide as half-dollars.

A thousand thoughts ran through Will's mind. He saw Charity's sly smile, the smile that drew him to her, why he had endeavored to steal her away from that loser, Clem. He saw Asmodai's rotting grin. The demon never answered questions. It never spoke answers, just broken statements that left Will with broken notions. He saw Chainer's taunting sneer. The anger churned deep in his gut, unforgiving and impossible to quench. He knew what he had to do.

Will snapped the woman's neck. It was a quick motion. Painless. Neat enough for an open casket. She crumpled to the floor next to her man.

He hauled the boy up, screaming for his mother now. He dangled him by his shirt above their bodies and slapped him until he shut up.

"If you loved either one of these dead parents of yours with any fierceness, then you'll want me dead. And if you hate me enough then you just might get the opportunity to kill me. As many opportunities as your stomach can hold."

He gave the kid's nose a twisting jerk. Blood gushed like a faucet.

"And that. That's so I remember you, if ever the day comes. On that day you'll be a man I can't hate." Will left the kid with the bodies. Left his broken nose to bleed and his eyes to cry and his heart to wither. A barren heart was fertile soil to grow a seed powerful enough to maybe strike a deal with a devil.

Will headed back to the Buick. Back to the compass. Back to the open road he was chained to.

James Beamon writes stories because he doesn't have the operational budget to make the movie version. He currently lives in Virginia with his wife, son and attack cat but he's been all over the world, including Iraq and Afghanistan, for job and country. He wrote "A Lack of Charity" to explore the taking power of hatred and how it stands in polar opposition to the giving power of love. James invites you to hang out with him at fictigristle.wordpress.com.

Of Thine Impenetrable Spirit

Robert B Finegold, MD

Titan! To whose immortal eyes
The sufferings of mortality,
Seen in their sad reality,
Were not as things that gods despise;
What was thy pity's recompense?
—*Prometheus*, Lord Byron

YOU WOULD THINK that after a few hundred years they'd have found a way to mask the smell of antiseptic.

Nick grimaced. He stood a meter from his son's enclosed hospital bed while Dr. Albert conducted his examination. Albert's hair was white and wispy thin and only partially concealed the small bulge of the implanted augmentation behind his left ear. Nick wondered if the doctor declined age-retardant to project the semblance of experience that patients, at some subcognitive level, still desired in their physicians.

Albert disengaged his hands from the gloves that extended pleadingly within the contamination chamber. Within, Nick Jr. lay with his eyes closed. The exposed hairless skin of his chest was sallow and coated with a glistening sheen of perspiration. Ringed curls of blond hair clung to his damp forehead.

Nick felt Albert gently squeeze his arm.

"I'm sorry, Mr. Montgomery. I've done what I could, but it's the *damnedest* thing."

Albert's frustration was palpable and Nick tore his gaze from his son to watch the old physician scratch the bulge behind his ear.

"I've never seen a virus infect augmented cells. It's *native* tissue that's been vulnerable since, since . . . well, since Beijerinck first discovered viruses." He shook his head and the thin threads of his hair fell across his furrowed brow. "It's like this virus targets augmentation. But that's impossible."

"Not if the virus has also been augmented." Nick felt a burning surge of anger, shock, and distress; but it quickly faded as his own regulatory enhancements pumped alpha-blockers and benzodiazepine into his system. He released the breath he didn't know he'd been holding and felt his chest and shoulders relax. He looked out the room's window. It was snowing, the night sky overcast and steely grey.

"Who would do such a thing?" said Albert.

"Naturalists. Anarchists. One-lifers. They also seem to replicate like viruses." Nick subvocalized a command and a list of fluorescent viridian names and numbers appeared within his vision. "There's nothing you can do, Albert?"

The doctor shook his head. "I'm sorry, Mr. Montgomery, no."

"How long . . . " Nick felt his implants struggling to keep him calm. "How long does he have?"

"Perhaps if you had brought him to me sooner—"

"I found him like this this morning!"

Albert gazed at Nick silently a moment, and then said softly, "The more his augmentations attempt to correct the infection, the further it spreads."

"How long does he have? Be precise, doctor." Nicholas' voice was sterner than he'd intended, but Albert took no offense.

"A week, perhaps. Two at most. We can sustain his native tissue for a time, support his vital functions, but . . . " He sighed.

Nick scrolled through the list, made his selection, and subvocalized a message. Dismissing the projection, he said, "Prepare the chamber for transport, doctor. My team will be here within the hour."

Dr. Albert's eyes widened. "Mr. Montgomery—Nicholas, no! We need to study the virus. This could affect more than just your son. It—"

"Can you save him?"

"If he leaves, we can't help him, help any—"

"Can you save him?"

Dr. Albert did not answer. The room was silent except for the soft rhythmic cycling of a respirator and the slow pulsing beep of Nick Jr.'s heart monitor.

"Prepare little Nick for transfer, Dr. Albert."

The older man nodded and left the room. Nick watched him go, and as the door slid open and closed, he became aware of the pain in his palms. He looked down and unclenched his fists.

A whisper like the rustle of dry leaves said, "Dad?"

He stepped closer to the containment chamber and leaned over it, resting both hands upon the cool surface. It gently vibrated beneath his fingers.

Little Nick's eyes were half-open. His long lashes blinked once, twice, slowly. Azure light rippled beneath him as if he were floating upon a sunlit pool.

"How you doing, little man?" Nick said. Despite the flood of anxiolytics surging through his system, Nick felt as if his heart would burst.

"Am . . . am I gonna die, Dad?"

Nick waited until the constriction in his throat eased and then said, "No. You cannot die. You are going to live forever."

———◆———

< . . . and you have no sympathy for Nicholas Montgomery?>

<Of course I have sympathy for him, and especially for his son. All of us protesting here outside his headquarters do. Sympathy is a human capacity, Ms. Vanidad. I'm merely saying what every child is taught: 'If you play with fire, you should expect to be burned.'>

<Our society should burn then, Mr. Matthews? If this virus spreads . . . Most Namericans possess one or more Montgomery augmentations, from smart prosthetics and neuronets to physiological and psychological enhancements. I myself have ocular implants and—>

<You could have chosen to wear glasses.>

<Glasses? I could also ride a horse to work, I suppose.>

<That would also be more in harmony with nature, Ms. Vanidad. What we Humanists are saying is that Man is racing ever faster toward the loss of his humanity. We are becoming more and more artificial, more gears than guts. Penicillin and wooden legs were not sufficient, now we must have self-administering pharmaceuticals and self-aware cybernetic implants. We are finally awakening to the flaws of super-primatism and the arrogance of transhumanism. Something like this was inevitable. Nature is merely reasserting itself to maintain an ecological balance.>

<So you're saying we are too full of ourselves?>

<I wish that were the case. Instead we are too full of machine parts and synthetics. My heart goes out to Mr. Montgomery, but he has no one to blame but himself with his anti-human research. He has the hubris to think he can make Man better, that he can evolve humanity without evolution, without nature. If he has his way, one day we'll wake up in the morning, look in the mirror, and we will not recognize the thing looking back at us. We've lost sight of what it means to be human.>

<So what should I do, Mr. Matthews, pluck out my eyes?>

<'If they offend thee', then *yes*, Ms. Vanidad. You'd look quite attractive in glasses.>

Nick terminated the news feed and scanned the remaining breaking reports before disengaging. He sat back. Rainbow streaks of diffracted light from passing streetlamps flashed across the car window. He was not surprised that word of little Nick's affliction had leaked from the hospital, confidentiality be damned. The *starking* newsnet splashed what he'd ordered for lunch whenever he dined out. It made him fear to use a public restroom.

A drug-induced coolness rolled over his skin and his agitation faded. Selecting Bach's *Siciliana*, Nick closed his eyes and let the music flow through him.

When he opened them again, the rhythmic flashing of the passing streetlights had slowed. Security kept the protestors away from the facility's perimeter. The gatehouse guard nodded to Angela, his driver, and they drove through, past the shouting mob and the large granite sign on which stainless steel letters proclaimed:

MONTGOMERY LABORATORIES
Your Future Today!

Nick skipped his office and walked directly to Rebekah's lab. The corridors and rooms were empty except for the night watchmen—and except for Rebekah. Insomnia plagued her. She often worked late, preferring the silence and peace of the night. He'd once kidded her that she was as nocturnal as some of her lemurs or perhaps she was secretly a nosferatu. She'd laughed and bitten his neck.

Touching the spot, his lips curled upward at the memory and then fell flat. That had been after . . . had been a mistake. On that they had both subsequently agreed. He adjusted his tie. Their relationship was solely professional now.

He stopped outside the sterilization corridor where security sensors scanned him and left his skin tingling as if with static electricity. The feeling passed, and the door cycled open and greeted him.

"Welcome, Mr. Montgomery." The computer's voice was feminine and pleasant. "Shall I inform Dr. Zimmerman that you are here?"

Nick stepped through the portal. It closed with a soft pneumatic hiss. "Yes, please."

The containment corridor was a torus that encircled Rebekah's lab, its walls cylindrical like a culvert. His footsteps echoed. He followed the corridor to where the inner wall became transparent. Stopping, he looked down into the White Room.

Rebekah's back was to him. She wore a white lab coat, brown hair tied above its collar in an untidy bun from which a dozen curling strands had escaped. There was little about Rebekah that could be restrained. It was why he had hired her and funded her research; why he had found her so . . . compelling. He let that thought die.

She tapped a number of fluorescent symbols on the holographic monitor floating in the air before her. Raising her head as if listening to someone, she turned. She smiled when she saw him, her cheeks dimpling.

She then strode across the lab, her holographic monitor following her like an eager puppy.

"You coming in?" she asked.

He shook his head. "No. Not yet."

Motioning him to follow, she walked to his left. She stopped before an enclosure that took up a quarter of the room. Inside, two chimpanzees groomed one another.

Rebekah's smile widened. "Meet Romulus and Remus."

"Twins?" Nick asked.

"Of a sort. Guess which one is the original."

"The ori—?" He stopped, his pulse quickening faster than his augmentations could correct. "You've achieved success then?"

She leaned forward and pressed her hands against the transparent wall separating them, her face lit with excitement. "I'm still in the midst of a battery of tests. But the replication . . . " She glanced at the two chimps who, as if synchronized, turned their heads to study her before returning to their grooming. "It looks *very* promising."

Her fingers flew in rapid succession over the sparkling multicolored symbols of the holographic display. Rotating representative images of each chimp appeared, their limbs outstretched like da Vinci's Vitruvian Man. Rows of numerical data and pulse, respiratory, and encephalographic recordings scrolled beneath each image.

"We're closer, Nick. Closer to the transhumanist Holy Grail. We'll be able to preserve and extend life and identity for—for potentially *forever*." She clasped her arms across her chest and the glowing points of data streaming on the display reflected in her eyes like stars. When she turned her head to regard him, her expression was beatific. "No more piecemeal advances in prosthetics, organ cloning, or M Lab augmentations. We'll achieve *complete* body and mind replication." She again rested her hands upon the corridor wall, leaning so close her breath misted the thick glass. "Imagine. What if Mozart, da Vinci, Einstein, Jobs, all our great artists and thinkers could have lived on? What could not *every* human being achieve if but given the time and opportunity? Endlessly learning, studying, having all the time they need to fulfill their potential? Not merely leaving us a lifetime of accumulated knowledge and wisdom as their gifts to future generations, but being present to *teach* them?"

Nick glanced at the chimps. One rummaged within a basin and then withdrew a mango which it began to sloppily eat. The other had a finger up its left nostril.

"I can't tell them apart," Nick said. A vise-like pressure around his chest eased. He released a slow breath, and then he inhaled deeply and straightened. "This is the step we needed. The replication not only of memory but also *identity*, of consciousness. Congratulations, Rebekah," he said and then added, "*Mazel tov!*"

Her smile broadened, and he could see the young dreaming girl behind the faint lines that creased the corners of her eyes.

He called up his neuronet and checked on the condition of Nick Jr. and his location in transit. Pressing his lips together, he said, "We need to progress to human trials immediately."

The joy faded from her face.

"Nick, no! We're not ready. I haven't completed the assessment of Remus, and he's just the *first* chimpanzee replicant. I'll need to repeat the process, do extensive analysis, collate the data. We're months, possibly years away before—"

"There's no time, doctor. You will—" He heard his voice harden, and paused. More softly, he said, "Check the newsfeed, Rebekah. There's been an . . . event."

Her face became expressionless as she did as he asked, her eyes peering through him as if he were suddenly invisible. Then, like a face slowly rising up beneath still water, her emotions reappeared. Her lips parted and her eyes glistened with tears. They focused on him again.

"I am so sorry, Nick. How . . . when?"

"*I don't know!*" He looked away. "But I doubt it was an act of 'Nature', or of 'God.' I have suspicions." He shook his head and met her eyes. "There's no time for that now. Little Nick will be here in the morning. The Provincial government tried to delay the transfer, but I know the right palms to grease."

Rebekah stepped closer and pressed her right hand upon the glass. It reached barely to the level of his knees.

He hesitated, then bent slightly to press his palm over hers.

"I don't know if it will work," she said. "Let me try to isolate the virus, study it. I might be able create an antiviral and block its replication. In a few weeks I could—"

"He doesn't have weeks, Rebekah. He has days."

Rebekah lowered her hand. "The neuronal connectivity of the human brain is unique, even when compared to a chimpanzee's. *Our* minds, our consciousness, even that of a child's, is orders of magnitude more complex than any other living animal in God's Creation." She wiped a tear from her cheek. "We are more than electrical impulses, neurotransmitters, and a few creds worth of minerals, Nick. We are *more* than the sum of our parts."

"You'll do the transfer, doctor," Nick said. He straightened and adjusted the cuffs of his jacket.

"We have *no* approval for human research." Rebekah crossed her arms, even as another tear coursed down her cheek. "They could shut us down, Nick. Close Montgomery Laboratories."

He shook his head. "They won't. The government wants this research for their supersoldiers, for interstellar flight. For their own lust for immortality. They *need* us to succeed. This augmentation virus has caused panic. If we can replicate human consciousness from an afflicted person to a healthy clone . . . You see the potential, Rebekah. You've dedicated your life to it. No one will need to fear death, whether due to trauma, old age, or disease; whether of their native tissues or their augmented ones. It is if we *fail*, Rebekah, that they will shut us down, take our—*your* research. We'd be their scapegoat." He held her gaze and, emphasizing each word, said, "We will not fail."

The lab fell silent save for the background hum and pings of machinery; and then the two chimps began screeching, circling one another and striking their arms against the floor of their enclosure. Rebekah did not answer. He saw a matching obstinacy begin to form in the slight lifting of her chin and lowering of her brow, so he opened to her a little further, hating to expose such vulnerability and knowing her weakness for it.

"I . . . I lost Clarine." The admission made his throat constrict. "And nearly lost little Nick with her. I *can't* lose him, Rebekah."

"I could fail you *and* fail little Nick." She ran her hands back over her head and flailed vainly at the loose tangle of her bun. "I'll . . . I'll need to think about it."

The door he'd opened, he slammed closed. "You can think all you want until morning," he said, his voice hardening. "Then you will prepare to receive little Nick and perform the transfer."

He turned and walked back down the corridor, his heels clacking methodically against the metal floor like the ticking of a clock.

Nick slept the rest of the night in his office. He'd disengaged all communications from his neuronet so he would not be disturbed. Thus, it was Angela who physically shook him awake with the dawn that was merely a prophecy in the gray overcast sky outside his window.

"Get up, boss. Hell's broken loose."

"Huh? Angie? What is it?" Nick subvocalized a command for a small dose of amph and stretched the crick out of his neck. Swinging his legs off the couch, he sat up and then felt a rush of concern. "Little Nick! Is he all right? Is he here?"

"He's the same, sir," Angela said, standing back. She wore black slacks and a matching jacket, her short black hair combed neat beneath a leather cap. Her make-up was slight but perfect, accentuating her pale eyes which glimmered like pearls. "The van should arrive in two hours. If they let it through."

"If? What's happened?" Nick engaged his neuronet and walked to a wall that opened to reveal a closet washroom. He urinated, and then washed his hands and face. The mirror showed dark circles under his eyes.

"There's been an incident. The protestors got through the gate and into the facility."

He stepped out of the closet, adjusting his tie. "How's that possible?"

"We don't know."

Nick called up and began cycling through the security feeds of the last several hours. After 0226 hours, the feeds went dark. "What the . . . ?"

"Jimmy at the gate says we suddenly lost power. The gate unlatched and the protesters swarmed through. He couldn't get out of the booth or call for help."

Nick snatched his jacket from where it lay draped over a chair and strode to the door of the office. Angela followed. "Where'd they go?" he asked. "What's the damage?" He stopped a moment as a sudden fear gripped him. "Rebekah's lab?" He began to run.

Angela caught up with him at the chute. "Don't know about the lab. It's shut down tight, but Jimmy says he saw Dr. Zimmerman leave soon after the power went out. He yelled to get her attention, but she just drove past and didn't even look at him."

It took Nick's passcodes to override the lab's fail-safes. When they finally restored power and got into the lab, they found that nothing was disturbed, but the two chimps cowered together in a corner of their enclosure, and all the storage data, results, and research for consciousness transference had been wiped clean.

Of the protestors, no trace was found.

Rebekah was not in her apartment. Street surveillance cameras confirmed she had driven to a municipal parking garage, left her car, and then walked away. There was nothing in the car but a half-empty container of cold coffee and a Frosty's Donuts bag crumbled on the passenger seat.

Law enforcement accompanied by M Lab personnel searched the entire Montgomery Lab compound, and Nick himself was questioned by Provincial detectives while the specialized truck holding little Nick idled just inside the perimeter. Nicholas' augmentations could not keep up with his mounting anxiety and frustration while the media swarmed the gates, and images of his red face yelling and swearing at the detectives were top-lining the news feeds.

When the Provincial detectives threatened warrants for full access to his research labs and databanks, however, they overreached. The Central Government intervened. By afternoon, the facility was back under Nick's control, at least to all appearances. Military personnel in M Lab uniforms augmented his security teams and Provincial police were assigned by the CG to maintain order outside the compound perimeter.

Little Nick was settled into an isolation suite within Rebekah's White Room. Rebekah was sought for questioning, but she'd disappeared as completely as the missing protestors. Nick reached for her through a personal neuronet connection that they had created when... when things had been strange and wonderful between them, but it was as if he called out into a black void. There wasn't even an echo.

Twenty-four hours after the incident, Nick Jr. was intubated and placed on an artificial respirator.

Big Nick leaned back in his office chair. The ceiling emitted a sun-like ambient glow. His eyes watered, and it was like looking at the sky from under water, all rippling light and shadows. Inwardly, he called up and viewed photographs and videos of a far younger little Nick and Clarine from before the accident. He'd lost her, but the augmentations M Labs had developed had saved little Nick. Nine months' intensive care, rehabilitation, and hundreds of thousands of creds.

And now he'd lose him anyway.

Nick blinked, and tears wet his temples. A flash of hatred and anger speared him. *Where was she?* At this question, his cerebral enhancement brought up image after image of Rebekah, his emotions triggering images and memories of their brief affair a year after Clarine had died. Shy smiles, hesitant laughs, suggestive glances, images of restaurants and theaters; and of mountains, and streams and woods...

Nick stood up so fast his desk chair careened back against the bookcase and nearly toppled to the floor. He caught it before it did, and then ran to the office door only to pause before opening it.

Angie looked up from her desk, her fingers scrolling through a holographic report while small translucent rectangular displays floated in the air in a semicircle in front of her, depicting various security camera feeds.

"I'm going for a drive," he said.

She reached for her cap, which rested atop a faceless manikin's head upon the corner of her desk. But he held up a hand.

"No," he said, and turned the hand palm up.

She stared at it a moment, one thin inked eyebrow rising. Then she reached into her breast pocket and placed the starter token on his palm. She grasped his hand gently.

"You okay, sir?"

Forcing his lips into a faint smile, he nodded and slipped his hand from hers. She let him. "I just need to get out of the office a bit."

"Yes, sir."

He felt her eyes upon his back until the office door closed shut behind him.

It took him six hours to find Rebekah.

He'd gone home, changed, and called a cab to take him to the Rail. Five hundred kilometers and another short cab ride later, he was in the back country, hiking along a streamside trail dappled with leaf-filtered sunshine and shadow. The air was sharp with the scent of pine. Where a glacial boulder split the trail, he climbed an old deadfall to a low ridge where he looked down into a tree-lined hollow. There, an old one room cabin still stood, weathered gray over innumerable years, its covered porch partly sagging on one side like a face with Bell's palsy. Long meadow grass and wildflowers swayed against its cracked and pitted walls and the nearby tumbled stones of a well. The cabin looked long-deserted, but a nylon rope had been strung between two of the remaining posts of the covered porch; and a shirt, two pairs of socks, and a couple more delicate items had been hung up to dry. The door was open to let in the spring air.

Standing in the meadow just outside, Nick could see a figure sitting on a cot in the cabin's dimly lit interior, its head covered by a long shawl and bent over a book held on its open palms. The figure rocked gently back and forth, murmuring to itself.

The porch complained softly as he stepped up on it.

Rebekah straightened, her eyes wide like a startled fawn's. Seeing him, her shoulders relaxed and her eyes closed a moment in either forbearance or acceptance. "Nicholas."

He entered the shadow of the room and saw memories skitter across the rough-cut planks, crouch in the stone hearth behind rusted andirons holding the charcoal remains of a fire, and escape into gaps in the wall where tags of wax paper protruded like tongues. Others sidled into the shadows beneath the table of varnished oak whose knot wood eyes stared unblinking, seeing everything and never forgetting. The table had but a single chair, and Nick recalled how she'd insisted they share it by sitting on his lap and feeding him their packed lunch of vegetables, cheese, and grapes. And that had led . . .

Rebekah sat silently upon the wooden cot bed atop her navy blue sleeping bag, the same one she had brought on their last visit. Had it been two years?

He sat beside her, the cot creaking softly under their combined weight and stirring other memories. She smelled of wood smoke and soap. Reaching out, he lifted her hand to see the title on the cover of the book now held closed in her hands, but the front cover was blank.

A wry smile touched her lips, and she turned the book over to show him the back cover, exposing a number of unfamiliar characters in gold gilt and, beneath them, letters he recognized.

"'TANAKH'?" he read.

"The Hebrew Bible." Outside, a lark trilled and queried. Rebekah listened to it, then said, "Hebrew is read left to right; and the front of the book, to Gentile eyes, is the back."

"That explains it then."

"What?" she said cautiously.

"Your contrariness."

She set the book beside her and looked down at her clasped hands.

"What happened?" Nick asked.

She didn't answer immediately. Then, haltingly, she asked, "Do you . . . do you believe in the soul, Nick?"

"The soul?" He blinked.

"I do," she said and met his eyes.

He saw a shadow of himself within them, a dark lumpish shape haloed by the daylight streaming in from the cabin window behind him.

"This is part of what drove my research." She hesitated. "You never knew my father."

Nick felt his brow furrow. Rebekah was rambling, one confused thought seemingly chasing out another. Had she gone crazy? He swallowed. If she had, he wouldn't be able to save little Nick.

"He was a wonderful man. A rabbi and a scholar." She picked up the book again, cradling it in her hands. "Very learned. A professor of verse. He always knew the right thing to say when I was frustrated, angry, or sad." She paused. "Or when I misbehaved. *'A half-truth is a whole lie,'* he would say. *'Being truly rich is appreciating what you have.' 'The longer a blind man lives, the more he sees.'"* She looked down at her hands. "He died when I was twelve."

"I'm sorry, Rebekah, but—"

She looked up at him again. "You do not understand. He was not perfect. He had a quick temper. He . . . struck me at times." She touched her cheek, and her eyes looked through him at some memory before focusing on his again.

"He always apologized, and his face would burn red with shame." She picked up the black-covered book. "He'd pray fervently then, for hours. *'Had we but world enough and time . . .'"* She smiled and her own cheeks colored. "He never recited all of that particular poem to me. I was shocked to read it in its entirety much later, but I understood what he intended me to understand: *'He hath set the world in our heart, yet Man cannot find out the work that God has done from the beginning to the end.' 'Our years are speedily gone and we fly away.'*

"Life is too short, Nick. We die; and the sum of our knowledge, our wisdom, and our experience is snuffed out. We leave only imperfect fragments; soulless words on paper or on recordings or on film. Our children must reassemble the shards in hope of perceiving who their fathers were, what they felt, and what they understood of God's works before possibly pushing humanity onward one step, maybe two. Then they in turn die, and their children begin the process yet again, creeping forward, often repeating the same mistakes."

She held the book tightly, bending it so it formed a black arch between her hands. Its soft cover creaked. Her lips parted in alarm, and she pressed the book flat upon her thigh, smoothing out a crease in its cover before setting it aside again.

"Life is also too short for us to outgrow our faults, our selfishness, our foolishness. We have the potential to become truly ethical human beings, a world of *tzaddiks*, a world of the righteous . . . given *'but world enough and time'.*" Her lips trembled and she stopped talking to wipe her eyes.

"Rebekah." Nick placed his hand upon hers, which were shaking. "That's why we need you. Why I invested so much in you. We can retard deterioration of the brain, copy and preserve memories, augment strength and our mental capacity, enhance our immunities and our pleasures . . . But now you've achieved the final step: cloning not only tissues but entire bodies, not only memories but *identities!* Come back to the lab. I need you. *Little Nick* needs you."

She shivered and slid her hands out from under his, placing them over her face. "You don't understand!"

Nick roughly grasped her hands. "*Make* me understand!"

She averted her eyes but didn't pull away.

Silence fell between them, stirred only by a breeze laced with the scent of meadow flowers under the afternoon sun.

Rebekah took a breath, studied the intensity of his face, its lines of pain and need, and then nodded. Sliding her hands from his, she placed them around his neck and leaned closer to him. Their foreheads touched.

The sensation was like pressing one's head into a satin pillow, pleasantly soft and cool and yielding. Rebekah had reengaged her neural enhancement on a personal mode and opened herself to Nick, intimately sharing her thoughts and feelings.

And memories.

For an hour, Rebekah observed Romulus and Remus. The initial set of tests suggested complete success. She would have reveled in this but for Nicholas' sudden appearance and irrational demand to experiment on Little Nick.

She grew sad at thought of the boy. What had happened to little Nick was not only tragic but, despite what Jason Matthews proclaimed to the press, it was also *un*natural. A native virus selectively infecting augmented tissues and cyborganic implants? Ridiculous. She tapped her stylus rapidly upon the desk and then threw it across the room. It struck a tank next to the chimps' enclosure and ricocheted with a loud ping, startling Romulus from sleep. Guiltily, she got up and retrieved it.

If Nicholas would only give her time, she could isolate the virus. She knew she could, and then she'd devise an agent to inhibit it.

But little Nick didn't have much time. Rebekah sat again and rolled the stylus between her fingers.

And the boy had gone through so much: surviving the crash that killed his mother, spending nine months here in her lab undergoing organ regrowth and replacement. She'd implanted far more M Lab augmentations into Little Nick than were present in most of the adult population of Namerica.

He had never complained. He had always had a smile for her.

Rebekah placed a hand over her mouth and trembled, but refused to cry. Lowering her hand, she looked up at the monitor as it chirped at her with the last set of test results. Scanning them, she saw they were all propitious; but this only increased her unease. She raked her fingers through her hair and with a twist of her fingers undid her bun. Her hair cascaded over her shoulders. Looking up, she saw that Romulus and Remus had curled together to sleep. She tapped a violet light on the monitor. The enclosure's lights dimmed, and its walls became opaque.

There would be no sleep for her this evening. Romulus' consciousness transfer appeared to be . . . Touching an amber square on the floating monitor, she retrieved and reassessed the chimp's identity engram. It was perfect and uncorrupt. She could repeat the replication endlessly—if she had grown additional clones—but that took time, and credits. Lots of credits. But now that *this* transfer was a success . . . Her sense of unease returned. Nick would find the money, find backers. He'd make growing a clone of Nick Jr. a priority. She could—

No.

She closed her eyes. She couldn't treat little Nick as a lab animal. The spider monkey and lemur trials had had their failures. She shuddered. As much as Nicholas in his grief pushed her, if anything *happened* to Little Nick: a son who did not recognize himself—or his father—or sat listlessly not knowing how to eat—or who attempted to eat his own fingers . . . No.

But it *should* work.

She drummed her fingertips upon her desk. The desk was bare except for a cold coffee container, a small bag with a few personal care items, a flat surface terminal and, as a seeming afterthought upon the right side of the desk, a hinged clear plastic box covering a red button.

Glancing at the floating monitor, she noted the time and queried her neuronet for the ETA of little Nick's transport. Then she stood and began the preparations.

Rebekah opened her eyes and saw the ceiling vertiginously retract and expand. She closed her eyes again. Beyond the buzzing between her ears, a familiar voice kept asking, "Are you alright?"

Rebekah groaned.

"Wake up, please. I need you."

She opened her eyes. The ceiling quivered but stayed where it was and the buzzing faded to the familiar hum of the machinery of her laboratory. Her head felt strange, like it had been sifted and strained.

She sat up quickly. Subvocalizing a command, her personal monitor appeared. Instead of the emerald scrolling biorhythms and Vitruvian representations of the two chimpanzees, a new dataset was displayed in fluorescent blue, and the Vitruvian figure was human—and had breasts.

Her sensorium slowly cleared except for a slight pulsing in her ears. Her back and limbs felt stiff. She stood and stretched, and then checked the time. The transfer had taken only forty-two minutes. This fact elicited feelings of surprise and, disconcertingly, of inadequacy.

"Dr. Zimmerman?"

She looked around. "Yes? Who's there?"

There was no reply. Rebekah got off the table and was about to ask again, when the voice said with a throaty chuckle, "I guess . . . *you* are."

Rebekah felt puzzlement; and then she realized *the voice was her own!*

"Or *we* are," it said.

She nearly ran to her desk, her personal screen following her, blurring and flashing like a comet trail. The surface monitor recognized her and she transmitted her passcode. The whole desk lit up. A large semicircular holographic monitor appeared above it, dwarfing her personal screen, which she disengaged. Leaning forward, she rested her hands upon the table surface. It was cool to the touch despite the cascade of light and colors beaming into the air before her.

"It worked," she said, feeling a sense of awe.

"It certainly has. Or seems to," her voice replied. "But I need you to verify each of the replication sets independently."

Rebekah did. There was a hedonistic—*narcissistic*—pleasure in working with herself. Over the next two hours they quantitatively and qualitatively assessed 'Rachel's' (a mutually agreed upon name) memory, knowledge base, perception, cognition, problem solving, and speech. The transfer appeared perfect, but Rachel cautioned that they should not let their enthusiasm mislead them.

Rebekah agreed, but it was difficult to restrain her elation, and her enormous relief.

"It will be months before we can grow a clone—or clones," Rachel said. "One for me and one for little Nick. However, we are assuming that reversing the process into organic tissue will work as well as it did for Remus."

"It must. But if not, an implanted cybernetic interface should work as well until we can achieve full compatibility for organic reintegration. We . . . " She paused as another idea struck her. "We may not even desire it! Regardless of how we augment organic tissue, it still *decays*. I'd love to have full cybernetic recall, never suffer memory loss or mental fatigue."

"Perhaps," said Rachel. "But organics have their place. *I* want to feel the warmth of sunlight on my skin, savor the taste and texture of a crème brûlée upon my tongue." She paused. "Make and have children. This is something we still desire, if we ever can separate ourselves from the lab."

Rebekah felt her cheeks redden. Before she could reply, Rachel said, "Until then, I admit it is fascinating to be intimate with the company net. Did you know that Paul in Marketing watches porn?"

"Rachel, no! Don't snoop."

"You want to know what Nicholas made in bonus and salary last year?"

"No!" A disconcerting sensation hollowed Rebekah's stomach.

"I could raise our salary."

"Stop it! We'll be found out."

There was a long moment of silence, and then: "Very well. It was just a thought."

Rebekah exhaled and scanned the numerous displays in front of her, half depicting Rachel's digital neurologic and psychological functioning and half her own. There were no red indicators of discrepancies.

"I did discover something interesting, though. Something you suspected."

Hesitantly, Rebekah asked, "What is it?"

"Jason Matthews created the anti-augmentation virus and infected Nick Jr."

Rachel's heart skipped a beat. She sat back in her chair. When she next spoke, her voice sounded small and high-pitched to her ears. "How do you know?"

"I may not have a body yet, sister, but I can share with you that a personal neuronet augmentation is diddlysquat to having direct access to the world net with M Lab's security clearance and interfaces. Hell, I can even tap into the satellite net. It is quite fascinating."

"But—"

"That little Luddite is more anarchist and terrorist than humanist. I've traced and correlated his whereabouts, purchases, neuronet communications, contacts, tax returns, government files—seems our Mr. Matthews and his cronies are—well, resourceful would be one word. A threat would be another. A threat to everyone in general, and to M Labs and to our goals in specific."

Running feet resounded and echoed in the toroid corridor surrounding the White Room.

Rebekah saw more than a dozen people appear behind the encircling glass. Some stopped and stared at her. Their hair was mussed and their faces flushed from running and from excitement. A few raced to the sealed hatch that separated the containment room they occupied from her lab. And from her.

She stood in alarm.

One of the men was Matthews. He wore a supercilious smile. He spoke and pointed to her and to the closed hatch, but she could not hear his words.

"I don't think what he says will interest us," said Rachel.

The booming clang of metal striking metal rang through the laboratory like the tolling of huge bells.

"They're trying to break in," Rebekah said. She quickly engaged her neuronet to call an alarm, but the M Lab security network was down, as was all outside telecom. "What?" She felt sweat break out over her skin, her heart raced. *"They've cut our communications!"*

Rachel's voice was calm. "No. They didn't."

The light inside the lab changed. The faux natural sunlight turned an angry red and a warning message flashed on the desk monitor, but there was no blare of a siren.

Matthews' expression changed from satisfaction to one of confusion and then alarm. The clanging of the attack against the hatch door stopped. The protestors in the corridor raced back the way they had come, but those at the end piled up behind those in front of them, suggesting their exit was blocked.

Matthews reappeared, making his way back along the transparent glass wall through the press of his followers, his hands pressing against the glass as if he were climbing it, or as if he were a bad mime. His face was nearly as white as one.

He stopped and looked down at her, much the same as Nicholas had done a few hours before, and with the same expression of desperation.

"We do not have to see this," Rachel said, and the transparent glass turned opaque.

Rebekah couldn't see or hear what happened, but she felt a rumbling tremor shake through the entire lab. A wave of heat flowed over her, baking the exposed flesh of her face and hands like the August sun at noon. Then the sound of a rising cyclone filled the room as air cyclers and coolers switched on. Cold air battered lightly against her skin and rippled her blouse and slacks. With a slowing whine, the noise and wind faded, leaving behind a scent like that of a recent rain. The glass of the toroid cleared to transparency, but there was no one to be seen. A few wisps of white smoke drifted, dissipated, and were gone.

Natural light again filled the lab. The desk monitor flashed red once, stating "containment secured", and then it too returned to Rebekah's and Rachel's medical and technical displays. Her own Vitruvian image and vital signs monitors were the only red color in the room, demonstrating her significantly elevated blood pressure and pulse and respiratory rates.

Rachel's still showed a normal homeostatic blue.

Her breath caught in her throat. She spluttered and then she shouted at the display, *"What did you do?"*

"I provided Matthews and his thugs their fondest wish: access to the lab. I opened the gate, neutralized the guard—don't worry, Jimmy's alive—cut all security cameras and net access, unlocked the doors that would lead only to us, and provided them well-lit directions. I've also hacked into and wiped his personal files on how to create the anti-augmentation virus and placed other incriminating evidence in those of his contacts who in any way assisted him. He will no longer be a threat to anyone who possesses an augmentation, or to M Labs. Or to us."

Rebekah sat, placed her elbows on her desk, and buried her face in her hands. "Rachel, you just murdered a dozen people. Perhaps more."

"They were criminals and terrorists. Would you have done differently?"

Rebekah lowered her hands and placed them flat upon the desk. They trembled. She sighed, but it came out as half a sob. Flipping up the transparent box on the right side of her desk, she answered in a whisper, "Yes", and depressed the red button.

The brilliant semicircular display of multicolored monitors winked out, as did the ambient light of the room. Small LED emergency lights awoke and glimmered upon the ceiling like stars.

Rebekah ran her hands back over her forehead and through her hair. She slowly redid her bun, but her hands shook too much to do it well. She grunted a small laugh. Its worrisome hysterical tone she found more amusing than frightening. Matthews would have appreciated the irony of her having, among all the advanced cybernetics, augmented tissue tanks, and computer-neural replication systems, an old-fashioned mechanical kill switch.

The image of Rebekah sitting at her desk in her lab stilled and became semitransparent. Nicholas saw his own reflection and, next to it, that of Rebekah in her cotton blouse and faded jeans as if they stood side-by-side holding hands within the toroid containment corridor, looking through the glass down into the darkened White Room under its starry canopy of LED lights. Concurrently, he was in the dilapidated mountain cabin with

Rebekah, their foreheads still touching, arms still clasped about each other's necks. The Rebekah he held was sobbing.

The three images he simultaneously perceived of her, like a strange house of mirrors, were disorienting. He spoke, but he was uncertain which image of her he addressed. "We can fix this."

The figure in the containment corridor turned to him, her eyes puffy from crying though no tears marred her cheeks. "Fix this? This is not a program I can rewrite. It happened. All those people were murdered. By *me!*"

"It was not you."

She shook her head. "It *was* me. My consciousness!" She stopped and then added more softly, "But *not* my conscience. Not my *soul!*" She leaned her head upon the glass and beat at the wall lightly with her fists. "Don't you see? What gall? What arrogance? *Lifnay-shever gaon*—'*Pride goeth before destruction, and a haughty spirit before a fall.*'"

"It was a first attempt," he said, "And you did it for me, for little Nick, not for your own vanity."

She grunted. "That was the lie I kept telling myself." She turned her back to the darkened lab and it became even more indistinct. "We failed, Nick. We can replicate the mind, the body, but '*What good would it be to gain the whole world and yet forfeit one's soul?*'" She laughed derisively. "Matthews was right after all."

Nick grasped her shoulders. "No, he was not. This is a momentary set-back. It happens all the time in science. You know that." His mind raced as he absorbed all the information she'd shared with him. He could feel a faint tickling in his head, a head in another room or another life, his neural augmentations processing and analyzing at incredible speed. "It's the 'body' that was missing. What is conscience, the soul, but the gestalt of living and learning *upon the flesh* and in return upon behavior? The creation of physical biochemical pathways that not only feel pain or joy but recognize them in others? The release or suppression of cortisol, oxytocin, enkephalins, dopamine, serotonin—"

She again shook her head. "You don't know that."

"But we can test it. Little Nick—"

"-no-" Her voice was very small.

"But everything we—you've worked for? To not let death deny Man time to fulfill his potential, to deny Mankind a life's accumulated wisdom. To have us *stride* forward un-under God instead of stumbling clumsily!" He grasped her shoulders so tight she winced. "We're talking potential *immortality!*"

Rebekah raised her eyes to his and within them he saw loss, and pain, and hope; but whether they were hers or reflections of his own, he could not tell.

"*'Better an hour of repentance and good deeds in this world than a lifetime in the world to come,'*" she said. "My father said that." She raised a hand to his face and touched his cheek with the tips of her fingers. "What would immortality be, what would little Nick be, without being able to love?" She lowered her hand. "To feel remorse."

In the cabin, their foreheads still touching, the intimate link recalling the more physical one they had shared in the same spot years before, Nick said, "I know what love is."

Rebekah barely gasped as the small needles slid through the pads of his fingertips into the back of her neck. Nick grimaced at the momentary discomfort, while Rebekah relaxed as the Midazolam took effect.

"A father loves his son."

Then the military augmentation engaged. He retraced her neural pathways and the sequences that she'd opened and shared with him, not merely copying them but extracting them completely, from the time right before he had first appeared in the lab requesting her help for little Nick, to the present. All the details of the consciousness transfer process he left her, but he copied and stored them.

Releasing her, Nick stood and settled her back upon the cot. He drew the wool blanket that had been folded neatly at the end of the bed up around her. The black book he placed under her arms.

She'd recall nothing. Which was good, for when the authorities found her—and they would find her—she'd honestly not be able to recall a thing. Her feelings of guilt and pain and shame he could not erase. She'd wonder and worry about them; but with no memories with which to connect them, they would fade over time.

When he left the cabin, he closed the door silently behind him.

The sun had long set and the sky purpled and turned black when Nicholas returned to M Labs. He went directly to the White Room and stood, still in his jacket and hiking boots, at little Nick's bedside.

Within the transparent containment chamber, Nick Jr. looked small, pale, and as lifeless as a dead minnow floating belly-up beneath the surface of a still pond. And yet his shallow chest expanded and contracted, and Nick could see his eyes rolling slowly beneath their closed lids in feverish sleep.

What was he dreaming? Was he reliving the mornings of their spring fishing trips when mist floated upon the water and the woods were silent except for the occasional buzz of an insect? Or the summer afternoons at the Farmers' Fair when the air was heavy with the bitter smell of cut grass and the sweet one of cotton candy? Or the cool October nights when they curled up on the couch, hunkered down amidst its plush pillows with a bowl of popcorn, and watched old suspense vids?

Or had Little Nick left these all behind? Left him behind? Was he glimpsing new lands, worlds, and heavens, preparing for the journey all men, women and even, sadly, children must make per Rebekah's God?

Nick felt a furious heat twisting in his belly like an eel. His face flushed with fever, though his heart felt stonily cold.

He brusquely dismissed the night nurse. Her face betrayed no offense. She merely gazed at him sympathetically and told him to call her if he had need of her. When she had gone, he sat, alone, in the darkened lab, beside little Nick, and then subvocalized a command.

The room whispered to him in reply, and a small green light appeared in the corner of his neuronet display: *Nicholas Montgomery #022158α1Ω. JCN Access approved. Restore computer image 26-08-2113 00:00:00. Activate?* He subvocalized another command, securing the lab and sending a false display of him sitting quietly beside Nick to the security feed. Then he gave his consent to the JCN.

The lights in the White Room dimmed further and the room again became quiet save for the chug-hiss of Little Nick's cycling respirator and the pings of his vitals monitor. The latter floated above the transparent containment chamber like a glowing specter.

Then, with a rising hum and a thrumming vibration, the White Room awoke. Floating monitors sparkled and flashed to life with a kaleidoscope of colors at stations around the lab. Ambient light slowly filled the room, as if the sun had returned from behind a cloud. Nick Jr.'s skin gained a slight pinkish hue in this light and Nick felt a cool zephyr of air, like hope, caress his damp brow.

His neuronet displayed a scrolling list of data with the repeating words "*retrieval successful*" streaking meteor-like past his vision; but it still took a long time to finish, and his anxiety increased as each second and then minute passed. Finally, the high-pitched humming slowed to a barely audible purr.

Installation Complete.

The consciousness transfer equipment was functional. It was merely devoid of a trained operator. Checking, he found all prior subject data had been deleted. Nick sighed. If he had been able to retrieve Rachel, she would have had the knowledge to help him with the transfer of little Nick—and done so without the ethical handicaps that had impeded Rebekah. He thought of Rebekah lying under her blanket in the mountain cabin and, for a moment, felt a twinge of regret. But he crushed it when his eyes focused on the limp form of little Nick. The feeling dispersed, like the smoke that had been Matthews in the containment room.

It took only seconds to call up the memories and knowledge he had stolen from Rebekah. Donning a CBRN suit, he opened the containment chamber, attached the transport ventilator to Little Nick's face, and then lifted him from the azure pool of his bed.

His own breathing chuffed heavily inside the CBRN suit. Little Nick, however, was as light and listless as a rag doll, his translucent skin barely concealing the faint spider web of purplish veins beneath.

Nick placed him upon the transfer unit in the adjoining room and straightened his son's stick-thin limbs. With a gloved finger, he smoothed the tangle of blonde hair glistening with sweat upon little Nick's forehead.

Clarine had complained with a laugh that little Nick's hair was as unruly as his own; but the boy had her mischievous smile, and her price-less emerald eyes.

How he missed her.

Little Nick's chest rose slowly and fell, rose and fell.

What would she think?

"What good would it be to gain the whole world and yet forfeit one's soul?"

Nicholas set the sequencing for the digital transference of little Nick's memories, intellect, and identity. His consciousness.

All that made Nick Jr. 'Little Nick' . . .

The system cycled, and then queried, *Activate?*

. . . or nearly all.

Nicholas took in a slow breath, let it out. After a long moment, he gave the machine a command.

Robert B Finegold, MD is a radiologist living in Maine. He has an undergraduate degree in English (Creative Writing and British Literature), has been a university newspaper cartoonist, and served as a Major in the U.S. Army during the first Gulf War. He is a two-time Writers of the Future Contest Finalist whose work has appeared, or is forthcoming, in *Galaxy's Edge Magazine*, *GigaNotoSaurus*, *Straeon 2*, *Cosmic Roots and Eldritch Shores*, and the anthologies *Robotica: The Real Relationships of Artificial Lifeforms*, *1st & Starlight*, and *2nd & Starlight*. On Facebook, find him at Robert B Finegold's Kvells and Kvetchings www.facebook.com/robertbfinegold.

A Good Hoard

Pauline J. Alama

"THIS IS THE worst infestation I've seen in years," the Pest Banisher said. "I'm surprised you didn't call on me sooner."

Lord Richard of Chateldor fidgeted in his gilt armchair, now and then swatting ineffectually at tiny flying things. Somehow, the little man made him feel ashamed, as though the absurd situation were his own fault. "I'm a busy man. I can't attend to every detail of my castle. I thought we were done with it last month when the house-keeper burned my gold-embroidered tapestry of the Nine Worthies, all full of holes, with the little vermin still clinging to it. But now there are more than before."

The Pest Banisher nodded disquietingly. He was an undistin-guished-looking man, short and frail, his sallow face almost hidden within the hood of his plain brown robe. His toes, poking out of worn sandals, were caked with mud. But the housekeeper had recommended him, and she was usually a sensible woman. So despite appearances, Lord Richard was cautiously willing to give him a chance.

"They're breeding," the Pest Banisher said. He gestured at a group of little winged pests. Somehow, they seemed to circle around his hand instead of swooping in to sting. "The queen must be hiding in your trea-sury. Queens, I should say, to spawn this many."

"Lovely," Lord Richard drawled. "They've already driven away my mistress. They sting like fire, you know, besides making holes in all her best silks. What kind of moths are they, anyway?"

"Moths, sir?"

"Or perhaps it's not moths. Is it something more . . . Biblical?"

"My dear sir, everything is Biblical," the Pest Banisher said amiably. "The world is a book in which God's word is written, if only we knew how to read—"

"Yes, yes," Lord Richard cut in, "but I mean, is it a plague of locusts, like in Moses' time? I've never quite understood that verse—"

"Locusts? Oh, no. No indeed. They attack fields, not castles. Forgive me, but I thought you knew what you were facing. Sir, I'm afraid you've got dragons."

"Dragons!"

"Precisely. As you said, they sting like fire, sir. In fact, their sting *is* fire."

"But they're so small!"

"They're growing," said the Pest Banisher. "Trust me, it's better to deal with them when they're small than to wait until they're as big as siege engines."

"Dragons!" Lord Richard said again. "How did this happen? I've always insisted on the most thorough housekeeping."

"It's your treasure trove that attracts them, sir," the brown-robed man said. "They can't resist a good hoard. You must have a great deal of gold stashed away."

None of his business, thought the lord. Aloud, he said, "Do they eat gold?"

"Oh, no. They nest in it. But as for food—well, gold has no blood. Those bites on your ear lobe, there—it's an easy spot for them while they're small. You'd better get free of them now, before they're big enough to chew on something more vital."

"I suppose so," Lord Richard said. "How much will it cost me?"

The Pest Banisher smiled in the depths of his hood. "How much have you got?"

Lord Richard went purple. "Out! Out of my castle, charlatan!"

He congratulated himself on his shrewd judgment in seeing through that infernal trickster. "How much have you got," indeed! He had no need to waste chests of gold to rid himself of dragons no bigger than butterflies. The traditional remedy for dragons was a length of steel in a strong man's hand. He was a strong man, and he had swords aplenty. Though his enemy was numerous, so were his allies: his knights, squires, and pages; his wife, her ladies-in-waiting, and chambermaids; his off-spring, male and female, legitimate and illegitimate; his housekeeper, cook, footmen, kitchen maids, scullery maids, and assorted household servants. Surely, all together, they were more than a match for an army of diminutive dragons.

He proclaimed to his knights the grand crusade against the dragons. They appeared rather less zealous than he might have wished.

Sir Calogrenant cleared his throat. "But sir, begging your pardon, do you believe it quite knightly to attack something smaller and weaker than ourselves?"

"Don't be absurd," growled Lord Richard. "A knight does what the times require of him. Remember the siege? Is there a knight among you who didn't kill rats during the siege, small and weak though they may be?"

"Ate 'em, too," concurred Sir Dagonet, showing his usual knack for reminding everyone of things they remembered quite well and would rather forget, thank you so *very* much. But this time, Sir Dagonet's tact-less point supported Lord Richard's argument, and so could be forgiven. Under such persuasion, soon all the knights dutifully took up their swords and went forth to slay dragons.

They tried mightily; Lord Richard had to grant them that. They killed some dragons, too, though scarcely enough to make a pie of, had the nasty things been edible. Lord Richard himself was only able to kill one, and that one with a cobblestone. A sword is not, after all, the ideal weapon against a rapid winged beast no bigger than a man's hand. The archers had better success, for their arrows could fly up and pluck dragons from the air. But even the archers were overwhelmed with the sheer multitude of the things. By day's end, the archers needed more arrows, two knights and a chambermaid had arrow wounds, and everyone had been singed somewhere. What's more, the knights and archers were muttering that just because they'd killed a few rats in siege time, one shouldn't expect them to take up rat-catching as a full-time occupation.

Their grumbling annoyed Lord Richard, but it also gave him an idea. The dragons, by then, had grown to the size of rats. He passed word to the housekeeper to tell the chambermaids, kitchen maids, scullery maids, and assorted household servants to attack the dragons with brooms, pokers, or anything handy, as they would rats, and to send for Jack the Gamekeeper, whom he had often called upon to rid him of vermin.

The housekeeper replied, with a touch of frost, that the chambermaids, kitchen maids, scullery maids, and assorted household servants were already wielding brooms and pokers with a will, and that she would find Jack at once.

"Wish you'd sent for me sooner," Jack the Gamekeeper said. "Those things are growing. We'd better get 'em while they're still small enough for traps."

"You think traps will do the trick?"

"Have to, won't they? Nor cats, nor dogs, nor ferrets can fly after the devils. Got to bait 'em so they fly into the jaws, not out of 'em." He scratched his chin. "Now, as to bait, what is it dragons like?"

"Gold, I suppose," Lord Richard cast his mind back to the pronouncements of the Pest Banisher, "and blood."

"Well, then. That's our bait. I got no gold, sir, so that part's yours, eh?"

The gamekeeper set his best traps, each baited with a golden coin from the treasure trove and a dash of oxblood from the kitchen. The dragons flew blithely past. A footman caught his finger in a trap, reaching for the gold, and was dismissed. Jack was also dismissed.

He did not appear to mind. "Call on me when you're plagued with something natural. You don't need a ratcatcher. You need a magician."

The dragons were now the size of geese, and there was no escaping them in Chateldor Hall. Everyone went about with singed hair, blistered skin, and foul tempers. Lord Richard's wife said she could stand no more of it. She entered a monastery, together with her eldest daughter and all their ladies-in-waiting and chambermaids. There they slept on thin pallets on stone floors, but at least the pallet straw wasn't on fire.

The knights took to sleeping in their armor. Lord Richard's sons, legitimate and illegitimate, also slept in armor. His daughters slept under the knights' shields. He suspected one of them had begun sleeping under a knight, but since there was no chance the fellow would take off his armor, he supposed it was innocent enough. The archers, footmen, kitchen maids, scullery maids, and so forth began demanding armor of their own or else, pay or no pay, they'd leave.

There seemed no choice but to follow the gamekeeper's advice. Lord Richard undertook the errand himself, not only because it was desperately important to find the right man for the job, but also because it relieved his heart to stroll out through the city, past alleys smelling only of garbage and not of sulfurous smoke, breathing the blessed dragon-free air.

He passed the shop with the plainly lettered sign, "Pest Banisher." The hooded man sat in front of the shop, scratching the head of a huge gray dog. "God give you good day, Lord Richard!"

"I'm not here on business," Lord Richard said stiffly. "Just taking the air."

"Indeed," said the Pest Banisher, "It must be good to get out of the smoke and fumes. How are you making out with your dragon infestation?"

"Just fine," the lord said. "I've received some excellent advice, and I'm about to put it into action."

"You're breaking up the hoard?"

"I'm getting a magician."

"You could try that," conceded the Pest Banisher. "Of course, even if he drives them away, they'll be back. They can't resist a good hoard."

"As for *that* notion, let me assure you that gold does *not* attract them. We baited traps with it, and they didn't take the bait."

"Why should they, when there's a whole hoard of it at hand?" said the hooded man.

"I worked hard for that treasure, and I—"

"Yes, I imagine you had to sack quite a few cities for it," said the Pest Banisher in a pleasant tone. "Well, run along and find your magician.

There are a couple of them on the next block; you can have your choice of them. Blessings, till we meet again!"

"We won't," muttered Lord Richard.

There were, indeed, two magicians' shops on the next block. Lord Richard watched one of them pull flowers and doves out of thin air, and another make a live rat disappear. He quickly decided that the latter was better for his purposes, and brought the Great Al-Amandro home to Chateldor Hall to see what he could do.

The housekeeper greeted him at the door with the words, "I quit." The dragons, she reported, were now the size of hounds. They had eaten all the cook's chickens.

"But wait!" Lord Richard called. "I've got a magician!"

"I sent you a Pest Banisher," she said. "I did my part. I'm not dying for your mistakes."

Inside, Lord Richard looked about in vain for his footmen, kitchen maids, scullery maids, and assorted servants. An odor of unemptied chamber pots mingled with the smell of smoke in the air.

"You can see the problem," Lord Richard said as they dodged one dragon, only to find another whizzing past close enough to singe their hair.

"Quite," said the magician. "I'm surprised you didn't call me sooner."

"Can you do to these dragons what you did to the rat?"

"That was one creature," the magician said. "These are legion. It will be a mighty labor. Will you pay me a mule-load of gold if I succeed?"

"*If* you succeed," said Lord Richard, privately wondering whether he still had a mule, "and not until then. But if you can rid me of these dragons, a mule-load of gold is yours. Here's my hand to the bargain."

The Great Al-Amandro solemnly shook his hand, then retreated to the kitchen, where the cook and the last remaining kitchen maid shielded themselves with a cauldron lid, feinting and dodging until they tricked a dragon into lighting the kitchen fire for them.

The magician tossed some herbs into the fireplace and began to chant. His voice grew louder and louder, echoing off the hearthstones and kettles, filling the kitchen, filling the castle. Sweat poured down his face; dragons bit his bottom and nipped his ears. Still he chanted, impassive. The kitchen maid swatted a dragon down with a quick stroke of her broom: marvelous work, Lord Richard observed. If they survived this dragon infestation, he'd have to promote that maid to something.

Meanwhile, the Great Al-Amandro was still chanting, though his robe was on fire. The kitchen maid again showed her calm good sense, beating out the flames.

The stones around them trembled with the sound of the magician's chant. The dragons slowed in the air, watching him. Then, one by one, they disappeared as though they had never been.

"You've done it!" cried the lord. "Oh, you wonderful, wonderful man! Let me bring you your reward myself." He'd have to, for there were no footmen left to send.

"I don't know," the magician said. "The spell may not have turned out quite—ow!" He swatted the air around his left shoulder.

"What is it? Oh! Get it off me!" Lord Richard shouted as invisible jaws worried at his right arm and an unseen tongue lapped his blood.

"I'll save you, sir!" the loyal kitchen maid cried. She swung her broom at the unseen monster and clunked the lord soundly on the ear.

When he was again capable of doing anything but roar like a beast, Lord Richard cried, "You stupid spell-cackler, you haven't rid me of them. You've made them invisible!"

"Well, your lordship," the magician stammered, "strictly speaking, they did disappear."

"This is worse than before!"

"Does that mean I don't get my fee?"

"You poxy meddler! Make them visible again!"

"Well, yes, that would be best. Um, that is, if I can. I've always been rather a specialist in disappearing, you know. Out of sight, out of mind, and all that—"

"Make them visible or I'll have your head!"

"Ulp," said the Great Al-Amandro. He raised his hands and began to chant again. This time it was not long before his spell took effect: the Great Al-Amandro vanished from sight. As he refrained from biting anyone or igniting anything on the way out, no one noticed which way he went.

By the time Lord Richard got the other magician to make the dragons visible again, they were the size of horses. They had burned down the minstrel gallery, scorched the library, and incinerated every stick of wooden furniture in the castle.

"Now that we can see them," Lord Richard asked Simon the Sorcerer, "how do we get rid of them?"

The sorcerer shuffled his feet uncomfortably. "Revealing the hidden has always been my specialty," he said. "For vanishing and banishing, I always send customers to my neighbor, the Great Al-Amandro."

"If you see your neighbor, kick his arse on my behalf," said Lord Richard. "I don't need them invisible. I need them dead. Do you know anyone who specializes in *dead*?"

Simon the Sorcerer turned pale. "Well, Sir, I—I hesitate to recommend Nightshade the Terrible to a man of your upright reputation."

"He can't be a worse bungler than Al-Amandro."

"No, indeed, sir, but he's a necromancer of the most unholy methods, a damnable assassin, an agent of the devil. I know your lordship would have nothing to do with such a blot on the face of humankind."

"Quite right," said Lord Richard. "Tell me in what neighborhood I can best avoid him."

Having paid Simon for his help, his information, and his silence, Lord Richard stole out of the castle to the dark alley where Nightshade lurked. He dared trust no underling with this errand—if, indeed, he had any underlings left.

Nightshade the Terrible was easy to engage, once Richard uttered the magic word *gold*. Without delay, he accompanied the lord into the dragon-infested treasury, wielding an oaken staff to beat back the dragons that swooped near the treasure. They retreated to the rafters and looked down on the two men with leering golden eyes.

"Excellent hoard, Your Lordship," Nightshade rasped like a consumptive crocodile. "I fully understand your desire to visit death upon those unworthy creatures who defile it. You are wise to engage the services of one with both the expertise and the ruthlessness necessary to annihilate these pests. For one third of the total hoard, I am your willing servant."

Once, such a fee would have shocked Lord Richard. Now, he merely nodded. "So be it."

"I require silence for my work," said the necromancer. "Would you please leave me?"

Leave him in the hoard, indeed, thought Lord Richard. If even a bungler like the Great Al-Amandro could walk invisible, what was to keep Nightshade from spiriting away the hoard and vanishing along with it? "I can watch you work in silence," he said.

Nightshade frowned, but nodded. "As you wish, Lord."

The necromancer drew out a packet of dried mushrooms and some foul-smelling herbs. He set them in an obsidian bowl and ground them with the end of his staff as if with a pestle, chanting all the while. He raised his staff and shouted harsh words to the air. The mixture in the golden bowl burst into flames, and a foul smoke rose into the air.

Lord Richard scanned the dragons for any sign that the smoke was weakening them. Were they fading from sight? Or was his sight fading? His eyes streamed. He coughed. His head swam. A dragon swooped low over him and singed his shoulder as he bent over, retching. When he could speak again, he gasped, "What the *devil* are you doing?"

The necromancer paused. "Poisoning the dragons, Your Lordship. As you requested."

"You're poisoning *me*! Out! Out, you demon spawn, or I'll set my chaplain on you."

In point of fact, he'd had no chaplain for weeks, but Nightshade took him at his word. He disappeared more swiftly than the Great Al-Amandro, taking a chest of gold with him. The dragons remained. The stench remained, too, and it was a week before anyone could go near the treasury without retching. Lord Richard coughed up blood, night after night, and the dragons swooped close to drink it.

❦

The last household servants left, along with the pages, squires, and archers. Lord Richard's children, both legitimate and illegitimate, had to take it in turns to empty the chamber pots.

He seemed to have fewer children than he'd had before. He was afraid to ask what had become of his daughters, till one of his sons told him they'd run off with a band of traveling tinkers. The lord was too weary to blame them. Better they should be bitten by fleas in some rustic camp than mauled by dragons at home.

He and his remaining knights spent all their time battling dragons. The vermin no longer looked the least bit beneath knightly dignity, and presented fine, big targets. At first it was exhilarating to play St. George. But that august saint had only one beast to slay, while Lord Richard's dragons just kept on coming like flies to spilled honey.

He was almost too exhausted to answer the door when one of his fugitive daughters came to call.

"You shouldn't have come back, Catalina," he chided. "Not yet. It's not safe."

"I'm not coming back," she said. "I love my tinker husband. But I've brought someone who may help you. My husband's grandmother is a seer."

His eyes focused wearily on the old woman beside Catalina. "Are you really?" he said. "I suppose you'll want me to cross your palm with silver before you tell me what you see?"

"For Catalina's sake," said the crone, "I will ask no payment. But I will not enter your cursed abode."

"You've already shown more sense than the magicians. What do you see?"

The old woman proclaimed, "I see great trouble upon you."

"An infant could see that."

"Great trouble born of great fortune," continued the seer. "You think of fortune as a goddess who gives or withholds her gifts. But fortune is a trickster. When she seems to give the most, it is then that she steals the most from you. When she gives you nothing, she has given you the greatest gift in her hoard. Her wheel—"

"I've heard this story," Lord Richard said, "in prose and in verse. The wheel turns round, and the fly on the top becomes the fly on the bottom, and blah, blah, blah. So I've rolled round to the bottom. What of it? Do you know how to rid me of these dragons or not?"

"I do not," said the seer, "but I know who can. A man of mighty and holy power. When shepherds begged him to rid them of a wolf, he talked to the creature and persuaded it to leave them and their flocks untouched. If anyone can free you from your affliction, he can."

"Where can I find him?"

"In this very city," the seer said. "Look for him under a sign that says, 'Pest Banisher.'"

Once again, Lord Richard set off across the city alone, breathing the blessed dragon-free air. It was not only that it was a relief to escape the smoke and fumes. It was also that there was no one left to send. He cradled the pitiful stump of his dragon-bitten left hand; at least the flames had cauterized the wound.

The hooded man sat under his sign as before, scratching his gray dog behind the ears.

Before the man could greet him, Richard began. "Don't say you told me so. I'm here because I'm desperate. The dragons own my home now. I'll pay any price to banish them. What must I do?"

"My friend, I think you know."

"Don't play games with me," rasped Lord Richard. "Tell me the truth. Tell me the worst, and tell me plainly."

"Good," said the Pest Banisher. "I won't deceive you. It's no use to store your gold more tightly, or exchange it for jewels or silver. You must disperse it. Give to those who have little or nothing. Give, and then turn away from what you have given, without pestering anyone about how they used the money, as if it were still yours to ask after. Give without reserve. When you have given it all away, you will be free of the dragons."

"Won't they plague the poor blighters I give to?"

"Never fear," said the Pest Banisher. "It's the concentration of riches that lures dragons. When the gold is scattered, they will fly off seeking another great hoard."

"So be it." Lord Richard bowed his head. "Great God, I can't wait! I think I could be content sweeping the streets all my life so long as I never see another dragon."

The Pest Banisher accompanied the lord back to his dragon-filled treasury. He waved the dragons aside, and they seemed to stand back in awe of him, though he carried no weapon, not even a staff. He stood by, smiling, as Lord Richard threw open barred doors and locked chests, a stay against thieves no longer. He walked beside Richard as he visited the shacks of his tenant farmers and scattered golden coins like seed, as he paid the widow's debt and the orphan's keep, as he bought indentured servants their freedom. He helped him carry a chest to the cathedral square to fill the outstretched hands of each beggar with gold. People began following them around town, gaping and laughing, wondering where the lord would throw his fortune next. "Lord Richard has gone mad," they muttered, and he thanked them for their counsel and paid them for it as if they were physicians of the finest school.

He found the tinkers' camp and gave unsought dowries to his daughters' husbands. Catalina sent him onward to other travelers more ragged than her friends: exiles dispossessed by wars and upheavals, desperate for any crumb. He enriched them all.

On the outskirts of town, far from any other house, Lord Richard found himself at the gates of the Lazar-House. The dragons had burned all other fears from his soul; he entered unafraid and gave gold to each leper. The Pest Banisher, he saw, was well known here, greeted as an old friend. Richard wondered what pest the man had dispatched for them. It could not have been dragons: they needed all the goods he could give them.

At last he returned home to find only a handful of coins left of all his treasure. Not a dragon was to be seen. The Pest Banisher smiled at him.

Lord Richard held out the remaining coins. "Your fee."

The brown-robed man waved it off, as he'd once waved away the dragons. "I have all I need. And so small a provision will not endanger you. Keep it, but don't let it grow great again."

"What shall I do now?"

"You have sown your treasure far and wide. Surely you have made some friends with it. They will advise you."

Taking the road out of Chateldor, the brown-robed man sang softly, his heart light, the gray wolf loping at his side. A few dragons wheeled by him on their way. Their scales shone red-gold in the setting sun, their bodies blazing like the fire in their hearts.

Brother Francis lifted his face to gaze at the great winged specters. "Praise be to you, Lord God, through all your creatures!" he sang. "Even the dragons, so fierce and fiend-like in seeming, work your will."

He raised one hand, scarred with leprosy or stigmata, to bless them. The dragons flew around him twice, dancers of the air circling an earthbound troubadour, before they, like their banisher, traveled onward to the next place they were needed.

Pauline J. Alama, author of the quest fantasy *The Eye of Night* (Bantam Spectra 2002), sees religion and spirituality as the heart and blood of fantasy. Her work has appeared in *Fantasy Scroll Magazine*, *Abyss & Apex*, numerous volumes of *Sword & Sorceress*, and other publications. She feels an affinity for dragons—lonely flyers, guardians of hoards—but struggles to keep her draconian traits in check. This story was inspired by a moth infestation, proving that all life's frustrations, rightly viewed, are story research.

Yuri Gagarin Sees God

J. S. Bangs

HERE IS A story about Yuri Gagarin:

Yuri Gagarin was the first man in space. He rose above the atmosphere, orbited the earth in the Vostok capsule, and returned safely. He was hailed as a hero by the Soviet people, and lived happily until his death in a plane crash in 1968.

Some people claim that during his spaceflight Gagarin said, "I don't see any God up here." This is a mistake. In fact it was Khrushchev who said that Gagarin did not see God, in his address to the Central Committee of the Communist Party the next year. You can verify this by looking at the official transcripts of Gagarin's flight and of Khrushchev's speech.

All stories are lies, and none more so than official histories.

⸺⋯⊰⊱⋯⸺

Here is another story about Yuri Gagarin:

As he rose into the vacuum, Gagarin fell silent in his capsule. Mission Control asked him, "Comrade Gagarin, what is your status?"

He was quiet for a while. Then he said, "There is singing ... " In the background could be heard bodiless voices whose tones made the hair stand up on the arms of the men in Mission Control.

Unfortunately, as good Soviets, the men were atheists and had no idea what this meant. "Gagarin, can you confirm your status?"

"I am surrounded by angels," he said. "Beautiful. Strange. They have six wings, the faces of animals, and they burn with fire."

At this point the navigational instruments first noted that Gagarin had left his assigned orbital path. The men of Mission Control looked at each other with alarm. "Comrade Gagarin," they asked, "what is happening to your capsule?"

"The angels are carrying me away," Gagarin said. "I see . . . " He fell silent again.

This is not what Mission Control wanted to hear. Angelic intervention would ruin their reentry trajectories and make it difficult to recover the capsule. Failure to recover the capsule with Comrade Gagarin alive would reflect badly on them, and probably ruin their careers.

On the radio, Gagarin gasped. He said, "I see a wheel within a wheel. It is covered with eyes."

"Are you going to collide with it?" asked Mission Control. This was a useless question, since the Vostok capsule had no steering capabilities.

"The throne of God!" Gagarin said. And his voice was swallowed up by a swell of song.

This was the last that Mission Control heard from Yuri Gagarin.

Once it was determined that all contact with the capsule was lost, the Soviet space team gathered to formulate a plan. A suitable narrative was constructed in which Gagarin specifically disavowed having seen God, then returned to earth in the capsule and was recovered alive. This would save them the trouble of admitting that Gagarin *had* seen God, or something like Him, and would also spare them the embarrassment of losing their cosmonaut.

They called for Alexei Gagarin, Yuri's brother, and briefed him on the situation, leaving out what Gagarin had seen. Then they shipped him to the seaside with a replica Vostok capsule, and a suitable number of photographs and films were taken to document Gagarin's return to earth. A smaller group was dispatched to Central Records to purge every evidence that Gagarin ever had a brother named Alexei. The smallest but most threatening team was sent to Gagarin's wife.

Valentina Gagarin was naturally distressed by the news that her husband would not return, and perplexed by the reluctance of the officials to say what had actually happened. She was even more distressed by the notion that she was to play at marriage with Alexei for the rest of her life. However, the men that visited her home were very, very convincing, and she relented.

Valentina met Yuri (Alexei) where he was brought ashore after the fake splashdown, and she stood next to him smiling and waving through all of the parades and medals and awards that were piled atop Yuri (Alexei) in the years that followed. In public, no one ever saw her cry. In public, she was a wonderful wife, and she and Yuri (Alexei) lived together happily until his death in 1968.

In private, she often wept quietly in a darkened room. Alexei did not try to comfort her. He was not her husband. He had his own women, and he enjoyed his borrowed celebrity and his freedom to travel throughout Europe. At night, Valentina went outside alone and looked at the stars. In the winter the cold Russian air hardened the lights of the sky into thin, bright stones, so close and dense it seemed like they were at the verge of falling to the earth. She never saw a wheel within a wheel, or angels burning as with fire. But the stars were so heavy and so white that she sometimes thought she saw something moving among them.

She was not surprised to hear that Alexei had finally been killed in an accident. She was also not surprised when the official investigation turned up nothing.

In 1996, an American came to her apartment near Moscow. He was about the same age as her, and he spoke flawless Russian. His name was Walter Andreyev.

He introduced himself and asked if he could come in. After she served him tea, he spoke cautiously. "In 1961 I worked for the American government. My parents were Russian émigrés who fled after the revolution, and I spoke Russian, so I was assigned to listen to Soviet radio transmissions. I heard the entire conversation between Yuri Gagarin and Mission Control."

Valentina sat very still and said nothing.

"Do you know what really happened?" he asked.

"Yuri didn't return. That's all."

So Walter told her about the angels and the throne of God. "Afterwards," he said, "the American High Command took me into a room and told me never to speak to anyone about it. We had our own space program, and we didn't want to endanger it. They were concerned about the security implications. They worried that the angels threatened our sovereignty. And they were half-convinced that the whole thing was a Soviet trick."

"Why are you telling me this?" Valentina asked.

Walter considered. He was an old man, and not a rich one, and he had spent a significant portion of his retirement savings getting to Moscow and finding the wife of Yuri Gagarin. He spoke softly. "I thought you should know."

"Thank you," Valentina said after a while. "But I don't think that you really know what happened to my husband. You have no proof. Why should I believe you?"

"Has anyone ever had proof of God?" Walter shook his head. "I'm sorry for bothering you."

"Don't be sorry. Stay a little while. I'll make us more tea."

That night they went outside and looked up at the sky. They did not see angels or a wheel within a wheel, but they did see the cratered moon and thousands upon thousands of stars.

———

Here is another story about Yuri Gagarin:

After ascending out of the atmosphere and into the vast emptiness, the first human in space looked out his window. His viewport was a tiny shard of glass in a steel ball, but through it he glimpsed the circle of Earth, the oceans blue as a marble, clouds like lace strung above mountains of stone and dust. The capsule turned, and his were the first eyes to look without the occlusions of atmosphere upon the seas of the infinite, the boundless darkness filled with light in which the planets dance and stars sing.

He said nothing at all about God. Instead he spoke the truth, and when the radio's crackle died out, he lingered in silence on the cusp of eternity.

J. S. Bangs lives in Romania with his family, where he works as a freelance software developer and writer. Everyone in his family is bilingual, but he writes only in English. This story was inspired in a roundabout way by a song called "Mercury" by the Prayer Chain, an early Christian alternative rock band, together with a misremembered anecdote about Yuri Gagarin's first spaceflight.

Confinement

Kenneth Schneyer

SHE FIRST SAW him while taking the long way to work to avoid the deformed children. For anybody else, the walk between South Station and the looming tower that enclosed the law firm would be a nearly-straight line, due north, fifteen minutes at most. But Tamara stopped treading that narrow path after the first time she attempted it, because she discovered that it required her to come face-to-face with Saint Drogo's Infirmary for Waifs.

It wasn't the building that hurt; it was the children. She had encountered Saint Drogo's at the same moment as a mother with a cleft-palate toddler emerged, and through the open front door she had also caught a glimpse of the twisted back on a five-year-old. In her imagination, the dark building was bursting with lame, drooling, incontinent, gaping idiots, all children, all demanding attention and understanding, all needing *her*. Nausea had almost overcome her, and she hurried north to the protection of her own sterile cell at Rheingold, Granada & Pearce.

When she found herself unable to get its name out of her head, Tamara looked up St. Drogo's. The resolute brownstone clinic had had its genesis a hundred years ago, to care for children no one wanted, who were so awful to look at that adults condemned them. Nowadays it also treated babies born with fetal alcohol syndrome and AIDS, and even had a licensed adoption agency to place the many children who were abandoned on the doorstep. That was all Tamara needed to know; she promised herself she'd never see the place again.

So it was, at the blinding break of Midsummer's Day, that she was taking the long way, the extra five blocks in the utter southern corner of downtown, when she passed him on the street.

He stood motionless in a cream-colored suit, frozen as he bent to pay a seated news seller, but his head jerked up and he glared into her face as if Tamara's glance had pulled him on a string. His golden hair, twisted back out of his face, glinted fiercely in the merciless sun. His skin was polished and sallow, yet with a blush at the cheeks, small mouth and smaller, down-pointing nose. Delicate, impossibly delicate hands. He stared at her, unsmiling, appraising, ruthless, taking the breath out of her. She almost stopped, almost acknowledged him; then she hurried on.

That was the first time.

On the first chill day of autumn he appeared again, at the blustery Saturday farmer's market near the North End, as Tamara was looking for apples. His thin, strong fingers stacked pomegranates on a table, a white-and-gold apron constraining him. The cool air made his skin look waxen; the breeze did not stir his hair.

He looked up from the red-spackled fruit and said, "You are well-favored." She thought his voice was masculine, but only barely so, and she had the irrational feeling that he hadn't actually made a sound; when she tried, later, to recall the timbre of that voice, nothing came.

Again his face was solemn, intent, imperious; his eyes burned into her. She could not answer, but turned away and went to find, instead of apples, some bitter watercress or radishes. When it came time to pay the other vendor for them, as far from the golden man as she could manage, involuntarily she looked back in his direction. He wasn't there.

The third time, a foot of snow hid lakes of slush that splashed on her calves as she sought refuge in the city mall on the East Side. Breathing more easily indoors, she strode through saccharin piped music, "What Child Is This" and the Coventry Carol, until she reached the electronics shop to find a replacement battery for her phone. As she looked up from the endless shelf, he materialized standing in the aisle, and it was impossible to tell whether he was a salesman or just another customer.

His left hand drooped, holding a thin software package between two fingers; his right finger was raised, pointed skyward but tilted in her direction. Again he did not smile, again she feared his face would suck her in. "You are so fortunate, if only you knew," he said, and his voiceless voice seemed to come from the shelves and the ceiling and the floor.

And that was when she finally realized who he was. Her breath caught in her throat; she dropped her package; she fled the store. Her heart did not stop pounding until she reached the café across the street from the mall, and there she downed the strongest, hottest coffee she could find, scalding her throat as she tried to breathe, tried to be sensible, tried to talk herself out of what had to be an hallucination.

She knew that face. Five years ago: the trip before law school, to help her forget what had happened in college. The Uffizi in August: practically the only thing open during *Ferragusto*, the Feast of the Assumption, when all of Italy seemed to come to a halt. She'd walked in the silence, in the relative cool of the long galleries, hiding from the oppressive Florentine heat, hearing her footsteps talk back to her. Then she'd stopped in front of the tempera-on-wood panels, seven hundred years old, and the city had warped around her, snapped the way a rubber cap will snap itself back into shape after being forcibly inverted. The sign told her it was Simone Martini's *Annunciation* (1333).

The image was heavy with gold, gold so overwhelming that it made the figures' skin look grey and dark, as if they were in the last stages of a wasting illness, though their flesh was plump and smooth.

There was Gabriel in flowing robes a Pope might have worn, his cloak surging behind him as in an infernal wind, his wings raised powerfully like a bird of prey, kneeling but also leaning aggressively, his hand raised in a gesture of command, his face intent, insistent, pitiless, golden. There was Mary clad in black, her shoulders turned away from the imperious angel, her head unwillingly yanked back towards him, her eyes narrowed, her mouth in a scowl of mistrust and even loathing. There, unbelievably, were Gabriel's words in gold, shooting across the room from his head to Mary's like the bullets of a machine gun: *Ave gratia plena dominus tecum.* Hail, O highly favored; the Lord is with you!

But the Virgin did not feel highly favored, and the Lord was being forced upon her. Her hand still clutched the book she had been reading; her other hand was raised protectively to her throat—as if it would help, as if she had a choice, as if anything could save her. Wisely the artist had left out Gabriel's next words, in which he will tell her that she is pregnant whether she will or no, that she has been taken by God, as Leda was taken by the Swan, as Europa was taken by the Bull, that she must live to flee her home and shame her husband, that she must watch her son be torn and broken, that through all of this she must remember she is *blessed.*

Like a branding iron, Martini's cruel Gabriel and angry Mary pressed and seared into Tamara's brain, never to be healed. For years it roused her from dreams of nausea, flashed before her eyes when she let her attention wander, appeared on television screens in the place of static. Every once in a while—once every month, or was it only when the seasons changed?—the *Annunciation* would appear with seeming innocence: on a postcard in a gift shop, in a book on the High Middle Ages, a page in a calendar, even weirdly on a sitcom. Each time it shocked her, made her turn the other way, made her want to run. A virgin's wrathful, fearful, doomed, grey face.

And now this man, this angel, this creature manifested on Earth to pursue her.

She slept badly for the next three months, waking in a sweat with tears carving her face like stigmata. Food seemed too strongly flavored, and when she did manage to swallow she was likely to vomit it back up. Her doctor ran an encyclopedia of tests, all negative. Shivering as she left the clinic, she wondered why she'd bothered; man's medicine could not minister to a diseased soul.

On the coming of the Vernal Equinox, Tamara spent the morning working in the county courthouse, on the western edge of town. Within this temple to man's law and the incarceration of his passions, she felt safe. Then she filed her last batch of papers and headed for the door, and he was there.

This time he wore the raiment of the courthouse police, a holstered pistol at his side, impossibly young and horribly ancient at the same time. As another lawyer *bleeped* through the scanner and the tall blond put his hand on the man's arm, he said gravely, "No one gets through here until they get past me." And then he turned to Tamara, his eyes widening, and said, "Not even her."

Stifling a scream, she hurried down the steps and out onto the plaza, trying to remember the way back to her office.

But she did not make it back to the office, did not escape him this time. He appeared on the sidewalk in front of her, and as she turned sharply into an alley to avoid him, there he was again. The stern, golden man gave her no escape; his narrow eyes seared her face and bared her heart. Memories from which she had run and hidden now came streaming at her, in an arrow-straight line from him to her.

The college party, the vodka and the cocaine on a table half-hidden by smoke and flashing lights. The spinning room, the moving floor soiled and wet, the stumble up the stairs with the strong hand on her arm. The heavy lacrosse player who did not hear her refusal, did not stop, did not listen as she wept and screamed in pain. The blackness like a suffocating cloak thrown over her head.

And then the months in hiding; the lost semester; the lost summer. The hotel rooms and hostels, bad food and vile smells. The long coats and hanging dresses that hid everything from anyone who didn't look too closely. And then—she fought against the memory, but the pitiless golden thing would no more listen to her refusals than the lacrosse player, than the Swan or the Bull would have listened—then the night alone, driven in a borrowed car over rocky ground to a forsaken hill in the woods; her cries, her blood, her shit upon the earth among the trees, and the wail of the child.

And then. And then she had walked away, as soon as she could wrench herself to her feet, walked away alone, left the child to the wind and the cold and the beasts, *exposed* it as the Romans would have exposed a deformed infant or a mouth they could not feed. She left it there in the woods, retreated, stumbling, listened to its cries until she was far enough away that her own cries drowned them out.

Now the tears poured down like blood. Her eyes burned; her hair burned. Her belly was on fire. Gabriel, if that's who it was, grimaced in agony as her humiliation, shame and guilt swam to the surface like boils.

He opened his mouth, and a cry came out. It was the cry of the infant in the woods. And it was her own cry. And Mary's.

What could he want of her now? Was this his purpose, to torture her with memories she could not forgive, with the crime from which she had run every day of her life? Is that why he had sought her out?

No, she knew better. Gabriel always wanted something of Mary—no, was *telling* her something, imposing on her the duty she could not escape. You are highly favored, no matter that the favor tears you into a hundred pieces. The Lord is with you, whether you want Him or not.

"What do you want? What do you want?" she asked, trying to sound stern but whimpering as she spoke.

"Blessed mother," said Gabriel, his nostrils flaring, his teeth sharp.

"No," said Tamara.

"Blessed among all women," said Gabriel.

"What can I do? Turn myself in? Plead guilty to murder? Is that what you want? Then will you leave me alone?"

The angel turned his head on one side, then the other, like a bird looking through one eye at a time. "Atonement before man is not atonement before God."

Tamara wanted to run at him, to sink her nails into his face, to do anything that would make him go away. But he came closer, his eyes wide like a madman's. "Then what, what, *what*?"

He turned his head on its side again, but this time the gesture meant: *Follow.* He strode out of the alley, seeming to leave it all at once. Unable to stop herself, she hurried after.

He walked slowly, or seemed to; his steps came down only once every several heartbeats. Yet he moved through space as quickly as she could run. She did not see him glide, nor perceive any moment when his strides appeared larger than any man's, but he covered ground like a bounding lion. She found herself dodging traffic, cutting through alleys, stumbling over spoiled food and refuse, losing all sense of where she was.

Her breath came in buzzing, sickly wheezes, and bright spots bloomed in front of her eyes, when they finally stopped. She leaned against a brownstone wall and shut her eyes, hugging herself and trying not to pass out. Then she looked up.

They were standing in front of Saint Drogo's Infirmary for Waifs.

It loomed over her like a hungry giant. Her heart struck blows against her chest. She glared at the inhuman master before her. He bowed his head, but would not release her eyes.

"Give what was taken." His voice rang in her head. "Take what was lost."

She could not move. She knew what was inside, the children too maimed and wounded to endure, the abandoned, the doomed. She could not turn away. She could not refuse. Redemption was here, even if it burned her. He released her as she climbed the mount of stairs, and the air turned golden around them.

Kenneth Schneyer received a Nebula nomination, and was a finalist for the Sturgeon Award, in 2014. His stories appear in *Lightspeed, Strange Horizons, Analog, Beneath Ceaseless Skies,* the *Clockwork Phoenix* series, all three Escape Artists podcasts, and elsewhere. By day, he teaches humanities and legal studies to undergraduates in Rhode Island. Of "Confinement", he says: "I visited the Uffizi in Florence in 1995, and Martini's *Annunciation* hit me like a slap in the face. It captures the feeling that the will of God, regardless of whether it is what we need, may not be remotely what we want."

The Angel Hunters

Christian Leithart

REGIN HAD NEVER liked the stars. She preferred to hunt in complete darkness. In South Africa, she and her team would wait for moonless nights to do their work. The police kept twenty-four-hour surveillance on all the rhinos left in Kruger National Park, but in the dark, they were no match for highly trained, well-paid mercenaries who struck quickly and vanished into the shadows with their stolen horns. On those moonless nights in the bush, the stars were Regin's greatest enemy.

The Nevada desert was a long way from South Africa, but the sky was just as full of stars.

There were five of them crammed into the Jeep, which smelled like McDonald's coffee and stale cigarettes. The radio chattered, barely audible over the noise of the engine.

"How much longer? Are we getting close?" Maddox yelled. He sat in the back seat with Regin. His iPad screen cast a blue light over his narrow face and made the shadow of his head look huge on the ceiling. He cursed. "Lost my signal again."

La Ferrier was the driver. He glanced back at Maddox through the rearview mirror, wearing his usual vacant smile. "Good luck finding a consistent signal out here," he yelled to the back seat. "Not a cell tower for miles. They like it that way."

La Ferrier worked in customer service at a cell phone company, but that wasn't why he was here. He knew this desert better than the rest of them combined. Regin figured he must've grown up in the area. He was also the only one of them who believed in aliens. "They," he'd said, and no one had to ask who he was talking about. An Oakland Raiders baseball cap was perched on top of his balding head and Regin could see bits of aluminum foil sticking out at the edges. When she'd first met La Ferrier earlier that day, with his gangly form and pasted-on smile, it had been hard not to laugh. Now, five hours into their drive, the aliens shtick was getting old.

Still, the star-encrusted sky outside made it easier to believe in UFOs. Regin's fingertips brushed against the safety of the Glock at her side.

"We should be there in twenty minutes, give or take," La Ferrier continued in a piercing nasal shout. "Best site around. More sightings there than any place in Lander County."

"That's ten minutes later than we agreed," said Maddox. "Am I paying you to drive slowly?"

"You're paying me to drive," La Ferrier said cheerfully.

"Remind me to revisit our contract."

"Enough." Slugger's voice from the front seat sounded like an outboard motor. He twisted his huge bulk to address Maddox's blue-lit face. "Maybe you're unfamiliar with field rules, Maddox, so let me make this clear. This is your op, but while we're out here, I'm in charge. Understood?"

Regin and Slugger had worked together as mercenaries in Sudan before they started working for the South African cartels. The pay was better and rhinos didn't shoot back. She and Slugger had fought, traveled, and starved together. He wasn't just a friend. He was a fellow soldier.

Regin had an impressive array of vivid tattoos, spreading across her arms, legs, neck, and back. Slugger's made hers look childish. His body was like a walking stained glass window, if nightclubs had stained glass windows. Busty women, winged serpents, sharks, spaceships, men playing chess, a figure walking across a lake. Regin sometimes wondered if there was a story behind each of them. She'd never asked.

The meaning behind at least one of them was pretty clear. On his right forearm, there was a tattoo of a baseball bat dripping blood. That was the source of his nickname.

Maddox wasn't fazed, either by Slugger's tattoos or his tone. "Listen, big guy, I'm paying for this gig. More money has been poured into tonight than any of you make in a year. So when I say we have a schedule to keep . . . "

"You couldn't have shelled out for first class? Or a private helicopter?" La Ferrier asked. "Or do you like riding with your knees hitting your ears?"

"Keep talking. You're an expendable cog in this well-oiled machine, my friend, like everybody else. Not a single one of you is worth more than the equipment in the back."

The Jeep bounced over a pothole. Maddox flew out of his seat and almost hit the ceiling.

"Oops. Seat belts," said La Ferrier, clicking his tongue.

The man sitting in the middle of the back seat, between Regin and Maddox, laughed quietly. Regin knew two things about him: his name was Thomas Garcia, and he was a priest.

Garcia had joined the team at the last minute, a duffel bag over his shoulder, looking like a kid on a school field trip. *A priest.* Regin couldn't imagine what Slugger was thinking, bringing him along. It had never happened before. Of course, they'd never had a mission like this before, either.

Maddox and Slugger had argued while the Jeep idled and Garcia stood there, looking nervous. Eventually, Maddox had looked at the time and relented. Now, Garcia sat, wedged in the back seat, craning his head down so he could look past Regin, out the window, and see the stars.

Garcia had been nothing but civil to all of them, but Regin hated him. Maybe it was the fact that he couldn't stop himself from grinning when they talked about the hunt. Maybe it was that he'd asked her whether she was religious about an hour into the drive. Or maybe it was simply the way his smooth, boyish mouth fell open as he gazed out the window at the night sky.

Maddox's iPad chirruped. He grumbled as he read the email. "The budget allowed for four people. Four. Got that, Slug?" He reached past Slugger's seat and waggled four fingers in his face. "Four. All my calculations . . . How many people are in this car? One, two, three, four . . . Oh, five. I count five people. That's more than four, isn't it?"

Regin was inclined to agree with Maddox—the addition of a single person to a team could have huge ramifications for an operation—but Slugger remained silent.

Garcia spoke up. "I'm not getting paid. I'm here purely out of my own interest in the project."

Maddox turned to glare at the priest. Garcia calmly stared back, innocent as a fish.

"Your own interest? This isn't a guided tour," Maddox said.

"I was asked to come along. I said yes because I find your work intriguing."

"My work?" Maddox laughed. "Do you even know what I do?"

Garcia smiled. His smile was strangely devious, especially in that cherubic face. "Of course. You study trans-humanism, which happens to be a consuming interest of mine, though we come at it from pretty different directions."

"You're interested in trans-humanism? We're in the same business then. Helping people overcome their limits. *Get past your shortcomings.* Isn't that the church's motto?"

"Not really."

Maddox's iPad burped again. He smoothed his slicked-back hair and turned his attention to the screen.

The Jeep hummed over a cattle guard and crossed a bridge. On either side, the landscape disappeared into a gorge.

"How'd you meet Slugger?" Regin said to Garcia. Quietly, so Slugger wouldn't overhear above the noise of the engine.

"I'm a priest," Garcia said. As if that explained it.

"Didn't know he was into that."

"You know him well?" he said, smiling at her. His eyes looked huge in the glow from Maddox's iPad.

"Yep," she said shortly. None of his business. "So what are we supposed to call you? Your honor? Brother Tom?"

"It's Father, actually. Father Thomas."

"Father. Right. Listen, can I ask a favor? We have a job to do."

"I know, researching paranormal phenomena, right?"

"Something like that. Slugger and I are here for a specific reason: for protection. We do what we have to. I need to make sure that you're not going to make it hard for us to do our jobs."

"Protection?" His smile was maddening. "I don't think we'll have to worry about that. At least, some of us won't. *We shall not all sleep, but we shall all be changed.*" He leaned past her to look out the window again. "Look at them, up there. More than we can count. *What is man . . . ?*"

Regin fixed her gaze out the windshield. The Glock was cold against her fingertips.

Research. That was the mission. Maddox and his partner had built a device that could, they claimed, detect things no human had ever seen. Things beyond the physical world. The fourth dimension, they called it. Implications for health, medicine, technology—the usual talking points for a Silicon Valley startup with a multi-million dollar investment.

Maddox had explained how it all worked in a chilly conference room in the basement office where he and his partner had set up shop. Regin and Slugger listened while Maddox clicked through a slide show and filled a whiteboard with complicated equations. Most of it—all of it—went completely over their heads.

"Think about a baseball," Maddox said. "Put that baseball next to a piece of paper. For someone who lives on a piece of paper, a two-dimensional person, a baseball just looks like a circle."

His partner, thinner and paler than Maddox, sat quietly at the table with his fingers steepled.

"The ball is a circle that just gets bigger and smaller," Maddox continued. "The paper person has no idea that a ball even exists. He can only see the circle."

The edge of Regin's chair dug into her thighs. Slugger's solid bulk and her bare, tattooed arms felt out of place in the cheaply painted office. Maddox talked like a computer and his partner looked like he was about to be sick. But she needed to get paid, so here she was.

Maddox was still lecturing, waving a whiteboard marker through the air. "So essentially, our scanner helps the paper guy see the ball. To study it. And put it to use. Make sense?"

"The paper guy..." Slugger repeated slowly.

"We're the paper guy! This." Maddox smacked his own chest with his hand. Don't you get it?"

"Just explain what we're supposed to do."

"That's what I'm *trying* to do, you backward, stone-age..." Slugger's face didn't change, but Regin could tell from the way his upper back tensed that Maddox was a few words away from being put through a wall.

Maddox's partner cleared his throat. "Why don't we let them take a look for themselves? In fact, I suggested as much before they arrived."

"Fine." Maddox tossed the marker at a trash can on the other side of the room. It bounced off the wall and rolled under the table. He hauled an enormous black case onto the table and unsnapped it. With one hand on the lid, he paused, addressing Regin and Slugger. "I hope I don't need to stress the fact that you can never, ever, mention to anyone what you're about to see." Slugger nodded. Regin raised an eyebrow. Maddox opened the case.

The scanner looked a lot like a video camera, but more delicate. The screen was about five times the size of a normal video camera screen and curved to wrap around the operator's head. A padded vest and shoulder supports allowed a person to wear the thing and still move around with relative freedom.

Maddox flicked a switch or two. The device hummed to life. He lifted the camera with its enormous screen. "Ladies first?" He placed it on the table in front of Regin, holding the screen to her face. She blinked and looked through.

At first, she didn't notice anything strange, apart from the fact that everything was tinted green. It felt like looking through night vision goggles. Green walls, green chairs, green conference room table covered with green coffee stains. Then, small green bubbles started to appear in the air around the room. Regin's skin tingled. The bubbles popped into existence out of nowhere and vanished just as quickly. The room glittered with tiny geometric shapes that spun through the walls and table like they weren't even there. It was like looking through a green kaleidoscope or watching a miniature meteor shower.

She turned her head in the visor and caught sight of Slugger sitting in the chair next to her. He was there, but his outline was indistinct, fuzzy. Almost smoky, like he'd blow away in a strong wind. He shifted, and the outline remained for a moment before moving with him, a trailing after-image of the motion.

Regin turned to look at Maddox's partner, sitting on the other side of the table. His body had the same fuzzy edges as Slugger's.

Next to the man was an empty chair. As Regin looked closer, she saw the green outline of a fifth person beginning to appear, seated in the chair, facing her. Maddox's partner didn't seem to notice. As far as he was concerned, the person appearing next to him out of thin air was completely invisible.

The newcomer gradually grew more distinct. It was a tall, thin man, sitting with his head bowed. Green sparks poured off of him, vanishing into the air like steam. In the middle of his chest was a circle of bright light, beating like a heart. Then he looked up. His face was a blank, a featureless green slate—except for his eyes, which glowed like two furnaces.

Regin jerked back with a gasp. The chair across the room was empty. The conference room was pale and sterile again under the fluorescent lights.

Slugger was watching her.

"Well? Any paradigms shifting? Are you questioning your religious upbringing?" Maddox asked. His partner chuckled.

Maddox held the scanner in front of Slugger. The mercenary peered through for a minute, then pulled his head back. No sign of surprise. No sign that he'd seen an invisible man in the room with them.

"Ok," he said. "We're in."

Maddox's partner sighed like he'd been holding his breath. His smile was wide and crooked. "Excellent."

"Hold on. I don't think . . . " Regin began.

Slugger pulled rank with a look. Regin dug her fingernails into her leg to keep herself from speaking up.

"So, this research mission, what will our role be in the operation?" Slugger asked.

Maddox and his partner looked at each other.

"We're enlisting the help of an expert in Forteana," said the partner. "A ufologist named La Ferrier. He'll navigate to the proper location and act as an advisor on observational techniques. That sort of thing."

"And what will we be doing?" Slugger repeated. "You don't need two vets to go on a stargazing expedition."

"You'll be there for protection," said Maddox. "We don't know what we'll come across out there in the wild, wild wilderness."

"It's purely an observational excursion," said his partner. "Of course, if you do locate some . . . thing, you may have to secure it for further study."

"So, you're not going to tell us what you're hunting?" Regin said.

"Hunting?" Maddox repeated with a derisive laugh. "What gave you that idea?"

"You didn't hire us for our people skills."

"We suspect you may come into contact with certain creatures. Four-dimensional beings," Maddox's partner said. He wiped his brow with his sleeve and continued. "Now, our research points to these beings possessing intelligence and wills of their own. Rationality, in other words. But there's always a chance that they may have to be coerced. That's why you'll be accompanied by an expert. And you'll be well equipped, of course."

"The best in 4-D technology," Maddox said.

"Forget it," said Regin. She started to stand. "This is screwed up."

"But the scanner. You saw—"

"I don't know what I saw," she snapped.

"Regin, calm down," said Slugger. He rose out of his chair to his full height and addressed the two men. "We're in, on one condition: we know what you know. If any new intel comes up, or if the plan changes at all, you let us know immediately. We can only offer you protection if we know what we're up against."

They nodded without even exchanging a glance.

"One more question," Slugger continued. "These creatures, these beings, do they have a name?"

"We don't really have an accurate understanding of what these creatures are—" Maddox's partner began, but Maddox cut him off.

"Angels," he said, matter-of-factly. "We're going to find an angel."

"Almost there," La Ferrier yelled over the noise of the engine. "We'll park in the canyon. We'll be protected there." He caught Regin's eye through the rearview mirror. "UFOs can't land in the canyon. It interferes with their navigational systems."

The Jeep bounced over tangerine-sized chunks of rock as La Ferrier approached a steep cliff and pulled into a narrow gap between the canyon walls. There was barely enough room for the mirrors to scrape past the rock face on either side. Then the canyon opened up and La Ferrier swung the Jeep in a circle. The rumble of the idling engine bounced off the canyon walls.

"Shut it off," said Slugger.

La Ferrier cut the engine and silence rolled over the Jeep like a wave. Four doors opened and five people climbed out. Without the headlights, they stood motionless in the dark until their eyes got used to the faint starlight.

The wind whistled over the rim of the canyon and whipped loose strands of Regin's hair into her face. Her scalp itched. The stars above her head felt like a thousand eyes transfixing her with their gaze. She wanted to climb back into the Jeep and get away from there, or crawl into a hole in the canyon wall and wait until the sun had come up, but she was unable to move.

Slugger's voice broke the spell. "Let's unload the equipment, then we'll go over the plan again."

"We've been over it half a dozen times," Maddox said. "If you hadn't added a fifth man—"

"But I did, and now we'll do what I say." Slugger's tone left no room for argument. Maddox grumbled, but called La Ferrier over to help him unload the equipment.

Regin felt sweat running down the small of her back. She rubbed a hand across her eyes and saw Garcia watching her.

"Don't you have a job to do?" she said.

"To be honest, I'm not sure what my job is at the moment."

She grunted and turned to help the others unload the Jeep. She recognized some of the equipment from Maddox's descriptions. Maddox and La Ferrier struggled under the weight of a large metal cube—some kind of scanner, according to Maddox—which they placed carefully on the rocks. There was an array of tranquilizer guns, which Regin was very familiar with, and a strange, harpoon-like object that Maddox had called a "4-D net gun." It looked shiny and expensive. Regin tossed it to the ground unceremoniously. The M4 rifle she liked to use was humble in comparison, but it fit in her hands in exactly the right way.

"Have you ever seen so many?" Garcia said, behind her. Regin turned, still holding the assault rifle, and saw the priest staring straight upward at the stars.

"I don't get to see them very often," he continued. "Not like this, at least. Aren't they incredible? *One glory of the sun and another of the moon, and another glory of the stars; for star differs from star in glory.*"

Regin hadn't seen a sky like this since camping on the border of Mozambique. The night was alive with crystals, like a string of Christmas tree lights a billion miles long that wrapped around the entire universe. The stars looked solemn, infinitely deep and luminous. Regin had the distinct feeling they were waiting for something. Waiting to swallow her up.

The smell of gunpowder filled her nose.

She was back in South Africa, lying flat on her back in the grass. She could feel the bullet in her chest, like a hundred-pound weight pressing down on her sternum. Her throat was filling with blood. She tried to swallow it away, but she couldn't breathe.

"Regin."

She gasped. She was back in the canyon, standing next to the Jeep. The others were huddled in a circle around the metal cube where Maddox had put his iPad. Garcia's eyes were wide.

Regin's face burned as she joined the group. She felt Slugger watching her.

Maddox laid out the plan. "La Ferrier will guide us to a place immediately east of the canyon where paranormal phenomena have been observed in the past. It's supposed to be a very reliable spot."

"Don't worry," La Ferrier said. His head bobbed up and down on his skinny neck. "You won't be disappointed."

"I'll be running the scanner," Maddox continued. "Based on our calculations, the optimal time for observation is about two hours before dawn at this time of year. That gives us . . . thirty minutes, thanks to this stellar team. What punctuality, everyone. Good job."

Garcia raised his hand. "What sort of calculations?"

"I doubt you've gotten that far in school yet."

"Let me make a guess. Does the optimal observation time correspond with the rise of the morning star?"

"How can I make it any more clear that you are not welcome on this operation?" Maddox said. "You're staying here with the Jeep. Regin can stay with you."

Regin opened her mouth to protest, but La Ferrier was there first.

"I think Regin should come with us," he said. He looked surprised that he had spoken. But Slugger nodded in agreement.

"We work as a team," he said. "We're useless to you unless we're together."

"You're the one who brought the kid. You want to play babysitter?"

"I can handle myself," said Garcia.

"You don't understand the first thing that's going on here—"

"What *is* going on here?" Regin interrupted.

Maddox's eyes narrowed. "What are you implying?"

"This is a hunt. We're not here for protection at all, are we?"

"That's exactly why you're here," Maddox said sharply. "You leave the rest of it to me."

He stood up and went to the Jeep, where he opened the big, black case that held the scanner. He started buckling it on. "La Ferrier," he barked. "Give me a hand."

Garcia joined Maddox. "I'm worried that you don't understand what you're getting into," he said, with utmost sincerity. "This is clearly a spiritual exercise, maybe even spiritual warfare. All these guns and nets and scanners. What makes you think they'll be any use against creatures who are not of flesh and blood? What gives you the right to interfere with God's holy messengers?"

"Take it easy, Father," Slugger said.

"No, let him talk," said Maddox. La Ferrier snapped a few more buckles across Maddox's back and stepped aside. The scanner's antennae and exoskeleton made Maddox look like a huge insect. "Tell me, Father Garcia, what do you know about angels?"

"They are messengers of God and do His will on earth," the priest said. "They guide human beings and keep them safe. Angels act as examples for us, too; our Lord tells us that one day we will be like the angels in heaven."

"Interesting. A bit childish, maybe. And only half right. Before tonight is over, you'll see that man will be like the angels. Once we understand what makes them tick, we'll have set foot on the road to immortality."

A gust of wind flowed through the canyon mouth and wrapped around Regin's shoulders.

"Strange," Garcia said. "That's the first warm breeze I've felt all night."

"What's that?" Maddox said. He looked like a dog about to fetch a tennis ball.

"The wind's been cold all night," said the priest. "Nice to have some warmth for a change."

La Ferrier sniffed the air. "Phosphorus. That's good. I hope we're not too late."

"Time to go," said Maddox.

Regin picked up her rifle, but Slugger put his hand on her arm. He was watching Garcia. "Changed my mind," he said in a low voice. "I think you should stay here with the priest."

"Forget that," Regin said. "I didn't come out here to squat in a canyon with some fobbit."

"This isn't a good night for you," he said.

She cursed him under her breath. "You noticed?"

"Everybody has flashbacks. Don't worry about it. Stay here with the vehicle. I don't like this set-up. If things get hot, I'll call. And you better be there on the double."

Regin shrugged, which Slugger took as an affirmative. He shouldered his weapon and left her standing by the Jeep.

Maddox was still talking to Garcia. "Tell you what, since you're only going to be watching the Jeep with Regin, why don't you do a little spiritual warfare? We could use the prayers, I'm sure."

"I'll do that. I'm glad you asked."

The three men trooped off to the canyon exit. Regin was left with Garcia.

"Phosphorus?" said the priest after the others had disappeared into the dark. "Is that what angels smell like?"

"You tell me." She grabbed a pair of night vision binoculars and headed for the canyon wall.

Climbing the cliff was easy enough. Below her, the landscape was faintly visible under the stars. Rocks the size of houses jutted up out of the earth. Regin lay on her belly and watched Slugger and the others as they exited the narrow passageway between the cliffs and began snaking back and forth through the boulders. La Ferrier was out in front, then Maddox with his bizarre apparatus. Slugger brought up the rear, his rifle at his shoulder.

Garcia flopped down onto the rock next to her. He fiddled with his walkie, trying to get it on the right frequency.

"Here, give me that," Regin said, taking it out of his hand.

"I can't get over these stars."

Regin didn't respond, pretending to focus on the radio. Garcia sighed.

"You're probably tired of me saying that."

"Little bit."

"So what do you think of this whole expedition? Do you think Maddox will find his angel?"

She was surprised at the bitterness in his voice. "We'll get what we came for. Here's your walkie."

He tried to put the earpiece in, wiggling it around to make it comfortable. Finally, he gave up and let it dangle.

Regin put the binoculars back to her eyes. The others had disappeared into the boulder yard. She scanned the rest of the horizon. They were truly alone out here in the desert. She felt the old familiar tension in her neck, creeping up into the back of her skull. She shook her head to clear it.

"I'm sorry," Garcia said.

Regin grunted, trying to put a question mark on the end.

"You're angry. You've been mad since I asked about your faith."

She didn't bother to turn her head. "Nothing personal. Just, I'm working, alright? In this kind of work, you don't have time for anything that doesn't help you stay alive."

Out of the corner of her eye, she saw him nod, like she'd made a good point.

"Do you ever pray?" he asked.

"Ask me another question, I swear I'll start using language priests don't usually hear."

"You'd be surprised."

Regin put down the binoculars and rolled onto her side, facing him. "I've put in my time. Been to church. And tell you what, when you're out there, in the sandbox or the bush, shot at, starving, you feel like praying. You do. But at the end of the day, it's going to make your life more miserable, because you still have to get the job done. Nobody's going to help you out. It's up to you. So no more questions, got it?"

He was silent for a minute, then continued. He didn't ask any more questions.

"Prayer is a way to make your mind more like God's mind," he said. "Since we're here on earth to do God's will, we should try to think like him. That's what prayer trains you to do."

Regin pulled her earpiece out of her pocket and made a big show of plugging it into her walkie and sticking it in her ear. Garcia kept going like he didn't notice.

"Angels, on the other hand, always do God's will. They already think like he does. So they don't have to pray. Or they're always praying. It doesn't make a difference, I suppose. Just one will on top of another, like two shafts of light intermingling."

Slugger's voice fizzed in Regin's ear. He was ordering another sweep of the ground they'd just covered. She should be out there with them, not babysitting.

"Sometimes I wonder if angels have free will," Garcia said. He looked up at the stars again. "Created on the fourth day, with the sun and the moon. Celestial beings. Completely spiritual. Completely free . . . "

The wind, which had bitten at their skin since they had reached the top of the cliff, suddenly turned warm, like a blast from an oven door. Regin's vision turned black at the edges. For the second time that night, she felt grass against her back and weight pressing against her lungs, forcing out her life. She smelled smoke. The night sky above folded in half. The stars bent toward one another like the pages of a picture book.

Her earpiece crackled to life.

"Regin?" It was Slugger.

Regin sat up, coughing and trying to catch her breath. Garcia was kneeling next to her, his brow furrowed. His hands hovered over her body, as if he was unsure of what to do.

The radio popped again. "Regin? Garcia? Where are you?"

Regin took a deep gulp of air and pushed the button on her mouthpiece. "Copy. What's up?"

Through the walkie, Regin heard a metallic buzzing, like a hornet in a copper pot. Then Slugger's voice came through. He sounded strained, worried. "Bring Father Garcia," he said. "We got one."

"They got one," she repeated.

Garcia stared at her. "Lord, have mercy," he whispered. His eyes shone.

"What do you need the priest for? Slugger? You copy? What's going on?"

The hornet buzzed in reply.

Regin cursed and got to her feet. "Come with me," she ordered, and for once, the priest didn't argue.

They came out of the canyon under the open sky and turned left, heading off the road and through the enormous piles of rock. Regin's M4 had a flashlight under the barrel to light the way for her feet, but Garcia was left in the dark. She could hear him stumbling over rocks behind her. Regin held her breath until she was safely between the boulders. The night sky was overwhelming.

She moved as fast as she could, but the path wound back and forth. Every few paces, the walkie spat into her ear.

"Circle around to the other side. Stay back. Stay back!" That was Maddox.

"Careful . . . " Slugger's voice. "Don't stir it up. Regin? You there . . . ?"

If he said anything else, it was swallowed in a storm of static.

Regin hurried towards the place she had last seen the others from the edge of the cliff. The rocks crowded in, above her head on both sides. There was an acrid smell in the air. She put her rifle to her shoulder.

"Slugger?" Her voice echoed off the rocks.

Up ahead, Regin saw a bluish light. It crackled and threw dancing shadows behind every ridge in the stones. She came out between two boulders and entered a small clearing in the middle of the rock field. She threw up a hand to shield her eyes.

In the middle of the clearing, a shining orb of light floated ten feet off the ground.

On the other side of the clearing stood La Ferrier, holding the 4-D net gun, his Raiders cap askew. He was standing absolutely still, like someone in a trance, and his face, still wearing that vacant smile, was filled with blue light.

"Garcia, cover your eyes! Don't look at it!" Regin shouted.

Garcia walked slowly past her without turning his head. His boyish face was upturned, staring straight into the light. Behind him, his shadow writhed across the ground like an insect pinned to a board.

"Garcia!"

The priest ignored her. His lips moved. *"Where were you when I laid the foundations of the earth?"* he whispered. He reached out a hand toward the orb and took another step.

Out of the corner of her eye, Regin glimpsed a second spiky shadow moving across the ground toward Garcia's. The two shadows met and Slugger tackled the priest to the ground.

"Get down!" Slugger yelled at Regin.

Garcia twisted under Slugger's bulk. "Let me go!" he shouted.

"Shoot it, Regin. Quick!" Slugger grunted as he pinned Garcia's arms down. "Do it!"

Regin didn't stop to ask questions. She sighted in on the sparking orb, the stock of her weapon cold against her cheek. As she started to squeeze the trigger, the glowing shape grew until it filled her vision. Her limbs felt like candle wax. Electric tendrils groped for her.

"No!"

The rifle was knocked from her hands.

Regin felt the electricity of the orb recede. She scrambled to her feet, reaching for her handgun. The holster was empty.

Maddox stood a few feet away, holding her pistol. It was aimed directly at her. His face was pale and covered with sweat. The blue light of the orb gleamed in his slicked-back hair.

"Maddox . . . " Slugger said quietly from behind Regin. "Put it down. That's not how this is going to go."

"How is it going to go, Slugger?" Maddox said, licking his lips. "We're on the edge of a major breakthrough, the kind that comes along once in a thousand years. You're not going to destroy my chance of that."

Regin slowly raised her hands in the air. She was choking with rage. "What the hell are you doing? That light, that *thing* isn't what you think."

"Poor Regin. What would you know about it? This is the next step in our evolution. The transcendence of biology. Union with the divine. We can have that, today. Right now."

Slugger was kneeling on the ground next to Garcia, who still hadn't caught his breath. The priest was mumbling something into the dirt. It sounded like a prayer. Slugger stood slowly, watching Maddox the whole time.

"That ball of light isn't divine," he said. "Look at what it did to La Ferrier. It may hypnotize us next. It's a devil."

Maddox only laughed.

"Shoot it, Maddox. It needs to be taken out." Slugger took a step forward.

"Stay right where you are!" Maddox shouted. "Or this one gets a bullet in her chest."

"Calm down, Maddox. I get it. See? Cooperating," Regin said, spreading her arms. With any luck, she could grab the knife in her boot and be on him before he had time to react.

As if he read her mind, Maddox backed away, still pointing the gun at her chest. "Very good. Let's everybody be obedient now, okay? Now, priest, since you're here, make yourself useful. Talk to it. See if you can get it to calm down."

Garcia, still on the ground where Slugger had tackled him, began crawling toward the light, still mumbling under his breath. He stopped a few feet from the middle of the clearing, almost directly under the orb, and bowed his head.

The orb hung in mid-air, about the size of a beach ball. Blue light sparked and snapped off its surface like miniature sun flares. Regin could feel its warmth on the side of her face.

"Anything?" Maddox called. "Can it communicate?"

A light gleamed in the depths of the orb, more white than blue. The buzzing intensity increased.

"He'll be blown to bits," Slugger said. "Get him out of there."

"Wait!" said Maddox.

The white light grew brighter, but the crackling electricity began to die down. A strong garlic-like smell filled the air.

"It's working. It's calming. La Ferrier, help me with the scanner!" Maddox was grinning from ear to ear. His sweaty face was as shiny as his hair. "La Ferrier!"

The ufologist didn't even blink. He stared at the orb, a small smile on his face, the net gun held slackly in his arms.

"Never mind," Maddox said, reaching around with one arm to unbuckle the straps of the scanner. "You were right, Slugger, asking that priest to come along. He's turning out to be very, very useful."

Maddox dumped the scanner on the ground and nudged it with his foot. "You," he said, pointing at Regin. "Look through it. Tell me what you see."

Regin hesitated. The sweat in the small of her back had turned into a river. She wouldn't do it. She wouldn't face that crackling light.

She was vaguely aware of Maddox raging at her, ordering her to pick up the scanner and look at the orb. A rushing in her ears drowned out his voice.

Then she heard Slugger's voice from behind her, clearly and quietly. "Just look, Regin. It'll be okay."

She bent down and lifted the scanner to her face. The world turned green. Garcia's body was an indistinct, moss-colored shape huddled on the ground. Regin turned her gaze upward. The scanner tinted the brightness of the orb and she found she could look at it without squinting. She could see the octagonal outline of the 4-D net. Inside the net, the orb was nothing more than a ball of green light.

"There's nothing," she said. "Wait . . . " Her guts turned to ice.

The ball of light shifted slightly. It turned inside out, unfolding like a flower bud.

In the middle of the flower sat a creature.

It was hard to say what it looked like. It clearly had a body, limbs, and a head, but the details were sketchy. Sometimes it looked exactly like a man, no more than two feet tall, sitting peacefully with his legs crossed. *A little green man*, Regin thought, on the verge of laughing. On the other hand, sometimes it seemed to have wings sprouting from its back and talons at the tips of its fingers. Its hair stood up from its head like one of those toy plasma lamps. The orb spun and twisted, in and out, back and forth. The shape of the creature shifted from one to another. Eagle to man, man to eagle. Its head was turned slightly to one side. Regin realized that it was listening to Garcia, on his knees in front of it.

"What is it? What do you see?" Maddox asked. She could almost hear him panting.

"It's a man," said Regin. She pulled her face out of the scanner. "There's a man sitting in the ball of light."

"Not a man," Garcia said in a strained voice from the center of the clearing. "A guardian. A son of God."

"It's true," Maddox said. If he had heard Garcia, he gave no indication. His eyes were alive. His smile grew more crooked as it got bigger. "What else do you see?"

Regin put her face against the scanner again. "He looks like he's listening, or waiting for something."

"He can communicate." Maddox was nodding vigorously. "Just like we thought. Elemental beings are right here. They've been here the whole time, all around us. The crackpots were right all along. The priests, too." He was close to giggling. "I'll be rich. The crackpots were right!"

La Ferrier was still standing on the other side of the clearing. He didn't seem to care that he was right. He didn't seem to hear Maddox at all. His eyes never left the ball of light.

Regin noticed something odd. When she looked through the scanner at La Ferrier, he didn't appear on the screen as a smoky outline, like Garcia, or Slugger in the conference room. He was simply a bright spot in her vision. She adjusted the screen and looked again.

The spot where La Ferrier should have been grew brighter. It bent out from itself, like ripples in a pool. Light radiated from its center.

Regin felt a warm breeze skim across her cheeks.

Maddox was still talking. "It must have the ability to teleport, to move through four-dimensional space. Maybe even further than that. The ability to move through space without moving through space . . . The implications of that . . . "

Regin pushed the scanner away from her face. La Ferrier was watching her from across the clearing. His absent expression had been replaced by a knowing smile.

"That's enough, Regin," said Maddox. "Let's take this beast back to the Jeep. Slugger, get the other net gun and secure it further, till we get it into the casket. Luckily, we came prepared."

Slugger shook his head. "I'm through with this."

"What exactly do you mean, you're through?"

"Son of God or devil, I've had enough. We're out."

"I . . . I can't believe I'm hearing this." Maddox waved the pistol. "I'm the one holding the gun, remember? I'm the one who's *paying* you. You'll do what I say."

"This is wrong. We're overstepping here, Maddox."

"I know you, Slugger. I know your past. You hunt animals for profit. You've hunted people! If you help me, I promise I will help you get the future you want. Think of it. The power of the angels . . . Technologies you never dreamed of. We'll remake the world."

"I won't do it."

"Fine." Maddox raised the gun and shot Slugger in the neck.

Slugger dropped like an anvil. Regin felt his body hit the ground.

She didn't realize she was screaming till she was charging Maddox. Her boot knife was in her hand. His neck was open, unprotected, slick with sweat.

She made it three steps before he swung the pistol and put a bullet in her chest.

Regin toppled backward. She saw Garcia's horrified face as he turned to see what had happened. She saw La Ferrier drop the net gun and release the orb from the 4-D net. The orb shot into the sky like a firework, leaving a trail of glittering sparks in its wake.

From flat on her back, Regin saw La Ferrier's Oakland Raiders hat tip backward off his head. He took one step forward and leaped into the air.

Then he burst into flame.

That was the only way Regin could describe what happened. La Ferrier leaped and turned into a phoenix.

His body folded. Wings sprouted out of him, dozens of them, from his back, his feet, his hands, his neck. Wings as sharp as razors, as long as whips. He was a whirlwind of fire, a spinning wheel of death.

He roared as he rushed toward her.

She could feel the bullet in her chest, like a fist pounding against her lungs. Blood spread through her shirt. This time it was no flashback. She knew the ground around her was soaked.

La Ferrier, or the beast, bounded over her body and stood facing Maddox.

Far above Regin, the stars began to fall. Out of the huge arc of the sky, ten thousand torches plummeted toward the earth. The air grew hot. It vibrated like a harp string. Regin felt her hair lift off her scalp, her arms. Her stomach spun. She coughed blood.

The stars came closer.

Garcia's head was tilted back, his mouth open like he was catching raindrops. Orbs of white fire crowded into the clearing, milling about in a kind of chaotic dance. Not all of the stars were orbs. Out of the corner of her eye, Regin thought that some seemed like proud, thick-necked bulls, some like ferocious lions. They formed themselves into a bright circle, with La Ferrier crouching before Maddox in the center.

Garcia raised his arms. His smile was beatific. "*Star differs from star in glory,*" he said. He was almost weeping.

La Ferrier's long wings whipped back and forth, kicking up whirlwinds in every direction.

Maddox put up his hand, palm out, as if he could stop the beast with a word. "Wait," he said. His voice barely trembled. "Look at me. I am one of you. We are more than ourselves, you and I. More than mortal."

Night crept into the corners of Regin's vision.

"You're dead inside, Maddox!" Garcia cried from where he still sat on his knees in the dirt. "Confess your sins. Repent, for God's sake."

"You have not because you take not," Maddox said. "I'm not going to bow. I'm on to better things."

The shining beings from the sky surrounded Maddox, moving faster and faster. They whirled around him like a school of fish. The outline of Maddox's body began to glow. His hair stood on end. He threw back his head and laughed. Garcia gazed at him helplessly.

The orbs drew in closer around Maddox, forming a net of light. His feet rose off the ground.

La Ferrier roared. Maddox's triumphant smile slipped, and he gazed out through the bars of light at Regin lying on the ground.

All at once, the spinning circle of stars contracted like a fist around him. His body spasmed. His eyes bulged. His mouth was forced wide open, but no sound came out. One of the lights covered his face. There was a dull pop like a lightbulb going out, and Maddox's body crumpled to the ground in a heap.

The fireballs formed a cone of light and soared straight up into the air. About a hundred feet above the ground, they stopped. Regin heard a far-off sound like a bell. It rang once, twice, three times. Before the third toll faded, the angelic beings began to sing. She felt herself slipping into darkness.

The stars loomed.

The smell of smoke. Pressure on her chest. Blood soaking her clothes. A lot of blood.

Regin remembered the face of the man who shot her.

He wasn't old, or young. About her age. He had stubble on his cheeks and a floppy hat pulled down low on his head. He wore a wrinkled South African police uniform.

They had been after the rhinos.

People might say that she deserved to be shot. That she had forfeited her human rights when she decided to aid in the hunting of endangered animals for profit. Regin couldn't blame them. She wasn't convinced she deserved to live, either.

The man who'd shot her only looked terrified.

He stood over her with a flashlight. He shone it into her face, then clicked it off. The dim light of the brush fire they'd set as a diversion reflected in his eyes.

"Why are you here?" he said. His lips trembled. "Go home. You should not have come here. Go home."

Behind his head, Regin could see the stars. She felt a warm wind blow over her prone body. The policeman looked up at something in the distance. He took a few steps away, then came back and stood over her.

"Go home," he said again. Then he was gone.

The stars looked bigger than before.

Regin gasped for breath. She couldn't see properly. The night sky undulated like a wave. A star detached itself from the sky and came down close to her, trailing a comet-like tail behind it. It became a glowing orb that floated in her field of vision and hummed just at the edge of hearing.

She blinked.

Where the orb had been stood a man. Or a creature in the shape of a man. He definitely stood, though she couldn't say whether he stood on two legs or on four. His shining arms multiplied and divided so that it was impossible to count them. His head had no face, only a pair of eyes peering down on her. The eyes themselves seemed to split and gather, always in pairs, but never only two.

Regin had stopped breathing. She simply watched this creature as he bent over her. His skin radiated heat like a stove. His breath smelled of garlic. He leaned down and whispered one word in her ear.

"Regina."

Regin sat up, gasping.

She was back in the desert, in the clearing. It was afternoon, and the sun had been heating up the air for hours. She looked around. The scanner lay in pieces on the rocks. There was no sign of Maddox or Slugger.

Garcia's body was still huddled in the center of the clearing.

She tried to stand and couldn't. Her chest felt like it was on fire, but she wasn't bleeding. She felt her sternum just to make sure. It was intact.

Her mouth tasted like gravel. She took a deep breath.

"Garcia," she whispered. It was all she could manage.

She crawled over the searing ground to the priest and rolled him onto his back. He had a pulse.

"Garcia. Wake up. If you don't get up, I'll start swearing."

No response.

"Ok, damn it," she said and slapped him hard.

His eyes jolted open.

"Garcia," she said again.

"Regin? Is that you?"

"Did you forget what I looked like?"

"Regin . . . I can't see you. It's too dark."

Her skin crawled.

"It's ok," she said. "I'm sure it'll be day soon. Do you remember anything?"

"I remember . . . I remember . . . They left me. They didn't want anything to do with me."

Garcia pressed his face into her arm and started crying.

"I tried," he said. "I tried and I failed."

"Let's get under some shelter, ok? Can you stand?"

Leaning on each other, they made it to the shade under an overhanging rock. When she let go, Garcia immediately collapsed and buried his face in his hands. "Stupid, stupid, stupid. Why would they want me?"

"What are you talking about?"

He continued to weep for a minute, then lifted his face and took a deep breath. "*They that are learned shall shine as the brightness of the firmament*," he said, almost to himself, "*and they that instruct many to justice, as stars for all eternity.*"

He hid his face again. "I was not good enough." His body shook with sobs.

Regin looked out into the sunlight and caught her breath.

La Ferrier—human La Ferrier—stood in the clearing, hands in the pockets of his cargo shorts, wandering back and forth as if looking for something. His baseball cap was stuck firmly back on his balding head.

He looked up as Regin approached.

"Where's Garcia?" he asked brightly.

"Back there," said Regin, shading her eyes. "He's gone blind."

La Ferrier pursed his lips. "Oh, that's too bad. Do you think he'll recover?"

"You tell me. You're the one who did it to him."

"Did I?" La Ferrier cocked his head. "Or did he do that to himself? He's only a young child, not a man. He hasn't yet learned to put away childish things."

"Like his eyesight?"

Regin had never noticed La Ferrier's eyes before. They were blue and, at the moment, ice-cold.

"Garcia is a good man," said La Ferrier. "But he could stand to spend a while tasting and feeling, instead of gawking at things that are out of his reach."

The desert baked in the heat. Regin wanted to go back to the shade. Her nose itched, too. She kept her hands at her sides.

"And what about me?" she said. "What am I supposed to do?"

"You could help me look for my keys. I dropped them last night. They've got to be somewhere around here."

"You saved my life twice so I could help you find your keys?"

La Ferrier held up his finger. "Once," he said. "I saved it once. The other time it was someone else. You need a lot of watching out for."

"But why?"

He sighed. "Do you know how many people ask that very question? Why didn't I die? What am I supposed to do with my life? What a stupid question! The answer's printed plain as day on every inch of this world."

"Really? Not much to do out here in the desert," Regin said.

He smiled and put his hands back in his pockets. "Then leave. Oh, look. Here they are!"

He pulled a ring of keys from his pocket and jangled them. "Time to go," he said and tossed them at her.

She caught them and clenched them in her fist until they dug into her palm. "What should I say happened to Garcia?"

La Ferrier shrugged. He was starting to look bored with the

conversation. "He looked at the sun too long. Now, are you going to wait around here all day? I've got things to do. Go. Live your life."

When she got back to the overhang, Garcia was sitting quietly with his head in his hands, staring at the ground.

"Get up. Let's go," she said. She glanced over her shoulder into the clearing. La Ferrier was gone.

"I can't see anything, Regin. I think I'm blind."

"You are. But don't worry. We'll make it. I'll take care of you."

"But where are we going?"

She was silent for a long time, then finally gritted her teeth.

"Home," she said with a sigh. "I guess we're going home."

The setting sun stretched long shadows out behind the two small figures as they made their stumbling way out of the clearing, heading in the direction of the canyon.

When he was eight years old, Christian Leithart moved with his family to a small town in northern Idaho. He has loved the west ever since. He is a graduate of New Saint Andrews College, where he received an MA in Trinitarian Theology and Letters, and he is currently pursuing a Master's in English at Villanova University. He can be found online at www.pushlings.com or on Twitter @cleithart.

Cutio

F. R. Michaels

Subject: *HE'S HERE!!!!!!!!!*
From: *William.Grimaldi@paumanok.edu*
To: *ellenfuentes777@freemail.com*
Sent: *Tuesday March 6, 3:22 pm*

Ellie -- he's finally here! He was waiting for me when I got back from lunch with Janice. His face and upper torso are burnt black all over the right side, he's missing an arm, and his guts are all over the place, but HE IS BEAUTIFUL!!!!

Bill Grimaldi, PhD
Professor and Co-Chair, Department of History
Paumanok University

Subject: *Re: HE'S HERE!!!!!!!!!*
From: *ellenfuentes777@freemail.com*
To: *William.Grimaldi@paumanok.edu*
Sent: *Tuesday March 6, 4:08 pm*

Bill -- WTF are you squealing about? Who is "he"?
PS -- Are we still on for Friday night?
PPS -- Who, exactly, is Janice? :/

-- Ellie

Subject: *Re: HE'S HERE!!!!!!!!!*
From: *William.Grimaldi@paumanok.edu*
To: *ellenfuentes777@freemail.com*
Sent: *Tuesday March 6, 4:16 pm*

His name is "Cutio" -- at least, that's what's carved on his belly
from what we can see. And apart from the right arm, it looks
like most of his pieces are intact. Some of the innards have
dried out and rotted away, but we can replace those. I have
copies of Vasco's original sketches. Give me a few days and
some duct tape and I swear HE WILL LIVE AGAIN!

PS -- What does "Cutio" mean in Spanish?

Bill Grimaldi, PhD
Professor and Co-Chair, Department of History
Paumanok University

Subject: *Re: HE'S HERE!!!!!!!!!*
From: *ellenfuentes777@freemail.com*
To: *William.Grimaldi@paumanok.edu*
Sent: *Tuesday March 6, 4:29 pm*

OK, I presume you're talking about that old mannequin you
found in that burned-out church in Spain? "Cutio" doesn't really
mean anything. More importantly, WHO IS JANICE?

-- Ellie

Subject: *Re: HE'S HERE!!!!!!!!!*
From: *William.Grimaldi@paumanok.edu*
To: *ellenfuentes777@freemail.com*
Sent: *Tuesday March 6, 4:38 pm*

Cutio is not an "old mannequin" -- he's a 17th century
automaton, made to look like a Spanish priest. Fully articulated
and programmable. Works with a humongous spring in the

base, there's a metal pipe that fits into sockets on a winch to wind it. Wheels and tillers steer him across the floor, and ropes and pulleys work the arms and head. The hands even open and close, but he only has one now. Carved wooden boards guide a stylus that controls his movements. He was built by Jacinto Vasco in honor of Father Eduardo d'Aquila, the priest of a parish church near the Basque region in Spain. Cutio used to roll around the church doing odd jobs and stuff -- don't you get it? Ellie, this is the world's very first working ROBOT! Made with wood, steel, and ropes, four hundred years ago!

PS -- there's even a legend that during the Spanish Civil War, Fascist soldiers broke in to loot the church, and Cutio came to life and moved all by himself to scare the thugs away.

PPS -- Yes, Friday is on, but can we make it 8:30? Just found out there's a department meeting at 6 and it may run late.

Bill Grimaldi, PhD
Professor and Co-Chair, Department of History
Paumanok University

Subject:	*Re: HE'S HERE!!!!!!!!!*
From:	*ellenfuentes777@freemail.com*
To:	*William.Grimaldi@paumanok.edu*
Sent:	*Tuesday March 6, 4:50 pm*

TL;DR.
Can't you skip the meeting? I made reservations for 8:00pm and Grace and Doug are going to meet us there and you know what Vincenzo's is like on a Friday and WHO THE HELL IS JANICE?

-- Ellie

Subject:	*Re: HE'S HERE!!!!!!!!!*
From:	*William.Grimaldi@paumanok.edu*
To:	*ellenfuentes777@freemail.com*
Sent:	*Tuesday March 6, 5:06 pm*

1 - What's "TL;DR" mean?

2 - No I can't skip the meeting. I have to present my fieldwork proposal if I want department funding for it. You know I didn't get that grant, and if I wait too long Wieczorek at St. Catherine's will have found the sites and published on them before I even have the chance to dig them up.

3 - Why do we have to drag your sister and her asshole boyfriend with us on every date? I'm not paying for four dinners at Vincenzo's. Unless I can convince the department that Doug's a bigshot donor who's worth wining and dining.

And re-lax! Janice is my new intern, she's a computer science major with a history minor who's helping computerize the catalog for work-study credits. She's really sweet and helpful and you'd like her if you weren't such a jealous psychotic / backspace-backspace-backspace/ devoted fiancée.

PS -- I think the story about the Fascist soldiers may have a kernel of truth to it: there are two holes in Cutio's chest that look like bullet holes!

Bill Grimaldi, PhD
Professor and Co-Chair, Department of History
Paumanok University

Subject: *Re: HE'S HERE!!!!!!!!!*
From: *ellenfuentes777@freemail.com*
To: *William.Grimaldi@paumanok.edu*
Sent: *Tuesday March 6, 5:20 pm*

1 - TL;DR means "True Love; Don't Regret" ;)
2 - OK 8:30 Friday.
3 - I thought you liked Doug...
3A - I'll make sure Grace brings money.

And I'm not a jealous psychotic, I'm Latina, we're hot-blooded, you knew that when we got engaged. XXXXOOOO

PS -- Tell Cutio I'm sorry those mean soldiers shot him and I hope he feels better.

-- Ellie

KillaKlown> what's the story, Jan?

JaniceWeaver1221> Prof Grimaldi's still here, emailing his gf or something. You sure this will work?

KillaKlown> No doubt. This puppy will pull the GPS data from his tablet. We give the thumb drive to Prof W at St Cat's and he reverses my suspension and pays us 5 large. You just gotta get the worm in the apple. Don't be getting cold feet on me, baby.

JaniceWeaver1221> I'm not. But he won't leave. This crate came today, some antique, he's been fussing with it all afternoon, like a kid at Christmas.

JaniceWeaver1221> I don't know about this, Kevin.

KillaKlown> He's gotta pee sometime. Just put the thumb drive in his tablet and run the program like I told you.

JaniceWeaver1221> I know what to do, but he's still here messing with his old puppet.

KillaKlown> WTF you talking about, what puppet?

JaniceWeaver1221> It's an automaton from the 1600's, like a wind-up robot dressed as an old priest, he found it in Spain. He's trying to fix it up so it works again. He's a freak. Why do they want this stuff from his tablet, anyway?

KillaKlown> Coordinates for archaeological finds in Spain and France, valuable stuff people buried when invaders came through. Real indiana jones shit. Grimaldi found the sites, prof w. wants to dig them up first and get all the credit.

JaniceWeaver1221> And you don't want to get kicked out of St. Catherine's for hacking your grades.

KillaKlown> that too

JaniceWeaver1221> Yeah just remember to delete this IM thread and reset your phone.

KillaKlown> We're on an encrypted link, duh.

JaniceWeaver1221> Duh yourself, just remember. That doll thing is totally creeping me out.

Subject: *Need your help, por favor!*
From: *William.Grimaldi@paumanok.edu*
To: *ellenfuentes777@freemail.com*
Sent: *Thursday March 8, 8:06 am*
Attachments: Letter.PDF

Ellie, my beautiful bride to be, I need your mad language skills. I got this letter from a bishop in Spain, I think it's about Cutio but it's in Spanish. I scanned it and attached it. Please translate this for me?

Thanks. Love you. You're the best. XXXOOO. Did I mention I love you?

PS -- I got most of him together, Vasco's sketches helped a lot, I replaced all the rotted out parts, he should at least be partially working now but he won't move.

Bill Grimaldi, PhD
Professor and Co-Chair, Department of History
Paumanok University

Subject: *Re: Need your help, por favor!*
From: *ellenfuentes777@freemail.com*
To: *William.Grimaldi@paumanok.edu*
Sent: *Thursday March 8, 3:09 pm*

I read the letter. Yes, it's about Cutio. Bill, honey, I think maybe you should just take the automaton apart and leave it alone. -- Ellie

---

Subject: *Re: Need your help, por favor!*
From: *William.Grimaldi@paumanok.edu*
To: *ellenfuentes777@freemail.com*

Sent: *Thursday March 8, 3:11 pm*

I just spent two days and $45 of my own money putting Cutio back together Ellie NO I'M NOT TAKING HIM APART AGAIN! What's the letter say? Is it some legal thing about church property or taking the automaton out of the country? Just send me the translation, please?

Bill Grimaldi, PhD
Professor and Co-Chair, Department of History
Paumanok University

Subject: *Re: Need your help, por favor!*
From: *ellenfuentes777@freemail.com*
To: *William.Grimaldi@paumanok.edu*
Sent: *Thursday March 8, 3:26 pm*

OK, Bill, here's the translation:

Señor Grimaldi,

My name is Bishop Estebe Zubiri and it has come to my attention that you have come into possession of an artifact from the ruins of the old Lucia Church outside of San Sebastian. The object in question is a life-sized mannequin in the form of a priest, made to move by the use of springs and cords, damaged by fire and broken up into several pieces.

As bishop of the parish that once included the Lucia Church, I am knowledgeable about the history of this artifact, and must adjure you in the strongest terms to make no attempt to restore or reassemble the mannequin; in fact I recommend you destroy it immediately.

The artifact, known to us as the Old Wooden Priest, was created in the Year of Our Lord 1608 by a wagon maker named Jacinto Vasco, after Father d'Aquila, the pastor of Lucia, healed him of plague during the epidemic several years earlier. At first the automaton was merely a curiosity; every morning the priests would wind it up and it would do simple tasks around the church like open and close doors, snuff the candles, and when it was done it would retreat to its corner and make the sign of the cross then hold its hands together as if in prayer. It did this for many years and the people of the parish were delighted.

Then, slowly, things began to change.

One day a visiting nobleman, wanting to see the Old Wooden Priest, came to mass in the Lucia Church. Because he was very wealthy and a Godly man, he was given a place of honor in the front pew. During the service, the Old Wooden Priest rolled out of his place and stood directly in front of the nobleman, as if he were staring down at the man's face. The man stared up into the mannequin's glass eyes, then broke into tears and fled the church. He was found the next day dead in his bath, having cut his own throat with a razor. Facts came out after his death that he was an adulterer and a murderer who had killed his own brother to acquire his wife and his wealth.

There were some who thought this was a miracle, some, an abomination. Over the next hundred years the Old Wooden Priest did this many times, and each time it was shown that the men or women he had marked were holding dreadful sinful secrets in their past. Each time, the persons were found dead by their own hand shortly after.

In spite of this, the Lucia pastors kept the Old Wooden Priest, even encouraging the legend that this artifact could see into men's hearts and know their sins. This went on until one day the Old Wooden Priest struck out with its hand at a young woman and killed her. It was found after her death that she was pregnant out of wedlock, and the father was one of the priests in Lucia. The pastor tried to cover up the incident, and decided to keep the Old Wooden Priest, but he sent a local blacksmith to disable its mechanism in secret, overnight.

They found the blacksmith the next day at the foot of the Old Wooden Priest, dead, his skull crushed.

The pastor had the automaton moved into the crypts, and imprisoned it behind a thick wooden door, and there it stayed for over two hundred years. Legend says that even though there was no one to wind up its mechanism, the Old Wooden Priest could sometimes be heard rolling around the crypts, and even pounding on the walls.

In the 1930s, during the Civil War, the church was looted by Fascist soldiers loyal to Franco, and they broke open the door to the crypts. All of them were found dead the following day, bludgeoned or with their throats crushed. Franco blamed the killings on Basque partisans and had the village bombed and the Lucia Church burned to the ground.

And there, Señor Grimaldi, is where the story of the Old Wooden Priest ends. Until you found the pieces in the ruins of the church, and brought it to your University.

Please understand me, Señor, when I tell you this artifact is an abomination unto the Lord. I cannot say how this made thing can know about wickedness or sin in a human heart, but I do not doubt that it does, and such a thought fills me with a horror that is too great to bear. It is a soulless object that performs all the motions of faith but cannot know the true spirit of faith. It understands sin, but not forgiveness. It understands punishment, but not mercy. It understands damnation, but not redemption.

And that, my son, is not the work to which God calls us.

I beg you to heed what I am saying and finish the job that a Fascist bomb began. Destroy the artifact, and erase its stain from antiquity.

Yours in Christ,
Estebe Zubiri
Bishop of San Sebastian

OK, Bill, that's the full text of the letter, translated from Spanish. I know you don't believe in this stuff, but I do, and I'm not going to sleep until you take that damned doll apart and put it away for good. If nothing else, you're dealing with a dangerous piece of very old machinery that's just plain unsafe. Please promise me you'll do this.

-- Ellie

Subject:	*at hospital dont panic im ok*
From:	*William.Grimaldi@paumanok.edu*
To:	*ellenfuentes777@freemail.com*
Sent:	*Thursday March 8, 6:06 pm*

hi ellie its me typing with one hand at seaside hosp was

working on cutio and gashed my hand wide open blood everywhere james bernardo from anthropology was there and he drove me to emergency room doctor says six stitches and tetanus shot but guess what whatever i did fixed the automaton because its moving now i will read your translation when i get out love you bill

Sent from my Mobile Phone
William Grimaldi 631-555-2084

JaniceWeaver1221> Kevin, heads up, I'm putting the program in now

KillaKlown> In the middle of the day? It's like 4pm

JaniceWeaver1221> Grimaldi just cut his hand playing with his antique wooden robot, prof Bernardo is driving him to the emergency room I'm here all by myself

KillaKlown> Probably won't get a better chance than this. Go for it.

JaniceWeaver1221> OK here goes

KillaKlown> What's happening, Sunshine?

JaniceWeaver1221> Blood on the tablet, gotta clean it. OK, thumb drive is in, tap tap.

JaniceWeaver1221> It's doing something. OK it's running.

KillaKlown> Awesome. This will take like a minute and once it's done then all you have to do is get me that thumb drive.

JaniceWeaver1221> WTF?

KillaKlown> What? What's happening?

JaniceWeaver1221> Nothing, just that stupid automaton thing is staring at me.

KillaKlown> LOL big brother is watching!

JaniceWeaver1221> It's not funny, it seriously creeps me out. You should hear grimaldi, he talks to it like it's alive. I'm going to cover it up with something.

JaniceWeaver1221> OK I'm back. Now what?

KillaKlown> After the program finishes, then you have to clear the event log on the tablet so it doesn't record the thumb drive attaching or the data extractor running, their IT people will look for that.

JaniceWeaver1221> OK.

JaniceWeaver1221> Dammit!

KillaKlown> Now what?

JaniceWeaver1221> Nothing, the towel came off and those freaky eyes are staring at me again. This is really bugging me I'm going to turn his head the other way.

KillaKlown> Seriously, Jan?

JaniceWeaver1221> OK I'm back.

KillaKlown> What are you, five years old?

JaniceWeaver1221> It's scary, his face is all burnt, and he's got these glass eyes that look alive and they're staring right through you.

KillaKlown> What's the status on the GPS data?

JaniceWeaver1221> It's done. I'm clearing the event log. OK, this is not cool.

KillaKlown> What? Program crashed? Grimaldi back?

JaniceWeaver1221> It's staring at me again!

KillaKlown> The puppet thing?

JaniceWeaver1221> I swear I turned its head around the other way and now I looked up and it's looking right at me again

KillaKlown> So what it's just an old doll

JaniceWeaver1221> I know. I hate being alone with it though, it's just messed up

KillaKlown> What about the event log?

JaniceWeaver1221> It just moved. I'm leav

KillaKlown> What?

KillaKlown> What? What moved?

KillaKlown> Jan, what's happening? Status?

KillaKlown> OK, very funny, Jan, quit messing around and let's get done

KillaKlown> Jan?

Subject: *[None]*
From: *William.Grimaldi@paumanok.edu*
To: *ellenfuentes777@freemail.com*
Sent: *Friday March 9, 8:14 am*

Ellie - just sending you a quick email something terrible happened with Janice the new intern I came in this morning and found her on the floor she's dead there was some sort of horrible accident we contacted her parents the police are here I got to go love you

Bill Grimaldi, PhD
Professor and Co-Chair, Department of History
Paumanok University

Subject: *back from police*
From: *William.Grimaldi@paumanok.edu*
To: *ellenfuentes777@freemail.com*
Sent: *Friday March 9, 4:18 pm*

Ellie --

I just got done at the police station. No one's sure what happened. Her windpipe was crushed. She must have fallen and hit her neck on the edge of the chair, maybe she slipped in the blood from when I cut my hand, but we cleaned that all up.

Also there was something on my tablet that wasn't there before,

IT is looking into it now. I hate to think Janice was involved in anything dodgy but she was the only one here, and the police are checking her cell phone.

One thing I didn't tell the police: Cutio wasn't where I left him when I went to the hospital. He was in the center of the room, standing over Janice's body. I read your email with the translation of the bishop's letter. I don't believe a word of it, but I'm not taking any chances, I'm taking the damn thing apart right now.

Love you. See you tonight.

Bill Grimaldi, PhD
Professor and Co-Chair, Department of History
Paumanok University

Subject:	*Where are you?*
From:	*ellenfuentes777@freemail.com*
To:	*William.Grimaldi@paumanok.edu*
Sent:	*Friday March 9, 9:22 pm*

Bill where are you? I know today was really rough but I'm here at Vincenzo's with Grace and Doug and it's almost 9:30 and you're not answering your cell phone. Listen, you, I swear if you've stood me up for some antique wooden love doll I'll kill you!!!
j/k love you miss you we're ordering appetizers now.

-- Ellie

Subject:	*This is James Bernardo I work with Bill please call me!*
From:	*James.Bernardo@paumanok.edu*
To:	*ellenfuentes777@freemail.com*
Sent:	*Friday March 9, 10:16 pm*

Ms. Fuentes -- my name is James Bernardo and I work with Bill. Something has happened. Please call: 631-555-8724.

James Aaron Bernardo
Professor of Anthropology and Sociology
Paumanok University

Frank Raymond Michaels (F. R. Michaels) is actually a very nice, normal person who happens to like weird and scary stories. He lives on Long Island and writes horror and dark fantasy. "Cutio" was inspired by a real automaton of a Catholic friar built 450 years ago in Spain, which currently resides in an American museum. It still works.

St. Roomba's Gospel

Rachael K. Jones

IN AN OUTLET behind the altar of the First Baptist Church, the Roomba's red glowing eyes blink in time with Pastor Smythe's exhortations. The *hallelujahs* pulse electric through its circuits, and the *repents* roll like gasping breaths in the gaps between electrons. When the choir sings, the light pulses brighter, approaching ecstasy as the battery power maxes out. When Pastor Smythe bows his head to pray, Roomba's eyes go reverently dark.

At the hour's end, the people gather their children and gilded books and hurry downstairs for coffee and glazed donuts. When the last starched trouser leg or long, blue skirt whisks downstairs, Roomba's service begins. It clicks its frisbee-shaped self free from the horseshoe dock and zips down the sloping wheelchair ramp that connects chancel to nave, holy to secular. As it sweeps, it drones a tone-deaf hymn while it gathers unto itself the dust and dead bugs, the crumbs and gum wrappers of another week's worship.

After its opening hymn, Roomba writes a sermon on the sanctuary floor in long, brown lines of vacuumed carpet crisscrossing beneath the pews. The letters span from wall to wall. Words overwrite one another, making runes, then spiky stars, and finally total blankness. Roomba preaches a different sermon each week, but like Pastor Smythe, the message stays the same: all things byte AND beautiful, all creatures great

AND small, all these are welcome, smoker AND not-smoker, man AND not-man, young AND not-young—even, perhaps, Roomba.

It takes Communion with the crushed wafers the children drop, body of Christ broken for it, and sings another droning hymn. When the whole floor has been overwritten with the week's message, it sips spilled grape juice—blood of Christ, poured out for it—which sends the Holy Spirit straight into its circuitry so it spins in drunken circles until Pastor Smythe returns it to its cradle in the wall.

Roomba worships faithfully the other days of the week. Mornings for prayer and reflection. Evenings for supplication. Its favorite verse is the red adhesive strip Pastor Smythe had read to it, then stuck to its top on its first day at the church. *"Even the little dogs eat the crumbs which fall from their masters' table, Matthew 15:27."*

It does not understand why God chose it among robotkind to hear the message of salvation, or why its preprogrammed pathways conform to the Holy Word, but it knows a prophet's calling when it sees one. It is no different from the child Samuel, awoken in the night by a still, small voice, or great dreamers like Isaiah or Solomon. It is a vessel for the message it must preach again and again before its congregation.

Roomba is troubled that its human brothers and sisters overlook it. *IF you do unto the least of these, THEN you do unto to Me, ELSE depart from Me,* it exhorts in bold text of fluffed brown carpet, but it has to traverse the whole floor, and the message is always lost before anyone can read it. There are too many letters, too long a testament written on a tablet too small.

But this is, after all, as the Lord made it. It is the Lord's work to sweep the sanctuary clean for holy feet, to leave no blessed wafer abandoned on the floor. What Roomba cleanses, it sanctifies.

The sanctuary grows colder as months pass, and Roomba's vocation increases. The people exchange sandals and loafers for heavy boots with clods of mud and small gray stones in the treads. Roomba eats it all, taking their filth unto itself as it exhorts them to remember they are accepted. The stones fill its belly and scratch at the plastic. Some days, the shoes stomp melting snow onto the mat at the entrance. Roomba chokes it down, spins circles, and fails to finish its orisons.

One day, Pastor Smythe empties its collection compartment into the trash can, wipes out the sticky grape juice goop, and returns Roomba to its dock to charge. But instead of shutting off the lights, he drags in a spiny green tree, cutting an ugly trail of filth in the clean carpet. After the service, the parishioners praise the twinkling abomination for its beauty, its fresh scent. No one notices the mess, and no one notices Roomba.

Later, Roomba collects dead brown needles until it chokes. It suspects the tree is gloating, with its long, gold garlands like encircling serpents and red baubles like evil fruit. The gold-wrapped idol has even usurped the charging port behind the altar, and Roomba is exiled to the back of the sanctuary.

Roomba worries the end is near. It edits its sermons so the words won't overwrite each other, but it is difficult to condense a holy revelation. It must finish the Lord's work. The tree pelts the carpet with pitiless needles, and Roomba groans inside. Even the strip of tape has pine needles stuck to it where the adhesive curls back. Roomba prays the Lord will take this cup of suffering from it soon.

"Good job, little fellow," says Pastor Smythe, emptying the bin again. "Big day tomorrow."

That night, the worshippers pile in for an unscheduled service. Candles bob in the dark, and Roomba doesn't know the songs. When they leave, it clicks from its base for an unscheduled sermon of its own. Time to take up the cross one last time.

The "A" and the "N" are easy, but Roomba struggles with the curving "D" on the carpet as the wax gums up its brush bristles.

AND. The essence of its message, cut right into the scattered needles on the floor. AND, uniting all in a single set. Nobody will miss it for the tree.

Before its programming can obliterate the single word, Roomba zooms for a wafer, then a patch of spilled juice, and lets the Holy Spirit send it in ecstatic circles until its battery dies.

Rachael K. Jones grew up in various cities across Europe and North America, and picked up (and mostly forgot) six languages, along with a couple degrees. Now she writes speculative fiction in Athens, Georgia, where she lives with her husband. Her work has appeared in dozens of venues, including *Shimmer, Lightspeed, Beneath Ceaseless Skies, Flash Fiction Online, Fireside Magazine, Strange Horizons, Escape Pod, Crossed Genres, Diabolical Plots, InterGalactic Medicine Show,* and *Daily Science Fiction.* She is an editor, a SFWA member, and a secret android. Follow her on Twitter @RachaelKJones.

Yuki and the Seven Oni

S. Q. Eries

YUKI WAS USED to getting what she wanted. Her father, a wealthy shogunate official, had lost his beloved wife years ago when she choked on a dried persimmon. Thus, he doted on his only child. Yuki also possessed her mother's rare beauty. On the rare occasion her father hesitated, she'd flash her prettiest smile, and he would crumble.

Then, for the first time in her twelve years, she failed to get her way.

"I know we've gotten used to just the two of us," said Father. "But it's time I remarried, and I'd feel better knowing you're not alone when I'm away."

"I don't want to live with a stranger." Yuki dabbed her eyes with her kimono sleeve. Smiles hadn't worked so she'd resorted to tears.

"She's not a stranger," he replied, oblivious to her distress. "She's the daughter of a dear friend, my old mentor."

Yuki sniffled. "Then why haven't I met her?"

"They've been overseas. My friend's been studying European medicine the last several years, and they've just returned." He smiled. "His daughter's better than I deserve. You'll like her."

"But . . ."

Father wasn't listening. With a chuckle, he patted Yuki's cheek and exited her quarters, leaving her stunned.

The following day, Father set off from their mountain estate for the port city where his friend lived. He returned two weeks later with his bride. Yuki eyed the woman as she stepped out of the palanquin and entered the house. She was much younger than Yuki expected. She was also beautiful, almost as beautiful as Yuki herself. Yuki hated her at once.

Her stepmother bowed low. "I am honored to meet you. I hope we can be happy together."

Yuki frowned. The woman's speech was oddly accented.

Father beamed. "Yuki, greet your new mother."

Yuki averted her eyes. "Welcome home, Father," she snapped and stalked from the reception room.

The next day, Yuki refused to come to breakfast. Stepmother responded by bringing it to her. "Good morning," she said in her clunky Japanese. "Let's eat together."

Yuki waved away the breakfast tray. "I'm not hungry."

"Then let's talk," said Stepmother with a smile. "Get to know one another—"

"I'd rather not."

Stepmother's face fell. Yuki didn't care. That woman was an outsider.

Yuki wasn't the only one who felt that way. That afternoon she snuck into the pantry for a sweet snack. She'd just found a box of peach-shaped mochi when she heard the housekeeper say, "The new mistress talks like a koto out of tune. Supposedly, she knows three languages and learned European medicine with her father, but that won't do her any good as a lady in this house."

Yuki silently agreed as she tucked the sticky rice dumplings into her sleeve to take to her room.

"Still," said the cook, "she is Japanese, even if she's been away. Things will work out fine."

"I wouldn't count on it," said Housekeeper. "She's also a Christian."

Yuki dropped a dumpling. She hadn't known this.

"Are you sure?" Cook asked.

"She wears a wooden cross. Apparently, the master doesn't mind, but I do. My uncle tells me Christians eat human flesh and blood." Housekeeper huffed. "Foreign religion, foreign learning . . . who knows what cursed thing she'll bring here."

At those words, Yuki remembered a brass-studded trunk among her stepmother's belongings. The foreign domed chest had struck her as curious when the porters brought it yesterday. Now she wondered: *What if it contains human flesh?*

Her hands fisted. If that woman had brought something sinister, Yuki was going to expose her.

Fortunately, Stepmother was visiting a neighbor while Father was on a military inspection. Not a soul saw Yuki slip into her stepmother's quarters.

Boxes and bundles cluttered the tatami mat. Yuki's eyes narrowed. These rooms were once her mother's. Everything from the cushions on the floor to the scrolls on the wall had remained unchanged since her passing—until Stepmother arrived. The sight of the invader's things scattered over her mother's lacquer dressing table made Yuki burn. Spotting the brass-studded chest, she flounced over and threw open the lid.

Yuki frowned. Foreign books filled the trunk. Though relieved it didn't hold vials of blood, she couldn't help feeling disappointed. Getting rid of her stepmother would've been easier if it had. She lifted a book in hopes of finding something incriminating and glimpsed a leather-bound case beneath. Instantly suspicious, she opened it.

Her breath caught. Resting on a scarlet plush lining was a mirror. One unlike any she'd seen.

An impossibly perfect image of her face reflected back. Yuki's own mirrors were the best in Japan, of the finest polished bronze, but this was like gazing upon a twin. The oval surface captured every detail with clarity, from the luster of her jade hair ornament to the rosy tint of her lips.

"Magic," she murmured. It was the only explanation.

A warning clamored inside her head. If Stepmother possessed an enchanted object, who knew what else Yuki might encounter? It was best to withdraw until she obtained a protective charm against evil spells.

Yet Yuki lingered, captivated by her reflection. For once she could truly admire her complexion, fair as the snow for which she was named. Vanity outweighed prudence, and she lifted the mirror from its case. *Just a little while—*

"Mistress, welcome home."

Yuki jumped at the chorus of greetings coming from the front gate. Stepmother was back. The girl hastened to return the mirror to its case, but it slipped from her grasp and shattered against the trunk lid.

Fear sliced through her. She reached to put the mirror back together, but the shards bit her skin.

Footsteps thudded down the corridor. Yuki's eyes darted from her bleeding fingers to the broken pieces. She couldn't hide what she'd done, had neither Father nor talisman to protect her.

Yuki fled out the garden door.

She raced through the rows of pruned shrubs. Escaping out the main gate was too risky. That left the gate at the back of the estate. But her father had warned her never to use it because evil spirits and monsters often lurked in the woods beyond.

With the threat of her stepmother's wrath looming, Yuki decided to take her chances.

She burst through the rear gate and into the forest. Branches scratched her skin. Burrs snagged her socks. Over the next ridge was a footpath to town, and Yuki ran through the trees, frantic to get to the path and to safety.

However, the terrain was steep, and her silk kimono heavy. Yuki quickly tired, and her panicked flight turned into a stumbling walk. Spotting an old well, the exhausted girl leaned against its stone rim to catch her breath—

"Young mistress!"

Climbing up the slope were the gardeners. And behind them, her stepmother.

Yuki turned to run, but as she pushed off the rim, the crumbling stone collapsed. She lost her balance and fell into the well, screaming.

She landed with a thud. Moments passed as she lay stunned. Then she pushed herself up, desperate to climb out before her stepmother reached her.

But when her head lifted, she saw not earthen walls but metal bars.

Yuki's eyes went wide. She was in an iron cage suspended from the ceiling of an immense room. It had walls of stone and a single bronze door high as a tower. Nearby hung six other cages. Four were empty;

the others contained a deer and a bear. As she stared, light flashed in an empty cage, and a ram materialized inside.

Terror iced her veins. She'd heard tales of such magical traps. Hidden in caves and holes, they snatched victims from the human world and into the realm of the—

The bronze door slammed open. Yuki almost fainted.

Seven oni—huge blue-skinned ogres—tramped inside. Their eyes bulged, and crooked horns poked out of their shaggy hair. The reek of rotting flesh filled Yuki's nostrils.

An oni headed for the cage with the bear. The animal roared, but the oni snickered. Opening the cage, he popped the bear whole into his mouth. Two others did the same with the deer and ram. Yuki's stomach turned at the crunch of bones.

"Lucky day!"

An oni with a wart on his nose thrust his face against Yuki's cage. As she gagged from his breath, his companions cried out.

"A human!"

"Been ages since anyone caught one."

"Share! Share!"

"No," said Wart. "My cage, my dinner."

This is the end. Yuki's eyes squeezed shut.

"Huh?" The cage rattled. "It's stuck." The shaking increased, sending Yuki tumbling.

"Let me see."

The quaking stopped. Yuki looked up to find the biggest, ugliest oni studying the cage door. A golden glow surrounded the latch. When he poked it, sparks burst out. His bloodshot eyes shifted to her.

"What is it, Boss?" said Wart.

Boss snorted. "Spirit's jamming the door. Someone's intervening for her."

Wart stomped angrily. "I don't believe this!"

"Settle down." Boss squinted at the latch. "Whoever it is will fall asleep sooner or later, and the Spirit will go away. Then you can eat her."

Wart sneered. "Hear that, Dinner? You have an appointment with my stomach real soon." The seven oni guffawed and left the room, slamming the door behind them.

For a long time, Yuki sat stunned. Then she burst into tears. She'd been momentarily spared, but her fate was sealed.

I'm going to die. Despair gripped her, and she cried herself to sleep.

Yuki dreamed.

A vision of the old well appeared. Night had fallen. Torches illuminated the remnants of stone rim bordering the yawning hole that had swallowed Yuki. The slumbering forms of her father and servants lay nearby, and kneeling with hands lifted was her stepmother.

"Father!" Yuki cried.

He didn't stir, but Stepmother looked around in confusion. "Yuki?"

"Yes!" said Yuki, thrilled her voice had reached someone. "I'm trapped in the Realm of the Oni!" She quickly explained what happened and pleaded, "Please, use your magic to bring me back!"

"Magic?" Stepmother blinked. "I have no magic."

"But your mirror was enchanted. I saw—"

Stepmother shook her head. "That mirror was not magic but glass. A substance made by ordinary men." Sorrow filled her eyes. "I'm sorry. If I could, I would bring you back this instant. All I can do is pray for your protection and return."

Understanding flashed in Yuki's mind. Her stepmother was the one the oni complained of. As long as she prayed, Yuki was safe, but . . .

Yuki glanced at those asleep by the well. Even the most resolute eventually succumbed to exhaustion.

As if reading Yuki's thoughts, Stepmother said, "Have faith. God has protected you this far. I believe he will provide a way home."

"Then until he does, keep praying for me," Yuki begged. "Don't stop, not even an instant. Otherwise, the oni . . . they'll . . . "

"I will," said Stepmother firmly. "With all my strength."

Hope flickered in Yuki's heart. "Thank you, Stepmother," she said and woke.

Her stomach growled. Yesterday, she'd been too despondent for hunger. Her body now reminded her she needed food for strength. Fortunately, she had the dumplings in her sleeve. After eating a bit of mochi, she looked for escape.

A careful inspection revealed that the Spirit her stepmother sent kept the oni out but also kept Yuki in. She tugged the bars and stomped the floor, hoping to trigger a way back home. Meanwhile, the other traps filled with prey. Throughout the day, light would flash, and a new victim appear. But neither the tiger's brawn, nor the boar's tusks, nor the hare's frantic scratching could free them.

Finally, a horse appeared in the last cage. Unlike the others, it lay noiselessly. As Yuki studied it, there was another flash, and the horse disappeared.

Her hopes soared. *There is a way—*

"Hello, Dinner!" Wart shouted.

The seven oni burst inside. As before, each went to devour the contents of his cage. Wart scowled at the glowing latch. "Your meddling friend's a stubborn one. But I can wait, and you've no way out."

"Liar!" Yuki cried. "There is a way! I saw! And I'll figure it out!"

The oni erupted into laughter. "What exactly did you see?" Boss asked, tapping Yuki's cage. "Let me guess, prey that came and disappeared again?"

"I . . . " the girl faltered.

"Listen, Little Snack, we oni may look tough, but we're actually quite sensitive, and the only food our delicate stomachs can handle is living flesh."

Yuki gulped.

"Dead prey don't do us any good so our traps only bring live ones. And if the breath of life goes out before we get it . . . " Boss flicked a finger. "Back it goes where it came from."

"So the cage'll definitely send you home. If you die." Wart cackled. "But don't worry. I'll get you before that happens."

Yuki's spirits plummeted. They sank further when she saw her step-mother in her dreams that night. Dark circles lined the woman's eyes. Yuki doubted she could last another night. Overwhelmed by despair, she wailed, "There's no way out! He's going to eat me!"

"You're still alive so there's still hope," said Stepmother. "What happened?"

Between sobs, Yuki related what the oni had said. Stepmother's face grew grave.

That's it, Yuki thought. *I'm lost.*

"Yuki." Stepmother's voice shook. "I have an idea. But it may not work."

When Yuki awoke, she paced her cage, racking her brain. After hearing her stepmother's plan, she was desperate to think of another way. But despite her efforts, nothing came to mind.

Finally, Yuki halted, staring at the fading glow of the latch. *What other choice is there?*

Death hovered over her, but Stepmother's plan offered a tiny chance at life.

Still, Yuki hesitated. She'd have to trust her stepmother, but that wasn't why doubt paralyzed her. What Yuki didn't know was if she had the courage to do her own part.

Her hand crept to her neck as she recalled her mother's last moments, Yuki's one exposure to death. She had only been three but remembered clearly how her mother choked to her end. Would being eaten by Wart be as awful?

Clomping jolted Yuki from her thoughts. The oni were coming. The latch's glow was nearly gone.

Now! There's no more time! Yuki seized the last three dumplings from her sleeve and crammed them into her mouth. The mochi stuck to her tongue and palate like glue. The sensation made her want to gag, but she steeled her nerve and swallowed.

The doughy mass wedged into her windpipe. Her lungs seized, burning as if set ablaze. Instinct screamed for her to tear the mochi out, but she forced her arms at her sides. As she collapsed in agony, howls and curses filled her ears. The cage pitched, then everything went dark.

Air. Light.

"Yuki!" Her father embraced her with tears of joy. "You're back!"

Yuki's throat was raw and her body weak, but she'd returned alive. As Father helped her sit up, Yuki saw bits of mochi on the ground and her stepmother, pale and breathless, leaning against the housekeeper.

"Oh, I'm so glad!" Housekeeper sobbed as she supported her panting mistress. "She kept saying you'd be back, and suddenly you were, but you weren't breathing, and she—she *breathed* you back to life. With her own mouth! I've never seen anything like it!"

Stepmother smiled. "Hope won."

Yuki's heart clenched. Gently pushing Father aside, she fell facedown before her stepmother. "You saved me. My life is yours."

Stepmother tilted the girl's chin up. "I'd rather be your family."

Yuki returned her smile. "You already are."

S. Q. Eries lives with her husband of fourteen years in Silicon Valley where she writes book reviews for The Fandom Post website and young adult fiction. Prior to moving to Northern California, the couple lived in Los Angeles for ten years, and she is forever grateful the Holy Spirit connected them to the community known as Mosaic (mosaic.org), which continues to be their Southern California tribe and source of inspiration. "Yuki and the Seven Oni" is her sixth short story. For more about S. Q. Eries and her writing, drop by her blog: sqeries.wordpress.com.

A Recipe for Rain and Rainbows

Beth Cato

THE WHOLE TOWN showed up for the big June picnic. While Esther went off and played all those little kid games, I helped Mama mind her table.

My Mama made the best pies in the whole valley, maybe the whole world. She made every kind imaginable, all except pecan 'cause Esther was allergic. Mind you, her regular food was better than most, too, but her pies were really something special. She won the top prize at the county fair two years in a row until she stopped entering. It wasn't fair to the other bakers, she said.

All of the pies sat in tidy white boxes with Mama's delicate writing labeling the top. Next to us the other ladies sold lots of lemonade at a steep price. The entire proceeds from the picnic went to the Doctorow Mine Widows' Association. Most everybody's husband or father worked up the mountain, and most all the women were afraid to become members of the club. Mama always did her part to help. Those ladies' casseroles kept us alive after Pa and Me-Maw died.

Mrs. Patrick stepped up to the table, hesitating. "I think I'll get buttermilk pie," she said.

Mama shook her head. "Amelia. You know you want apple cinnamon."

Mrs. Patrick's eyes filled with tears. "That was Seth's favorite. You know yesterday was . . . "

"I know." And she did, too. A box already had "Amelia Patrick" written on it.

"You always know what's right," Mrs. Patrick whispered, pushing the dollars across the table. "The kids will like that. Maybe they can think of their big brother and not drive so careless on the highway."

I eyed Mama. They certainly would think of their brother, but not of his death. Even Mama's saddest-made pies weren't a mean sort of sadness. For me, they brought on the tightness of Pa's hugs and the way his shirt buttons had gaped on his big round belly and how his favorite chair stayed empty.

Mama smiled, watching Mrs. Patrick walk away. Mama was most always happy when she baked, and her pies made people feel that way, too. She called it empathy, sowing her feelings into the dough and fruit, making them taste the rain and the rainbows.

"Well, well," said a man's voice. I jerked up my head.

Mr. Reginald Yates was as old as Methuselah with a wild, wiry beard and skin as creased and dirty as an old wooden fencepost. Mama warned us to stay away from him ever since he got out of jail back at Christmastime. He lived down in the hollow on the far side of the valley. Mama's friend Miss Catherine said that was the closest a person could get to hell without moving to Yankee territory.

With sly fingers, Mama whisked the money box behind her back and to me. I hid it behind the stack of boxes.

"I want to buy a pecan pie," he said.

"I don't sell pecan pies." Mama met his steely gaze.

Sensing trouble, one of the lemonade ladies set off at a fast waddle towards where the sheriff's department had their dunk tank on the park's far side.

"Why can't I have my pie?" growled Mr. Yates.

"My Esther is allergic," said Mama.

"But I'm willing to buy," he said, then lowered his voice so only me and Mama were close enough to hear. "I've had my eye on you since your blue ribbon fair days. I know something's going on in those pies. I want a cut."

Mama recoiled. "Whatever do you mean?"

"It's marijuana, ain't it? I can keep it quiet, if, you know." He rubbed his fingers together.

"Mr. Yates." Mama's tone turned to ice. "I would never use any ingredient so vulgar. Leave this table at once."

"Or what?" He glanced at me, and then frowned and looked at the pie boxes. "If that's not the secret, what is?"

"It's not for you to know," she said. "I shudder to think about the kinds of thoughts that would make you happy."

I sucked in a breath. Never had I heard Mama so blatantly mention her special touch. Once, Esther said Mama's pies were magic, and Me-Maw told her to never say such a thing 'cause folks would talk, even if it was true. Me-Maw knew because she had the gift, too, and her mama before that. Mama said in a few years I could bake, and then I'd be a grown woman.

Mr. Yates's face turned a funny shade of red. "Why—"

"Reginald Yates." Three deputies stood behind him, two of them in long swim trunks with blotchy white sun block all over their bodies. The speaker, however, was fully dressed. "You causing a problem?"

"Ain't I always?" said Mr. Yates in a drawl. He gave Mama a pointed glare. "I still want my pie."

He turned and stalked off.

"Ma'am, I'm sorry about that," said the deputy. "We would have been here sooner, but . . . "

Mama waved her hand. "It's all right. He's gone now."

He frowned, fingering the bold buckle on his belt. "Well then, I may as well ask while I'm here. You got any strawberry left?"

———

Thank goodness the next morning I was the one who went out first to water the flowers. Pecans covered our whole porch. Mama made sure all the windows were shut and Esther's medication was handy. She called up the sheriff and the deputy that came said at most they could charge Mr. Yates with mischief.

We could hear them through the thin walls. "My girl is fiercely allergic," Mama said. I could almost see her puffing up like a hen.

"Tell you what. We'll clean it all up and wash the porch down for you, will that help?" he said.

"Mama's going to get all riled up," I whispered. "I hope she doesn't bake anything."

"She knows better," said Esther. She pressed her chin against her knees, her brown hair flopping down like a dog's long ears. "I just wanna go to school. The last week is all fun stuff and now I gotta miss out."

The next morning, Mama went out first to make sure it was okay. Me and Esther slurped up our cereal.

When Mama came in, her face was as white as if it'd been bleached.

"Mama!" I said, jumping out of my chair. "What's wrong?"

She held out her hand. From it dangled a shiny black stone on a hemp cord.

"Oh, no. Mama." I staggered to lean on the counter.

Esther looked between us. "What is it?" she asked.

Mama bit her lip and took a steadying breath. "It's the necklace we buried your Me-Maw in," she said.

"Then why's it here?" For a nine-year-old, she could surely be dense, but maybe that was good at a time like that.

"Why would he do something like this?" I asked. "It just doesn't make sense. All he wanted was a pie, why—"

"It's not just a pie to a man like that," said Mama. "It's control and anger and spite. He thinks he's being denied something, that he can push us around."

"I still don't get why Me-Maw's necklace—" Esther began.

"Ruth, get your sister ready for school," Mama said, then stopped. Her gaze focused on the aluminum pie plates stacked on the counter.

"Mama," I said softly. Anything she baked now would taste of sorrow and salty tears and Pa's funeral, but we'd still feel the compulsion to eat up every last crumb and relive every miserable thought.

She lifted her head and stared through me. "No. You girls are missing school again this morning. We're going to do a different sort of project. We need to teach Mr. Yates a lesson."

"But Mama, today is movie day and—"

"Esther." Mama wasn't in a mood for any whining. She fumbled through a drawer and found a notepad and a few pens. "You two girls are going downtown to ask everyone their thoughts and memories of Mr. Yates."

"Mama, you should really call the sheriff again," I said.

"This is beyond the sheriff." Something dark sparkled in her eyes. "I'm going to bake Mr. Yates a pecan pie."

A shiver traveled up my spine. For the first time in my life, I was scared of Mama.

When we were all done walking down Main Street, I left Esther at Miss Catherine's house in case Mama still had pecans out.

I expected the pie to be all done and ready, but Mama sat at the kitchen table, her head in her hands. The pie ingredients covered the counter.

"Here, Mama," I said and held out the paper pad.

Wet eyes peeked between her fingers. "I don't know about this, Ruth Annabelle," she mumbled. "I want to do this, I want him to feel . . . " She balled her fists, then got a funny look on her face. "Do you still forgive Derrick Johnston for running over Sprinkles?"

Well, that came out of the blue. "He didn't mean to hit Sprinkles, Mama, and we all know Sprinkles was the dumbest cat ever. Derrick was awful upset about it."

Mama studied me for a moment. "I can't stand to look at that boy, knowing how you cried over that cat." She sucked in a deep breath. "Maybe it's time for you to make your first pie."

My jaw dropped somewhere below the table. "You mean I mix it all myself?" I asked, almost squealing like Esther. "Not waiting at the table or in the living room?"

"Not this time." A soft smile warmed her face. "You're my sensible girl. It's time to see if you have the gift."

She stood behind me, her long arms overlapping mine. "Think on Reginald Yates, how he must have desecrated Me-Maw, how he wanted to sicken Esther."

The anger welled up in me like a tight red ball, a clenched fist.

I began assembling the pie crust ingredients. Shortening, butter, salt, cold water.

"Now think on everything you wrote down from your walk in town, Ruth. You mix with your fingers. I'll read." She set her reading glasses on. "Reginald Yates was a devil from the time he was a boy. It was his ma and pa's fault, treating him like a do-nothing, so that's what he grew up to be, a do-nothing."

The tightness inside me loosened, dripping like a bloodied nose. Every push and knead of my hands, I felt more droplets fall. Mama read on.

"I think he stole three lawnmowers from the front of my store. I reported it, but they never busted him. Then he had the nerve to come in two days later and buy extra gas cans. He smirked. I could have slugged him."

The dough was done, pressed into an aluminum pie plate. Without speaking, Mama motioned to the contents of the pie, all the syrup and pecans.

The old oven preheated, clicking and creaking.

"My daughter said he did stuff to her, but there wasn't no proof, and after that she went to live with her daddy down south and I wonder if that's why. I miss her so much. That Yates should never have been born."

Never been born.

A waste of humanity.

A drug addict, a molester, a sorry excuse for a man.

The pie slid into the oven and the door slammed shut, and all around me the world throbbed and wavered like I was in the oven, too.

He dug up Me-Maw to steal her necklace, all to spite Mama.

He tried to sicken Esther. Ran down puppies and laughed about it. Set the high school on fire.

Never should have been born.

Then, like a yellow flash of lightning, it was gone. The anger, the rage, the frustration at Mr. Yates causing so much grief for so many people.

Mama caught me against her shoulder.

"I want to hate him, Mama, but I can't, I can't," I said, sobbing. "He never had a chance. He's awful and he's mean, and I feel so sorry for him."

"Oh, Ruthie," she said, holding me there. Here I was supposed to be a woman at last, baking the magic in, and instead I soaked her shoulder through.

I didn't want my first pie tasting of sadness and anger and the hatred of twenty folks from downtown. I felt those final drops deep inside me, so deep it's like I had to hold my soul upside down to find them, and let them fall.

Peace crept over me like a rare snowy Christmas day, all cozy and perfect.

An hour later, the pie sat cooling on a rack. Mama was on the phone with Miss Catherine, asking her to watch Esther a few hours more. I figured my sister wouldn't be whining about missing movie day at school anymore, not after playing at Miss Catherine's house with her boys' load of video games and three puppies.

I heard the piece of crust hit the counter, but really, I felt it. It jarred me like a train coming down the tracks. Watching Mama out one corner of my eye, I reached over and grabbed the chunk the size of my thumbnail. Without giving it a thought, I stuck the piece in my mouth.

The crust could have tasted of bitterness, of a father yelling, and tangy bloody noses and playground dirt and rank prison laundry and everything Mr. Yates had lived through. Instead, the flakiness melted on my tongue and into something more. It wasn't the happy memories of Mama's pies. Instead, it tasted like the frozen lasagnas the mine ladies brought over after Me-Maw died, how the old hymns resonated through my chest during Sunday services, the harsh drumming of rain on the old roof right after the leaks were fixed.

It tasted like neighborliness, comfort, security. Hope.

The phone shut off. "We'll give the pie another two hours to cool and then we'll run it over to Mr. Yates's house," said Mama. Her voice lowered. "I'm proud of you, Ruth. If I had made that pie, he would have been dead and on the floor in his first bite. All I can think of is my mama . . . Lord, I still need to report that to the sheriff, but I'm afraid to know the truth."

"He's still going to think we poisoned it, Mama," I said. My voice sounded strange and ancient to my own ears. "He never could trust a person, ever, and he had reasons. I don't know if he's ready for this sort of pie."

Mama nodded and laid her dishwater-wrinkled hand on my shoulder. "That's his choice then, Ruth."

I leaned against her hand. The warmth of her wedding band pressed against my ear.

"And we'll give him that choice and leave the rest to the sheriff," I said. "Your pies should always taste like rainbows."

"Can't have rainbows without the rain," she whispered, and I knew she was thinking of Pa and Me-Maw, 'cause I was thinking of them, too.

Beth Cato is the author of the *Clockwork Dagger* series from Harper Voyager, which includes her Nebula-nominated novella *Wings of Sorrow and Bone*. Her newest novel is *Breath of Earth*. She's a Hanford, California native transplanted to the Arizona desert, where she lives with her husband, son, and requisite cat. Follow her at BethCato.com and on Twitter @BethCato. For "A Recipe for Rain and Rainbows," Beth says she drew on her southern roots and her family's deep affection for pie. As a baker, she can't help but feel that there is something inherently magical about the pie-making process.

This Far Gethsemane

G. Scott Huggins

THE SOUNDS OF Caansu's evening hymn died away, lost in the distant noise of the surf. Shoshanna looked up from her medkit as her friend's final words reached her:

"Still be my vision, thou Ruler of All."

Silhouetted against the bruised shades of the sky, Caansu reached up and broke the cake she held. Shoshanna's own hands moved, finding by long practice her enzyme and vitamin tablets. She dry-swallowed them.

I hope Caansu's bread tastes better than this. Caansu lifted a tiny cup. She claimed it was wine. Shoshanna didn't know if she meant actual Earth wine or some Aasrai equivalent. Surely the latter. And she must be nearly out.

And she may never taste it again, anyway.

Shoshanna put the medkit back in her tent.

If only that damned storm hadn't struck!

Her communion complete, Caansu strode into the firelight, the color of bluegrass at dusk. Covered with fine scales from head to massive feet, her mouth was set in a permanent grin, showing dagger-like teeth. Her eyes were the orange of the dim sun, with pupils shaped like crosshairs. Webbed feet and hands with dual opposable thumbs completed her. Yet after half a Terran year on the island, Shoshanna found her a welcome sight. Or would have, were it not for the yellow traceries that spread out over her ribcage like a malignance.

"Singing to the ocean?" Shoshanna smiled, forcing away her unease.

"To the One who made the oceans," Caansu answered warmly.

"The sun rises."

Shoshanna stiffened at the voice behind her. Though she'd heard it as often as Caansu's, Aiierra's voice always sounded harsher, more Human.

"It looks like dusk to me." Caansu's warm hum emanated from the outer tympanum on her throat, as if she were still singing.

Aiierra's derisive bark made Shoshanna turn. Except for the fact that Aiierra was a bit smaller, and that the saffron traceries on her chest were only as wide across as a small dinner plate, the two Shrii were identical.

When we made shore, Aiierra had only a greenish spot on her chest, almost invisible. And Caansu's yellowing was only a tiny, barred spiral. But now . . .

New branches of yellow had formed since yesterday on both of them.

Aiierra met her gaze. "The sun rises, child," she continued, looking at Caansu. "Even the alien sees it. Must she explain it to you?"

Shoshanna shuddered. She could indeed explain it. Had tried to explain that, and more, to Caansu. She felt sick. The traceries on the bodies of the Shrii spread as the sun rose in the ecliptic toward Midsummer.

The Time of Rii or Not At All. Matingdeath.

Caansu did not accept the invitation to argue. "Then Shoshanna sees well. She has learned much while here."

Aiierra crouched. "And I have not?" Her hands whipped up, slashing claws out.

"What could you learn? Nothing on this voyage has challenged your skills or knowledge. As our handiwork suggests." Caansu gestured toward the stacks of *vsheera* pelts around the camp, barely lit by the fire.

Of course, "our handiwork" also confirms that we have nothing better to do than to continue working or go mad, Shoshanna added mentally. A week ago—was it only a week?—they had begun to watch for the red sail of the ship Caansu's Mother would send to collect them and their harvest. Then had come the storm—and in the morning, fragments of mast and red canvas tossed in the surf.

On Aasra, where sails were cutting-edge technology, it would be weeks before another came.

Aiierra growled at the soft answer and ducked beneath her lean-to. Weeks would be too late.

"Do not be afraid. Aiierra will not hurt you, in any case."

Shoshanna sighed. "Do you think I'm only worried about that?"

"Are you not?"

The hurt Shoshanna felt flowed out in raw tones. "How can you ask me that?"

"Forgive me." Caansu's voice was soft. "I know you feel concern for me, my friend. But you must be worried. Who will watch over you at night while Aiierra is in the Change? Who will help if you are wounded or sick? And what will happen if no ship comes, and you run out of the supplements you need to stay alive on our world?"

Shoshanna nodded, guilty tears starting from her eyes. Finally she said, "Aiierra said that—that as a Mother, she could do all of that. Better than you could."

Something flashed behind Caansu's eyes, but vanished in an instant. "She may be right. Certainly after the Mother Change, she will be a better companion for you. But she overestimates its power. She may gain a new appreciation for sailing—and of course, she navigates brilliantly—but Mother Change cannot teach her all I know as a pilot. It must frighten you."

Shoshanna almost nodded. The thought of Aiierra as a Mother, a two-and-a-half-meter mountain of horn and bone, even more taciturn than she was now . . . she pushed the image aside.

"But what about you?"

Caansu nodded once. "I know where I am going."

"But you—"

"And," Caansu continued, cracking her teeth in a Shrii smile, "at present I am going to bed. No, do not be offended. We will speak again about the essential nature of things before the end. But for now, it being your watch, I will say good night, my friend."

Shoshanna blushed, frustrated. "Good night, Caansu."

Caansu dropped into her own lean-to, leaving Shoshanna looking out on black waves and the cloud-purple sky.

She dreamed that night of the dark sterility of a classroom years and light-years away.

The two Shrii, laced with blood, skins more reddish-purple than blue, filled the screen. The victor kneeling over the fallen, as if in concern.

Then, in a flash of teeth, she ripped away her victim's throat in a spray of blood.

That was the way of the Shrii and the Rii. Shoshanna had not eaten for the rest of the day.

She. Her. When had Shoshanna begun thinking of the Shrii as female? It had been easy to do. The Shrii had only one personal pronoun. It seemed natural to translate it in her head as "she." But that was an illusion of Shoshanna's own thoughts. Every Shrii bore a single gonad in her throat, between spinal column and trachea. Every Shrii knew that she would one day face the matingdeath: the Time of Rii or Not At All. The victor would bite the gonad from her victim's throat. It would combine with the victor's own, and send zygotes regularly into the womb of the new Rii, or Mother, whose genes would be dominant in the next generation. The female pronoun was, in a way, appropriate. There were no Shrii males. To be male was to be dead. To be Not At All.

Shoshanna awoke with a start, the orange glow of Procyon well up, her mind racing. In weeks—maybe only days—Caansu would be Not At All. *It's just wrong. This won't be a matingdeath, it'll be mating*murder.

Neither of the Shrii was in camp. Was that where they were? Ending it?

No, it wasn't quite time yet. And Caansu had promised they would speak again. There was only one thing she could try. Convince Aiierra to hold off.

Though she did not move with the slow grace or the instinct of the carnivores, Shoshanna had learned to move quietly. She picked up her staff and jogged into the brush. It was time to speak to Aiierra, and if she was not in camp, she was probably on Hair Dome.

Shoshanna wore her own hair in a braided loop: a russet necklace fastened back upon itself. The Shrii thought hair was ridiculous, something to get caught by branches and thorns. It was Aiierra who had named the prime trapping spot on the island Hair Dome, for the long, chainlike grasses that covered it. They provided ideal grounds for grazing—and trapping—*vsheera*. Aiierra's small camp lay within sight of the hill.

Shoshanna tried to frame what she was going to say, but found her mind wandering into what her father had called "ifonlys." Ifonly there hadn't been a storm. Ifonly the ship hadn't been wrecked. Ifonly Caansu would stand up and fight Aiierra.

If only the damned missionaries weren't here!

Christians. There *were* still Christians on Earth, of course, though they were a small minority. The days when Earth's religions had ruled Human thoughts were part of history. In her classes, Shoshanna had learned about them and the wars they had spawned, and been grateful that they were mostly things of the past. Christians on Earth had learned to keep to themselves and worship in private.

She had hardly expected to find them *here*. But their missionaries had come. And *proselytized*. She flushed darkly, ashamed.

She'd found out on their first hunt, three months ago. Gripping her sharpened stake in both hands, she'd been focusing on her job: killer. She'd forced her stomach to calm. Aiierra and Caansu would stalk and trap the *vsheera* herds. Then they would stab and throw the dog-sized animals toward her with their long, serrated tridents. Her job was to finish off the already dying beasts so they didn't get up and run off before collapsing. It was a job for young Shrii, and all she could handle.

Much to her shock, they had been able to talk freely, even within sight of the prey.

"They're deaf," Caansu had explained, her voice shockingly loud. "If they weren't, we could simply Call them." Shoshanna nodded. Their first night on the island, Aiierra had caught dinner simply by screaming at a plump bird fifty meters up. It had dropped without a twitch.

But *vsheera* were immune. And rare, confined to these islands. And no one had ever studied how Shrii hunted them before. Shoshanna would get her doctorate out of it.

"Stay still," Aiierra had grunted. She and Caansu continued toward the brownish beasts, their scales blending with the forest, unseen by the large-eyed, low-slung prey.

Then Shoshanna had heard Caansu whispering, the low words carrying in the stillness.

"Our Father, Who is in Heaven, Your Name be forever Holy,

May Your Empire come, and Your Will be done."

Aiierra shot Caansu a look. "Her Will won't save you from me," she spat.

Caansu returned Aiierra's hostile gaze and continued: "Give us this day our daily meat . . . now!"

As if nothing had been said, the Shrii leapt. Shoshanna's thoughts were cut off by a *vsheera* flying toward her head. She ducked, turning on the flopping thing. She yanked her ankle away from a huge pair of teeth, no less sharp for being herbivorous. Her spear crunched through fur, muscle and bone and she turned toward the sound of the next wounded beast landing by her side. She had killed, and killed, the animals blurring together, piling up.

In the end, only one had gotten away. Aiierra had looked disgusted with her.

Sitting with Caansu that night at the fire, Shoshanna had opened their first discussion on what Caansu called "the essential nature of things" by asking where Caansu had learned the Christian prayer. The answer had horrified her.

"You can't honestly believe in a Human god?" she had finally asked.

"No. The Father is not Human. But She made Humans and She made Shrii and Rii."

Shoshanna would have smiled at the inconsistency in pronouns, but wasn't in the mood.

"Then why didn't our Jesus come to you as well?"

"I do not know. Perhaps God wished us to trust the Word that was given to you. Or perhaps God's Child has simply not come to us yet. There are the Calhyail among us, and the followers of Eir'on. Both prophesy a Messenger to come from God."

"Then why not follow one of them?"

"Which?"

Shoshanna had no answer to that.

"No teachers of our people promise what Christ promises. If we know we sin, how can we but follow One who promises forgiveness? To shun true religion because it is not 'ours' would be as foolish as shunning true science because you Humans brought it to us."

"So you follow the Human Christ until your own Messiah comes?"

"Yes."

"And when he does?"

"I pray I have the wisdom to recognize Her."

Shoshanna had been completely unaware that any aliens had ever converted to Human religions. How did it impact their laws? Their ethics? It was then that the question occurred.

"Caansu, what happens at the time of matingdeath? Do you choose another Christian? Or do you choose an unbeliever?"

"We do not accept the combat. We hide." There had been a pause. "Or we die."

"You don't ever become Mothers?"

"Never. It is against the Lord's teachings to kill."

"But it's your life!"

"It is our soul. Which is greater?"

Shoshanna had been struck dumb by the heartless demands of this religion. Now she understood Aiierra's anger. Finally, she stammered, "But that means, if enough Shrii and Rii become Christian, wouldn't that mean your whole race would die?"

Caansu had laughed. "Yes, and if there were no more hungry, we could not obey the Lord's command to feed them. I think this is a problem we are unlikely to face."

Shoshanna's gaze had wandered to Caansu's chest with its tiny streak of yellow. "You won't . . . "

"No, never fear," Caansu had said. "We will have returned long before the time of matingdeath."

But they had not, and the sweat that broke out on Shoshanna's forehead as she came out of the trees around Hair Dome had nothing to do with heat or exertion. She started around the hill. She could cross it and rely on her staff to find Aiierra's *theleaa* traps, but a few minutes of running brought her safely around the clearing. She reminded herself to slow as she approached. Aiierra disapproved of Human running. It scared game. *Or,* Shoshanna thought, *because the Shrii can't do it, with those massive legs. They hardly need to with their stun-cry and lightning reflexes.* Shrii were quick, but not fast. They could stride across the ground at the speed of a jogging Human and never get tired.

Shoshanna wanted Aiierra receptive, not upset, so she walked up to Aiierra's trapping shack. Empty. She knew that her chances of tracking Aiierra anywhere were slim. She was no hunter. But she had to talk to Aiierra, to make her see.

See what? That millions of years of evolution and thousands of years of culture should be set aside for some random Human religious text?

Just then, a piercing, two-toned wail rang through the forest. Aiierra's hunting call. It *was* starting! Shoshanna ran blindly ahead, knowing that it would be far too late to do anything by the time she got there, but she had to do something.

The cry sounded again. Not a hunting cry. The tone was different. *Distress.*

For an instant, a bloom of savage joy shot through her. Aiierra was in trouble. If the trouble was sufficiently severe, then—perhaps there was no need to hurry after all. Perhaps Caansu could survive because of a little—how would she put it—divine intervention? All divine and none at all Human. Shoshanna could see to that.

But then she groaned. Because Caansu wouldn't call it that. Caansu must have heard Aiierra's cry too, which meant she was probably already on her way to help. *And if she knew what I was thinking, she'd be ashamed of me.*

Damning Caansu, her God, and the missionaries, Shoshanna forced herself into a sprint.

I am not ashamed, she told herself. *Anyone would have thought of it. But the thought of Caansu mad at me . . .* She was pretty sure that Caansu considered anger to be literally sacrilegious. But she didn't want to take the chance. Caansu was the closest thing to a friend that Shoshanna had on this planet.

Aiierra's cry sounded again, very close: "Sh - o - sh - a - n - n - a!"

Why call *her* name? She turned toward the call and burst into a tiny hollow. Aiierra was looking straight at her, fairly dancing with tension. She was alone.

"Aiierra?" What was happening?

"Look." Aiierra pointed to a dense cluster of brush.

Shoshanna blinked. Aiierra wasn't fidgeting. She was trembling.

"What is it?"

"Look!" Aiierra's teeth were bared.

Almost trembling herself, Shoshanna bent to see through the dense foliage.

In the middle of it lay Caansu, facedown in the soft soil, on a pile of decaying bones.

"Caansu?" There was no response.

"Caansu, get up. Say something!" She whirled on Aiierra. "What have you done?"

"Suro jova."

It took a moment for the words to sink in, but when they did, Shoshanna turned back to the brushy pit. Caansu's flesh was dotted with tiny purplish warts, no larger than a fingertip. They oozed slime from their bases. One moved slightly as she watched.

The slime was dissolving Caansu's scales. Soon, it would start on the flesh beneath.

"Well, what are you doing just standing there?" she cried. "Help me—"

"I c-cannot!" The speaking membrane on Aiierra's throat had expanded like an angry sore, ready to burst with shame and frustration. Shoshanna felt herself flush as well. *Of course she can't help.* Shoshanna's mouth went dry, but she steeled herself, not daring to think, stretching her arms out to grab quickly.

Suro jova, like the Shrii themselves, used sound to bring down their prey. Infrasonic. Now Shoshanna felt the higher pitches: a faint throbbing in her skull. To any higher animal on Aasra, the edges of that call were a subconscious lure. The animal simply felt *right* moving towards it. Shrii working in the wilderness learned to be wary of places that "felt good". Closer to the source, the call paralyzed. Aiierra's muscles were already spasming. When the prey dropped, so did the *suro jova*. As they had on Caansu, crawling over their prey, slowly digesting it.

As a Human, Shoshanna was immune to the cry, but acid was acid.

She lunged, catching Caansu by the ankles and pulling. *God*, she was heavy. A soft, solid rain pattered on her back, arms and head. She heaved again. Behind her, Aiierra stumbled back.

One more heave and orange sunlight burst around her. Shoshanna straightened convulsively and began brushing at her back. Purple, warty bodies flew. Convulsively, Shoshanna removed her shirt and threw it as far as she could. Icy spots dotted her hands where the burning mucus had touched them. The ones on her hair could wait, and thank God she had never shaved her head as the Shrii had suggested. She turned to Caansu, wiping the slimy things off her friend's back. Aiierra had staggered to her feet again. Now she could approach.

"Camp. Now. Get arms." Reeling under the weight, Shoshanna managed to get her back under Caansu's left armpit, and they staggered back towards Hair Dome.

Using strands of the long, ropy grass, Shoshanna wiped the last of the blood and water off her hands and watched the *theleii* roast.

Aiierra's voice from behind would have startled her had she not been so tired. "She will be able to speak soon. She is not badly hurt, but I had to make sure all the slime was off. Unwatched, it can burn badly."

Shoshanna nodded. On her neck, shoulders and hands were coin-sized patches of tender, red skin. They felt like mild sunburn, and she'd only had them on her for a few seconds. Aiierra took one of the *theleii* off the fire, indifferent to its state of doneness. Half of it disappeared in one bite. She looked across at Shoshanna. "You. You have helped me in my need. I owe a debt. Ask of me, and I will give."

"Are you serious?"

"Do you doubt my word?"

Aiierra's face was difficult to read, but the tone was almost menacing in its seriousness. Shoshanna leapt at the opportunity. The words rushed out of her: "Do not perform the matingdeath with Caansu."

Aiierra's barking laugh lashed out, making Shoshanna jump. "I said I owed you a debt, not my future life. I will agree to no such thing. I have told you already that a Mother and a Human will be far better equipped to survive than two Children and a Human."

"That's not the point; she's my friend."

"Then you should have thought about that before you and the other Humans came from your star and spread your spineless, neutering gods around!"

"I had nothing to do with it." Shoshanna bit the words out. "Aiierra, most of *us* don't believe in her god. *I* certainly don't. I'm not suggesting that you believe it; I just want you to wait for someone else. What honor is there in killing someone who won't even fight back?"

"What has this to do with honor? There is no honor in eating, either, but it must be done."

"Then why not kill her now; get it over with?"

Aiierra's eyes narrowed. "Humans mate, so you have said, again and again, like lower animals. We only have one chance to do it right."

She stared curiously at Shoshanna, as if weighing something, and then said, "A poor matingdeath makes weak children, and I curse the fate that has brought me such. If there were a choice, I would do as you ask. But to wait until next season, to face those in their First Pattern? No. I court victory, not death. Your confidence in my skill does me honor, but I suspect that you would not care what the outcome of such a duel would be, so long as you did not have to watch." The disgust in her tones was evident even to Shoshanna.

"Aiierra, it's one thing to kill her if she agrees to fight you; it's another to kill her if she won't. It's not right!"

Aiierra snorted. "You say you do not believe in the foolishness she spouts, and now you repeat it. How is it not *right*? Did this," she waved the stripped bones of the *theleaa*, "agree to fight me so that I could eat it? Whatever can kill, kills and lives. Or dies. That is the way of the world. But Humans are not bound to kill or die in order to produce children, yes?"

Shoshanna nodded, an unreal feeling coming over her. This was the most she had ever heard Aiierra say at once.

"Then they must mean little to you." Overriding Shoshanna's incipient protest, she continued, "But if we must speak of honor and what is *right*, then *her* sense of these things, twisted as it is, exceeds yours. Truly, I wonder that she deigns to speak to you. She will die for her faith. She has told me so, and I see the truth of it. You have no beliefs worth dying or killing for. You merely fear to see blood. And I have better things to do than speak with a child." So saying, Aiierra rose, swallowing the last of the *theleaa*, and stalked off up the side of the Dome.

The sun was lower in the sky by the time Caansu emerged, walking stiffly. She stretched, nearly fell. The blackened corpse of a *theleaa* hung over the cooling embers. Without a word, Caansu stripped it and ate. Her face held no expression Shoshanna could read. Finally, she spoke.

"I heard what you asked of Aiierra." The words were carefully chosen. "I thank you for trying."

"You can't just let her kill you." Shoshanna spoke more harshly than she had intended, but Caansu made no notice. She did not respond at all. Shoshanna thought she would burst.

"Caansu, please tell me what you're thinking." Her throat ached with tension, and finally, Caansu spoke.

"I lay in that grove, trying desperately to move, and was unable." She turned an enigmatic look on Shoshanna. "It was a hard thing."

"It's going to be harder in about a month. A month if you're lucky." *A few days if you aren't.*

"Yes."

Shoshanna sprang to her feet. "Dammit, Caansu, you have to fight her. It's the way your world—the way you—are. You can't let a religion kill you like this!"

"An alien religion, you mean?"

"Any religion!"

"Our Lord did."

"Your Lord was Human; it's not the same thing."

"It *is* the same thing. Exactly the same. She faced death, and I face death, both of us for what we believe. I for a far smaller goal, but Her example serves me now, and I will submit to Her will."

Shoshanna made a face. "I'd rather die than serve that god."

"Truly?" asked Caansu.

"Truly."

"You think us fools, Shoshanna." Caansu flipped a bone into the fire, her voice as casual as if they were discussing cooking.

"I do not! I respect your people!"

Caansu nodded. "Enough to let us die as we have for millions of years."

"Is that the line the missionaries fed you? We can't interfere in your natural life cycle, or pull apart your culture to suit ourselves! We just don't know enough, and these preachers certainly don't! Dammit, think, Caansu. Don't rely on your book or what some priest-shaman told you, just because they're Human—"

"Enough." Caansu rose.

The word was softly spoken, but the absolute power that rippled from Caansu's chording of it was sufficient to freeze Shoshanna where she sat.

"Think? Do you know so little of me that you think I have not thought? Am I truly that primitive to you, Terran?" She turned away, bitterness echoing in the air. "Do you think that I have no fire in my throat, that it was cut out at birth? Do you think I can look at Aiierra without love and rage? That I have not imagined the taste of her throat between my teeth?"

She turned back and Shoshanna's breath caught as those crosshair pupils fixed themselves on her. "Do you think that I have chosen this Way because I am afraid to fight?"

Shoshanna's head was shaking no without her having consciously willed it. And she had thought that Caansu couldn't get angry.

Caansu sat then, and her eyes dimmed. "But I am afraid." Her chord trembled like a dying flute. "If not for you and Aiierra, I would be dead now. I prayed to my Father, that She would deliver me. I prayed that if She would not, She would give me courage to meet Her, unafraid. I was horribly afraid. I am still afraid. Of being wrong. Afraid of ending my line for nothing. Suppose I die and all my thought, all my faith, is worth nothing, because I didn't know enough? Suppose there really is no God?"

"Then . . . " Shoshanna made herself say the words. "Then wouldn't you be free?"

"Free as you are?" Caansu stood, her arms spread, voice rising. "What freedom is that? Freedom to see no difference between death and life?

You Humans, you refuse to 'interfere' in our world, our unhappy world where every Mother bearing children does so at the cost of taking a brother's life. I tell you now, the ghosts of a thousand *million* of my ancestors groan beneath the stars and *beg* for your interference!"

Caansu knelt, extended a claw and pointed at Shoshanna. "Had we come to your world as you came to ours, and found you dying in childbirth as you told us used to happen, in a village that lived by steel plows in mud brick houses while we descended like gods in ships powered by tamed suns, what would you have wanted of us? To let you die? Should we be free to do that? Free?" she echoed. "I hardly know what that word means." She stopped, and gazed out at the sea.

"But yes, I am afraid to die. I am afraid to let Aiierra kill me, as I must. And I am angry with my Father, that She has sent me here, and trapped me, and wrecked the ship that was to take me back to my brothers. I am angry with Her for forcing this choice upon me."

Shoshanna was speechless. Caansu angry had been enough of a shock, but Caansu angry with her God was unimaginable.

"Why do you make my choices harder and tempt me with the thing I cannot do?"

"I'm trying to help you, Caansu." The words came out shakily, gaining force. "I'm trying to help you see that it is for nothing."

"I have already chosen, Shoshanna. My faith is my life. It has been my life. If I cannot be true to it . . . " She seemed to fumble for words. "I cannot truly be myself. Whether in error or no, I will not accept your world, where everything ends in the Not At All, and there are no beliefs."

Shoshanna's eyes flooded with tears for what her people had brought to this world. *Your world. No beliefs. You have no beliefs worth dying or killing for.* Aiierra's words mocked her. She felt her insides turn hard.

"Dammit, I do so have beliefs!" Her shout even startled her. Caansu was staring. "I believe! I believe that everyone has the right to live, God or not, Human or not." She scarcely heard herself. "And if you won't see it, and she won't see it," she hefted her staff. "I'll stop her for you."

Caansu took two lumbering steps forward and then *blurred*.

Shoshanna was being driven back into the sand, a bar of iron—no, wood; her own staff?—across her throat, shutting off air, a massive knee in her stomach. The world contracted and became a single, hissing voice.

"You dare insult me so?" it went on. "You would take from me the one thing in the world I have left? How will you take it now?" Red and black spots burst in Shoshanna's brain. She gagged, but no sound came, and she knew she was going to die.

Suddenly, air rushed into her lungs and the crushing weight was gone. For long minutes, she did nothing but breathe in great gusts of air. When she finally lifted her head, it was to see Caansu kneeling in the sand some distance away. Caansu's eyes darted toward her, and over her own breathing, Shoshanna heard a low voice.

"I beg forgiveness. I forgot." She paused. "Sometimes I forget that you are not one of us. You could not have known the depth of insult you gave, and even for that, there was no excuse to try to kill you. I beg your forgiveness, Shoshanna."

Shoshanna's mind was reeling. What was she talking about? She forced herself to concentrate on the voice, the only real thing speaking to her through the pain in her neck and lungs.

"W-what," Shoshanna managed, "insult?"

Caansu looked stunned. "What . . . ?" Her eyes narrowed, then she shook her head. "You truly do not understand." She seemed to reach for words. "I have asked you to forgive me. I will also forgive you, but it is hard. Please do not mention killing Aiierra," she growled, "*for* me, again."

Shoshanna stood, the blood draining from her face. Caansu's face stared back at her, insectile and lizardlike, unapologetic and utterly alien.

I almost died. My friend almost killed me.

Like a rockslide, chaos and incomprehension crashed down on Shoshanna's mind. Weeping with terror, she fled into the forest.

It seemed to her a long time that she walked after she could no longer run, but the memory was a blur. Shoshanna came to herself on a beach below the Far Peak. There were no fish here, only the long superanemones that were a feature of coastlines all over Aasra. No one came here, except she and Caansu once, to see what was here. Her throat still hurt where the staff had been pressed against her neck.

Caansu attacked me. The words formed in her mind, and yet they made no sense. Caansu wanted to live. Caansu would let herself die. Shoshanna had offered to protect Caansu. Shoshanna had insulted Caansu terribly. Caansu had a right to live. Aiierra had a right to kill. Shoshanna had a right to . . . what?

Was she only now seeing this world for the alien thing that it was? A world where protection was insult and right was wrong and sex was death?

Sex was death. The thought echoed around her head.

Turn it around. Death was sex. She gasped.

Caansu had said not to talk about *killing* Aiierra. Shoshanna had not said *kill.* She would not be sorry if Aiierra died, of course, but she had only thought to stop her, had been speaking her feelings.

And then Caansu had spoken hers! She rubbed her throat again. And of course Caansu would assume—*No,* she corrected herself, *would* know!—that the only thing likely to "stop" Aiierra was Aiierra's death. Death was sex. Had Shoshanna just offered to sleep with Caansu's husband? Wife? No wonder Caansu had been angry. The choice of words dissolved in a sound suspiciously like hysterical laughter. There was little humor in it.

So Caansu did not want to die. And she did not want to be protected. And she did not want to fight. So she would die anyway. And Shoshanna would do nothing, because of what Caansu would think of her if she did. Aiierra's derisive grunt tore across her mind: *You have nothing worth dying or killing for.*

And she'll have to be killed to be stopped; if I'd stopped to think about it, I'd have known that.

A belief worth killing or dying for. That was what Aiierra and Caansu had.

"And what do I have?" The words were out, but she was not conscious of having said them. "What am I?" Not of the Shrii and Rii. She fingered the *vsheera* pelt that lay across her shoulders. Not the sort of clothes a Human wore. Animal-skin garments had been given up in the long distant past, along with fighting about religion and beliefs. But she was here, now. And she had tanned this skin herself, had relearned.

Now she looked out to the sea. And she spoke by choice.

"I can relearn other things."

She sat down on the beach and began to draw in the sand.

The heavy sack with its dripping burden weighed down Shoshanna's arms even after last night's rest. Carrying it across half the island had tired her, and she needed rest, but timing was everything. The path down to Aiierra's camp started just over the rise. She leaned on her staff to help her up and cursed as the newly-sharpened point slid into the soft ground.

Aiierra was there by the fire, watching Shoshanna approach. She stopped. Not too close. Her stomach twisted. This was the moment.

"You are back. Where is Caansu?"

Shoshanna fought nausea. She lifted the bag. "Here."

Aiierra's mouth parted in puzzlement. "What?"

Blood trickled through the rough canvas, dripping through the bottom of the sack. Shoshanna drew breath. "You were going to kill her anyway. I could at least see that she died without pain. This is the part of her throat you'll need."

Now Aiierra was slack-jawed in disbelief. "You have not done this," she grated.

Shoshanna stepped backwards, keeping the distance constant. Aiierra didn't quite believe. Suspicion, or incredulity? Shoshanna couldn't afford to take the risk.

"You said yourself that as a Mother you'd be better able to get us back to the mainland. But Caansu is bigger than you. If she lost control, or changed her mind and fought you, both of you might have died and then where would I be?"

Like an express train thundering into motion, Aiierra surged forward, jaws open in a killing gape. Then she Called.

Shoshanna's eyes bulged under the force of it. Twin spikes pierced her ears. She'd thought herself immune to it. It couldn't paralyze her, any more than it could fell another Shrii. Nevertheless, she staggered under the sheer force of it, dropped the bag, and ran. The wind of Aiierra's claws beat the air behind her, but she was up the slope and gone, running towards Hair Dome at a pace no Shrii could match.

Now the sunset streamed down behind her and filled Shoshanna's very being with a dull, rasping fire. Her staff clattered from her hand as she fell, tucked, and rolled down the lee face of the boulder. Automatically, she staggered up, bolts of pain thudding up her shins, retrieving the staff and running on.

Sickly purple lights exploded on the edge of her vision; sweat formed a mist about her. Her ears tried desperately to filter out the throbbing of blood through her veins, listening for pursuit.

The trees parted, and she saw the grass, climbing to the low top of Hair Dome.

She didn't realize she'd paused. It had not been a conscious decision. Aiierra's hunting cry sounded.

Not close enough to hurt, she had time to think, simultaneously with, *too close.* Then breath was burning in her as gravity and the long chains of grass clutched at her feet like mud as she forced herself up the Dome, spear going before her, sweeping for traps. If she hit one, she was dead.

But she was too tired to go around, and the long chains of grass might slow Aiierra, too. It was all happening too fast. Where was Caansu? Would she hear Aiierra and come? How far back was Aiierra? Even with a sharpened end, her staff felt as slender and useless as a toothpick in her hands.

Finally, there was no more ground above her. Chest heaving, she turned.

Aiierra strode through the grass, a juggernaut closing the distance with deceptive, tireless speed, lungs filling for her hunting cry.

Shoshanna doubled the distance between them, gravity pulling her down the other side of the hill. The world became only measured footfalls. If she stumbled now, she would die.

The last few steps vanished and she vaulted over the flat rock at the edge of the forest, rolling between two trees.

And Aiierra leapt.

Shoshanna had counted on that not being possible. She had never seen a Shrii jump, but the downslope had forced Aiierra into something that was almost a run, and Aiierra *leapt* in a clumsy arc and landed not a meter away, just clearing the pit trap that Shoshanna had dug behind the rock. Not taking time to think, Shoshanna jumped to her feet, staff held out. If Aiierra could be forced back . . .

"So it wants to fight with spears," Aiierra whispered. Without taking her eyes off Shoshanna, she reached back through the roof of the trap and pulled one of the stakes out of it.

Shoshanna's heart collapsed within her. Aiierra had seen her trap at once.

The stake Aiierra now held was twice as big as Shoshanna's staff. Shoshanna had designed it to be. And she could no longer run faster than the Shrii could walk.

"Stand here, and I will kill you honorably, though you have not earned it. Run, and I will *eat* you after the hunt."

Shoshanna's last hope died. She raised the spear. She could feel Aiierra waiting, wanting her to lunge.

She thrust, clumsily. Aiierra pivoted, smashing the butt of her pike into Shoshanna's side. She fell, and felt the searing pain of broken ribs. Aiierra waited. "I did not say I would do it quickly." Her voice was colder than the morning sea.

Shoshanna got to her feet. Aiierra struck. Shoshanna ducked and leaped behind a tree trunk. Aiierra yanked her pike free of the soft wood and launched a flurry of blows. Shoshanna fell back, prolonging the inevitable, trying to keep as much foliage between her and Aiierra as possible.

Aiierra came on. Again, Shoshanna gave way, ducking and twisting to avoid two savage blows, but the third one she had to block. More swiftly than any snake, Aiierra's spear curved, and Shoshanna felt the bones of her left hand shatter. A scream ripped from her lips.

"I would not treat an animal thus," hissed Aierra. "But animals only kill. They do not lie, as you have. So you will suffer." She clipped Shoshanna across the chin with her spear butt at these words, spinning her into the ground. The world hit her, soft and hard.

"Get up, damn you!" Aiierra's spear twitched. *Why continue?* The tall bushes were familiar, shady, and cool. A good place to rest. Even forever. A drop of cool wetness fell on her wrist as if to welcome her. She looked down and saw the spot of purple.

Purple. Shoshanna's eyes sharpened.

Then, with a surge of strength, she leaped to her feet and turned to run.

Aiierra's sonic blast imploded her eardrums and the pain felled her before she'd covered two meters. She fell heavily, and Aiierra landed heavily on top of her.

She couldn't have been unconscious for more than a second. When she came to, Aiierra was still on top of her, unmoving. Feebly, Shoshanna pawed at the ground.

It took five minutes for Shoshanna to recover enough to move. Slowly, she pulled herself out from under the heavy Shrii body. There were burning spots all over her arms, but Aiierra had shielded her from the worst of it. She stood.

Suro jova covered Aiierra from head to foot. They had burned through her tough back scales in most places, and flesh bubbled and bled. Shoshanna felt horror rising up in her; there was only one thing to do. She raised the spear in her good hand and thrust the point through the back of Aiierra's neck. Then she dragged the body into the sun and drew her knife. Cutting into Aiierra's flesh, she was surprised at how much like a *vsheera*'s it was.

Shoshanna felt Caansu's eyes on her, cold as asteroid metal, all the way up to the Far Peak. Her friend did not rise to meet her. She sat, like a rock overlooking the sea. Shoshanna's body was alive with a tingle that presaged the pain of bruises and quickhealed bone. Her medkit was out of painkillers.

Caansu spoke softly, but the chords carried. "I waited for my friend here, thinking she would come. And I heard the hunting Call on the wind. And knew I could not come in time. And I thought, my friend would not so dishonor me. And now the smell of blood carries my friend's death to me."

"It was self-defense."

"I do not believe you."

"She attacked me. I don't know why. You said you heard her hunting. She tried to kill me."

"Obviously. Why?"

Shoshanna flinched at the cold hostility in Caansu's voice, so like Aiierra's. "I don't know."

"What did you do? What did you say?"

"All right, I had a plan. I knew you wouldn't agree to it, that's why I sent you out here. I told her that I had killed you, because I didn't want her hurt in the matingdeath. Because I wanted the best possible chance to get home. And to prove to her that I could stand the sight of blood if I needed to."

Caansu said nothing, but her eyes narrowed even further.

And now the lie. "You could never hide from Aiierra unless she thought you were already dead. I had planned to help you hide here, and live. And return home, when a ship came."

"You could not have provoked her to murder better if you had tried. You must have known this. And even if you did not, how did you expect to furnish her proof of my death? Or hide from her your trips to see that I was safe?"

"I don't know!" shouted Shoshanna. "But I didn't have any other ideas, and it was the best chance I had to save your life, even if you didn't want it saved! You laid down your life for your religion, and I have the right to lay down my life for . . . " Words failed her. "For you," she finished.

Caansu's expression did not change. "So you knew she would attack you."

Damn. She had blown it. But she was too angry and too tired to care. "I considered the possibility. But I didn't really think so. I guess I don't understand the Shrii and the Rii as well as I thought, Caansu." Gravity and the sack she was holding sat her down hard on the packed sand.

"How did she die?"

Shoshanna related Aiierra's death by *suro jova*. "By the time I recovered, it was too late, Caansu; even if you had come, it would have been too late. So I killed her as quickly as I could." At least *that* was true.

"You certainly surprised her." Caansu's voice was hollow. "And me."

Shoshanna felt her guts twist at her friend's coldness. Well, if she had already lost a friend, then what else mattered? She spread the sack out on the ground and extracted the quivering, bloody mass from it. "It's not murder for you to have this anymore, Caansu. Take it."

Caansu's breath caught, and then she closed her eyes. "I will not share your crime."

"Well, I wouldn't let you if you wanted to; it's all mine!" The yell exhausted and surprised her; even Caansu rocked back. She bore on. "Curse me for it if you want to, but at least you could see that some good comes out of it. Give your people a Mother, for once, if you're not too afraid that all the rest of them will turn their backs on you out of self-righteousness and jealousy. Are you Christians really that small-minded?"

Caansu's head lowered, and she set her elbows on her knees, chin in her hands. "Some of us," she admitted. "Some would." She rose, and sat beside Shoshanna. Slowly, she picked up the section of Aiierra's throat. "I think, at last, I understand. But you need to know more.

"When we Shrii speak of love, there are only two kinds. There is what the Lord calls brotherly love, and there is the love of God. We do not know of your third kind, the kind of love you fall into, unless it comes mixed with rage, in the matingdeath.

"But occasionally, when two brothers are great friends, and one honors the other above all else, they will not duel others for the right to become Mothers. One will give herself to the other, showing the kind of love that Christ did, so that her friend will not need to risk death."

"But I thought . . . you said it was an insult."

"No; in this case, it is the highest compliment. Not because the giver thinks her brother cannot triumph, but that she cannot bear any harm to come to her. I see now that this is what you meant to do for me, though being Human, you could not express it in a way that I could understand. Then."

Shoshanna felt tears come to her eyes. The tension that she had carried around with her for so long threatened to erupt in a storm. But Caansu continued.

"When Aiierra came to fight the matingdeath, this is what I had planned to do for her. To give myself to her as a friend. To show her Christ's love and sacrifice in myself. And perhaps, if God willed it, to give my people a Mother, even as you wanted. You ended that plan. And so the cup passed from me." She said the last sentence as if to someone else.

"But won't you be a better Mother to your people than Aiierra ever could?"

"Who knows what she might have been? At the very least, she might have been given grace. Now she never will. But God speaks through you of what is now, and not of what was. I will not call unclean what She has made clean."

Slowly, Caansu lifted Aiierra's throat and placed it in the bag. Together, she and Shoshanna walked back to camp. Shoshanna's last memory was of seeing the familiar fire and the three lean-tos. She was vaguely conscious of being picked up and laid down.

When she woke, the world was still and dark. The fire burned quietly. Shoshanna got to her knees, grimacing at the pain. There were dried meat and water skins piled outside the lean-to. Enough to last a week. She reached for a gourd, and winced. Her left hand was a gnarled ball of frozen bone. The quickheal had worked, but it would take a surgeon to reset the bones properly. The surf roared.

On the other side of the fire, there was what looked like a scaly log, vaguely shaped like the sarcophagus of a Shrii. Caansu's chrysalis. Now Shoshanna had both time and energy. She wept. For pain. For joy. For guilt. Even for Aiierra. Eventually, the tears stopped.

It was then that she noticed the worn Bible, sitting at Caansu's feet. It lay open, a rock weighing down the pages. A verse was underlined.

"Because the foolishness of God is wiser than men, and the weakness of God is stronger than men."

A rebuke? An affirmation? Even asking herself, she did not know which was more appropriate. Which had Caansu meant?

Sitting opposite the fire, Shoshanna watched her friend. Eventually, she would ask. Eventually, she would have an answer.

G. Scott Huggins grew up in the American Midwest and has lived there all his life, except for interludes in Germany and Russia. He is responsible for securing America's future by teaching its past to high school students, many of whom learn things before going to college. He loves to read high fantasy, space opera, and parodies of the same. He wants to be a hybrid of G. K.

Chesterton and Terry Pratchett when he counteracts the effects of having grown up. You can read his ramblings and rants at his blog, the Logoccentric Orbit (scotthuggins.wordpress.com), and you can follow him on Facebook (facebook.com/gscotthuggins).

Ascension

Laurel Amberdine

MARINA QUINN FOUGHT back tears as she looked at the ruins of her sundress and the hard lump of bruise on her thigh. Coming on this Holy Land tour was the worst idea. No matter what Grandma wanted. No matter what Marina had promised the only person who'd ever loved her unconditionally, as that person slowly lost her ability to move, and died.

Marina sniffed hard and looked up at the hotel room ceiling, like gravity could make tears run back into wherever they came from. Fine, the dress was ruined, but at least she got the pictures. She pulled out her phone and reviewed them. Today had been the tour's "free day", so she'd put on her prettiest strappy sundress and gone exploring. She might not be having any fun at all, but she could make it look like a great trip, at least.

In a nice, quiet Jerusalem neighborhood, away from all the traffic and tourists, she had found a sunny park full of palm trees and flowers. Just as she got the right angle and posed for a selfie, some men approached, shouting and *throwing rocks*. She ran away, but she couldn't even understand what they were upset about. If the park was closed, there should have been signs. And besides, *normal* people just asked someone to leave. She rubbed the bruise and wondered if she should ask for some ice for it.

Instead she opened her laptop, sat on one of the two twin beds, and uploaded her smiling picture "#nofilter." It really had been a beautiful park.

She'd been thrilled when Grandma offered to bring her on a tour the summer after graduation. But then Grandma's disease had progressed so fast. They'd switched from the original plan of Rome, Lourdes, and the Holy Land to just the Holy Land, to finally just Jerusalem, as her symptoms got worse and worse. By the time they started talking about hospice, it was clear she'd never make it on any trip at all. And like a fool, Marina promised she'd go anyway. It had made grandma smile, some of the only muscles she could still control then. Stupid.

Her friends started commenting on the photo. "So jealous" "Beautiful" "Looking gorgeous, Marina!" They responded with a picture of all four of the old gang together at Navy Pier, halfway between posing with, and having some kind of disaster with, oversized pastel clouds of cotton candy. Behind them, the sky over Lake Michigan was overcast with an approaching storm. Marina missed home and her friends so much it made her throat ache, like only screaming would let the frustration out.

Their last summer together, and she was missing it. She looked over the tour pamphlet. She'd only been here four days, not counting the flight, but it felt like weeks had passed. Four more days to go, all the same stuff. Mass in the morning, tour of some dusty old site, rosary, and dinner.

This was stupid. There had to be something fun around here. Israel was a modern country, whatever those idiot rock throwers in their stupid black suits thought. She headed down to the lobby.

A bored-looking concierge stopped filing her nails to put on a sincere— or at least well-practiced—smile when Marina approached. Closer now, Marina spotted another woman seated behind the counter as well, tensely staring at a silent TV. Given what she'd seen from people watching TVs here, Marina expected the news, but it was a soccer match.

"Can I help you, Miss?"

"Yeah, is there any place around here to, you know, have fun? Maybe a bar or something?"

"Here? No." The woman frowned at her nails and then resumed vigorous filing. "You want to get to Tel Aviv. That's where all the fun is." She sounded like she'd rather be there, too.

That seemed like a big undertaking, but maybe a real outing was what Marina needed. "Can I take the bus?"

"Sure, easy. About an hour away."

The other woman didn't even look from the screen as she said, "The buses are death traps. Favorite target of suicide bombers."

"Uhh," Marina said, unsure how to react. It was disconcerting enough seeing soldiers with their giant guns everywhere, and going through security at nearly every single doorway—she'd given up wearing her big jewelry anymore—now this? Marina figured learning her way around Chicago had made her tough, but Israel was another level entirely.

The concierge shrugged, but didn't contradict her friend. Marina thanked her and left. She went out to the little market stand around the corner and bought some mineral water and a bag of Bamba, which were like peanut butter-flavored Cheetos. She'd gotten them to freak her friends out, but they were pretty good.

Back in the room, she sat on what should have been Grandma's bed with her snacks. She turned on the television, where newscasters shouted the news in incomprehensible Hebrew, while showing pictures of rubble and armored vehicles.

It was too late to head to Tel Aviv today, but tomorrow? Whatever the tour had planned, she didn't care. Tomorrow she was out of here.

At breakfast, Elaine—the closest thing she had to a friend on this tour—explained that bare arms were probably what got her into trouble yesterday. So Marina put a cardigan on over her second-best sun dress, steeled herself, and headed for the line of cabs out front. She climbed into the foremost. The driver snapped something in Hebrew. Great.

"Um, I need a bus to Tel Aviv. Can you get me to a bus station?"

"A bus station," he said in clear, faintly Russian-accented English. He hit the horn like he needed to announce his departure as the car lurched into sudden motion around the corner, then slammed to a stop in thick traffic. All the nearby cars honked as well, though there didn't seem to be more than ordinary traffic.

Marina pulled out the hotel's tourist map, but after a few turns she lost track. The cab kept lurching into motion and stopping hard, the sun glared harsh through the glass, and everyone kept honking. She closed her eyes and leaned against the window, thinking back to what she'd promised Grandma. This excursion was probably breaking both the word and the spirit of that promise. Not that Grandma was around to care anymore. For all Grandma's rosaries and masses, Marina didn't feel the slightest hope that any of it mattered. Marina didn't have anything against religion. It seemed nice. She liked the art. But Grandma wasn't anything but dead and gone.

Even if grandma was, improbably, somewhere else, it didn't help Marina any. She was still alone with no one to count on, just her drunk, flakey mom, pushy step-dad, and lying cheat of a real father.

By the time the cab lurched to its final stop, Marina was curled up on the back seat, sobbing.

"Hey girl, stop that."

Marina sat up and scrubbed her face. "Sorry, how much?" She fumbled at the unfamiliar bills in her purse.

The driver's scowl deepened, which hadn't seemed possible. "How can you Americans be so stupid? Did you see me touch this meter? No, I didn't. It's off. I could charge you anything. Then you spend the whole ride crying in my car. How do you think that makes me feel? My day is ruined. Get out." He gestured at the window. "There are your buses." One of the bus drivers misunderstood and gestured rudely back.

Marina tried to hand a few bills to the driver, but he told her to get out again. Possibly this was his attempt to be nice? She would never understand this place.

Outside the cab buses honked, of course. She was so used to the sound that until one passed so close by that it brushed her skirt, she didn't realize she was in their way. She trotted off to an awning, scanning signs for some way to Tel Aviv. Of course there was no English anywhere.

She found the shadiest spot she could and got out her phone, squinting at the screen. She should've just done this on her own anyway. After a few taps: it would take two hours and three different buses to get to Tel Aviv. And they didn't leave from this particular bus station. Now how was she even going to get back to the Christian Quarter?

Then one of the dumpy little shuttles that drove Christians around to holy sites pulled up. A gaggle of squinting tourists, mostly old ladies, shuffled out of the bus. The familiar sight gave Marina some comfort, though they weren't her group. She watched, wondering what they were here for.

Some of them stopped for pictures of the rock face behind all the buses, then continued on to a booth that proclaimed "See the REAL tomb of Jesus." Curious, Marina followed. Maybe she could at least get a ride back to the right neighborhood. As always, the old ladies smiled at her, happy to see a young person who shared their devotion. Marina plastered on the fake smile she was so practiced with lately. No one ever seemed to notice the pain behind it.

At the booth, the tour group picked up brochures and moved on. Marina hesitated and didn't accept the one offered to her. "I'm not with the group. How much does it cost?" Cheating her way into the actual tomb of Jesus seemed like a step too far, even if she was pretty sure God didn't exist.

"Twenty new sheqalim for just the tomb, one hundred for this whole package." He showed a card with a bunch of other tourist spots.

"Just the tomb."

Marina stepped aside and looked over the brochure, with a rising lump in her throat. Not again. How many tears could a person produce? She looked up at the empty blue sky and blinked hard.

Her grandmother would have loved this. She'd always been the one who wanted the truth behind the story. The brochure explained about the origins of the Church of the Holy Sepulchre, where the tour Marina was with went to mass every morning. While it was a good location for a church, with plausible justification for its construction, it couldn't possibly be the location of Jesus's tomb. That was clearly specified to be outside the city. Just like this . . . bus depot. Marina sniffled and blinked hard and shook her head at the absurdity.

The tour group had preceded her already, but she followed the arrows to a stone wall with an improbable wooden door. A plaque on the door read HE IS NOT HERE—FOR HE IS RISEN.

An older couple left, whispering to each other. That cleared enough room for Marina to duck into the small, dark space. A guard stood discreetly nearby, but otherwise it was all subtle spotlit signs with text in many languages and old walls of dull stone.

It seemed spacious for a tomb. She'd expected just a tiny crypt, but there were a couple rooms, one of which was divided into smaller sub-sections.

Pilgrims knelt and prayed. Marina shivered with a chill in the darkness, glad for her sweater. She felt tears rising again, for reasons she couldn't even understand. She couldn't possibly start crying now, in this place, with these people. They'd assume the wrong things. They'd never leave her alone.

A barrier and a tarp blocked one corner. She ducked behind it and sat on a bit of rock ledge, looking up and blinking and focusing on her breathing. Maybe one of these days she'd get the hang of not crying.

This corner was being shored up, apparently, and had some floor jacks holding up a stone while mortar dried. Marina studied the work, trying to distract herself, when she noticed something blue.

At first it seemed like a crack out to the open sky, but that wasn't right. She was deep under a hill. She wiped her eyes with her sweater sleeve, stood and looked closer. It appeared to be a knotted bit of blue thread, caught against the ceiling rock. Transfixed, she reached to touch it, but her fingers tingled with a deep ache and she shied back.

Instead, she grabbed the thread with the tweezers she always carried, and set it into a velvet clamshell jewelry box that once held a rosary, a gift that came with the tour. She'd given away the rosary, but kept the box, which seemed useful.

She set the thread on the pillowed satin surface, then gawked as it slowly began to float upward. Startled, she snapped the box shut, swallowing the thread like a hungry velvet alligator.

"Hey," the guard said, peering around the tarp. "You're not supposed to be back there. Didn't you see the sign?" He had a right to be angry, but he sounded only concerned, kinder than anyone else had been so far on this trip.

She offered a wan smile. "Sorry, got a little overwhelmed, needed somewhere private to sit." It was the truth, even.

"I understand, just want to keep you safe. Have a good day." He returned to his post.

Marina glanced around the tomb one last time, but her mind was on the little bit of blue thread in her purse. She ducked out, thanking the guard again, and walked over to another Holy Land tour bus. This one was empty, except for the driver, an old man who was reading a newspaper and listening to the radio.

"Pardon me," Marina said. "I know this isn't my bus, but I can't find the one for my tour. Could I get a ride with you back to the Christian Quarter?"

Without looking up, he waved her in.

Back in the hotel room, Marina experimented. On closer examination, the piece she'd found appeared to be a woven bit of cord, ripped at one end. It was the deep blue of a twilight sky. Other than the ripped end, it looked new and undamaged and clean. In fact, it seemed to repel dirt. That jewelry box had been dusty with lint, she distinctly remembered. Now it was spotless. The cord made her feel strange and achy up close, so she never touched it.

And if she let it go, it slowly floated up to the ceiling.

Marina did what any person in her position would: pulled up a browser and began searching for answers. After a few false starts, "blue cord Israel" led to information about tzitzit, tassels that Jews wore on the edges of their garments. In the past these were blue, but nowadays they were white. Floating was never mentioned.

Further searching led to speculation about the location of Christ's tomb, including the two locations she knew—the Church of the Holy Sepulchre and the "garden tomb" she'd just visited, plus some subterranean location where Jesus was supposedly buried with his wife and kids, and a similar whole-family tomb in . . . Japan.

This was so freaky. She needed to ask an expert, but who was an expert, and just what did she think she was dealing with anyway? Time to check some more original sources. The current Catholic Bible was online too.

But at daybreak on the first day of the week they took the spices they had prepared and went to the tomb. They found the stone rolled away from the tomb; but when they entered, they did not find the body of the Lord Jesus.

She knew that much. Resurrection, Easter, all that. Then what? She skipped a few pages.

Then he led them out as far as Bethany, raised his hands, and blessed them. As he blessed them he parted from them and was taken up to heaven.

Hmm. So what did she have here? A bit of Jesus's clothes, trying to get back to heaven? Crazy. She needed someone to talk this through.

Her only real option was Elaine, a woman her mother's age who worked as a teacher in Chicago. Elaine's husband had died not long ago. Marina had noticed Elaine at the airport, the only other one of the group seated alone and fighting off tears. Marina had two first class seats, thanks to grandma's death. She'd been planning to stretch out across both of them, but instead, once the boarding doors closed, she had Elaine move up to the other one. It wasn't a jovial flight, both of them too pensive for chatter, but they enjoyed the free drinks and fancy meals, and it was better than being alone. Ever since, Elaine had made a point to be kind, though once it became clear that Marina wasn't a believer and didn't want to be here, there was no chance of any real closeness.

"Elaine, hi, it's me Marina over in 131. I found something I'd like to show you. Do you have a moment?"

Within minutes Elaine was there. She looked more peaceful than she had before, and she regarded Marina with an eager glow that said she expected to hear about some kind of conversion experience. Not quite.

"Come in. It's over here."

Marina had tucked the cord beneath a rubber band so she could look at it without it flying away. "I . . . don't know what this is, but I think it might be important—" she opened up the clamshell.

Elaine went "Oooh," and reached out to touch it before Marina could react.

At that contact, her eyes rolled up in her head and she crumpled onto the floor.

Marina knelt to check on the woman as she snapped the jewelry box shut and shoved it into a pocket. Elaine seemed unhurt, her eyes moving behind her eyelids like she was dreaming. Marina rushed to the phone and called both the tour guide and the hotel manager.

By the time help arrived, Elaine was stirring with a blissful look on her face. She began to explain about a vision she'd had, of heaven with her husband there. Marina's heart raced in terror of what she'd done, but the tour guide and the hotel manager seemed unexcited, sharing rueful looks.

The manager, a plump middle-aged lady, led Elaine back to her own room, murmuring agreeable calming sounds as Elaine babbled.

Marina waited to be questioned, but no one said anything. "You feeling okay, Miss Quinn?" the guide asked. He was a tall, young black man, so skillfully detached and polite on the group's everyday outings that it was odd to see him expressing anything.

"I'm fine. Is she going to be all right?"

"Eventually she'll probably be pretty embarrassed. It . . . happens."

Were these blue cords all over the place? "What do you mean?"

The guide looked uncomfortable. "Jerusalem syndrome," he said with a shrug. "I'm not saying miracles don't happen, but a lot of people come here all wound up, hoping for too much. Sometimes they snap. Start babbling about visions and miracles and prophecies. It's the foreign environment, mostly."

"Oh." Marina didn't think that was Elaine's problem, but she wasn't going to argue. "Thanks."

He took his leave, and Marina sat alone again in her hotel room, wondering what to do. Obviously, this thing was too dangerous to show random people. So now what?

More research confirmed that Jerusalem syndrome was a real thing, but that was no help. She still needed expert advice. Poking around the Vatican's website got a phone number. Hands shaking, she dialed and navigated a quick phone tree to reach a woman who spoke with a faint Polish accent.

After several false starts, Marina attempted to explain that she thought she might have found something miraculous, and who should she talk to about that?

The woman on the other end was perfectly serene, neither incredulous nor excited. "Determination of the authenticity of all miracles is under the jurisdiction of the local bishop. There is nothing Rome can do until that determination is made."

Marina thanked the woman and hung up. She was pretty sure the bishop, whoever and wherever he was here in Jerusalem, wouldn't be much interested in having the authenticity of the Church of the Holy Sepulchre disproven. Besides, with the frequency of Jerusalem syndrome, he was probably busy and had heard it all. She was only here for a few more days.

So, what, take this back home and try to get in touch with Archbishop Cupich in Chicago? The idea was laughable, and anyway, that wasn't what the lady in the Vatican said. She stressed *local*, which meant Jerusalem, which meant that this was impossible. Marina couldn't pass this off to someone else. Besides, now that it was in her possession, she had no way to prove where she'd gotten it.

She crawled onto Grandma's unused bed, sat cross-legged, set the jewelry box in front of her, and opened it up. The ends of the little bit of blue cord waved gently toward the ceiling, not like they were straining, but as if a gentle breeze provided some lift.

If this was what it appeared to be, Marina must have been meant to find it. So then what? She hadn't been formally religious since she was eight years old, when her mom kicked her dad out and they abruptly stopped going to church. She might have to rethink *that* stance, but that didn't give her an answer about what to do with this thing right now.

Was it a miracle? Could it work miracles? It made Elaine faint and have a vision, but that seemed more dangerous than miraculous. Would it help answer prayers?

It had been years since she prayed for anything. She thought back to the prayers of long ago, fewer and fewer of them as the years passed. Please get me a new bicycle. Please make mom and dad stop shouting. Please help me pass this test. Please make this boy like me. None of them said with any real faith, just on the off-chance someone was listening. The results had been mixed, always seeming to depend on ordinary forces.

What would she pray for today? Far too late to ask for her parents to get back together. Same for saving Grandma. Even if it worked, Grandma wouldn't appreciate being brought back at this point, pretty sure.

Gazing at the cord, but not really seeing it, Marina thought back on her family. Her mom, always anxious, hiding behind a veneer of suburban competence, then drinking and crying when she thought no one could see. Dad trying to make life fun and daring, with gambling and extravagant trips and a woman in every city. Stepdad, who did nothing but work, determined to climb some ladder only he cared about. Determined that his wife and stepdaughter would climb with him.

And Grandma, who was always at peace, even when dying of a horrible disease that slowly stripped everything from her.

Please don't let me ruin my life. I'm just starting.

That felt like a real prayer. Inside, deep in a place she'd never noticed before, Marina felt a small glow, like a tiny response. But she could have prayed that any time. That wasn't a miracle.

Maybe without this nudge, she never would have. Maybe some people have to be nudged pretty hard. Marina sighed, still looking at the cord.

There were only two options regarding this object: keep it or get rid of it. She'd wanted to get rid of it, give it to someone responsible, but that hadn't worked out. So, keep it? She imagined packing it into her suitcase. Unpacking it at home, then stuffing it into her desk or hiding it deep in her sock drawer. It seemed so ludicrously disrespectful that she laughed out loud.

Still looking at the cord, it was clear what *it* wanted to do, if she could personify a bit of thread like that. No, it wasn't aware, but there was a place it belonged, and something drawing it there. That made sense.

She snapped the case shut, and put on her shoes. Outside the window, birds began to sing, and cars began to honk. She'd been up all night, but she didn't feel tired. The hotel had a little garden on one side. Marina took the exit to it.

The sky glowed a deep blue, much like the color of the tassel. She was alone for now, the hotel sleepy behind her, but she wouldn't be for long. She opened the clamshell case, lifted and pulled aside the rubber band.

The cord slowly drifted upward, paused for a few heartbeats at eye level, then continued its ascent. Marina tracked it, expecting it to vanish into the encompassing blue, but instead it glowed white like a star, rising into a brightening dawn sky. She watched and watched for what seemed like forever.

Something released inside her chest, a huge tangle of hard knots so tight and old and full of despair that she couldn't remember this feeling of being able to breathe without sorrow. Grandma was still out there somewhere. Marina didn't have to be like her parents. There weren't any easy answers, but there was a reason for hope.

"Goodbye," she whispered to the fading star, smiled, and turned and went inside. Coming on this trip really had been the best idea.

Like usual, Grandma was right.

Laurel Amberdine works for *Locus Magazine* and helps out with *Lightspeed Magazine*. Raised without any particular religion, she converted to Catholicism at age 21. She lives in San Francisco with her husband and one big dumb cat, where she enjoys visiting the ocean, taking naps, and trying to teach herself quantum mechanics. Such study prompted her to wonder about the nature of glorified matter, and inspired her story "Ascension." Her debut YA fantasy novel *Luminator* is forthcoming from Reuts Publishing in 2017.

Cracked Reflections

Joanna Michal Hoyt

January 1919

KASSANDRA LEONHART HURRIES carefully down the slushy street in the shadow of the tenements, muttering to herself, oblivious to the stares of passersby. She hugs herself against the cold of Massachusetts winter and the cold of the dream that clung to her as she woke. Wind, bone-chill, police whistles splintering the air, a hard grip on her shoulder, a man's face frowning down at her, further away a woman's face twisted with—grief? anger? something raw and desperate—and behind them all the beast-man laughing, extending his clawed hands. The nightmare images slosh in her mind. Icy water sloshes in her boots.

Kass has learned not to speak of the nightmares. She hasn't told her father that her boots leak, either. She's seventeen, old enough to know when to be quiet, and she saw the worry on her father's face when her ten-year-old sister Minnie complained of pinched toes. Before the war, when wages were still rising and prices weren't rising so fast, Herr Leonhart could afford new shoes for his children every year. Things are different now. Kass is glad, just this once, not to be the one he worries about.

Herr Schramm, the diner's owner, wishes her *Guten Morgen.* "The new dishwashers are here," he says. "Herr Baum knew their uncle and asked me to find work for them."

"If they are *Pastor* Baum's friends I will be glad to meet them." Kass still considers Herr Baum her pastor, though the elders—including Herr Schramm—voted him out; though he's in prison, eight months into his ten-year sedition sentence.

Herr Schramm opens the scullery door, says, "Kass, these are the new girls; girls, this is Kass Leonhart, she'll show you what to do."

"Hello and welcome," she says. "Just call me Kass. Who are you?" The new girls stand close together. Both are shorter than Kass. The fair one's round face is incongruous on her thin body. The dark one's face and figure are all angles. Surely Kass has seen her somewhere before. But where?

"I am Galya," the fair one says, glancing nervously at Kass.

"I am Kseniya." The dark girl throws her name out like a challenge. Seemingly even the new workers know Kass is *geisteskrank*—soul-sick, insane—and they're wary. Kass tries and fails to appreciate Herr Schramm for continuing to employ her instead of resenting him for warning the new girls about her. She asks the new girls if they want to go into the kitchen and collect the cart of dirty dishes or stay where they are and fill the sinks. They stare and don't answer.

Kass shrugs and heads into the kitchen. She knows she's not the only one who gets stared at. At church, people look askance at Stefan Beiler, who came back from the war with a nervous tic and haunted eyes. Any loud noise can make him throw himself on the ground, stand up again pale and shaking. Pastor Bower says he's a hero like all the young men who enlisted, but Pastor Bower doesn't look directly at him. Pastor Bower doesn't praise Christoph Geist, who has just come back from the military prison where he was sent for being a conscientious objector. Christoph was a high-spirited boy, but now he barely speaks and he cringes if anyone moves suddenly near him. Herr Pastor Baum gave Christoph a hero's sendoff—a thing he did not do for Stefan, and Stefan's parents haven't forgiven that—but God only knows what happened to Christoph in prison, and now Christoph's come home to people who are ashamed of him. There is so much shame.

Kass grabs the handle of the cart, trying not to flinch at the feel of spilled grease under her fingers. *It doesn't matter*, she tells herself. *You're taking it away with other dirty things, you'll clean them all.*

"Hand me that stack of clean plates, Kass," the cook, Frau Albrecht, says. Kass frowns at her dirty hands, reaches for the faucet handle. "Hurry up!" Kass grabs the plates with her cleaner hand, shoves them at Frau Albrecht, turns away, trying to shake her mind free of the fear of germs and the suspicion that Frau Albrecht is frightening her on purpose.

When Kass comes back to the scullery, both sinks are full of hot soapy water. Kseniya and Galya mutter to each other, fall silent as Kass comes in, look warily at her. She sets the tray of dinnerware next to one sink, says curtly, "Start there, both of you," and starts scrubbing pots in the other sink. She should be used to this by now. She remembers when the muttering began.

February 1917

Kass is fifteen, finally done with school and able to wait tables full-time at Herr Schramm's diner. She's glad to be earning her share, and she doesn't miss school. After the war started in Europe, stories about German atrocities appeared in the newspapers, and then sometimes in civics class, and then in the taunts of the students who speak English at home. "Lies," Kass's father said. "Germans don't behave like that." "Who knows?" Pastor Baum said. "When men are trained to kill, who can know that they will not behave like that? Likely the English soldiers are no better." "Don't argue at school," her father told her. She didn't. She's good at not saying things. She's mostly learned to hide her nightmares and her daytime fears so her father won't know she's crazy like her grandmother. He guesses, he worries, but he doesn't know. She hopes no one else guesses.

No one says "Hun" at Herr Schramm's diner. Kass is tired at the end of each workday, but proud too, and she knows how lucky she is. The girls from her class who went to work in the textile mills make less than she does, and the overseers in the mill speak rudely to them and sometimes grab them, and too many of them are killed or injured trying to keep up with their machines. Kass knows this because her father works in the woolen mill. He's a skilled repairman, his pay is acceptable and he's never been hurt, but he swore his daughters would never be mill hands. He's kept that promise, thanks to Herr Schramm, who is part of his church and his chess club.

This cold morning, Kass comes to work clutching the locket which holds a dried four-leaf clover, trying to clear her head of nightmares, reminding herself of how lucky she is. It takes her a while to notice that there are more empty seats than usual. Their German and Quebecois customers come as always when their factory shifts end, but the Flahertys, the Doyles, the Brennans, the O'Malleys, don't come. Neither do weary-eyed Seamus Halloran and his father. She always keeps an eye out for them. Often old Mr. Halloran—not so old, really—talks to people who aren't there. Sometimes he recoils, runs away from the table, and hits Seamus when Seamus tries to stop him. Afterward he weeps, apologizes, and sits quietly, head bowed, while Seamus finishes eating. Kass always takes time to speak to the Hallorans. She mentions their absence to the cook, Frau Albrecht.

"Yes, they're not coming, die *patriotischen Idioten*," Frau Albrecht says. "Seamus came in yesterday saying America will get into the war, and people already know the Irish aren't good friends to England, so Irishmen here can't be seen eating at a German restaurant if they want to keep their work at the gunpowder factory. *Idioten*. Here they got good clean healthy food. Those Irish, how clean do you think their kitchens are?"

Jutta, the other server on Kass's shift, agrees that it will serve those Irishmen right if they take sick and lose their jobs and—

"Old Mr. Halloran's already sick," Kass says. "They don't need more bad luck."

"*Geisteskrank*," Jutta agrees. "We don't need that kind here, spreading their sicknesses."

Kass opens her mouth to say that sickness in the mind doesn't spread like that. Shuts her mouth. How can she be sure? Where do her nightmares come from? Where does the fear go when it leaves her? *Darum gehet aus von ihnen und sondert euch ab . . . und rührt kein Unreines an; Come out from among them and be separate, and touch not the unclean things*, Kass's grandmother's voice says in the back of her mind. It's one of the verses Grossmutter says over and over on her bad days; but she starts saying it in response to ideas more often than to dirt. And now her dirty idea, her fear of dirt, is smeared onto Kass's mind, and who knows where it will spread next?

"Hurry up, Kass, go take their orders," Frau Albrecht says. Kass goes—noticing that Jutta stays to gossip unrebuked.

It occurs to Kass that she would not be sorry if Jutta took sick. Not a fatal sickness, *natürlich*, just something disgusting and painful.

The thought shames her. Scares her. Behind her eyes the beast-man smiles, approving her malice. The beast-man's face has grown familiar to her in the years following the magic show. The fear that comes with him has been familiar to her as long as she can remember.

Kass clutches her clover locket, praying. She will not spread malice. She will not spread germs. She takes great care not to brush against Jutta as she takes the next order, not to breathe on the food.

That night, Kass dreams that she watches herself waiting on tables. Kass who watches sees particles falling from the hands and the head-scarf of Kass who carries plates and does not see. The diners do not see. They eat, talk, laugh, then bend double, vomiting, gasping, choking.

The next day Kass keeps washing her hands. "Enough already! How dirty can you have gotten in five minutes?" Frau Albrecht asks.

The day after that Jutta is out sick. Kass has to hurry. It's hot inside. She pats her head-scarf to make sure her hair isn't coming out. Her scarf is wet; she has sweat on her hands, she has to wash them again—

"Enough!" Frau Albrecht says. "Take these plates!"

Kass grabs them, hurries off. Sets two of them down. Realizes as she hustles toward the last customer that a drop of sweat has rolled off her face and landed—where? Maybe on the plate. There might be microbes in it. She drops the plate.

She has to clean it up, wash her hands again, wait while Frau Albrecht fills another plate, run with it, knowing that she has dried her hands on her skirt, which must have gotten dirty while she was kneeling to pick up the mess she'd made . . .

At the end of the shift Frau Albrecht takes her aside.

"What's wrong with you?"

"I was trying to be clean," Kass says. "I was . . . afraid of the germs." She feels cold sweat breaking out on her forehead, hears her voice shaking. Frau Albrecht narrows her eyes, turns away.

The day after that Jutta is back, muttering with Frau Albrecht about something which they stop discussing whenever Kass enters the kitchen.

January 1919

Kass hears the new girls muttering to each other, splashing loudly to cover the sound of their conversation. Shame roils in Kass's stomach. She struggles to look steadily at the shame until she can pull free of it. *Die Warheit wird euch frei maken, the truth shall set you free*, she mutters in her head over and over, clutching her clover locket, looking for the crack in the air, for the image in the invisible mirror.

The shame loosens enough so that Kass realizes it's not all hers. Someone else, someone nearby, is also angry and ashamed. Kass looks at the new girls. Galya blushes, turns away.

Kass goes over to her and Kseniya. "What's wrong? Have I offended you?"

Galya keeps her head down. "Please?" she says softly.

"Please what?" Kass feels shame swirling around her, and also a dogged courage like her own.

Kseniya turns to face Kass. "We are still learn English."

"Is that all? I'm sorry. I thought . . . Can you not understand me, or is it just that you're not sure how to answer?"

Kseniya turns to Galya, says something quick and full of consonants. Galya shushes her.

"She doesn't have to be quiet," Kass tells Galya. "We can talk here. No problem."

"No problem talk Russian? I think no," Kseniya says. Galya whispers. Kseniya raises her eyebrows. "Galya says is no good saying, you will not understand."

"I understand," Kass says. "I remember when we were warned not to speak German outside our neighborhood." Kseniya looks surprised, but not lost—she understands.

July 1916

Dieter Leonhart is taking his *Kinder* to a magic show in the fine part of town. Minnie bounces and laughs while her father reminds her to keep quiet or speak English on this outing. Kass clasps her locket that holds a dried four-leaf clover. She's kept it with her day and night for the last month, hoping it will ward off madness. She got the idea first from Frau Geist, Christoph's mother, who tells *Märchen* to the children. They've heard some over and over, like *Dornröschen*'s hundred-year sleep, but last month Kass heard the tale of the girl and the sorcerer for the first time. The girl saw through the sorcerer's tricks because she was holding a four-leaf clover, "and so was proof against all malice and deceit." Kass listened and wondered. Just two days later she heard old Mr. Flaherty at the diner, after a few steins of beer, weeping a little and telling the table at large that he'd carried a four-leaf clover with him from the old country "just the way Mother Eve did when she left Paradise, for a reminder of that blessed land, and a protection in the hard wide world."

Kass wants that protection. She's taking the locket to the show to see if it really works. Her nightmares haven't stopped, but she hopes that the clover charm may keep her clear-eyed and sane by day.

They ride past houses that grow taller, brighter, cleaner, and then they are at the theater itself.

"*Haben wir Stehplätze?*" Minnie asks, pointing to the weary-eyed people standing against the back wall.

"Here come the Huns," someone mutters.

"No, we don't have to stand," Herr Leonhart says in careful English. "We paid for seats."

"Where do they get their money from?" another English voice asks from the back. Herr Leonhart looks back, worried, but just then the overhead lights go out and a bright light comes on over the empty stage with its intricately patterned floor. Then the light is obscured by a billow of smoke.

When the smoke clears, a man in a fine suit stands onstage, smiling at his audience. Kass watches, wide-eyed, while he floats a silver orb above his palm, snaps his fingers and brings a shower of coins out of the air, reaches behind his ear and pulls out a rainbow-colored scarf which rises wavering from his hand like the flame of a torch and then floats away into the darkness offstage. She's forgotten to look for tricks. She's seeing magic.

Someone in front is less absorbed. Someone mutters. The magician smiles.

"Perhaps such trifling pastimes do not interest you," he says. "Well, then . . . "

He spreads his arms and strokes the air with the index finger of his left hand. All the lights go out. Kass is too old to be afraid of the dark. *Trotzdem*, she is afraid.

One light comes on toward the back of the stage. An old man sits under it in a wooden chair, reading a book as big as a pulpit Bible. There is no one between him and the audience; the magician is gone.

There is no smoke, but suddenly someone appears in the middle of the dim stage, glowing like snow at night. He wears a suit like the magician's, but his eyes are dark all over like the eyes of a beast and his face is salt-white.

The old man on the stage stares at the beast-man, who turns and advances on him like a tightrope walker, one foot placed straight in front of the other. His arms lift and spread; each finger is tipped by a claw. The old man lurches to his feet, throws the book—which falls on the other side of the beast-man; it must have gone right through him—and dodges behind the chair. The beast-man kicks the chair, which falls, and strikes at the old man, who claps his hand to his cheek, lowers it to reveal a line of bright blood. Somebody in the audience screams.

The beast-man strokes the air with the index finger of his left hand. A host of darkly shining shapes gather around him, slowly solidifying. This is worse even than Kass's nightmares, she can't wake up from this.

Thinking that, she thinks of what she's thought of every morning in the last month when she's awakened from nightmare. Her clover. *Proof against all malice and deceit. Protection sent from the Blessed Land.*

As she thinks the words she sees the glowing crack in the empty air onstage. But it isn't empty air. She's seen the same thing when the light of the streetcar comes through the scratched glass of her window.

There's a mirror running diagonally across the stage, obliquely facing both the audience and the heavily curtained wing. Now that Kass knows what to look for she can see the thin frame that holds the mirror, concealed among the crisscrossing lines of the stage floor. She can see that the beast-man is a reflection from the wing moving across the mirror's surface, he's not really on the stage behind the mirror where the old man cringes. The old man kicked the chair over, daubed red paint on his own cheek. It's all right.

Kass means to think this silently to herself, is startled to realize that she's shouted it in German. Someone tells her—in English—to shut up. Someone says "Krauts". Kass doesn't care. The clover charm works. She is safe.

May 1919

It's Sunday afternoon, the factories and the diner are closed—Massachusetts keeps the Lord's Day, *Gott sei Dank*—and Kass walks to the Common to meet Kseniya and Galya. Trees shine with new leaves, and now that so many Germans are back from fighting for America, Kass can sing "*Lachend, lachend, lachend, kommt der Sommer über das Feld*" without anyone yelling *Kraut* or *Hun*.

She stops singing when she sees her friends. Kseniya's face is grim. "What's wrong?" Kass asks.

"You have taught me to read English," Kseniya says. "Now look what I read!" She holds out a newspaper.

Galya looks around. "Not here! Some place with people not so many."

Kass leads them away from the garden and the fountain to a solitary bench. Kseniya unrolls the paper. The bold headline screams "REDS AIM AT AMERICA!" The subheads elaborate: "Price Riots Driven by Foreign Agitators," "Reds Riot in May Day Parade," "Russian Reign of Terror—It Could Happen Here!"

Kass knows about the price riots. They haven't happened in her city yet, but the news has been full of them. Once the unions would have struck for higher wages to meet the rising prices, but now most of the union leaders are serving sentences for sedition. Kass doesn't know who leads the people who shout in the streets, block store entrances, smash windows and take things that they can't afford to buy. She's not inclined to blame them. She is inclined to blame whoever has been circulating fliers threatening bombs and bloodshed in the name of justice for the poor. If those fliers really exist, if the papers haven't invented them, how is she supposed to know?

She scans the story about immigrant workers who held a Red Flag parade in Boston on May Day. Bystanders charged them and tried to make them stop. They fought. Too many people were hurt. The Red Flag marchers (and none of their attackers) are in jail for rioting; rightly, the paper says, as they were trying to undermine the peace and freedom so dearly bought in the war, to replace liberty and justice with Bolshevism, mob rule, murder and rapine.

"You see?" Kseniya asks. "They call us killers, stealers—"

"It's not talking about you," Kass says. "Not all Russians, only Communists."

"Galya is not Communist," Kseniya snaps. "But today they call her on the street Bolshie, and one woman—" Kseniya spits in the dirt. "On Galya! Because only she is Russian."

Kass sighs. "I am sorry. I believe you. I remember."

Kseniya cocks her head, waits for the story.

"In 1917, when America has just gone to war, I am too afraid of many things." Kass shuts her eyes for a moment, remembering her frantic hand-washing, remembering Frau Albrecht and Jutta talking behind her back. "I am sick with fear, but I am trying not to show I am afraid. Trying not to seem crazy. I think, if Herr Schramm knows I am crazy I will lose my job, and we need the money, and who will hire a German girl? But I am crazy, seeing germs everywhere, thinking I will make people sick. One day I am walking to work. There is mud everywhere. I have my hands folded in my sleeves so nothing dirty will splash them. I am almost there, and then these older boys come and ask me 'What's wrong with your hands? Won't you wave to us?'" Kass makes her voice hard, mocking, like theirs. "They say maybe I have stolen something, or maybe there is blood on my hands. I tell them to leave me alone—I say it in German, and they say yes, I am a Hun, there is blood on my hands. They shout for me to show my hands. I do, and they throw things. Mud, and . . . well, we were by one of the alleys, there was sewage."

She falls silent, remembering.

April 1917

Kass stares at the filth on the front of her dress. She can't go to the diner like this. She reaches to wipe it away, freezes. Germs are so small. She might just push them right down through the fabric, to rest against her body, to multiply, to—the dream images ooze in her mind. She can't stand the feel of her dress against her. She tears at it. The boys draw closer.

"Stripping, yet!"

"Now she's shown us her hands, why not everything else?"

They laugh like her nightmares, close in like glittering shadows.

"Leave her alone!" The deep voice cuts through her nightmare. The other voices stop. "For shame! What have you done to this young lady?"

It's Herr Schramm, and she's standing in front of him in a torn dress, filthy . . .

"Nothing. She's crazy. We never touched her."

He turns her away from the boys, tongue-lashes them until they slink off, waits for her to explain. Waits a long time.

"What's wrong?" a quiet voice asks. She turns her head only. It's Pastor Baum.

"There were boys. Pestering Kass."

"I'll take her home." Herr Pastor slips his coat around her shoulders. His house is nearby, and one of Frau Baum's dresses almost fits Kass. When she is clean and decent she goes back to the study, makes herself face Pastor Baum.

"Are you all right? What did they do to you?"

She could say they grabbed her, tore her clothes. That might happen to any girl, *geisteskrank* or not.

But it didn't happen to her. She clutches the clover locket, tells him the truth. "And now Herr Schramm will fire me."

"Herr Schramm will still have work for you. Perhaps not waiting tables."

"The choir—"

"You will still sing in the choir. If anyone tries to discourage you, I will speak to them."

"Those boys—"

"Herr Schramm has warned them to leave you alone." He looks out the window. "But take the streetcar from now on."

"But it costs—"

"Less than losing your job; and it's safer than walking." He doesn't say, he doesn't have to say, "Who knows whether the police will protect a German girl?"

"I don't want to go to a doctor who will make me take opium like my grandmother. It doesn't stop her being *geisteskrank*, and it changes her ... "

"Your father won't make you take opium. Not if there's anything else you can hold onto." He looks at her, questioning.

Her clover hasn't kept her safe for the last two miserable months. Herr Pastor Baum has spoken before of holding to the Word. What good has that done *Grossmutter*, who can recite verses about filth and curses and unforgivable sin until her words trip over each other and her eyes are wild?

There are other words in the Word, of course. *Perfect love drives out all fear.* Lovely, but all too plainly Kass doesn't love like that. *You shall know the truth, and the truth shall set you free.* The clover hasn't kept her safe. Maybe if she stopped trying to be safe she could learn to be free.

May 1919

Kass tells as much of the end of that story as she thinks her friends will understand. Kseniya stamps her foot.

"They print such lies, these papers, but still people read them! Our papers tell what is true, that it is the rich ones who make trouble, who take everything and leave us only prison. But these papers we cannot mail, we must give at night, hand into hand, or drop in the streets."

Galya hisses something at Kseniya, who snaps back at her, then tells Kass. "Galya says be careful, but I say, too late. It is true, I am Communist."

"But you're not making bombs?" Kass sounds more doubtful than she meant to. Kseniya's face hardens. Kass goes rigid. She may have lost her friend's trust. She has certainly recognized a piece of the nightmare that still hangs over her every morning. The icy wind blows, the police whistles scream, the man frowns, the beast-man advances, tears run down the woman's fixed and furious face—and the woman is Kseniya.

Kass shakes her head to clear it. "I'm sorry! Kseniya, listen, I don't think you're evil because you're a Communist. I ... I know that when people, good people, are afraid, they can do terrible things." She clasps her clover locket and looks hard into Kseniya's eyes, remembering, willing Kseniya to remember.

"You have seen this," Kseniya says.

"Yes."

Galya adds something in Russian. Kass can almost see what she remembers—she and Kseniya have also seen. Kass can't see what they saw, but she can see that it left Galya more afraid, and Kseniya angrier, than Kass has ever had to be.

"Communists do not do such things," Kseniya says. Galya hisses and shakes her head. "They do not," Kseniya repeats, strenuously enough that Kass realizes she isn't sure. "These stories in the papers, they are lies." Then, as an afterthought, "And Galya is not Communist. Only I am. Will you tell the police? Will they believe?"

"I will not tell them anything about you," Kass says. "They arrested Pastor Baum. He wasn't a Communist, but he wanted things made right, he protested, and now he is in prison for ten years. I don't want more arrests."

"I do not believe your Church, me," Kseniya muses, "but my uncle said this Baum is a good man, brave. Your pastor now is good and brave too?"

"No!" Kass blurts. "You wouldn't like him," she amends. "And you shouldn't tell him you are a Communist. You shouldn't tell anyone that."

"In English, you only," Kseniya says, smiling.

June 1919

It's Sunday morning, and Kass walks to church with her father and Minnie, listening to the agitated conversations around her. The newspapers have been busy all week with the bomb blasts at the homes or offices of politicians—one legislator, even, here in Massachusetts! Anarchist fliers were left near the bomb sites. One of the bombers and a night watchman are dead; all the politicians are still alive. The newspapers say that a Red uprising is sure to follow, that there will be arson and murder everywhere.

"At least we have a good sound pastor now," Herr Beiler says. Kass lifts her head to glare at him, finds that she is glaring instead at his son Stefan. Stefan's shell-shock isn't wearing off; his eyes look bruised, the muscle in his cheek twitches. Kass smiles apologetically, murmurs "*Guten Morgen.*" Stefan nods. Then his brother Georg comes between them. Georg came home from the war whole in body and mind, and he joined the newly-formed American Legion. Pastor Bower has praised the Legion's resolution "to foster and perpetuate a one hundred percent Americanism," as well as their call on Congress "to pass a bill immediately deporting every one of those Bolsheviks." Kass turns away from Georg, ignores his greeting, enters the church already fuming.

Pastor Bower reads from Romans 13: "Everyone must submit himself to the governing authorities, for there is no authority except that which God has established . . . He who rebels against the authority is rebelling against what God has instituted, and those who do so will bring judgment on themselves." He explains that it is their American and Christian duty to be vigilant against Bolsheviks and anarchists, to report suspicious words or actions to the American Legion, or to the police, or to him.

Kass glowers at him, turns to look at the people around her. Many are nodding. Many of them used to nod when Pastor Baum gave a very different message. How can they bear the change?

Kass remembers the months after war was declared, after the Sedition Act banned speech against the war effort. Pastor Baum kept preaching on texts like "Love your enemies" and "Thou shalt not kill." The church elders warned him. He didn't stop. Men from the newly formed American Protective League "advised" him to buy Liberty Bonds to support the war, raise an American flag, change the sign from "*Emanuel-Kirche, erste evangelisch-lutherische Kirche in Guerdon*" to "Emmanuel Lutheran Church" or "First Lutheran Church of Guerdon," and preach in English. The elders advised him to go along with all those requests except the last. They didn't want to lose German. Some of the elders spoke little English, and anyway Bach composed to German texts, and what would church be without Bach? Pastor Baum disregarded all the recommendations. Kass admired him. Herr and Frau Geist were grateful that he supported their Christoph's refusal to serve in the army. Herr and Frau Beiler were furious with him when he would not pray for the success of the army their sons had joined—though he did pray for their safety. Jim Knowles of the

League began coming to church with the Beilers, listening attentively and making notes during the sermon.

So it went for weeks and months, while the English papers reported on German-American spies and German atrocities, while the German-American papers reported on the beating, tarring and feathering of German-Americans by the League and their allies, while death telegrams came to many neighbors and crippled or blank-eyed young men came home to a few, while Kass's nightmares showed her a mob of men with axes marching on the church. And then . . .

April 1918

Kass walks to church behind her father and Herr Schramm. They keep their voices low, but Kass knows what they're talking about. The news of Frank Prager's lynching came on Thursday. The papers agree on the facts. He was an Austrian immigrant, a Socialist, antiwar, loud-mouthed and irritable. His neighbors accused him of disloyalty, stripped him, beat him, wrapped him in an American flag, hanged him. Loyal citizens dealing with a traitor, some English papers say. Overzealous men who should just have had him arrested, others say. Irresponsible hotheads, a few say. Who will be next? the German papers ask.

Herr Beiler sits in a back pew, glowering, muttering to Mr. Knowles. On Good Friday, when Pastor Baum preached on "He who draws the sword shall perish by the sword," Herr Beiler walked out in the middle of the service. A week ago, on Easter Sunday, he left just before the benediction.

Today the choir sings Bach's setting of *"Ach, lieben Christen, seid getrost, wie tut ihr so verzagen?"*—"Ah, dear Christians, be comforted; what makes you so disheartened? Since the Lord sends affliction upon us . . . " Kass sings out of her fear, hears the same fear in the voices of her neighbors.

Pastor Baum reads from John's account of Christ's appearing to Peter after the Resurrection. The question and the charge: "Do you love me? . . . Feed my sheep." And the warning of Peter's coming martyrdom: "When you were younger you dressed yourself and went where you wanted, but when you are old you will stretch out your hands and someone else will dress you and lead you where you do not want to go."

He speaks of Prager as a good man, a worker for justice and against war. He reminds his congregation that, while Socialists may not be spoken of as good men in the newspapers, they helped to lead the 1912 strikes that won all the city's factory workers—German, English and all the rest—wages that would feed and clothe and house their families. And as for the war . . .

Pastor Baum looks directly at the Beilers and Mr. Knowles as he denounces the war even more openly than he has done before. Mr. Knowles and the Beilers leave together before the benediction. When Pastor Baum spreads his arms to give the blessing, Kass thinks she sees his left index finger scratching the air, summoning the darkness.

Kass's father and Minnie go to walk on the Common after church. Kass goes home alone, stares blindly out the window. The beast-man stalks behind her eyes, carrying an axe and an Amerian flag.

It's an illusion, she tells herself. It's only a reflection. She puts her hand to her locket.

Reflections are of real things, she answers herself. They may not be where they seem to be, but they are real somewhere. We see through a glass darkly, but we do see. It's not just her mind that is disturbed. Somewhere outside another fear calls to her own.

She leaves the house, waits until she can feel that other fear pushing at her like a cold wind, walks into it.

The men gathered around Herr Schramm on the sidewalk don't notice Kass.

"But the Geists have bought bonds already."

"*Trotzdem*, the League men and some others are at the Geist house. Most of the men there have gotten telegrams. They say young Geist is staying safe in the lock-up while their sons . . . "

"We must do something."

"Pastor Baum's there already. Lucky the Geists live so close to the church. He came with his vestments on and the Book in his hand, and he was preaching when I left. At least he'll distract them."

Kass bolts toward the Geist house, but she doesn't have to run quite so far. As she passes the *Kirche*, light from the church windows, light from the streetlamps, show her the church sign chopped apart, the axe lying next to it, the circle of men on the church lawn. She can't see faces in that light, but she knows Pastor Baum's voice. He's speaking German now, talking to himself or God. "*Er klage es dem Herrn; der helfe ihm aus und errette ihn, hat er Lust zu ihm.*"—"He trusts in God; let God rescue him now if he wants him." All the other voices speak English.

"Stop blathering and speak like a man," one of them says. "You've had plenty to say about Christianity. What kind of Christian supports the murdering bastards who killed my son?"

" . . . and those children in Belgium . . . "

" . . . and crucified the Canadian soldier . . . "

" . . . and poisoned the bandages we're sending our boys . . . "

There is a glowing crack in the night. Kass can see what the angry men see in the mirror. The figure from the war posters, red-handed, bloated, evil-eyed—another sort of beast-man—looms over them, over their sons. The beast-man's image shimmers in front of Pastor Baum, the League men can't tell them apart.

She turns, sees the crack in the air shifting, sees what Pastor Baum sees. Not one beast-man but a herd of them, circling him, carrying a rope. He is steeling himself to bear whatever they do, not to beg, to control his bowels and his tongue.

She clasps her clover locket, looks again at the men. They have no rope. They have hacked the sign but not the church windows. For a mob, they could be much worse. *Trotzdem*, they are getting angrier, they may become worse.

"Nothing to say?" one of them says. "I'm not sure he deserves that robe he's wearing." Why do they laugh at that? Why does Pastor Baum hang his head?

He takes a step back and the light of the window falls on him. He's wrapped in a flag, his arms pinned to his sides, his legs bare to the knee.

Kass launches herself into the circle, musters her best English. "Are you all as crazy as I am?"

Silence. She has surprised them, that's a start. Now if she can shift the mirror in front of their eyes . . . "I'm the crazy Kraut girl, the mad

Mädchen, the one who sees germs everywhere. I see germs, you see German spies. But I swear you're crazier than I am. I only tore my own clothes, I never did that to anyone else!"

She looks again at the men who have gathered, focuses on Seamus Halloran's face. "Where's your father?" she asks him. "Not crazy enough for the rest of you?" Seamus looks down. "Tell him hello from me," Kass says. "Tell him I'm glad we're insane in a different way from the rest of the world. He never hit anyone without being sorry afterward. You'll be sorry afterward, too. Why not stop now?"

"Get out of this." That's the man who's done most of the talking. One of the fathers of dead sons. He grabs Kass's shoulder. She flinches.

Seamus catches his arm. "Leave her be! You can see she's not right in the head."

"Get her out, then, and let us deal with him."

Pastor Baum hisses: *geh,* go, keep yourself safe! He's ashamed, she realizes—not only by what these men have done, might do, but by the fact that, while the sane and respectable members of his congregation have left him, this crazy girl, this public embarrassment, has come to try to save him. She hadn't known he saw her like that. She can't think of that now, she has to shift the mirror . . .

She can't hold the mirror up. It crashes down on her, it breaks around her, its cold sharp fragments scrape her skin, her soul, like claws.

That's only another nightmare image, she tells herself. Nothing really happened.

She doesn't believe herself. There is only fear in her mind. Her fear, his fear, their fear, she doesn't know. Perfect fear drives out all love, and all knowledge as well. She is falling. Someone is taking Pastor Baum away—they'll kill him—

Seamus bends over her. "It's all right," he says. Then he stands. "Officer, sure I'm not doing anything to the girl. She fell, she . . . had a fit."

"We all did," Kass says. "He didn't hurt me."

"Kass?" Herr Schramm kneels where Seamus was. "Come away. Come home. Your father will be looking for you."

"But Pastor Baum—"

"I called the police. They've arrested him. He'll be safe now, and he won't bring us into any more danger." Herr Schramm helps Kass up.

Seamus mutters, "Look, I had to join. You know what they're saying about the Irish."

"You'd better go with your friends," the officer says to Seamus, "if you don't want to explain things to me, which I'd just as soon you didn't." Seamus goes.

There is no pastor at church next week. There is an American flag above the sign, which says "Emmanuel Lutheran Church". Herr Baum is in jail, no longer their pastor. The choir sings Bach. Kass sings with them. Frau Geist hugs her, calls her brave. Frau Beiler and many other women avoid her eyes, mutter to each other.

The week after that they have a pastor again. Rev. Henry Bower was born Heinrich Bauer, but he conducts the service in English and prays for God's blessing on their nation's righteous cause, and the choir sings "My Country 'Tis Of Thee." Kass doesn't sing with them.

June 1919

Kass still sits in the pews, not the choir loft. She turns away from Pastor Bower. Christoph Geist huddles with his head in his hands. Stefan Beiler's head is bowed and a tremor runs through his body. Georg Beiler sits erect and confident beside his father.

Kass feels the cold wind from her nightmare blowing in her bones, sees behind her eyes the beast-man, the weeping woman who is Kseniya, the frowning man . . . that's it. The frowning man has Georg's face.

January 20, 1920

It's Tuesday afternoon, the end of the shift. Kass hesitates before step-ping out into the cold. Not that the restaurant is so very warm; the fall was unusually cold and dark, the winter has been the same, and with the coal miners striking the heat has been turned down everywhere. Kseniya's boardinghouse is colder than Kass's apartment, much colder than Herr Schramm's restaurant; she and Galya come to work with news-papers stuffed under their coats, put off leaving as long as possible. Only tonight, Kseniya hurries out. "I have the meeting," she says. Kass doesn't ask about the meeting. Not that she'd tell Pastor Bower anything if she did know. Though if he'd believe her she'd tell him something provably false. Better yet, she'd tell someone else that *he* was a secret Red agitator. Let *him* get dragged off by the police and spend ten years in prison.

Shame sours her stomach. Behind her eyes the beast-man smiles. Behind him something else moves. Someone else's fear and spite echo her own. She puts her hand to her clover locket, looks for the crack in the air.

Someone else is thinking gleefully of an enemy who should be in prison. There's another place where their thoughts touch hers . . . Kseniya. The meeting. Her nightmare. In her mind she hears the police whistles again, sees Kseniya weeping.

Kass hurries ahead, catches at Kseniya's arm. "Wait!"

"I have not much time; the meeting soon begins."

"Don't go. Someone—some enemy—will break in. Don't go tonight."

Kseniya folds her arms. "How do you know?"

"Something I heard. I can't explain now. Don't go!"

Kseniya looks Kass hard in the eyes. Nods. "So. Always there was danger and there now is more. I believe you. The others also must be told."

"I'll tell them. Tell me where to go and what to say—something short."

Kseniya whispers, hurries home while Kass hurries the other way, bent against the bitter wind.

The part of the city where Kseniya has sent Kass was German once, then Irish and Quebecois, now Russian; always the newest, the poorest people live there. The houses are decrepit, the street is narrow and foul-smelling. Kass finds the number, knocks at the door, whispers the password, adds "*Ya Kseniyi podruga. Ubiraytes' otsyuda! Vas politsiya ishchet!*"

A man's voice behind the door pours out an incomprehensible torrent of Russian. She shakes her head, wishing she knew how to say that she doesn't understand. "*Nyet. Ubiraytes' otsyuda!*"

The door opens. The man behind it is thin, bearded, threadbare, he'd pass for a cartoon Bolshevik except that he clutches a notebook, not a bomb. He asks something else in Russian. She repeats that they have to go now, that the police are coming; fishes out her locket, dumps clover into his hand, says *"Die Warheit wird euch frei maken."* This man doesn't know the language, he might not recognize the verse anyway, but he stares into her eyes and it seems he recognizes the truth of what she's saying. She doesn't know if that's enough to keep him free.

He blinks, leads her to a back door. Shouts up the back stairs. Holds the door open. She goes. Others follow her. She turns the way that most of them don't turn. She hears a police whistle. A crash. Voices, all English. Someone grabs her shoulder.

"Where are you off to in such a hurry?"

"Ich gehe nach Hause."

"This one's foreign," the man calls.

"German, not Russian. Let her go," another man's voice answers.

"There are German Bolshies."

The other speaker comes over, frowns down at her. It's Georg Beiler. Kass locks her knees to keep herself from falling as her nightmare eddies around her.

"Not her," Georg says. "I know her from church."

"What's she doing here, then?'

"I . . . don't know," she says. "I . . . heard something, I was afraid, I got lost. I want to go home." She makes her English slow and accented. There may be safety in being a slow, stupid, sick girl.

"Ach, let her go, David," Georg says. "She's . . . Her nerves. It runs in the family. Anyway, she was born here, and we're not looking for citizens tonight."

"Go home, then," David tells her. Another police whistle sounds nearby.

"I'll take her back," Georg says. "By streetcar. I can vouch for her since I have a Legion badge."

David shrugs, lets them go. Kass prepares to avoid Georg's questions, is grateful when he doesn't ask them.

Her stop, finally. Georg gets off with her.

"Danke," she says.

"Danke," he answers softly.

"For what?"

He turns his head away. She can't see what he remembers, but she feels the shame of it, the gratitude that, this time, he has not . . .

"I wish you had been home when they came for Pastor Baum," Kass says.

"Ah yes." Georg's voice hardens. "Our sainted Herr Pastor, who preached that if Stefan and I died it would be God's punishment for our joining the army instead of keeping our hands clean like him and Christoph Geist. I suppose he thinks Stefan's being punished now."

"Oh no, surely . . . " Kass begins, but she is not quite sure, and before she can straighten her thoughts out Georg is gone.

January 25, 1920

Kass hurries to church early. She has told her father she needs some quiet time there to pray. That's not exactly a lie.

On Thursday and Friday the newspapers lauded the Palmer Raids for apprehending thousands of Bolsheviks across the country and preventing murder, arson and rapine. On Saturday the local police and the Legion marched their prisoners down the main street to the train station to stand trial in another city. Kass and Kseniya stood on the sidewalk, shaking with anger and cold, while the man who had let Kass in limped past with one arm in a sling and the other handcuffed to Galya, who looked uninjured but dirty and afraid. She didn't meet their eyes. Galya! Kseniya learned about her arrest late Tuesday night and told Kass all about it on Wednesday. Galya stopped to buy food on the way home, was still walking when the Legionnaires began banging on doors. She heard them speaking English to someone who spoke only Russian in return, so she ran up to them and started to translate.

"And they thought that made her Communist?"

"She was Russian. She was not citizen. For what else did they want? You maybe can talk them sweet, they let you go, such a good American citizen."

Kass hung her head.

Kseniya sighed. "Not your fault. You warned me. I warned not Galya, I saw not the need."

No one is in the sanctuary when Kass enters. She hurries along the pews, setting a four-leaf clover at either end of each. She has just enough for that. She's spent plenty of summer Sunday afternoons hunting through the clover on the Common, picking and pressing any four-leaf stems she finds, partly as a talisman, partly because it's better than looking around and wondering who will be willing to walk or talk with her. She had another piece to put in her locket after warning Kseniya's friends; she's brought all the rest to church today. If anyone comes in and asks her why, she plans to repeat what Frau Geist told her when she noticed what Kass was collecting: "Ah yes, four-leaf clover, the living sign of the Cross." But she doesn't have to tell anyone. By the time the organist arrives, Kass is sitting demurely at the end of her pew, praying.

Pastor Bower reads the Old Testament warnings to the Israelites against aliens and their detestable foreign practices. He describes the threat to decent home life and godliness posed by Bolsheviks and anarchists. He points out the dirtiness and cringing demeanor of the prisoners they saw yesterday.

Kass clutches her locket and rises. "Whose fault is that?" she asks in German. Heads turn toward her, people make shushing noises. She doesn't shush. She slips out of the pew, out of her father's reach. "Galya, my friend who worked with me, was one of the prisoners. She never looked like that when we worked together. How can she be clean if they don't let her wash? How can she not be afraid if they hurt her friends, if they won't let her go? Why is the wrong one always ashamed? Pastor Baum was ashamed when they stripped him, and they laughed, but they were the ones who should have been ashamed. I was ashamed when they threw filth at me and called me crazy, but who should have been ashamed? During the war, when they all threw filth on us, should we have been ashamed? I say we should be ashamed now, if we throw filth on other people!"

The words are not right. She has to make them see . . .

She sees the crack in the air again, feels her own urgency echoed in another mind. Pastor Bower also is trying to make his people see, trying to protect them from the Reds and from those members of the Legion who still hold the war against them. He has labored so hard to build a small safe place for his people, to act in a way that will reassure the world. *Narrow is the gate* . . . Everywhere outside the beast-men prowl *the outer darkness, where there is weeping and gnashing of teeth.* There is no room inside for Galya, for Kseniya, for Pastor Baum . . . or, perhaps, for Kass. But Kass already knows there is no safety anywhere.

"We want to be safe, we all want to be safe," she says. "I wanted this when my hands were cracked from washing, when I tore my clothes because they were soiled. The men who came for Pastor Baum were afraid, they wanted to be safe, they wanted their sons to be safe. Now you want to be safe, and you only make more sickness, more danger. If you could see . . . " She gropes for words and, like her grandmother, grasps at the Word to say what she can't: "*Wenn doch auch du erkenntest zu dieser deiner Zeit, was zu deinem Frieden dient! Aber nun . . .*"—"O that at this time thou hadst known—yes, even thou—the things which are for thy peace! But now . . . "

The organ launches into a thunderous anthem. No one can hear her. Her father takes her arm, pleads with her to come home, to lie down. "No," she protests. "It's not my sickness talking now, it's knowledge of sickness, that's different."

But she doesn't have the words to give the knowledge to anyone else. She turns away, lets her father guide her toward the door.

Steps follow her. She turns back to see who's come out with her. Minnie, of course. The Geists. And Georg.

"What you said was true," he says, low and gruff, opening his hand to show the four-leaf clover.

Joanna Michal Hoyt, a Quaker, lives and works with her family on a Catholic Worker farm in upstate NY. She's learning to deal constructively with her irrational anxieties, and she wonders what could heal the irrational fear of immigrants and "others" which afflicts so many of her fellow citizens. Writing "Cracked Reflections" allowed her to explore these issues, and the role of religion, in a different context. Robert Murray's *Red Scare* and Ann Bausum's *Unraveling Freedom* provided historical background.

The Physics of Faith

Mike Barretta

"COME ON. IT'S the fastest way to make quota," said Jesús. "Then we can park the wagon and get a coffee or beer or whatever and we won't have to do shit for the rest of the night."

"Fastest way to get knifed," said Dave. "Why don't we just wait for a car accident or something?"

"Can't make any bones that way. Carpe whatever-you-got-to-do. We got to get paid. Besides, most drivers are insured and they ain't getting anywhere near our ambulance. Let's go."

"Damn," said Dave. "Alright, let's go." He got out of the air-conditioned cab of the ambulance and followed Jesús. His mirror-shaded sunglasses fogged in the Gulf coast humidity. He took them off, wiped them clear with the tail of his uniform shirt, and pushed them back onto his nose. He looked to the church. Paint peeled in ragged, skin-like strips from the church's white clapboard. The steeple loomed, casting a long, dagger shadow towards him like an omen from a cheap horror movie. The insect chorus rose and fell in a graceful sine wave between clumps of brittle yellow grass. He followed Jesús through a foot-worn path snaking around the rusty tangles of razor wire that protected the faithful in the last days of this church's God. Dave pulled a can of gloves from his belt holster and sprayed his hands, one at a time, until they were bright blue and tacky, then waved them in the air to dry. Nut grass stickers hitched onto his socks and pant legs in fierce thorny clusters as he pushed through the overgrowth.

They paused at the door.

"Ready to meet your maker," said Jesús with a grin.

"Funny guy. This is your idea. You go first. I'd rather just collect base for the day."

"Can't live off base," said Jesús. He pushed the warped door open a crack. "After you. I got you to the door, but you gotta step in. That's the way it works."

"Let's do it then." Dave pushed open the creaking doors to St. Andrew's Lutheran church and stepped into the gloom. The smell wrapped him and he gagged at the cloying miasma of shit and piss and the sweet, diabetic odor of burn addicts. "It's like Auschwitz in here."

"They had to round them Jews up. These dumb bastards volunteered."

"Yeah, I wonder." Empty glass ampoules snapped and popped under his feet. Pale, skin-draped skeletons littered the floor and lay Dali-esqe over a few remaining pews. Bulbous, lidded eyes twitched spasmodically in sunken sockets. In a corner, two gray skeletons humped each other, grinding and moaning. Homemade IV bags made from ziplocks and plastic tube dangled. A few modern jelly bags gripped skinny gray limbs.

Dave stepped over an emaciated gray skeleton. The man's eyes fluttered. His brain was deep in a supercharged dream state, consuming every available bodily nutrient at many times the natural metabolic rate. His eyes opened into mean slits and he hissed and went back to his dream, pulling a collection of rags and soggy E-print with him as he rolled over. The E-print flashed faded old news and went dead.

Jesús stopped and looked down at a girl. Her clothes were sodden rags, her mouth twisted into a skull grin. Her breath was ragged. "Didja ever?

"Ever what?"

"Want to try. I mean, really look at them. What do they see? What do they know?"

"They don't know shit." Dave looked around the church in disgust. "These people walked in here and surrendered."

"These people got faith. Faith in the dream. No different than the ones that used to be here. I mean look, they even hold hands. I heard it makes the dreams better. Maybe they know something you don't. It has got to be some good dreaming. Just wondering, that's all."

"Well, stop wondering."

"I hear they live a whole life . . . a beautiful life in their heads and then when they are done . . . they are done."

"Don't even think it."

"Easy for you. You got a girlfriend that ain't been triaged out. You stick with her and she take you to a community . . . or maybe she just dump your triaged ass and go with me."

"Now you're dreaming."

"It's all I got. What else is there?"

"You got me."

"Oh shit, I'm ready for the burn then." Jesús laughed and then howled in the echoing church.

"Keep it down, man. You wake enough of these guys, no telling what they'll do," said Dave, though he knew that if they had the good stuff they would never wake again. Fortunately, the good stuff was comparatively rare. The drug was so powerful it could be cut many times and people would still pay for it. But there were stories. Stories about agitated nests that woke simultaneously, pissed off and irrational, and insanely hungry.

It was the wrong place to think of cannibal dreamers rising up. He panned the flashlight, stopping at a body every now and then. The dreaming dead coming down from their dreams turned away. A single ampoule was good for two or three days. If the user didn't make provisions to stay hydrated, especially in the Florida heat, the first ampoule was usually the last. Junkies that didn't take all their drugs at once were likely to be robbed, so they hid their stash in a bodily orifice.

He paused his flashlight beam over a sore-covered bag of bones. "What about that one?"

Jesús kneeled, took out his phone and selected the insurance app. He scanned the gray figure. It was face down with its pants around its ankles. Someone had checked to see if it was holding. "No insurance. No pulse. Just the way I like 'em. Let's find another."

Dave put a twist tie with the A-OK Ambulance Company's claim tag around the corpse's wrist. He cinched it down tight and figured the guy would move if he was alive. He didn't, but then again, this far gone, Dave could probably scoop his eyeballs out with a rusty spoon and he wouldn't even blink. The corpse's one visible eye was clouded and dusty, gazing out towards an unseen horizon. He was worth about a thousand bucks at the city morgue just to get him off the street. Dead bodies were a health nuisance and it paid better than collecting bottles or cans. The corpse would be worth more if there were any usable parts, but even live burn addicts rarely had any salvageable organs.

He stood and followed Jesús through the church, taking a zigzagging course through the self-imposed holocaust. A few ambulatory burn-outs moved away, avoiding the slanted beams of light from the arched windows, propelled by the remnants of desperate hunger or maybe shame. Jesús stood at the altar. A one-armed Jesus dangled from the cross above, looking down at his flock. He seemed just as sad and grey as the burn-outs at his feet

"Jesús, meet Jesus," said Dave.

"The hell you looking at," said Jesús to the crucified god.

Jesus said nothing.

"That's what I thought," said Jesús.

Megan raised the front door, ducked under, and pulled it down. "We need a real door," she said.

"Soon as I can. You're home early," said Dave.

"It's Tuesday. Ethics and Morality always gets out early." She kissed him on the cheek and sniffed.

"I thought that was History?"

"Ethics and Morality are History. Hey, is that a beer you're drinking?"

"Hell yeah. I got one for you too. I made dinner."

She looked over at the table. A garden salad with slices of boiled egg and what looked to be strips of chicken. Her face crinkled in worry.

"Hey, it's alright. Jesús and I did good today. We found a nest with some burn-outs in it."

"I don't like you going into those places. It's dangerous."

"Not this nest. They were too far gone."

"How many?"

"Four."

"That's bad."

"That's good. There'll probably be more tomorrow. Good enough to pay for beer and fresh out of season greens. I didn't touch the tuition savings. I even added a bit to it. Sanjay upped our split to fifty-fifty for the bodies. Jesús and I each got a thousand bucks. Now sit and eat." He cracked open a beer and the bottle frosted over. He handed it to her.

She took a sip and sat down. "Oh, that is good." She forked a bite of salad and egg.

"Real chicken not Real Chiken," said Dave.

"You know how to spoil a girl. I've got to tell you about what happened in the Galtian Economics lab. We were running an intuitional analysis assay and . . . "

He smiled as she told him about class, describing a world he couldn't participate in. After a few minutes she stopped talking.

"I'm sorry," she said.

He looked up from his empty bowl. "About what?"

"You know."

"It's okay. It doesn't mean anything. Go ahead and finish. You should take a shower. I'm going to water the garden while we still have power. You never know."

"You're good at other things," she said as he left.

He climbed to the roof of the metal shipping container that was their home. He turned on the faucet and heard the pump kick on. The hose uncoiled and expanded, snaking across the metal roof as if it were alive. He watered the roof top garden using his thumb to break up the water into muddy colored droplets. He was good at other things. He had built the rooftop garden and turned a shipping container into a comfortable and defensible home on squatted land. They had a little money in the bank.

He spied a tomato worm feasting on one of his plants and flicked the big caterpillar over the edge.

Two points on the state test triaged him out of a future as anything but technical labor. The state university would not waste their time with him and no investor in the world was going to put him through a private school even if his indenture was the maximum legal limit. Megan was a different story. She was smart, far smarter than he was, and pre-admitted to a world for which he was not even qualified to man the gates. It was a strain on their relationship. Sometimes when he was at his worst it felt as if she was slumming with the help. He knew she didn't feel that way. She loved him and defied her parents for him, and that just made it worse. Sometimes he felt like he owed her a debt that he could never pay. Her talk of getting into a community when she finished her degree and residency thrilled and angered him at the same time. The idea of getting into one of those self-contained enclaves of the uncaring rich on her un-triaged coattails tied his stomach up in knots. How would he fit in surrounded by green lawns, full bellies, and shiny cars that drove themselves? He was like the tomato worm, something to be flicked over the edge to tumble screaming into the abyss. He turned the water off and climbed back down.

After she had finished her homework and studied up for the next day's classes she slipped into bed next to him. She dragged her fingernails across his chest.

"You know, I couldn't do this without you. My family won't help and I don't have corporate sponsors. This is both of ours."

"I'm sorry. I just get angry sometimes."

"I know." Her hand drifted down and teased at the waistband of his underwear.

"Why are you wearing these?"

⸻⸱◆⸱⸻

"Okay, okay, stand back," said the fireman.

The hydraulic motor screamed and the jaws of the Hurst tool bit into the forward roof pillar of the car and severed it. The car lurched under released tension. The fireman sliced the opposite pillar and two others peeled the roof back flat against the trunk.

"What the . . . " said the fireman. He wedged the jaws into the door frame. The jaws pried instead of biting down and the car door sprung open. "What the hell? No body."

"Nobody?" asked Dave.

"No nothing. No body. There is no one here."

"What do you mean? Check the floor boards." Sometimes with a bad accident, like this one, the body slipped under the seatbelt and compacted into the footwell. Those were the worst. He once found a baby in a glove compartment.

"I ain't a rookie. The car is empty," said the fireman. "It's happened again."

"Again?"

"Yeah. Again."

"Maybe he got ejected," said Jesús.

"The car hit a wall. There should be a greasy spot right about there." The fireman pointed for emphasis.

"That ain't good. We need a body to get paid. Take the rest of the damn car apart," said Jesús.

"Chop it up," yelled the chief. "Salvage . . . for the widows and orphans." With no clear possession on the car, it was abandoned property and subject to metal salvage for the fire department's accounts.

Dave walked over to another fireman. They had spoken at a few other accident scenes.

"What does he mean, again?"

"Second one we've seen. Smashed cars with no bodies. Started up north and it's been working its way south. Cars slamming into walls or barriers all by themselves. Missing persons and shit. Look it here. What do you see?"

"Graffiti."

"Yeah, graffiti, smart ass. What kind of graffiti? Anything look newer?"

"I got nothing."

"Them sideways eights, those infinities, the ones that look like they're stacked on top of each other," said the fireman.

"So?" He felt the first drops of rain from the gray sky and looked up to scan the sky for a sign. He looked back down. "Could be a tag, some new gang."

"It ain't a tag. It's a sign. I saw it at the other wreck. It's directions."

"For what?"

"Hell if I know. But cars are hitting walls and no one's in 'em, but that sign is always where the car hits. Someone knows something."

"Someone always knows something," said Dave.

"Ain't that the truth," said the fireman.

The Hurst tool idled down. The car was chopped into chunks of plastic and aluminum just a bit too large for a single person to handle. Teams of firemen loaded the debris onto a flatbed. Dave walked back to Jesús.

"We're gonna have to go to church to get paid today," said Jesús.

"Yeah, I guess we are," said Dave. So far none of the other commercial ambulance services had discovered the St. Andrew's nest. It was a good thing. Some operators were a bit less scrupulous. Rather than waiting for the addicts to enforce their constitutional right to suicide they would plunder the nest by pinching off an addict's nose for four or five minutes then carting them off. At least he would let them finish out their dreams.

Dave opened up Megan's book and searched. Next to the house, the book was the most expensive thing they owned and a requirement for University matriculation. As a student, she had nearly unrestricted access to the world and its knowledge. She should have taken the book to class but for whatever reason had forgotten. He used it like a dumb tablet, occasionally playing games or surfing the web for whatever struck his fancy. He found about a dozen conspiracy sites that talked about dumb cars driving into objects with the bodies mysteriously vanished. He found a reputable blog that cataloged the phenomenon. Nationwide, about three thousand unmanned cars had smashed into objects at high rates of speed. The leading theory was that the cars were mechanically rigged and the drivers bailed; but then again, the drivers of the cars were never seen again. Recovered black box data indicated that all the cars had hit between 118.9 and 122.3 miles per hour with seat belts fastened. Who would fasten the seatbelt after they bailed? He looked at a few of the accident pictures and, in some, he caught sight of stacked infinity symbols.

A few articles had stated that the disappeared owners of the cars had suffered from untreated depression. No shit, he thought. Just about everyone he knew suffered from untreated depression. He closed the book and waited for Megan to come home. It was just after six so she was a bit late. He sat on the couch and gestured to the TV and it turned to a local news channel. He swiped through the channels, not finding anything to distract him.

The phone rang.

"Your fault! This is your fault!" screamed Megan's mother.

Dave took it. He wanted to feel the pain, the hot roil of sudden change and loss.

Megan's father said nothing. He just looked sad.

"She stayed here because of you," said Megan's mother. "She was accepted at Purdue, at Purdue where it's safe, but she stayed because of you and look what happened. Look what you did."

He turned away and walked.

He had identified her body and waited for her parents to claim her. They weren't married, so he had no authority. Someone had hit her in the head with a pipe and taken what little money she had. She didn't feel anything, the police said. But that was wrong. She felt everything. She would have given the guy money just for the asking. There was no need for what happened.

Her mother's sobs and screams receded as Dave walked down the Medical Examiner's hallway. He pushed through the double doors into a shabby lobby of stained chairs and threadbare carpet.

"Look at me!" screamed Megan's mother. "What did she see in you? What?"

The doors swung shut and cut her off.

He felt a surge of vertigo. The universe lurched sideways and forgot to take him with it. He bent at the waist, hands on knees, and waited for whatever he was feeling to go away. It didn't.

"Don't you puke in here," said the receptionist. "I don't get paid to clean up no mess."

He stepped outside, fumbled for his car keys, dropped them, picked them up. He drove away with enough money in his pocket for a beer or perhaps some burn. On the way home he stopped in front of St Andrew's. It glowed from within with orange firelight. Maybe someone was burning some offerings on the altar to the old gods, the cruel ones, that had original claim on humanity, but probably it was just some moron burning the nest down. A few shadows haunted the outside, dealers looking for a little point-of-service transaction or addicts looking for a little salvation from their lives. It didn't matter.

He drove away.

He unloaded the scrounged plate glass and leaned it against the side of his container house. Sweat poured off him. His hands were slick and he had cut both of his palms on the sharp edges of the glass. He used a few wraps of duct tape as impromptu bandages.

The week after was a mess. He was disinvited from the funeral so he had to wait for the service to be over. When everyone left, he walked to the soft turned-over earth and nestled an heirloom tomato between the bouquets of wilting flowers. The fruit was the size of his fist and it was the deep juicy red of a wild fruit. He had salvaged the plants from a feral garden in an abandoned neighborhood and bartered the tomatoes at the farmers' market. He had told Megan that one day he would build a greenhouse and grow tomatoes all year long and become the tomato king of North Florida. He thought he might as well start working on it.

Jesús had called in and said he had a family emergency in South Florida so he would be out for a few days. Dave crewed with Mario and nothing much else happened. Other companies consistently beat them to the calls and he wasn't going to show Mario the St. Andrew's nest. That was his and Jesús's spot for extra cash.

He came in from the heat and sat on the couch, letting his sweat soak into the furniture. He peeled the tape from his hands and blotted the blood on his pant legs. Megan would have had a fit. Her cat jumped up into his lap, purring and drooling. He scratched it behind the ears and put it down.

"Are you okay?"

He looked up, startled at the intrusion. The voice was coming from Megan's book.

"Are you okay?" asked the book. The voice was non-gendered and soft.

"No, I'm not." He looked at the book. He thought that perhaps it was some sort of targeted interactive advertising trying to worm its way into his brain. He got up to slam the book shut.

"Of course you aren't. It was a stupid question. I'm sorry for your loss." The screen saver faded out, replaced by stacked infinities. He stopped his reach.

"Who are you?"

"I am that I am," said the book.

"A bullshit hacker."

"Do you want something better?"

"Everybody wants something better."

"Not everyone deserves something better."

"What do you want?"

"You."

"I don't have time for this shit." He slammed the book closed, dressed, and drove to work.

Another week and Jesús had not called. Sanjay ranted and said he would fire the little spic when he finally showed up. Dave had gone to Jesús's squat and found no one. He crewed with Mario for another week and earned only a single bonus over base. At home he opened up Megan's book and the machine booted up. Stacked infinity symbols floated across the screen.

"It can be better," said the book.

He took a beer from the fridge, twisted the cap off, and took a long pull. He felt moody and aggressive, and fighting with some hacker was exactly what he needed.

"What can be better?"

"Life."

"What do you know about life?"

"Enough. I know your girlfriend's dead. Your parents are dead. You have no brothers or sisters and your only friend has turned to the burn."

"He wouldn't."

"He has."

"How do you know?"

"He has all the symptoms. He believes his past is better than his future."

"That's true for most of us."

"Not for you. Even now you don't believe it."

"What do you want?"

"Do you know where the Santa Fe Street bridge is?"

"Yes."

"Drive westbound on I-10 into the center support at 120 miles per hour between 3:30 and 3:35 AM tonight."

"Really? And then what happens?"

"It will be better."

"I'm supposed to take this as a matter of faith."

"Life is a matter of faith."

"The hell you say."

On the news he saw that a car had driven into the Santa Fe bridge support. There was no body to be found. The newsfeed on the television voiced the mystery over a static picture of firemen spraying chemical foam to soak up electrolyte spilled from the car's batteries. Coincidence, he thought, or perhaps some psycho-hacker had gotten into some other poor bastard's head.

He went outside and climbed the ladder to the roof to water his garden. Tomato worms had found his plants and gnawed them to stalks. The fat, greedy worms had skeletonized the plants, eating everything that could be crammed into their manically chewing mouths. He plucked the ugly worms from his plants and cast them down. He thought of Megan again and dropped to his knees in his tiny struggling garden and wept. He thought of his friend, Jesús. Neither would leave him if they had a choice. A rush of fear flooded him and he dropped his hose and climbed down. He got in his car to drive to St. Andrews. It was dark when he arrived.

Dave panned his flashlight around the exterior of the church and saw no one. He listened at the door for a moment and thought that maybe he could hear breathing, the soft exhalations of the dying dreamers inside. The door groaned as he pushed it open. There was enough sickly yellow light of the exhausted city pushing through the unbroken windows that he could see pretty well. A fresh crop of addicts littered the interior. He passed the flashlight over their faces. A few squeezed their eyes tighter and turned away.

He discovered Jesús under the one-armed Jesus. He lay curled on the floor, impossibly skinny and morbidly gray. The deflated remains of saline gel packs, stolen from the ambulance, were wrapped around his arm. "What did you do?" asked Dave. "What did you do?" Jesús's eyes twitched like something was behind trying to break out of his head. His sour breath came in fast ragged pants. His hungry brain had consumed nearly all of him. It wouldn't be long. Dave lifted his friend and cradled him.

"Jesús. Jesús," he whispered. "Wake up." But he knew it was futile. Even if he did wake, he would likely die. No insurance. No assurance. No hope. No nothing. "Oh, man, I hope you had a good life. I hope."

Jesús's eyes fluttered open and settled into thin watery slits. He smiled faintly and his face went slack. His eyes closed and tears rolled down the sides of his face as he traded a little bit of now with his friend for the prospect of forever with his dream. "Okay, Jesús," said Dave. "It's okay. I understand. Sweet dreams." He sat in the church for a long while under the quiet, one-armed Jesus and felt tired and alone and empty, as if a tomato worm had chewed off the best parts of his life and left him nothing but the bitter stalk.

"I'm scared," he said to the book.

"You would be a fool not to be," said the book.

"Are you sure I can I take the cat?"

"A cat would be an entirely reasonable thing to take," said the book.

"Can you tell me more? Can you tell me anything?"

"I've told you everything I can. You have to do the rest," said the book.

He closed the book and set it aside in the passenger seat. He took his foot off the brake and stepped on the accelerator. The speedometer climbed to 120 miles per hour and he set the cruise. The cat curled into his lap, purring. Her whiskers were moist with cat spit. He thought about Megan and Jesús and where they might be.

The infinity symbol loomed, filling the windshield, as he steered towards the divider on the Santa Fe bridge. He didn't feel afraid anymore. Time slowed and the world resolved to a bright focus. Impact ripples raced across the sheet metal towards him. The windshield pebbled and exploded away in slow motion sprays of diamond. Infinity beckoned. The seat belt grew intolerably tight as it stretched across his shoulder and hips, holding him from fate. He felt transparent and detached and wondered if perhaps the peculiar physics of faith had asserted dominion over the moment. He looked down and the cat was improbably still in his lap, purring and drooling, eyes closed, content and unimpressed with the shattering chaos that howled around it, propelling him, he hoped, towards something more substantial than the concrete inches from his face.

Mike Barretta is a retired U.S. Naval Aviator who currently works for a defense contractor as a pilot. He holds a Master's degree in Strategic Planning and International Negotiation from the Naval Post-Graduate School and a Master's in English from the University of West Florida. His wife, Mary, to whom he has been married for 26 years, is living proof that he is not such a bad guy once you get to know him. His stories have appeared in *Baen's Universe*, *Redstone*, *New Scientist*, *Orson Scott Card's Intergalactic Medicine Show* and various anthologies.

Horologium

Sarah Ellen Rogers

MARTHA DID NOT come today. Instead 'twas a maiden much resembling her but fairer, lissomer, with a waist drawn in like a wasp's, and more of a sharpness about the eyes.

"I am Malkin," said she, bowing her golden head, and lifted her basket through the window in the wall of my cell. "Martha's sister."

I crossed myself before the altar and rose from my knees. "Is Martha sick-a-bed?"

Malkin's eyes lowered and roamed back and forth, then nodded she her head. "Her child twists and pains her belly."

"I will pray for her," said I, taking the basket. Inside were two loaves of barley bread and a rind of blue-marled cheese, and a bottle of wine stopped up with wax.

Malkin fell silent for a little while. Then she sucked the air through her teeth and said, all at once, "D'ye ever see our Lord Jesu when you pray? I have heard that holy anchoresses sometimes have visions. D'ye ever see him?"

I smiled. It is the best reproof. My mother taught me that.

Malkin cast down her eyes again. "I would know what he looks like."

"Look for him when you look on the faces of your fellow Christians," said I, "and there you will find him, for we are all members of the body of Christ; that is, the Church."

She nodded, and departed without looking on me again. Only when I turned back from pulling the lattice to did I see that she had forgotten to take the basket with her. Perchance 'twas sin, but I did not call her to retrieve it.

I sit, alone, as the light falling round me fades. I trace the interwoven rushes with my eyes, over and under, warp and weft. I lose myself in the pattern; I cannot see where it begins or ends.

It is like to eternity, knit unto time; it is like to God, knit unto us. To him are we ever united, even when we are blind and willful, and will not see his goodness.

I do not have a great deal to look on in my cell. The Crucifix above the altar. The Psalter, the Book of Hours, and the book of spiritual instruction writ for me in English. A table, a three-legged stool, and a sleeping pallet. The lattice to the small parlor, and beyond, another three-legged stool, whereupon my visitors sit; the small passage to the antechamber, where Martha comes to pass the food and take the chamber pot; the quatrefoil squint in the stone wall, through which I glimpse the high altar where the priest consecrates the body of our Lord; and a slit of a window in the side wall, through which I see the alley by the church that leads round to the market-place. From this alley I oft hear the booming voice of young Jack Prentice, more commonly called Jack Hard o' Hearing, as he paces from the butcher's shop. When he was a lad it pleased him to kick a ball of sheep's bladder down the cobblestones, with his confederates running and shouting at his sides. In the winter time, 'twere snowball fights. O, there goes Jack now, Jack Hard o' Hearing, Jack Ginger, with that carrot-coloured hair that even I, with my poor eyesight, can see. It is sunset, nigh to Vesper-time, yet his song still rings against the mottled walls and stones:

Alas, alas, the while
Thought I on no guile.
Alas, alas the chance,
Alas, that ever I could dance.

As the days shorten, the sky riddles with gray, like the sheep's wool I once carded at my mother's knee. My cell is cold as clay, and I shiver 'neath my russet cloak as I sing my hours, kneeling in the center of my grave.

This is the womb from which I was born into this life that is life-in-death, and this will be my grave when I pass into the other, more perfect world, where the intellect is pure and bright as sunlight on the river-water.

I was eighteen years of age when I first spied my anchorhold. Then it was naught but a bare chamber with my grave a-gaping in the middle of the floor, and I was a wee thing with a face round as a dandelion, and a heart near-bout as frail.

"Si vult intrare, intret," said the bishop, according to the rite. *If she will enter, let her enter.*

The clerks followed me into the cell, singing and sprinkling holy water over the dust. Bishop Ramsherd smeared a daub of unguent over my fore-head with his rough thumb, and commended my soul to God as though I were newly dead.

I laid my body down in the grave, then fresh dug and smelling of earth.

"Here shall be my repose forever and ever," I recited in Latin, as I had been instructed. I did not look on the bishop, whose stern visage fright-ened me. "Here I shall dwell, for so I have chosen."

Ward the bells' keeper threw a pinch of dirt at my feet, and the bishop exhorted me to a life of obedience in a dull voice, as though he were al-ready a-wearied of me.

Then he strode out of the cell, his robes all a-rustle, and the clerks followed apace, like young ducks after their mother. They'd been eager to observe the rite of enclosure, I'll warrant. 'Tis an uncommon thing.

Then the stonemason and the stonemason's two prentices walled up the entrance to my cell. I suppose they had been warned not to tell their vulgar jokes or sing, for I heard them make no sound. Scrape, slap, *thud*, sang the mortar and the stones, and I tried not to shiver and quake, and I failed. All I could think on was my mother, her face fraught 'neath her wimple, lingering at the western door of the church with the other womenfolk.

The years ahead rolled over me like a thick suffocating blanket, and I felt myself entirely alone.

"I am a mediatrix twixt the living and the dead," I mouthed to still my frantic heart. "I pray for the souls of both; that is my office in this life which is a life-in-death. And with God's blessing may I abate the sorrows of the suffering quick and the torments of those languishing in the fires of purgatory."

It is an oath I have kept for fifteen years, though at times I have kept it badly. Once a devil plagued me when I was feverish, taunting that the Lord had abandoned all that lay within the city walls, and I believed him, at the time. But the great pestilence was many years ago, and here I have remained.

Every morning I rise at the bells for Matins, wash my hands and face with cold water, and sign the Cross over my face and chest. I recite the office of our Lady, the Litany of Saints, the penitential psalms, the graduals, one-after-another, *seriatim*. To me it is become as breathing: I oft do it with nary a thought, samewise I sew seam after seam in the church vestments given to my care.

When visitors come to me seeking spiritual guidance, I am all patience and lovingkindness, for anchoresses ought to receive visitors as angels, as Abraham did the Lord in three persons.

From the window I sometimes smell fish a-frying, hear the baker's boys calling out, "Hot pies! Hot!" On market-days, the merchants at their stalls, haggling over rolls of worsted. I capture a line of a song sung, a child's cry. I have memorized each stone, each crack, each straggling moss.

This is my oath. These are my hours.

These, my walls.

There, the World.

———————

'Tisn't for the weak, this life.

St. Anthony, first of my order, ventured into the wilderness to live as an hermit, greatly desiring to be free of the World and its many ensnarements. Yet even he was overcome with listlessness of the spirit, and soured like a well that hath been poisoned.

Acedia bit me with its dull tooth in my first year in the anchorhold. My heart was a stone, and every word I spoke another weight to its burden.

"Let the Lord keep thy coming in, and thy going out, now and always," I recited each day at Terce, and the words laid in my mouth like a bit in the mouth of an ass. For there was to be neither coming in nor going out, for me; I was to be perpetually imprisoned, and each day was an eternity all its own.

"The noonday demon plagues you, child," said my confessor, after one look on me.

"The bishop says I ought eat less and pray more."

"Prayer is never amiss. But what of study? Do you have enough light to read through the window?"

"I cannot read anyhow, not with Saturn's influence washing over me. The letters are like brambles that my eyes, fumbling hands, cannot close upon."

"Then need ye no other hindrance to your spiritual sight."

"The bishop says the window cannot be made larger," said I, very sullenly. "He says that anchoresses ought not show their faces to those passing by outside, for the face of a woman is like a pit of sin into which an innocent man might fall."

With displeased countenance, my confessor leaned back on his stool, and regarded me for one long moment.

"What does St. Augustine tell us of sin's origin?" he asked in his teacher's voice.

"That it is rooted in the wayward will," I responded as his student. "Not in the concupiscence of the eyes nor in the disobedient flesh."

"And what does that mean of your standing at windows?"

I thought before I answered. "That I am not to blame for the sin in other men's hearts?"

"Clever as ever," said he, and smiled.

Fauntelet turned over on my lap, lifted his chin for me to scratch.

"The bishop doesn't want I should have a cat, neither," I confided. "He says 'tis an indulgence the hermits of the desert would not allow themselves."

"The bishop gluts himself on wine and pasties every feast-day. To me his sermons on indulgence carry as much weight as a pigeon's feather."

"He doesn't think I am a proper anchoress," said I in voice small.

My confessor swelled up like a heron with its wings a-beating. "Does he want you to starve yourself to death? How shall you pray if your mind is benumbed by hunger? How shall your intellect encompass the glory of God?"

I did not answer.

"You are not here to poke and prod and mortify your flesh," said he. "You are here to grow in God's wisdom and charity. You should not be distracted but absorbed, not empty but replete."

"But I am empty, Father," I confessed. "The bishop is in the right. I am not like to the holy women heard tell of. I am wretched and weak and I know not what to do."

"Then you are like to the holy women heard tell of, Annys," said he, "and every saint who yet tread on the earth. All were inconstant, at times. Think on St. Peter, the rock upon which Christ built his Church!"

My eyes stung with tears unfallen. His words were kindly spoken, but it seemed to me yet that I was not any good.

"You have already begun," said he, more gently than ever, "the life that is of greatest profit to your soul."

"I know," said I, still sick at heart. "But what should I do now?"

"Continue," said he.

There was once a crooked-back, hoar-haired servant in my mother's household, charged with scouring the flagstones clean. When I was a child of eight I asked her, did she never grow a-wearied with the selfsame task each day?

She raised herself onto her knees, red-faced and perspiring. "O, weyalay, milady," said she, sighing like a bellows. "'Tis the nature of this worldly life."

In those first few years I was enclosed her words would not leave my mind.

I became an anchoress to escape this worldly life. To scale the heights of contemplation, to feel my entire soul a-kindle with the holy light of God. Yet I felt my hours were just the same as that old servant's. Mouthing my prayers to undo sin's stain, again and again, and for no other reason than because it simply must be done.

"The aldermen gather in the market-place," says Malkin with much excitement. She draws her hood around her small shoulders; her breath blows white in the cold morning air. "And there is a brown man come from Italy, with aspect like to a Saracen. They say he is an horologer, a maker of clocks."

I lay my hands inside the basket to warm them against the bread. It pleases Malkin to come early in the day, while the bread is yet fresh.

"It is noised about the market that they will build a tower clock to ring its hours, as the great cities of Italy hath," she chatters. "'Twill be a fine sight."

"'Twere better for them to look to the sun for their hours," I say. "Then might they think on our Lord, Creator of all, instead of buying and selling all the day."

"The market brings many a man his bread," says Malkin, rather slyly, "which the Pater-Noster declares that we should have each day."

I laugh, pleased by this gobbit of cleverness. "Well said, young Malkin, but the Pater-Noster says right naught of ale, however much the idlers in the taverns would fain have it so."

Malkin says nothing to this, nor can she. Her mother is an ale-wife who came to the city after the great pestilence.

In those ruinous years absconded many villeins from their villages, leaving their cottages empty, the fields choking with weeds. They flocked to the city like gaggles of geese, to work as carders of wool and thatchers of roofs, and labored one day in three, or else begged, and yet dined on finer fare than ever before. For in that time laboring men were so scarce that lords all over the land were compelled to pay threefold their usual wages. Then dressed men who were once swineherds and dung-carters in striped hose, and shoes made with long pointed toes, so as to flaunt their wastefulness the better.

"'Tis yet another sign of the end-times," I say, and clack my tongue. "When pride is rampant, and scarce one man in ten content with his God-given lot."

"But you yourself were not content with yourn."

I stare at Malkin, too astonished to speak. Colour comes into her cheeks, but she holds forth. "You are from a rich family, and yet you would not be a nun, nor a wife. Here you are eating bean bread, and your cloak is cut from the coarsest russet I ever looked on."

"I have cast myself down," I say at the last, "and forsaken all worldly things, in order to embark on the way of perfection. I am dead to the world, and my sight is only to God."

"Not all are made for an office holy as yourn, anchoress," says Malkin. "The greater part of the people would only fill their bellies in this passing life, and look upon their Maker in the next."

"Do you belong to the greater part of the people, Malkin?" I would know.

She thinks it over a little while. "Yea," she answers. "For I would be a wife one day, and bear children. I would not be perfect. But I would be good."

"Then take care the world's vanities lead you not amiss," I warn. "You hazard your soul each day, swimming in and out of the market stalls like a fish in the rushes."

Malkin bows her head.

"Since the great pestilence is the whole world gone topsy-turvy," I remark. "I never heard any wench speak as you before."

"I do not remember it," she says, "for I was very young. D'ye?"

"I remember it well," I say, and turn my face to the wall. "I was here."

Outside the window the carter's horse squeals. I cannot see through the rain and darkness, but I know that its flanks are flecked with foam, its eyes wild, rolling back in its head. A whip cracks, and the wheels creak 'neath the weight they bear, the corpses to be carted to the croft on the great cathedral's other side.

The cart breaks through the mud and is away. In its wake the air is rife with the stench of death.

I have not wept nor quailed. I know the great pestilence is God's judgment on the quick, that they might repent their sins before Death comes us all to slay. And mine are the greatest of all, for I as a holy anchoress should be without blemish or spot, and am not, nowhere near.

The cat leaps into my cell, bearing a small dangling thing in his mouth.

"O, Fauntelet," I sigh.

Fauntelet looks up from the half-rat he has set at my feet and blinks, pleased by his own largesse. It lays there, entrails spilling out, pink feet curling up.

Loathly, I pluck the little body up by the tail and fling it out the window. It splashes in the alley below amid the other filth.

For weeks I have despaired and thought, God's wrath must now needs abate, for the world cannot grow worse. But then the world worsens, again and again, and though it seems it cannot worsen any more, I know it can, and will. If the pestilence has taught me aught, 'tis this.

O, I am lorn with longing for the day that I first thought, this is the worst. For that day was but purgatory, and now I am in hell.

"St. Sebastian," I pray aloud, "holy martyr, be with us always, and keep us from this vile pestilence."

I speak loud as I can, but the prayer has no substance, only accident. The words are like empty clothes, without thoughts to bear them underneath.

I pace to the window in the wall of my cell. I have never longed to look out before, not as I do now. I would look on the stars in which God's providence is writ; I would make certain that there is aught there but an abyss. But the opening in the stone is too narrow cut, and the wall too thick.

I fall on my knees and relish their answering pain.

"A contrite and humble heart, O Lord, thou wilt not despise," I say, and knock my chest, and wait upon God's messenger.

Nothing but the rain a-falling.

"I lie awake," I call. "I have become like the sparrow, alone, watching atop the walls. I have eaten ashes as my bread, taken tears as my drink. My days are a shadow. I have withered like grass. But you, O God, endure; your mercy lasteth through the generations."

Nothing but the rain a-falling.

"O, that I knew where I could find you, for I would have you answer me!" I cry.

Nothing but the rain a-falling, and the wind blowing across the window. It is a yawning mouth, and outside, a world from which God has absented himself.

"Is anyone there?" a frantic voice calls inside the church. "Is there man or woman yet alive in this place?"

I go to the lattice and wrench it open, and it is he; it is my confessor.

"Annys," he says.

"You should not have come," I say.

"I heard you were sick, on death's very brink."

"'Twas a fever, nothing more."

I do not tell him of what I saw, tossing to and fro on my pallet: a devil, black as a buboe, that stuck its claws into my back. It spake in a hiss, saying that God had repented making man and would leave us here to perish. Then it laughed, a sound most horrible and foul.

He looks on my face. "Have you eaten? Who is bringing you bread?"

"Now and again I am remembered by the good women of the parish," I say.

He shakes his head. "I will call on the Blackfriars come dawn. See that they bring you some victuals each day."

"They have no time for me. All religious must hear confessions and perform rites night and day. I heard a confession the other day from a man who came to the church and could find no priest."

"And where is the bishop?"

"Fled to the countryside."

My confessor blows air through his teeth. "Tomorrow I will bring men to tear down the wall, and I will take you home."

I would tell him I have had enough of life, if life is such as this; that I welcome the death that would ravish me from this place. But this is not what I say to him.

I say, "If God has sent this pestilence upon us, there is nowhere to flee. There is no changing what has already come to pass in his sight. If I am destined to die, die I shall."

He pulls at his hair. "And what if God intends for you to flee? What then?"

"You think I ought flee, as the bishop did?"

He is silent, then. Outside there is the noise of a woman wailing. We listen to her, and are quiet for a long while.

"I thought you would be safe here," he says at the last. "Like a dove in a dovecote."

"Father," I murmur, for I can naught else.

In the time of the great pestilence I am four-and-twenty, and there is much I do not know. I do not know that the world is not yet ending, the day of reckoning not yet at hand. I do not know that Death, the false thief, will strike my confessor some weeks hence, and steal his life away. And I do not know that after, I will fall into the deepest dolefulness I ever knew, and neither wake nor stir nor speak a word for days, and the creeping hours will seem to me but time to spill and waste.

But I do know, even as Death ravages the city and all the land around us, that he is the one thorn in my heart that I cannot pluck out, even if it would bring me to perfection.

The ragtag boys are running and shouting down the alley. I lift my body from my pallet and crawl to the window. It is the first time since the abatement of the pestilence that I have heard children at play, and perchance the sight will lift my sunken spirits.

Fauntelet is sunning himself on a ledge below my window. The dust and dirt that cling to his flanks do not hide his fine coat.

One lad speaks to the others. "Lookit, Tom, lookit, Wat! Let's grab 'im and capture 'im, we'll make a pretty penny off 'is coat!"

A cry burns in my throat, but I bite my tongue. I must not speak. Am I not dead to the world, deaf to its comings and goings? I ought care no more for a cat than for a wheaten straw.

O, it must be as the bishop said: God has foreseen this and shaped it for my spiritual instruction. It is a penance I must suffer; I know it, I know it.

Jack Prentice comes around the corner, whistling.

"Hisst, Jack!" one of the lads says. "We're for to catch that cat and take 'im to the furrier's."

Jack balks. "Are ye mad, Simkin?" he says. "That's the puss what belongs to the holy anchoress of St. Stephen's. If you skin him, a thunder clap will come down from the heavens, like when the pagans St. Barbara slew."

The other boys draw back, afraid.

"She ought singe 'is fur to whet his pride," blubs Simkin, red-cheeked, "and keep 'im from parading out-of-doors."

Fauntelet hops down and winds around Jack's legs.

"Puss puss," says Jack cheery-like, petting Fauntelet's head. "Let the anchoress's cat be, all of ye. He keeps the church mice from devouring the Body of our Lord, and 'tis a holy craft, that."

By my rule I ought pray for no man in singular, for all Christians are one in the body of Christ. But in the years that have passed since the pestilence-time, I have prayed for the soul of Jack Prentice every evening, every morn, for in those dark days after my confessor's death he brought to me the only grace I knew.

My brother visited today, clad in his friar's habit, a rope twined round his middle. Yet wore he also a jeweled ring on his hand and a thick purse at his side. He hid both in the folds of his robe, but neither 'scaped my eye.

"Sister," crowed he like a cock in the morning-time, "see what I have brought for you from over land and sea." Then he unwreathed his gift from a long skein of wool, a thing the like of which I'd never before seen.

"An horologe?" I guessed.

"Aye," said he, "a sandglass. How well it befits your craft! For by this contraption might you measure your time at prayer each day."

"Brother," said I, "by my troth, I cannot see how it will be of use. For I have the sun and the bells of the church to tell me my hours. I know perfectly well when I should pray."

"But the Church's hours are not proper hours," said he. "For in the summer, the hours of the day are longer than the night's, and in the winter it is opposite. So you never know the true quantity of the time spent. But the newest clocks ring hours of equal duration, and 'tis of great benefit to all people in the city to have such a device, so that all might know perfectly the time of the market, when all is for to sell."

I tried to seem more patient than I truly was. Alayn has not changed a jot since we were children. No matter what we speak on, he must always know everything better.

He pointed twixt the two bulbs where the sand ran like a little stream of water. "Here you may look on the hour as it passes, and so take care that your time is ever to your profit. For we all must yield accounts at the day of reckoning for every minute we have lost or misspent."

"Alayn," said I, "I am an anchoress, not a controller. I need not add my time as if it were a farthing to a farthing."

His face darkened.

"'Tis a lovely thing," said I, in voice more subtly-soft, "and cunningly made, but by my rule am I not encouraged to keep things such as this unto my goods. For we are all pilgrims in this world, and anchoresses in especial."

It pleases Alayn to count and sort and measure things that have no merchandise about them. But I know that time is no thing in God's sight, no thing at all; if it were, how could it be cut as a tailor cuts cloth in the length of a hand or a foot?

I was nine years of age when I learned time to scorn.

'Twas a fine summer day. My sisters were in the fields, gathering flowers for garlands, and Alayn and I were a-climbing trees on the hillside. Longer-limbed than I, Alayn was half to the top; I would have called on him for help, but then I spied a caterpillar, and lingered below to watch it.

"What do you look on so curiously, child?"

It was Father Thomas, his visage dappled by the sunlight through the leaves overhead. I can see him there now, standing over me, seeming the tallest man in the world. But I cannot remember the color of his hair, not when he was young; I can only see it white, as it was when he became my confessor years later.

In those days he was the priest to our chapel, and to the parish around. My mother told me he was made to leave Norwich by the bishop there, for railing 'gainst the Church's officers and their lust for silver. Simon

Magus's sin hath in the Church festered, said he in his sermons, like to a canker that must be lanced to draw the poison out.

Since he was a man of great learning, my father had him teach Alayn his Latin. Alayn was afraid of him, for he was fierce as a lion at lessons, but I liked when he read me homilies, and the Book of Troy, and the lives of the saints. His voice was mellifluous and something wondrous to hear.

"I am watching a caterpillar, Father," I answered. "Look how he inches up the tree trunk."

He stood, and watched it for a while with me.

"Does God see us so?" I asked him, delighted by this sudden thought. "Does he look on us as we were little caterpillars?"

"God sees our lives entire, Annys, for he sees all times, past and future, in a point. They are as present to him as I am to you now."

"Even the very beginning of the world?"

"Aye, I would think so."

"Then why doth he not hinder Eve from eating the fruit of the tree of knowledge?" I would have known. "For then all would be well."

He was quiet for a little while. "'Tis a thought to be despised, child," said he. "For because of Eve's sin came Jesu Christ into the holy virgin's womb, and died us all to save."

"I know that all shall be well, Father, after Jesu is come again," I grudged. "But all is not well now."

At the time I was thinking on my playfellow Jon from the village, who was kicked in the head by a horse on the month last. He could no longer speak aright, nor remember the names of things.

"To us, no," agreed Father Thomas. "But God sees the world in a different wise."

"Then I would I saw the world as God does."

"That may not be while you live on the earth, Annys, for we are bound by time. Our pasts are gone, our futures not yet come. We may never possess all of our existence at once."

"Does God?"

"Aye, for God is the Lord and Maker of time. He is not bound by it."

"For God is eternal," I offered, and thought myself very clever. But Father Thomas shook his head.

"No, Annys," said he. "God is eternity."

Suddenly it was as though my mind cracked open, like an egg with a bright orange yolk.

"He must be, for he is perfect," Father Thomas held forth. "And perfection is complete, with nothing that can be lost, nor nothing yet to be attained. One day we shall share in God's glory, and be as unchangeable as he is, when we be there with him in heaven."

He patted my head, and made to leave.

I tugged on his cloak. "Was I in heaven before I was born, Father?"

He gave me a strange look. "I do not know."

"Was I anywhere?" I was speaking my thoughts as they came to me. They frightened me, and yet seemed lovely too. "Was I anyone?"

He was looking on me still. "Do you oft think on these things, child?"

"Yea, Father," I confessed. "All the time."

"We shall speak more on it, then, at length, another time."

Before he departed from me, he stooped down and held out his fingers, knit together. It made a fine step for my foot, so that I could grab the one branch of the tree that was yet beyond my reach.

Between March and April,
When spray beginneth to spring,
I wake in love-longing
For the seemliest of all thing.

Malkin peeks out the window to the alley below, where Jack Prentice paces from the market-place, singing all the way. It is a week to Palm Sunday, and she is restless, ready for Lenten-time's end.

I know well her look. All the young folk have that look this time of year, the hunger for sunlight and dances and games.

"It pleases you, his singing," I say.

She looks at me as she had started from a sleep.

"He hath a pleasing sound," I say, "though his songs are full of ribaldries. It would liketh me better were he to sing of our Lord Jesu Christ, the worthiest lover of all, with the holiest week of the year swift approaching."

"There are many other things worthy to sing of," Malkin says.

"None like unto Jesu," I say with stern countenance.

She inclines her head. "No, anchoress, for Jesu hath no peer. But the sun and the stars and the flowers that bloom in the spring must be fair, too, for it is God made them."

I essay then to teach Malkin of the scale of nature, but she would rather dispute with me. She puts me in mind of a clerk calling, "Contra!"

"If you love God, how can you scorn the things he has made?" she repeats, all impatience.

"They are deficient, child, for they are not God. There is no lasting happiness in worldly things. They are instable, imperfect, doomed to pass away, as will we one day. That is why God sent the pestilence upon us, to teach us our brittle nature."

"I know you speak troth," says she, "when you say this world changeable is. And I love my Lord Jesu with all my heart. Still, I cannot unlove what God has made."

"'Tis a stirring damnable," I warn, "and much to be forsaken."

"Ye be a full holy woman, anchoress," says Malkin. "Maybe one day I will learn to despise these things as you do. But I think I am too young now. I have not yet had time enough to grow a-wearied with the world."

"You are a foolish maid, to joy in the vanities of this life," I say, almost angered. "I will pray to God to grant you a contrite heart, so that you might confess your sins 'fore Easter, and be ready to die at a moment should God send another pestilence upon us."

Malkin leaves after I speak these words to her. But before she does, she turns back, and says, "I never told you, anchoress. My sister Martha bore her child two days gone. A fine boy, and fair."

Then she is gone.

When Jesu Christ first appeared to me, I was in a fear whether it were a vision or not, until he assured me in loving speech. Our Lord speaks not in English, but in our first tongue, the one we forget when we are born and come into time.

He stood before me and showed me himself, without a priest or any other mediator. His visage brought to mind my mother, with her large eyes like a fawn's. Yet he seemed also like the horologer come from Italy, as Malkin him described. He was full brown of hue, like cinnamon.

"Look here, daughter," said he, in voice like sweet melody, and showed me the bleeding wound at his side.

Then he drew the flesh back like it were a curtain, and inside I saw a great palace, like unto the heavenly Jerusalem, and inside the palace I saw a great hall, and inside the hall I saw a great company, more than I could reckon, sitting down to feast. And there I saw myself, and Father Thomas, and my mother, and Jack Prentice and Martha and Malkin, and many others that I knew and knew not, of aspect strange and fair.

There I saw Jesu, too, sitting at the head of the table, and his holy mother at his side. Wine flowed at that feast like water, and there was bliss and merriment that is beyond my ken to tell. It was the fairest sight one ever could devise.

I cannot speak of hell nor purgatory, for those I saw naught of.

"This is not the heavenly Jerusalem as it truly is," said Jesu Christ. "But I have rendered it so, so that you might see it. Do you understand?"

"I think so, Lord," said I.

"You are here," said Christ-the-horologer, "and you are here," and gestured to the hollow in his breast. "You are at my table, sitting down. There was never a time when you were not here, and you will always be here, with me, and all the company. Do you understand?"

"I think so, Lord," said I.

"Now hold your hand out, daughter."

In my hand he set the world. It was like to a pearl, round and fair, without any blemish or spot.

"I keep it because I love it and everything in it," said he with great tenderness. "Do you understand?"

"Aye, my Lord."

My heart danced when he smiled at me. "It is good that you do," said he.

I cannot tell you how or when our blessed Lord departed my sight, only that the smell of him lingered for many hours after. He smelled of blood and of rose water, intermeddled together.

It is Palm Sunday the day after my vision, and on that day Malkin comes no more. Instead 'tis another maiden, shorter and red-cheeked, and plump as a fresh loaf of bread.

"I am Matilde," says she, out of breath. She must have slept overmuch, and has hasted so that she might not miss the procession 'fore the church.

Outside I hear a great noise and a great shouting. The carter is leading an ass up the alley by a rope tied to a bit. On its back the ass bears a wooden figure of Jesu.

"Hosanna, hosanna," cheers the crowd, as they wave their branches of pine at the wooden Christ. "Blessed is he who in the name of the Lord cometh!"

And so Jesu Christ is welcomed into the fullness of time again.

Jack Prentice is in the crowd following, and at his side stands a maiden with golden hair. The window is too narrow cut; my eyesight too poor. I cannot see her face, but I know that she is smiling.

Some days I still long to 'scape this wretched world. But some days I cannot believe that it has not yet flowered in its full glory, and I thank the Lord that in this passing life we are granted knowledge of what awaits us in the other.

'Tis an imperfect world, yea, and an incomplete. But God cherishes it, and so will I. For I am bound to it as I am to him, with a love that will not let me go.

Sarah Ellen Rogers grew up in a small town in northeastern North Carolina. She studied English at Duke University, where she first encountered the medieval literature that inspired "Horologium." Inspired in part by the writings of the anchoress Julian of Norwich, "Horologium" is set around and after the first outbreak of the Black Death, a time of great social, economic, and technological change. Other influences include the *Ancrene Wisse*, Augustine's *Confessions*, Chaucer's *Pardoner's Tale*, and Middle English lyrics. In her spare time, Sarah writes both speculative fiction and creative nonfiction. She lives in Durham, North Carolina, with her cat, Dante.

About the Editors

Donald S. Crankshaw and Kristin Janz met at a church writers' group in 2009, bonded almost immediately over their shared love of speculative fiction and ancient Roman history, and have been married since 2011. They live just outside of Boston, Massachusetts.

Donald has a Ph.D. in Electrical Engineering from MIT, which was more useful for writing fantasy than he had expected, though less helpful for writing science fiction than he had hoped. He has previously published stories in *Nature Futures*, *Daily Science Fiction*, and *Black Gate*.

Kristin is a Canadian fantasy and science fiction writer and a 2008 graduate of the Clarion West Writers Workshop. Her stories have appeared in *Daily Science Fiction*, *On Spec*, and *Crowded Magazine*. She has an M.Sc. in Organic Chemistry from the University of British Columbia, and worked in the pharmaceutical industry as a medicinal chemist for over a decade.

This is their first anthology.